# LORI
## FOSTER

## SUSAN DONOVAN
### VICTORIA DAHL

*The Guy Next Door*

**HQN™**

ISBN-13: 978-0-373-77556-9

THE GUY NEXT DOOR

Copyright © 2011 by Harlequin Books S.A.

The publisher acknowledges the copyright holder of the individual works as follows:

READY, SET, JETT
Copyright © 2011 by Lori Foster

GAIL'S GONE WILD
Copyright © 2011 by Susan Donovan

JUST ONE TASTE
Copyright © 2011 by Victoria Dahl

Recycling programs for this product may not exist in your area.

# CONTENTS

# READY, SET, JETT

## Lori Foster

**\* \* \* \***

To Chris and Queen Janeen of
"Married With Microphones," WGRR radio, 103.5.

You guys keep me company every weekday morning
while I write. I love the banter,
the jokes *and* the wonderful music.

While Chris hasn't yet appeared on any of my book
covers (despite his claims otherwise), you've both
become a big part of my creative routine.

Thanks for the great entertainment!

Lori

Dear Reader,

Many of you have asked me if I'll have more SBC fighter stories, but for the foreseeable future, the answer is no. You see, I've launched into a new series of über-alpha hunks. The men are similar to private mercenaries, so they're big, capable and oh-so-sexy. When it comes to rescuing the innocent, they do what has to be done, however it has to be done. I think of them as men who walk the edge of honor.

My novella "Ready, Set, Jett" will introduce you to the characters in the first single title, *When You Dare,* hitting shelves in May. That will be followed by *Trace of Fever* in June and *Savor the Danger* in July.

To learn more about the books, visit my website at www.LoriFoster.com. And feel free to chat with me on my Facebook fan page—www.facebook.com/pages/Lori-Foster/233405457965.

I'm very excited about this new series, and I hope you will be, too!

*Lori Foster*

# *CHAPTER ONE*

HANDS ON HIS HIPS, impatience growing, Jett Sutter paced the length of his living room while his youngest sister, Betts, blathered on about God-knew-what. She'd been at his door when he arrived home, throwing off his intricate plans and putting a damper on his fevered expectations.

Never would he deliberately hurt his sister's feelings, but pretending interest had become impossible half an hour ago. A glance at his wristwatch showed that he needed to shower. He needed to…prep. When he thought of what he had planned, what he would do and with whom, his breath quickened and his muscles twitched.

It wasn't an unfamiliar reaction when dealing with his supersexy neighbor, Natalie Alexander.

Jett loved his family, he really did, but damn it, he needed privacy to deal with the blooming heat and anticipation of the next few hours. He needed…

The familiar sound of a Volkswagen Bug pulling into the apartment complex parking lot cut short his thoughts. Without caring what his sister would think, Jett took two long strides to the patio doors and parted the curtains just enough to look out.

And there she was: delectable Natalie Alexander.

Superstacked school teacher. Seduction personified. Enchanting enigma.

*His lover.*

Damn, she looked hot. Natalie was his most elaborate fantasy in the flesh, made up of scorching contradictions.

Long, corkscrew curls the color of dark honey danced around her face as she hurried from the minuscule cherry-red car with a bag of groceries in one arm, her requisite heavy book bag in the other, her enormous purse slung over her shoulder.

As usual when returning from work, she wore her school-teacher duds of a long dark skirt, flat shoes and a crisp blouse under a warm cardigan. For Jett, it looked like fetish wear—a modest ensemble to disguise the centerfold body.

Seldom had Natalie mentioned teaching, and that was mostly before they'd become intimate. Since then, she'd gone out of her way to keep all conversation to a minimum.

It really burned his ass the way she fought to keep him at a distance.

Not that her evasive attitude had done her any good. He knew what grade level she taught, that she enjoyed reading political dramas and true-crime novels, that she cried over commercials and laughed at birds when they visited the bird feeder off her balcony.

He also recognized the vulnerability she tried to camouflage with sexual bravado—at least, with him. Thinking of her utilizing that special brand of bravado with any other guy bothered him in ways he didn't want to analyze too closely.

He knew that Natalie came from a background of

extreme wealth and social influence, but the money and prestige hadn't guaranteed her a warm, loving family.

Though Natalie had no inkling of his research, he'd uncovered quite a bit about her, personal and otherwise. If she did know, she probably wouldn't like it.

Too bad.

At first he'd investigated her out of suspicion, because she'd come on so strong and had been so accommodatingly easy. As the quintessential school teacher, absolutely nothing about Natalie's outward persona said "uncommitted sex." Yet that's what they had.

Wild, hot, no-boundaries sex that left him burned and wanting more. A lot more.

Later, he'd done more digging because damn it, he wasn't used to any woman wanting *only* uncommitted sex with him. It didn't make sense. Natalie never asked him anything personal, never wanted to go out to eat or to a movie. She rebuked gifts and compliments and disdained social settings of any kind.

All she wanted was him, in bed.

That should have been the perfect setup for a man intent on maintaining his bachelor status, but for whatever reason, Jett felt uneasy about it. He wanted her to want more, damn it.

Why didn't she?

Now, as she exited her car, Jett watched her and knew by the way his muscles twitched and his skin burned that he was getting in too deep. Natalie had the most profound effect on him.

Confusion, he told himself. Curiosity and intrigue. Nothing more.

Once he knew why she'd built so many walls, he'd be able to scale them. They'd both have a good time for as long as it lasted, and neither of them would have regrets.

And with that goal in mind, Jett had a plan.

Using her hip, Natalie bumped the car door shut and, because of the brisk wind, hurried for the entrance. In late March, the weather was milder but still pretty chilly.

Along the way to the apartment entrance, she glanced up at his window.

Jett made sure she couldn't see him; God only knew what she'd think if she caught him watching for her. He'd look like a dupe, like a lovesick fool when, despite their burning compatibility between the sheets, she'd made it clear that she didn't want anything more.

Sex. For her it was the beginning and the end of their relationship. With every other woman he knew, he'd find that arrangement perfect.

With Natalie Alexander…no. *Hell* no.

Tonight, he had a plan to use her carnal nature against her. He'd keep her long enough to hash out a few things.

Thinking about his intent made him semierect and taut with urgency. He visualized her in his bed, stretched out, anxious for him—

"All right," Betts said from behind his right shoulder. "Give. Who is she?"

*Oh shit.* How had he forgotten all about his sister's presence?

Jett turned in what he hoped to be a nonchalant way. "A neighbor, that's all." With Natalie now home, his patience ended. He took Betts's arm, swiped up her jacket off the back of a chair and steered her toward the door. "The visit's been awesome, but I need to shower."

Laughing, Betts dug in her heels. "Get real, brother. I'm not budging an inch until you tell me every single juicy detail."

At twenty-six, nine years his junior, his sister wasn't old enough and, he prayed, wasn't experienced enough to hear *everything* that had gone on between Natalie and him. Never mind that Betts was only a year younger than Natalie.

"Not happening, Betts, so forget it." Knowing his sister, he added, "And don't you dare go blabbing to the folks, either." The last thing he wanted was his mother snooping around in his private life. His dad would shrug it off; his mother, like his sisters, would make him nuts with questions.

Being thirty-five and independent in every way didn't matter, not to his nosy family. He was the only son, with three younger sisters. For years he'd felt protective toward them all, and now they were determined to pay him back in kind.

Somehow, he got Betts halfway to the door.

"If you're seeing someone, I'd like to meet her."

Annoyed, he turned to stare at his youngest sister. "No."

"Why not?"

Because he wasn't *seeing* Natalie, not in the traditional way Betts meant. They hadn't had a single real date. The sum total of their time together had been spent either in bed or getting to the bed. Occasionally in the foyer against the wall, once on the couch, once over the back of the couch—

"Jett? Yoo-hoo."

"You're not meeting her, so forget it." Even if he wanted to introduce her to his family, Natalie stayed around only until the lovemaking ended. Then she high-tailed it right back out of his life.

Hell, outside of sex talk, they'd barely even conversed. Jett told her what he wanted to do to her, with her, and Natalie always gave enthusiastic agreement. Period.

She'd made it abundantly clear that he was good only for sex.

Actually, she'd said he was *great* for sex; she hadn't skimped on the compliments in that department. But she usually gave them while naked, draped over his chest, still breathing hard and rosy from a recent screaming climax.

Somehow, he had to work their combustible chemistry to his advantage so that Natalie would let him past her barriers.

"You look flushed, Jett." Arms crossed, Betts surveyed him through narrowed eyes. "What's wrong with you?"

Mood now soured, Jett said, "None of your business, so butt out." He wasn't about to explain to his youngest sis the scorching level of churning lust and…and whatever else it was that he felt.

Hell, how could he explain it to her when he didn't quite understand it himself?

Her foot tapped the carpet. "Jett…"

Struggling for patience, he gave her a tight hug and then held her an arm's length away. Dead serious, eyes narrowed and expression somber, he said, "If you love me, Betts, you will, just this once, let it go." She hesitated, and he waited, staring her down.

With a huff, she gave up. "Fine." Betts pulled free of his hold to don her jacket, jamming her arms into the sleeves with more force than necessary. "But it's only because I *do* love you."

Thanking her with great sincerity, he opened the door for her to go. Across the hall, Natalie's door remained closed.

Betts kissed his cheek and back-stepped out, watching him with expectation the entire way. Keeping a straight face with effort, Jett waited until he saw her go through the glass doors at the complex's entrance and until she reached her car.

Heading back inside, he stripped off his clothes along the way. In his bedroom, he turned down the blankets, leaving them at the foot of the bed. Determined on his course, he knelt near the head of the bed in the center of the mattress and wove a long specialized restraint through the headboard slats. A sliding "noose" at each end would be perfect for capturing Natalie's delicate wrists.

His abdomen clenched and his breathing hitched; he tugged experimentally and decided it would serve the purpose.

He glanced at the footboard, considered putting the restraints there too—but no. On a purely carnal level, he loved the idea of seeing Natalie tied spread-eagle to his bed, but he didn't want to push her so much that she felt compelled to object.

Now sporting full wood, Jett went to the shower. He had completed only the most cursory bathing when his attuned ears heard Natalie's familiar knock at his door.

Drawing a deep breath and shutting off the water, he propped a hand flat against the tile wall, dropped his head and took a moment to regain his control.

After doing a half-assed job of drying, he wrapped the towel around his hips and strode to his apartment door to let her in.

There wasn't anything he could do about the tenting of the towel. He wanted her, bad, more so with every minute that he knew her.

Today he'd make sure she wanted him just as much, in just as many ways.

HER HEART FLUTTERING in excitement, Natalie knocked twice on Jett's door. Anticipation rode her hard; she felt more alive, her every sense acutely heightened, whenever she was with him.

Even before leaving school she'd thought of this, of him and what they'd do, and now fire licked along her nerve endings, leaving behind a throbbing heat that pooled between her thighs.

Before Jett, Natalie hadn't been a sexual woman. But now, it didn't matter how many times she had him—she wanted him as if it was the first.

Maybe that was because the first time had been so mind-blowing, like the hottest of fantasies.

Even her sister, a bestselling author, couldn't write anything so amazing. The things Jett did, with precision and expertise and a complete lack of inhibition, were almost surreal.

The first time she'd laid eyes on him, she'd done an interested double take.

So had he.

Tall and strong with an athletic build, Jett Sutter was drop-dead gorgeous in a disheveled, comfortable, I-don't-give-a-damn way. His attitude was a refreshing change from the tailored, GQ men in suits, the type of men who sought her out because of her father's wealth and social standing.

She doubted Jett had any social standing; if he did, he wouldn't be living in their moderately priced apartment complex.

His body was enough to leave a woman tongue-tied, but it was his dark glittering eyes that had the ability to arrest all thought and movement. When he looked at her, his expression was teasing, interested, but also so intent that Natalie felt it in the most intimate ways.

She, decorum personified, had surprised herself by flirting with him.

She'd been surprised even more when he dished it right back. They spoke only a little, all of it light, sexy and…fun.

That in itself, the teasing and the flirting, had been a complete aberration for her, something she enjoyed but had never really indulged before meeting Jett.

Then one day, months ago, she'd found herself alone in the hallway with Jett as they'd each started into their own units. For the longest time they'd stared at each other, no doubt thinking the same thing, wanting the same thing. The tension had built to an excruciating level.

Natalie had waited, breath held, anticipation keen.

Without a word Jett unlocked his door and pushed it open, but then walked over to her.

Her heart had tried to punch right out of her chest.

Ever so slowly, he'd moved his hand over her cheek, under her wildly curling hair to curve warmly around her nape. Little by little his eyes narrowed and darkened even more, captivating her, making her knees weak—

until he leisurely bent to her mouth and brushed the lightest of kisses over her lips.

When she didn't pull away, he lingered, teasing at first, but then she leaned into him and he'd given in with a harsh, hungry groan.

In minutes, she'd found herself in his apartment, each fumbling with the other's clothes, arms and legs tangling while the kisses grew hotter and longer and deeper…

In mutual participation, they ended up in his bed having the hottest, most satisfying sex *ever*.

Other than a few moans and gasps and heartfelt expletives, neither had spoken a single word.

Afterward, as she'd tried to figure out what to do or say, he'd smiled at her, a smile of triumph, of confidence and cocky attitude.

Uncensored gratitude had left her bemused. She hadn't known sex could be so satisfying, or so consuming, and she'd spoken without really thinking it through. "That was…" She'd had no adequate words, so she settled on, "Thank you."

His smile slipped into a grin. "Anytime."

She'd been surprised and inexperienced enough to say, "Really?"

"Oh, yeah." His gaze went molten as he looked her over, making it clear that he liked what he saw. "All you gotta do is knock."

Natalie had taken him at his word, and from there they'd fallen into an unbelievable routine that was both scintillating and simple.

The first time she'd knocked at his door, feeling very tentative, alternate excuses at the ready, he'd answered a mere second later. His look of expectation had sharpened to satisfaction then quickly turned to lust. With that dark gaze devouring her, her worry dissipated as if it had never been.

After that, it got easier. And now, when she wanted him, she had no issue at all going to his door to let him know.

No, that wasn't entirely true, because she *always* wanted him. Minutes after she left him, she ached for him again.

Trying to keep her obsession with Jett under wraps wasn't easy, so at least three times a week she went to him. The rest of the time she lectured herself on moderation, on keeping things uncomplicated. If she pressed him, if she took up too much of his time, he'd grow tired of their uncomplicated arrangement.

But Natalie relished the lack of expectations. There were no awkward dates for her to flub or conflicting opinions to put them at odds or, God forbid, any uncertainty about his intentions.

So far, Jett had been very accommodating. Of course, one of these days he'd have other plans. Or not be home when she knocked. Or… She gulped.

One day he'd find someone else, someone important to him who wouldn't appreciate him having a no-strings affair with his neighbor across the hall.

But not yet.

*Not today.*

Natalie was sorting through her feelings about the indistinct future when Jett opened his door.

Her breath caught. Forget the future; she wanted to concentrate only on the here and now.

Wearing nothing more than a damp towel and his wet hair uncombed, Jett's dark-eyed gaze burned in a look she recognized only too well. He stood with his feet apart, one hand on the doorknob, the other on the frame above his head. The towel parted over one muscular thigh, showing an old scar, almost like a gunshot wound, on his right leg.

So many times Natalie had wanted to ask him about that scar. How had he gotten it, when.

*Why?*

She had no idea what Jett did for a living; she didn't know anyone who'd been shot.

It'd be so easy to ask him…but she knew she shouldn't. If she asked questions, it left him open to do the same. Eventually he'd find out that her father was ridiculously wealthy and well respected in the business world. He'd find out that she and her sister had been effectively disowned.

And he'd find out about her mother.

Her chest tightened with the thought. No, she didn't want that.

The effortlessness of their straightforward sexual relationship was too enjoyable to modify it with idle curiosity.

Shaking off all other concerns, Natalie stepped toward Jett. As if her movement broke a spell, Jett dropped his arms around her and drew her in close, taking her mouth in a hungry, devouring kiss. Still with his mouth on hers, he lifted her inside and kicked the door shut.

Wow. Today he rushed things, and she loved it.

In two steps Jett had her pressed to the wall in full-body contact, his big hands framing her face while he ate at her mouth with an all-consuming kiss. His tongue moved over hers as he adjusted his hold, turning his head for a better fit.

He smelled fresh and hot, felt damp and strong. Whatever his occupation might be, Jett stayed in prime physical shape with admirable stamina. In appreciation, Natalie contracted her fingers over his chest muscles. He made a sound of pleasure and ground his erection against her belly.

After her quick shower, she'd changed into a casual, oversized sweatshirt with a wide neckline, and loose drawstring leisure pants. The clothes weren't all that complimentary, but they were easy to remove, and she knew she wouldn't be wearing them for long.

When Jett's hand traveled down her spine to the waistband of the pants, then slipped inside to knead her backside, he discovered her lack of panties.

"Damn, woman," he rasped against her throat. "You know how to make me burn, don't you?"

Natalie couldn't reply, not with him touching her, drifting his fingers around to her belly, down between her legs. She went on tiptoe in reaction, her head back, her shoulders pressed hard to the wall.

Voice low with satisfaction, Jett said, "Ah, baby, you're already wet for me." While teasing her with his strong fingers, he lightly kissed her throat, behind her ear. "Been thinking of me?"

"Yes." *Always,* Natalie could have said, but she held back that telling confession. Right now her involvement with Jett was uncomplicated and burning hot.

So what if she occasionally got the urge to just *talk* to him? Thanks to a father who didn't care, a mother who'd left her and suitors who'd cared more about impressing her father than her, she'd learned to keep her relationships simple. If Jett got to know her, he'd get to know her family and the very misleading background of wealth.

Then how could she ever trust him again?

She'd found out the hard way that when most men looked at her, they saw only dollar signs. Never again would she put herself through that.

Near her ear, Jett whispered, "Hey, where'd you go, Natalie?"

Her heart softened; Jett was so attuned to her that he always sensed her mood, and he never failed to react to it.

She forced away the faint edge of melancholy, the niggling urge to reach for more than *this,* and said, "I'm here, with you, getting dangerously close to coming."

"Not yet," he told her. He took one step back, and when she reached for him, he caught her hands. With a level look of instruction, he kissed each palm and pressed her hands down at either side of her hips.

Breathing hard, Natalie acquiesced with understanding. Jett often liked to take control sexually, always with combustible results. He never, ever hurt her, never even caused her a twinge of discomfort. He was an openly giving partner, unselfish and talented. Regardless of any details that Natalie didn't know about him, she knew *him.* She didn't have a single doubt that anything Jett wanted to do to her was for her pleasure.

She could hardly wait.

After licking her lips, she said, "Why don't you take off the towel?" Looking at his body always thrilled her. She loved it that he was all man, hairy in the right places, solid and hard, so much taller and stronger than her.

"You first." He caught the hem of the sweatshirt and tugged it up. "Raise your arms."

When she did, he lifted the sweatshirt off over her head, baring her breasts.

Cool air-conditioning drifted over her skin. Her nipples were already tight, aching.

"Stand still." Jett lowered his head to dampen each one with his tongue, teasing, circling.

Her thigh muscles tensed, her belly hollowed. She waited for him to suck—but he didn't. He just kept teasing, lightly kissing, licking, but stopping short at what she wanted most.

She closed her eyes on a wave of sensation that felt sharpest between her thighs. "Jett…"

"Shh." He straightened again, cupped both her breasts in his hands and used his thumbs now to circle her wet nipples. "God, you have the most gorgeous body ever."

Both she and her sister were large-breasted, but the rest of her? Average at best. Not that you could tell that by the way Jett reacted to her. From the beginning he'd seemed very drawn to her physically.

While working her nipples with his thumbs, Jett took her mouth again. He kissed her soft and deep, and he kept on kissing her long after she needed and wanted more.

Growing desperate, especially with the mounting sensitivity of her breasts, Natalie turned her face away to catch her breath.

He recaptured her mouth, not giving her time to think, to speak. When she moaned, he only tilted in his hips, pressing his solid erection to her so that she'd know he was in the same shape. Situated between her thighs, he stroked against her in a parody of sex but without the ultimate satisfaction.

She loved how Jett built the need until her entire body felt alive, every nerve ending sparking. Sometimes he kept it up until she couldn't take it anymore.

She was there *now,* and still he seemed relentless.

When he pulled away suddenly, a haze of lust left her disconcerted. Without giving her a chance to regroup, he knelt and tugged the pants down to her ankles. "Step out."

Using his shoulders for balance, Natalie lifted each foot free and he pushed the material and her flip-flops away from her.

She was now naked, and he was still on his knees in front of her.

Her lungs struggled to get enough air. Slowly, far too slowly, Jett slipped his hands around her hips to her backside and held her secure.

Knowing what he would do, her voice quavered. "Jett?"

He leaned in, nuzzling against her, breathing deeply of her scent, and Natalie thought her knees would buckle. She wove her fingers into his cool, silky hair and inadvertently tightened them when she felt his open mouth against her. "Oh, God."

His tongue moved over her, *in* her, and then suddenly he stood to take her hand in a rush. "You're killing me, honey. Let's go before I lose it."

At that moment, "losing it" seemed like a pretty good idea to her. She gave him a look, letting him know that sex in his foyer worked just fine for her.

Wearing a half smile, Jett shook his head. "Sorry, honey, but tonight, that's not part of the plan."

"What plan?"

"Shh. Just wait." Gently, he urged her toward his bedroom. So that he could keep his gaze on her, he back-stepped all the way, staring at her breasts, how they jiggled with each step. His gaze sharpened and his jaw firmed; he made a sound of appreciation.

Beside his already turned-down bed, his voice gravelly with need, Jett said to her, "Lie down in the middle of the bed, on your back."

Natalie had no issue with that. Anything to hurry him along worked for her.

But the second her head rested on a pillow, Jett dropped the towel and came over her to straddle her hips. She was just reaching for him when he caught her wrists and raised them up over her head.

"Jett," she complained. She didn't think she could wait much longer. She wanted to touch him. She wanted to feel him alive, throbbing in her palms.

"Not yet." Holding both her hands loosely in one of his, Jett fiddled with the headboard—and then she felt the smooth, braided rope slipping over her hands, felt it pull taut with a gentle tug from him, closing around her wrists like a noose.

Alarm slammed into her.

She jerked her arms, but they remained secured over her head. "Jett?"

He surveyed her upper body, his face taut with lust. "Relax. You'll like this."

"But…" Again she pulled, and accepted that there was no way for her to break the hold. Her heart began pounding for an entirely different reason.

Satisfied, Jett stretched out next to her, propped on an elbow and rested his free hand low on her belly. He looked from her bound hands down her arms, over her face and to her chest. "Even like this, all stretched out on your beautiful back, you have an impressive rack."

Natalie tried to calm herself. She wanted Jett. But… she just didn't know about this.

Trying to decide what to say, she whispered, "I'm not sure…"

"Trust me." He bent and drew one nipple into his mouth, shattering her thoughts. She felt the gentle pull of his mouth everywhere: on her nipple, in her stomach, between her legs. It was a potent mix—sharp pleasure with an edge of uncertainty. Danger. Lust.

Again she tested the restraint, and this time, the feel of being powerless, at his mercy…excited her. She'd never been one to live on the edge; never, ever had she had this type of purely sexual encounter.

She remained nervous but not really afraid. However, she had to know.

"Jett?"

"Mmm?" Leaning over her, he switched to her other breast, licking, nipping with the edge of his teeth until she gasped and then enclosing her in the heat of his mouth.

Natalie moaned before managing to say, "I…I need you to tell me what you're going to do."

Movements unhurried, he sat up beside her and looked her over. "All right." His dark brows puckered, and then, as if making up his mind, he parted her thighs and knelt between them.

Before Jett had accustomed her to his unique brand of earthy sexuality, she would have felt exposed. Now, she just enjoyed his attention and the fact that he took so much pleasure in looking at her—in every way.

He trailed his fingertips down her inner thighs, tickling, adding to her tension.

"You and I are going to talk." He used his thumbs to part her, opened his big hands wide on the very top of her thighs.

The way he looked at her in such detail would have been distracting enough, but he…wanted to talk? "Jett?"

Giving up the perusal of her body, he raised his gaze to lock onto hers. "We'll talk, and when we're done, you're going to come for me."

# CHAPTER TWO

No woman had ever looked more delectable than Natalie did right now.

Worry softened the lust in her big brown eyes. Her keen intellect cautioned her of his intent, but her sensual nature was game for some risqué play.

In the dimmer light of his bedroom, her lashes left long shadows on her velvety cheeks. From her slender throat to her soft belly, heat flushed her fair skin. Her rosy nipples were drawn tight, her thighs open to him, her pink sex already glistening and swollen.

She chewed her bottom lip even while breathing hard. She wouldn't be able to free herself, and still she strained against the special restraints. Her legs, opened wide around his hips, flexed when her back bowed.

"It's all right, you know." Keeping his hands off her proved impossible, so he smoothed them down her ribs to her hipbones. Spreading his fingers wide, he used his hands to frame her sex. "Why are you worried?"

Her heavy-lidded gaze went smoky; she pulled at her restraints.

Damn, but he liked this. Too much. "You look sexy as hell like this, Natalie." He drifted his thumbs back and forth, brushing her pubic hair.

Closing her eyes to regain her wits, she took a deep breath then asked, "What do you want to talk about?"

Watching her was a unique pleasure. As he touched his thumbs to her vulva, he whispered, "Everything."

Breath held, she tipped her head back and concentrated on the way he made her feel. To most of the world, Natalie presented a modest sense of decorum. In bed with him, she became a complete hedonist.

Jett smiled at the sinuous movements of her perfect body.

Natalie might not realize it yet, but they were totally in sync. He was experienced enough to know it, even if she wasn't. Sexually, they were a perfect match.

It'd be interesting to see how they matched up out of bed too, but he had to tread lightly with that idea. If he came on too strong, she might mistake his interest for a commitment.

Looking at her voluptuous body, he told himself that he should take what she so freely offered and enjoy it while it lasted.

But deep down, he knew that someone in her past had hurt her.

Whether that person was still in the picture, Jett didn't know. He did know that Natalie wasn't married and never had been, wasn't engaged and wasn't seeing anyone other than him. But maybe the guy who'd hurt her was an associate or a family friend.

Jett scowled. Eventually he'd uncover all her secrets.

One thing at a time.

As a teacher, Natalie got extended time off for spring break. That meant plenty of grown-up time away from kids and papers, without the administration keeping tabs on her. No way in hell would he let her hit the dating scene without him.

Not without a fight.

And God knew, he never fought fair. Soon enough, Natalie would know it too.

"Honey, look at me."

Warily, she brought her gaze back to his, uncertain yet willing. "What?"

Jett kept one hand on her right leg, on her inner thigh. The other was still between her legs, playing with her ever so lightly. "I overheard you on your cell phone last week." Beneath his palm, her thigh felt sleek and soft. "You were coming into the apartment, talking about spring break."

She went utterly still, her eyes widening with caution. "Spring break?"

He narrowed his eyes at that evasive reply. "I know that you teach middle school, Natalie."

She shook her head but asked, "How?"

To distract her from what he had to say, Jett draped her legs up and over his, widening her even more and scooting in closer to her body. He was so hard that he hurt, but for now he could ignore his own need.

He heard her sharp inhalation at this new position, and he said, "You told me that you teach." Back before she'd decided she had to keep him out of her life. "Don't you remember?"

"No."

To keep her just as he wanted her, he put both hands on her thighs. "You didn't give me any details, but I have ways of finding out things."

Though he didn't look at her face, he felt her new nervousness, the burgeoning suspicion. Any second now, she'd demand that he let her go.

And of course he would. She needed to know that

she could always trust him, and that for him, no meant no, period.

To keep her from calling it quits, he cupped his hand over her mound again. "You are so hot."

She hesitated, just as he'd known she would. It had been that way from the beginning with Natalie. They were so sexually suited that a mere touch could ignite them both.

But despite Natalie's deliberate avoidance of emotional ties, he sensed that what she shared with him was more than sexual.

She definitely loved having sex with him, but sometimes she used sex as an excuse to seek him out for other reasons. After weeks of the most detailed physical exploration imaginable, he could easily read her frame of mind. Within minutes of Natalie knocking on his door, Jett knew if she was upset with someone, if she needed comfort, or distraction.

If she needed reassurance.

He always gauged her mood and then adjusted the lovemaking to reflect it. That meant sometimes things were fast and frenetic, sometimes slow and easy, and at times, even sweet and...loving.

Tonight she was worried. About what, he didn't yet know, but he hoped before the night ended, she'd tell him.

Natalie didn't recognize it, but an emotional connection played a large role in making the sex so damn good. She was too naive to realize that the thrill of a purely physical encounter quickly dimmed, that *just* sex, cold and detached, could never be as intense as the involvement they shared.

For a while now they'd been going strong. Neither of

them had tired of the other, and neither of them sought companionship elsewhere.

At least, that better be the case, because the idea of her doing *this* with anyone else felt like acid in his gut.

There were days when he knew she was in her apartment alone, and it kept him on edge wondering why she didn't come over. The urge to go to her, to change the dynamics of their relationship, prodded him more times than he cared to remember.

It wasn't until he'd heard her talking about taking off for vacation that he'd decided to push her for more than sex.

"I like you like this, Natalie." As Jett teased his fingers along her stomach, she shivered. "I like knowing that you're here and that you're not going anywhere."

Her lips parted, and then she dropped her head back to stare at the ceiling. After releasing a long, shuddering breath, she said with confidence, "You would never hurt me."

"I'd die first." He saw the tension leave her shoulders, and he smiled slightly. "What were you thinking?"

She squirmed in indecision.

"Natalie." He put his hands by her hips and leaned over her. "You can ask me anything."

"All right." Her gaze dropped to his thigh but then flickered away. "That scar on your leg…"

Though it still ached at times, Jett rarely paid it any mind these days. "An old bullet wound. What about it?"

Her eyes flared wide. Hesitant, she licked her lips.

Damn, but he felt that lick everywhere. "You are so fucking beautiful." He had to hurry this along so he could get inside her. "Now tell me, what about the scar?"

"I shouldn't have said anything."

Jett had to shake his head at her indecision. She was so damn vulnerable and so defensive of her privacy. She shared her body without reserve but feared sharing anything more. "But you did, so tell me, does it bother you?"

"No!"

He looked at the scar and shrugged. "I'm used to it. To me it's just a mark, but I suppose it's ugly."

"Oh no, Jett." Pure reaction tightened her thighs around him. "Nothing about your body is ugly. I didn't mean anything like that."

"Then what?"

She gave another small tug on her restraints. "This hardly seems the time to chitchat."

It was exactly the time to chitchat. "Why not now? We're neither one going anywhere, so we have plenty of time on our hands."

After a few seconds more, she got her backbone and met his gaze with an exasperated expression of daring. "It looked like a bullet wound to me, so I've sometimes wondered what type of dangerous man you might be."

His mouth twitched. She thought him dangerous? Perceptive of her.

"Is that funny?"

Given his background and his capability, it really wasn't much of a stretch. When necessary he could be deadly. "I guess not." He hoped she wouldn't be too put off by the life he'd led.

"So why are you smiling?"

Jett tried to look more serious. "I'm only a little dangerous, I promise." Encouraging her toward more conversation, he explained, "I do security work now, mostly domestic investigation."

"Security work?" Her expression sharpened. "What does that mean?"

"Means I'm a private eye." Jett watched her and saw her eyes widen with understanding. "It makes it pretty easy for me to uncover secrets." *Your* secrets.

Aghast, her brows came down and her mouth firmed. "Have you been snooping into my life?"

He gave a noncommittal roll of one shoulder. "Can't help myself. I'm the cautious type. See, I'm also ex-military and ex-FBI. Being well-informed is the name of the game, and I'm afraid old habits die hard."

She absorbed all that with a frown. "So that bullet wound…?"

"Is why I'm not still FBI. Other injuries I could brush off, but that one caused more damage and got me grounded, stuck on desk duty."

"You don't have the body of a desk jockey."

One brow lifted. "I guess not. That's because shuffling papers is not my thing, which is why I became a P.I. At least having my own setup, I can pick and choose the cases I want to take."

"Is it physically challenging?"

"It can be. I stay in shape because I need to." In an effort at full disclosure with her, Jett admitted, "I get most of my business from a surveillance firm that deals with divorce."

Even more aghast, Natalie said, "You *spy* on people having marital problems?"

He didn't like her tone. "It's not that simple, but if

you want to go bare-bones, then yeah." To make sure she got a clear picture, he shared details. "A few months ago, some bozo who'd been cheating on his wife and got busted for it decided he didn't want a divorce. He wanted her to give him another chance, and it didn't matter to him that she preferred to move on. Thing is, he was acting so weird, she didn't trust him, so she hired me to keep an eye on him."

Natalie frowned, but it seemed more out of concern than censure.

"I started checking up on him, learning his routine, his habits. A week later when the asshole bought a gun, I knew he had something planned."

Her lips parted. "A *gun?*"

Jett nodded. "That same day, he checked out an old barn at an abandoned farm out in the middle of nowhere. I didn't like it, so I followed him the rest of the day."

As if forgetting her naked pose beneath him, Natalie shifted then asked, almost breathless, "What happened?"

"He pulled the gun on his wife." Remembering it made Jett tense all over again. Abuse of any kind sickened him, but abuse against a woman, a wife, left him rigid with fury. "His plan was to force her into the car and take her to the barn."

Attention rapt, Natalie whispered, "Why?"

"He said he was going to do a murder-suicide."

"Oh my God. You heard all that?"

"And recorded it."

Her entire countenance softened. "What did you do, Jett?"

"I stopped him." Jett took great pleasure in giving

her that truth. It had been ugly, and he'd definitely lost control when the guy tried to stave him off by pointing the gun at his wife. More than anything, Jett had wanted to tear that guy apart. As it was, he'd done more than enough damage.

He waited for Natalie to ask him *how* he'd stopped the jerk and wondered just how much he ought to tell her.

Instead, she said, "You could have been killed."

She surprised him with that observation. "Maybe." Shots were fired that day. Luckily they'd only struck a tree, a car and the side of the house. "But I wasn't. Instead, the guy is now in jail on a string of charges, and the woman is free to live without always looking over her shoulder."

"I'm glad you were there to help her."

Jett felt compelled to tell her, "I'm damn good at any job I do."

She accepted that without comment then looked down at his thigh, currently under hers, keeping her legs apart. "Does it ever pain you?"

"Not often." He ran a hand up her leg to her hip. "For this, for you, I promise it's not a problem."

Her gaze went from his leg to his boner. "I'm glad."

Jett watched the rise and fall of her breasts as she rested there. He didn't want to push her, but… "Your turn, Natalie."

Her gaze shot up to his. "For what?"

"Share something with me. Something that I don't already know."

Her gaze immediately skirted away. "I don't think so."

"Why not?" He brushed a few of those honey-colored curls away from her face.

She turned her cheek into his palm. Sounding almost desperate, she said, "Because I like things how they are."

"What if I don't?"

Something close to panic darkened her eyes. Again she struggled against the restraint before giving up to say, "Try to understand, Jett." She took a shuddering breath, licked her lips. "Sharing is…difficult for me."

Because she didn't trust him—but he wasn't giving up. Not yet. "I'll make it easier for you." Leaning down, Jett kissed her lightly on her lips, then her throat and then each breast.

She held her breath as he sat up again, stroking his hands along her sweet, taut body, over her ribs, her hipbones, and coming to rest on her inner thighs.

Her breathing accelerated. "I don't see how—"

"I know what you want, honey. I know what you need." He eased a finger inside her, touching her carefully with slow, precise care. "Just relax now."

Her lids sank down over dazed eyes.

"I'll ask questions," Jett quietly told her, "and you can just answer."

He knew she was confused but also aroused, and he hoped that might help weaken her resistance. "Where are you going for spring break?"

She clenched, and he felt it on his finger. It was his turn to close his eyes as he struggled for control.

Voice very small and shaky, she whispered, "Jett… I'm not sure—"

"I know." But he couldn't let her uncertainty matter anymore. "Do you want me, Natalie?"

No hesitation. "Yes."

Coaxing, he said, "You're on the pill, and neither of us has been with anyone else since we started seeing each other."

He waited, and when she didn't deny that, a strangling tightness loosened in his chest.

It felt like relief.

With that confirmed, he made up his mind.

For the first time in over a decade, he wanted to skip the precautions to build on his special closeness with Natalie. It wasn't something he'd do with a casual date, and neither would she.

"I don't want to wear a rubber." Jett met her surprised gaze. "I want to feel *you,* Natalie. All of you." He eased his finger out then pressed in again. "And I want you to feel only me."

Her chest labored and, voice lower still, filled with heat, she said again, "Yes."

Damn. Maybe he'd overestimated his control. He took a second to regroup then took his fingers from her. Bracing on one arm beside her, he wrapped a hand around his erection and used it to tease her. Up and down, over her turgid clitoris—but he didn't enter her. Not yet.

She lifted up, trying to encourage him, but he held off. It sure as hell wasn't easy when every muscle in his body urged him to bury himself deep inside her. He had to remember his plan.

Locking his jaw, Jett pushed just the head of his cock inside her.

Slippery wet, silky hot and almost irresistible.

If he wanted only this, he'd be a goner. But he wanted more.

When Natalie squirmed, tightening her legs around

him, he damn near lost it. Giving her his weight to keep her still, Jett cupped her face, brushed his mouth lightly over hers and asked again, "Where are you going for spring break?"

She kissed him—until he leaned out of reach. *"I need you, Jett."*

"I know you do." Not as much as he needed her, though. "Tell me where you're going."

She paused in her fevered attempt to connect with him. "I don't understand you."

Closing his eyes, Jett stroked into her, filled her and relished her ragged moan of pleasure.

Then he pulled almost all the way out again.

"We both need this, honey." Talking wasn't easy, but he figured Natalie was worth the effort. "There's nothing I enjoy more than being inside you."

She stared at him with wanton concentration. "Then take me."

He touched his mouth to her jaw, her temple, in light, soft kisses. "Let's go one better, okay?"

"How?"

"We can start right here, right now."

She couldn't hide her skepticism. "What is it you want?"

A little trust. "Tell me where you're going."

She drew a deep breath—and relented. "To a vacation lake in Tennessee."

It was still chilly for that. He'd expected her to say somewhere farther south, maybe in Florida since that's where most people went on spring break.

His thoughts scrambled, but he couldn't think of a good reason for her choice. "Why there?"

"It's peaceful."

Okay. He got that. Peace and quiet sounded fine. But why go all the way to Tennessee for it?

Jett cupped her jaw. "What will you do there?"

Almost desperate, Natalie pleaded, "Make love to me, damn you."

He kissed her, longer and hotter this time, his tongue slipping over hers, twining. And because he couldn't stop himself, he stroked into her. Deep.

Immediately, she tightened around him, her heels digging into the small of his back as if to keep him there, a part of her.

Hell, he didn't want to move. Not yet.

He caressed her cheeks with his thumbs. "What's at the lake, Natalie?" Lust made his tone more urgent. "Tell me."

She struggled with herself but finally gave in. "Anonymity."

Jett froze. A hell of a lot of people headed south for spring break. She could run into a student or one of the faculty members. But so what? Seeing someone she knew would matter only if…

He stiffened, raising himself up the length of his arms. That position pressed their lower bodies closer together in exquisite contact.

They stared at each other, him hot and irate, her soft and susceptible, both turned on.

After a few seconds, her eyes closed and she shifted against him. "You're filling me, Jett, and it's so damn good. But God, I need you to *move*."

Instead, he pressed a hand down between their bodies until he could touch her. She jerked in reaction, clenching around him so tightly that he shuddered.

He wanted her. Bad.

But a horrible suspicion overrode other sensations, gnawing at him, as sharp as a blade. As his fingertips played over her, he asked silkily, "You planning to do this with someone else, baby, is that it?"

Her eyes flashed open and she gasped.

"S'that why you want anonymity?" He searched her face, turbulent with dark emotions. "So you can carry on another no-strings affair while you're away?"

"You're serious?"

Pressing deeper into her, until he felt her womb, Jett staked a claim even while asking, *"Is it?"*

Rigid indignation replaced the soft voluptuousness of her body. "Jerk!"

Now furious, she pulled viciously at the restraints. He rested between her legs—was still *inside* her—but she tried to kick at him. The frenetic movements only managed to push him closer to the edge, making him groan.

She twisted beneath him. "Get off!"

Taken aback by her reaction, Jett gave her all his weight, pinning her down. He held her arms near the elbows, not wanting her to hurt herself. "If that's not it, then *why?*"

Rancor had replaced the sexual haze. "You're the hotshot private eye. You tell me."

Usually, even under the worst circumstances, Jett could think fast, piecing together clues to come up with a viable answer to just about any problem. With Natalie, he stayed so damned confused, thrown off by overwhelming sentiment that half the time he didn't know if he was coming or going.

Taking a guess, he said, "Not to have a fling, then?"

Her head lifted off the pillow so she could say right into his face, "I'm already having a fling, you ass!"

With him. But damn it, he wanted to move beyond that now. There wasn't a single good reason for them not to be more social. He enjoyed dating. He wanted to take her to movies, to dinner…maybe to meet his family.

Shit.

He wasn't seeing anyone else, and she claimed that she wasn't either.

So why not?

Jett felt raw. "So this—" he pressed deep into her "—is enough for you?"

Dropping back again, she gave a broken laugh devoid of any humor. "It would be, if only you'd quit playing this stupid game and give me what I need."

Ah, hell. Even furious, her voice shook with desire. They were both in a bad way. "I guess that's my answer."

She turned her face to glare at him. "Don't you dare leave me like this."

"Wouldn't dream of it." He couldn't, even if he wanted to. Going back up on stiffened arms, he let his gaze wander over her. Fury pulsed through his blood.

Fury…and something more.

"Look at you. You think I could give this up? Not a chance." He didn't give her an opportunity to reply. "I love fucking you."

She gasped at the harsh words, and that gasp brought him a measure of sanity. He felt abusive and mean. Damn it, he knew Natalie held him at bay for a reason. Wasn't that why he'd started the whole bondage thing to begin with?

Well, that, and the fact that he enjoyed having her sweet body to play with.

Taking several calming breaths that didn't help one bit, Jett said carefully, "You're afraid of something, aren't you, honey?"

That did it. She went pale, rigid. "Untie me, Jett." Her eyes glistened. She sniffed. "Right now."

He would. Of course he would.

But those unshed tears wrenched his heart, even as his body throbbed.

He couldn't leave her like this. "If I untie you now, you'll storm out of here, mad and hurt."

Unsatisfied.

She blinked away the tears. "And if I stay, it'll be any different?"

Her breasts heaved in her ire, he was still inside her and they were both primed. It wouldn't take much to give her full relief.

That is, if he could change her mind about leaving.

Jett looked at her breasts, at her tightened nipples. "Yeah, it will." He lowered his head.

NATALIE SAW HIS INTENT, and she knew she wouldn't be able to resist him if he put his hot mouth on her again. Hoping to forestall him, to salvage her pride, she blurted, "I've been used before, damn you, so don't you dare."

He paused, then his piercing gaze flashed up to clash with hers. "By who?"

Memories, dark and filled with humiliation, brought a smirk of disgust to her mouth. "Men who thought my father's money was my own."

He was quick to say, "Bastards." And then, with his

hands cupping her face and his expression filled with tenderness, he added, "But, honey, that's not me. That could never be me."

Despite being restrained, she put up her chin. "That's what they all say." She wanted to believe him, but she wasn't a fool. Not anymore. "I'd rather not take that chance."

Jett flinched but rallied. "For just a moment, I'm going to forget you said that. Because, Natalie, when I look at you, I sure as hell don't see any family affiliations or connected wealth. I see *you,* only you, and that's enough for me."

He sounded and looked sincere, so maybe it warranted some discussion. But now that the sexual encounter had soured, Natalie couldn't bear the submissive position. "Untie me."

Seconds ticked by. "You enjoyed it."

"At first." Being tied to Jett's bed had been unbelievably exciting. "Until you ruined it."

"Right." His mouth tightened, his eyes narrowed. He looked at her breasts. "I could still—"

"No, you can't." Natalie didn't look away from his obvious regret. "Once you brought up fear, being restrained took on a whole new meaning."

His frustration wore on her until he finally reached beyond her to the headboard. She felt a tug on the restraint, it loosened and then she was free.

Jett didn't move away from her. Holding a wrist in each of his big hands, he lowered her arms. His thumbs moved over her skin as if to soothe, when that wasn't necessary. He hadn't hurt her.

But she was insane with unfulfilled need. The skin of her wrists felt too sensitive beneath his thumbs. His scent, heightened by arousal, surrounded her. His thick erection filled her. And the heat of their bodies mingled together.

No other man had ever made her feel this way.

Even now, hurt by his accusation, angry at being manipulated, she trembled with wanting him.

She'd accepted her response to him as a chemical phenomenon; whatever Jett had, it worked for her. In a thousand different ways.

But this…this attempt to change things…

Did she dare even consider it?

No. If she tried it, he'd see her for a fraud. He'd know that her daring in bed was all an act. She wasn't brave, or sensual or…free. She was a remote woman, socially inept, especially when it came to anything serious—like relationships.

Other than the kids she taught, and her sister, she felt out of place with most people.

Once again Jett seemed to read her thoughts. "Natalie." He lifted her hands to his hard, sleek shoulders and, curving his hands around her head, held her as a lover would. "Stop looking like that. I'm not trying to drag you off to the gallows."

"What are you trying to do?"

His long fingers kneaded her skull. "Just talk, honey, that's all."

"About personal things." And at an inappropriate time, not that she ever afforded him a better opportunity.

"About *you*."

"Why?" Men wanted sex. She *gave* him sex. God, sometimes she practically molested him. Why muddle things with conversation?

"It's a good start. A natural progression."

For what? Her brows furrowed. They'd talked before, of course, but not like this. Not about anything important.

Certainly not about her fear of commitment.

The fear remained a part of her, but now an aberrant optimism stirred inside her, filling her with warmth.

Knowing how easy it'd be for her to fall hopelessly in love with Jett, Natalie had set up deliberate barriers to keep her from getting too attached. Not that the barriers had worked.

She was already half in love with him.

Which was unacceptable, of course; she didn't want to be hurt again. Going away on spring break so she wouldn't be tempted to try to deepen their association had been her only solution.

But here they were, still in bed, still joined, still aroused. And Jett was full of insistence.

Natalie asked warily, "Progress toward what, exactly?"

His sexy smile melted her heart. "The thing is, I don't want to say something that'll maybe spook you."

Seeing the irony of that, Natalie shook her head. "If tying me to your bed didn't do it, I think you're safe enough."

The smile turned into a low growl. "You're probably right." He gathered her under him, his mouth to her temple, his strong arms around her. "Admit it, Natalie. You liked being tied to my bed, didn't you?"

"Maybe." This game was new to her and she wasn't certain how to play. "I'll enjoy a payback, too."

He went still before pushing back to see her face. His eyes narrowed. "You want to tie me down?"

She hadn't really thought about it, but now she did, and it stirred her. An image of Jett held captive, his strong body stretched out, at her mercy—she'd be free to touch him, taste him.

Ride him.

Her breathing quickened. She felt a rush of dampness and knew he'd felt it too. "Turnabout is fair play, right?"

"I can tell you like the idea." His jaw tightened. "You're so damn wet."

When he moved inside her, she made a sound of pleasure.

"You look so fucking sexy right now."

She *felt* sexy. "Mmm. How so?"

He continued the slow, easy thrusts, even as he whispered, "Your eyes are darker, your face flushed." He leaned closer, his mouth just barely touching hers. "You look just like you do when you come for me."

That should have embarrassed her, but it didn't. "I wonder how I'll look when I have you tied down."

Expression arrested, Jett went still over her. "I don't know if that scares me or turns me on even more." He kissed her hard and fast and then grew serious again. "I'm working on a hair trigger here, so before I lose it, I want to make a suggestion."

Would he switch positions with her right now? "I'm listening."

"Let me make love to you, because God knows, we both need it."

She couldn't agree more.

"But stay afterward."

Her heart tripped. Oh God, so many times she'd thought about how nice it would be to cuddle with him afterward, to just be with him. She dampened her lips. "For…what?"

"I like you, honey. I *love* having sex with you."

Natalie wasn't sure what to make of that.

"But sometimes I'd like to get out, too. Dinner, a show, whatever. Only I don't want to go with anyone else."

Her breath caught. "You don't?"

He shook his head. "And I don't want you with anyone else, either."

That wasn't a problem. She didn't date. Ever. "I don't—"

He didn't let her finish. "Since we're compatible, is it really such a big deal?"

"I don't know."

"You could try trusting me a little." He touched the corner of her mouth with his thumb. "Can you do that?"

She wanted to tell him that it wasn't about trust. But more than that, she wanted him. Right now.

Could it really hurt to stay, to talk?

Possibly. But at this particular moment, she just didn't care.

## CHAPTER THREE

THREADING HER FINGERS into Jett's silky black hair to keep him close, Natalie sought his mouth with her own.

With a ragged groan, he kissed her back, voracious and hungry and out of control.

As his tongue stroked hers he flexed his hips, withdrawing, entering her again, over and over in a driving rhythm that she knew would quickly take her to a climax. She suspected her agreement accounted for his enthusiasm as much as his heightened state of arousal.

She wrapped her legs around him again and wrung another groan from him. Each hard thrust rocked the bed and escalated the heat building inside her.

And wow, the man knew how to kiss.

He knew how to make love, too.

Natalie gave up trying to think; with Jett inside her, loving her, it was pointless to do anything but feel.

With one hand under her, he tilted up her hips so he could go even deeper, and with the other he cupped her breast, using his thumb to stroke her nipple. His mouth ate at hers, his tongue mimicking the movements of his body.

She breathed in his rich scent, felt the strength in his big body—and a climax shuddered through her, stiffening her legs, making her pulse and throb with the unbearable pleasure of it.

Just as her orgasm began to recede, Jett lifted his mouth away. He put his head back, fisted his hands in the sheet at each side of her and came with a deep groan of release.

Watching him through dazed eyes, Natalie admired his broad shoulders, his solid chest, the way his jaw locked as he spent. A light sprinkling of dark hair covered his chest, trailed down his abdomen in a thin line then spread out again at his groin. His bones were large, his body unyielding.

He had such striking good looks.

But he was so much more than a gorgeous body and face.

By small degrees, Jett lowered himself back down over her, balancing on his forearms to keep his weight off her. With his dark-eyed gaze now mellow and replete, he looked sexier than ever. They both breathed heavily for several minutes.

Natalie recovered first. Now with the gripping need temporarily eased, talking might actually be possible. Not that she looked forward to it, but she knew she couldn't dodge Jett without looking ridiculous. "Mmm. Much better."

Expression warm, his touch light and easy, he bent to kiss her mouth. "God," he whispered, "you're beautiful."

Natalie smiled. "I was about to say the same."

Eyes so dark they looked black in the dim light of his bedroom glittered with amusement. On other men, such long, black lashes might look effeminate; on Jett, they only emphasized his rugged masculinity.

He put his forehead to hers. "If you think I'm beautiful, then you must have come harder than I thought."

She chuckled. Now *this* talk she was used to; they often indulged in silly sexual banter before she slipped away from his apartment.

Natalie looped her arms around his neck. "You are beautiful, Jett Sutter. All over." She touched his jaw and realized she hadn't given him time to shave before coming over to knock. "It's a rugged beauty made up of oh-so-sexy eyes, a rock-solid bod and tons of irresistible charm."

"Irresistible, huh? I like the sound of that." He lowered himself down against her, and that sort of squished her boobs, leaving them plumped up high on her chest. He bent to kiss the top of each one. "Trust me, honey, I have no complaints about your body, either."

A safe enough topic. Being philosophical, she said, "Most men like big boobs."

He didn't smile when he looked into her eyes. "I like you, so your bra size wouldn't matter."

"I see. So…" Natalie tried not to grin at him as she shimmied her shoulders, making her breasts jiggle. "These aren't something you noticed right off?"

Still too serious, he said, "I did, sure. You, Natalie Alexander, are extraordinarily stacked." He toyed with her hair, letting one long ringlet twine around his finger. "But I also noticed your reserve and the way your incredible hair sort of dances when you walk."

Her hair was like dandelion fluff on humid days, but she enjoyed the compliment all the same.

"I noticed your smile and your pretty brown eyes that are always so sincere. How you greet every neighbor in the building and how you talk to yourself when you're trying to remember things."

Wow, that sounded as though he'd been plenty observant. "I talk to myself?"

He traced her lips with a fingertip. "You do, usually when you first get home. You come across the parking lot, arms loaded down with books and bags, and you say things to yourself, like *Check the mail, get the chicken out of the freezer, call Molly, sort the tests.*" As if he couldn't resist, he bent to her mouth for a soft but sensual kiss. "Things like that. Mental note-taking, I guess."

"I had no idea." But it sounded like the things she worked to remember each and every day.

"Molly is your sister, right?"

He'd admitted to snooping into her background, and now she knew he'd listened to her inane mumblings. Her defensiveness came crawling back in on her, but she tried to sound playful rather than offended. "You mean a supersleuth like you doesn't already know the answer to that?"

Sighing, he eased away from her and sat up.

Natalie realized that, without the use of a condom, she was on the…messy side. It was a novel thing for her. She'd never had sex without a rubber. She'd never before wanted to.

Being a sensible woman, she took responsibility seriously, and from the day she'd wanted to become sexually active, she'd been very cautious.

It went beyond that, though.

Jett was the first man she'd been with long enough, and trusted enough, to want to forgo condoms. Other men had asked, but her answer was always a resounding "no." Without the use of a condom, she didn't have sex.

Until now. Until Jett.

With his back to her, Jett asked, "Are you going to keep taking jabs at my profession?"

"What? No!" She hadn't meant it that way at all. "I wasn't ridiculing your work."

"Yeah, you were."

That annoyed her. "Wrong, Sherlock."

He eyed her.

"Sorry. Figure of speech." Natalie sighed. "I just don't like having anyone snoop into my business without permission." She looked beyond him to the open bathroom door. This was going to be tricky.

Why had no one ever told her about cleanup?

His gaze turned speculative, intent. "Hang around awhile and I'll explain about that."

Hang around—to be with Jett, to just talk, to learn more about him.

Oh, she wanted to, she really did.

But before she could even think about that… "Jett, I, ah…need to make a dash into the bathroom."

As her meaning sank in, his expression lightened. He smiled at her. "Stay put, honey. I'll take care of it."

Appalled, Natalie watched as he went into the bathroom. Through the open door she saw him dampen a washcloth under running water.

No way.

When he came back to her side of the bed, Natalie snatched up the sheet to cover herself. "What do you think you're going to do?"

"Clean you."

"Oh no, you are not."

As if she hadn't spoken at all he sat beside her, one hand on her thigh, his demeanor one of pure masculine possession. "I don't skip condoms, Natalie. Ever."

They had that in common. "Me, either."

He coasted his hand up and down her thigh. "Even though you're on the pill?"

With the washcloth held in his free hand, concentrating on the conversation took effort. "Doubling up is safer, and besides, pregnancy is only one concern these days."

"True enough."

And honestly, she hadn't been with that many men. For a twenty-seven-year-old woman, her sexual experiences were few and far between.

He studied her with lowered brows and grave intensity. "But you let me."

They both knew they'd just crossed some boundaries into new intimacy. Very softly she replied, "Yes."

Still holding her captive in his gaze, Jett whipped the sheet away from her, causing her to yelp. "I think you and I are going to share a lot of firsts together."

She tried to block his hands, but he laughed until he got her pinned down then coaxed her, saying softly, "Let me."

And she caved.

Jett didn't realize it, but he'd already been her first in many ways. Her first fling. Her first orgasm—at least through intercourse. Her first spontaneous encounter. Her first time being tied.

And now this.

It unnerved her, the complete and varied ways she enjoyed him. But it also felt so *right*.

She didn't fight him as he cleaned her body. She didn't look away from him either. What she'd expected to be horribly awkward just…wasn't.

Not with Jett.

He was so earthy, so comfortable with all things sexual, that he put her at ease with his attitude alone.

When he finished, he kissed the inside of her thigh then cupped his hand over her. "I like taking care of you."

Natalie wanted to touch him, to go to her knees and kiss him.

To have him again.

She started to move and he said, "Be right back." He returned to the bathroom but was gone only a few minutes.

Natalie stared at the ceiling, attempting to sort her thoughts, to order her priorities.

He returned to his side of the bed, sitting with one leg bent on the mattress, his gaze all over her body again. Neither of them could ever deny the physical attraction—it showed whenever they were together, in the way they watched each other, how they touched and that sharp level of awareness.

"Before we get sidetracked again, tell me that you're going to stay."

She wanted to pull him down to her, but she held herself in check. "How long?"

At her reply, his shoulders stiffened. "Is it really asking so much?"

Of course it wasn't. She felt like a heel. "Sorry. As you said earlier, old habits die hard."

One brow rose up. "Meaning you're used to deflecting guys in bed after they've just had sex with you?"

*That* brought her to her knees. She poked a finger at his chest. "Don't you dare judge me, Jett Sutter! You can't very well claim inexperience."

He eyed her breasts. "No." Catching her finger, he tugged her closer. "But you're different from every other woman I've been with, so I sure as hell don't want to be the same as every other guy."

Oh, God. He wasn't. Molly gave an exasperated sigh. "What I meant is that I'm not used to letting *anyone* get close, regardless of the circumstances."

"Not even family?"

She didn't want to explore the possibility, but if Jett did have any illusions about easy money, she could set him straight right now. "Especially not family. Well, except for Molly."

"Your sister."

She nodded. "We're close."

He caught her chin and lifted her face. "You're estranged from your father." It wasn't a question.

Damn. He really had been snooping. When she started to withdraw, he caught the back of her neck.

"It doesn't matter. I don't care about that." Then he shook his head, and his voice firmed. "No, that's not precisely true. I do care."

Of course he did.

As if he'd read her thoughts again, he gave her a look of censure. "It's one hell of an insult to be called a gold digger."

"I didn't."

"But you're thinking it." He dragged her in close for a hard smooch. "I bought land a few years ago and was saving to build my own house. I have about half the cash up front in the bank and can easily afford a loan on the rest. I would have started on the house already, but I met you, and since then I haven't been in a big hurry to move out of here. But I will eventually."

He'd stayed in the apartment complex for her? Staggered, she asked, "How much land?"

"Only ten acres. But it's secluded, and pretty. A stream runs through it." He gave her a look. "You want to see it? Maybe check out my bank account so you'll know I'm not in desperate financial straits?"

She couldn't blame him for getting nasty. "Jett…"

"What I have is nothing compared to your father's money. But you can believe me when I say I'm happy. I have what I want, and I got it on my own."

"I'm sorry." What else could she say?

"I care about your relationship with your father only because I think that's one of the reasons you're shutting me out."

And…he wanted in?

Natalie put a hand to her head, trying to think. Maybe all this could wait until she'd had time to think about it. "I'm leaving tomorrow for the lake. I'll be gone for a week—"

He surprised her by saying, "I'll go with you."

Her eyes widened; he couldn't be serious. But one look at his set face and she knew he was. She scrambled for a reply. "You don't have to work?"

"I take time off when I want—that's a perk to being your own boss." He stood, stretched elaborately and went to his dresser to get out boxers. As he stepped into them, he asked, "How long is your break?"

Well. Natalie knew he was bulldozing her, but the idea of having Jett along tempted her. She had almost dreaded the time away because she would miss him and their special time together.

She licked her lips. "Ten days."

"No problem."

But she emphasized, "In isolation." Jett might be expecting a real vacation with dinners out, live performances, something more than a quaint cabin on a secluded lot at an off-season vacation lake.

"Sounds great."

She couldn't help but fret. Never had she taken a vacation, especially such a lackluster vacation, with a guy. "You might get bored."

He shot her a look full of meaning. As his gaze went over her body he cocked a brow. "Not a chance."

And still she felt compelled to make him understand. "It'll probably be pretty cool there still. Even though the cabin is on a big vacation lake, there won't be any swimming. I'm not sure we'll even be able to take out a boat."

He found a T-shirt and jeans. "What did you plan to do there?"

"Not much." Watching him dress, Natalie decided that their bed activities must have ended. Disappointed, she slipped her legs off the side of the bed and stood. She realized that her clothes were in the other room, but she'd look foolish if she wrapped up in the sheet.

Instead, she folded her arms around herself—which really didn't do much for her modesty. Rather than tell him that she'd hoped to come to grips with her growing feelings for him, she said, "Walk, read, maybe catch a movie or two." She lifted a shoulder. "Unwind."

"How long is the drive?"

"Six hours or more, not factoring in time to stop to

eat or take a break." By way of additional warning, she said, "I take lots of breaks."

"Good. No reason it shouldn't be a relaxing drive." He found a flannel shirt in his closet and brought it around to her, holding it out so she could shrug into it. "You hungry? Because I could eat. How about I order up a pizza?"

Incredulous, Natalie pushed her hair from her face. She looked at the challenge in his expression and huffed. "You're changing things at Mach speed!"

"A warning for you, Natalie." He lifted her chin on the edge of his fist. "I always go after what I want."

*What did that mean?* "Um…" She swallowed. "I had planned to leave really early tomorrow."

"I'll be ready." He caught the collar of the shirt in both hands, pulling her a little closer. "But for now, you have to eat, right?"

"I…"

"You came here as soon as you got home and changed. You have to be hungry."

Expectation and apprehension set her heart to thumping in a wild beat. She bit her lip. "Jett, are we really going to do this?"

Knowing he'd won, he gave a half smile of satisfaction. "Relax, Natalie. I'm not asking you to marry me."

Her knees turned to pudding. Of course he wasn't asking for that!

"I'm not even trying to tie you down. We enjoy each other in bed—"

"An understatement, at least for me."

His eyes glittered, and he gave her a quick kiss. "So for as long as it lasts, why not enjoy each other out of bed, too? Just let it happen, and I bet you'll find it's not the hardship you're expecting."

A hardship, no.

But a heartbreaker? Absolutely.

She wouldn't admit it to Jett, especially now that she knew how casual he wanted to keep things, but she had to accept the devastating truth: she was already in love with him. More time with him would make it only that much harder when things ended between them.

But with him so persuasive, how could she possibly resist?

AFTER JETT ORDERED PIZZA, Natalie wanted to go back to her place and retrieve her cell phone. She needed a few moments alone to regroup, but Jett, seeming disinclined to let her out of his sight, kept finding ways to keep her in his place. He offered her the use of his cell phone, and she knew she'd sound silly if she insisted on running over for her own.

Silly, and as afraid as he'd already accused her of being.

She'd have to go back to her place soon enough, but for now, she accepted his phone. Moving to the other side of the room for privacy, she tried calling her sister. She wanted Molly to know that she'd be gone on spring break. They always checked in with each other, and neither made a big move without telling the other about it. They were best friends as well as sisters, and given the strained relationship they each shared with their father, they were the only real family either one had.

Molly didn't answer, so Natalie left her a message. Turning her back so Jett wouldn't hear her, she said low, "Hey, Molly. I'm leaving for spring break tomorrow.

Going to a lake. Not alone, either, if you catch my meaning. Call me and I'll tell you all about it."

She knew it sounded cryptic and that Molly would give her hell for that later. But she didn't want Jett to hear her gossiping about him, and she didn't want to leave anything serious on her sister's answering machine—just in case.

Molly was such a loner, especially now that she'd broken things off with her fiancé, that Natalie doubted anyone ever heard her sister's messages. But she didn't take chances with her privacy. God forbid her stepmother, Kathi, should get wind of her affair. Her dad would be disgusted—nothing new in that—but Kathi would flip out. She worried incessantly about appearances.

Glancing over her shoulder, Natalie saw that Jett was busy putting a movie into his DVD player.

He must have felt her gaze because he said, "All done?"

"Yes." After closing his phone and handing it back to him, she headed for her discarded clothes which were still on the floor just inside the front door.

Gaze heated, Jett watched her step into her pants. "Spoilsport."

Natalie rolled her eyes. "A pizza delivery guy is coming over, remember?"

"And you look like a woman who's just been tumbled." He didn't smile as he strolled over to her. "Since I'm starting to feel possessive, I suppose I should bundle you up."

"Possessive?"

He looped his arms around her waist. "Why did you think I was being such an ass earlier?"

Unsure of his meaning, Natalie ventured a guess. "When you asked me if I was planning another fling?"

"Yeah." He kissed the end of her nose in apology. "I'm not the sharing kind."

His attitude thrilled Natalie, prompting her to reciprocate. "How could I even notice other men when you're here?"

His expression changed. He cupped her face and kissed her again, lingering, enticing. Against her lips, he asked, "You already packed up for tomorrow?"

"Yes." Though now that she knew Jett would be coming along, she probably needed to change out a few things...like maybe a pretty nightgown in place of her thermal pajamas. And she'd need to pack the makeup she'd planned to leave behind. "If you want to get your stuff together now, I can—"

For only a second, his arms tightened around her. "It won't take me long. Don't worry about it." He stepped back. "We can start the movie after the pizza gets here."

He led her to the couch and pulled her down to sit in his lap. She felt awkward, unsure what to do. It was a novel thing, sitting with a man like this. Should she cuddle, be playful, or was this another moment of pure intimacy?

"Relax." Jett rearranged her so that her cheek rested on his shoulder and the starch left her spine. "Did you reach your sister?"

"No." A little wide-eyed at the sensation of being cradled, pampered, Natalie sought normal conversation. "I called her earlier, too. Molly always returns my calls."

Jett toyed with her hair, winding curls around his finger. "You're concerned?"

"A little." His heat surrounded her, his solid frame somehow very comfortable. She tipped her head to look up at him. "I know that sounds dumb, given that Molly and I are both grown, independent adults. But we're more than sisters. We're best friends."

He nodded in understanding. "So you always stay in touch."

"We do. If Molly was still dating Adrian, I'd think she was out with him, but that's over."

"Adrian?"

Natalie made a face. Even the mention of Adrian's name annoyed her.

"Ah, not someone well liked, I take it?"

"Not by me, no. He used to be Molly's fiancé." She stroked a hand over Jett's upper chest then into his sparse chest hair. Without a doubt, she knew he was far more honorable than Adrian had ever been.

"Used to be? Past tense?"

"Yeah. Molly thought she was in love with him, but then when her career took off, he showed his true colors." Hating to think about her sister with that ass, Natalie ducked her face. "I knew Adrian was a jerk long before she did. But when he started making demands of Molly, she caught on real quick."

Jett tucked her hair behind her ear and then trailed his fingers along her jaw, down her throat, until he cupped a breast. "She ended things?"

"Yes." Her voice sounded higher with the intimate touch. "And I tried not to look too relieved."

Still holding her breast, Jett bent down to kiss

her throat. "I'm sure she knows you're motivated by caring."

Did he expect her to talk while his hot mouth moved over her skin? "Even when Molly is in the middle of business, she usually takes my calls."

Jett opened a button on the flannel shirt. "She's an author, right?"

The depths of his research amazed her. Or maybe he was one of her sister's many fans. "Have you read her?"

"No. She writes suspense or something, right?" He shook his head. "I'm more of a biography kind of reader."

Natalie frowned. "So that's just part of what you learned while snooping?"

He paused with his fingers inside the flannel shirt. "Okay, let's clear the air on that one first." He put his hand down the front of her shirt, and now it was his hot palm holding her. "You say you've been burned? Well me, too."

Natalie bit her lip, part in reaction to his touch and partly because of the scenarios that ran through her mind. "Did you have a broken engagement?" Or even worse, was he divorced? Had he been madly in love with someone who broke his heart and now—

Somehow, Jett always knew her thoughts. "My heart is intact, honey. But I've had women come on to me to get insider information on cases, and let me tell you, being used like that burns."

Natalie drew back. "Spies?"

He moved his thumb over her nipple, and when it tightened he met her gaze. "Nothing that dramatic. But once I was investigating this influential businessman, finding all kinds of dirt on him, personal and professional, and out of nowhere, some hot babe wants to get under me."

*Hot babe?* Natalie scowled at how he said that. "Let me guess: you asked no questions."

He shrugged. "I'm not ashamed to say that I was a typical guy and just went with it. I thought we clicked sexually, that she wanted me that much."

He thought they had clicked sexually too. She wanted to groan. What was a very special and unique experience for her was apparently run-of-the-mill for Jett.

"I was interested enough that I didn't look for ulterior motives." He paid undue attention to his hand on her breast, pushing the flannel down, toying with her nipple—making her insane.

Natalie put her hand over his to still the distracting and provocative movements. After a deep breath to help regain her thoughts, she glared at him. "You had sex with her?"

"Yeah." He bent to put a kiss on the swell of her breast then met her gaze. "Afterward, while I was still in the bed regrouping from a freaking marathon of overindulgence, she said she was going for a drink."

Natalie could guess where this was headed. "But she wasn't really thirsty."

"Guess not." Looking only slightly chagrined, Jett shook his head. "I busted her trying to go through my computer files, luckily before she was able to find anything. See, she was a hacker hired by the businessman. Her end goal was to corrupt any data I'd already gathered."

Natalie didn't want to admit to her own deep jealousy,

but it was there, stewing inside her. Her lip curled a little when she said, "Bet that was one heck of a scene."

He laughed. "You have no idea."

"Meaning?"

"She was a hellcat who knew how to fight." His gaze went to her mouth. "Damn near kicked my ass too. I mean, I'd never fought a chick before. I didn't want to *punch* her, you know?"

Natalie gave him a sour frown. "How righteous of you."

He agreed. "Especially since she had no qualms about decking me. Even hit me with the damn keyboard, and broke it."

Natalie narrowed her eyes. "So what *did* you do?"

"I finally tackled her and then held her down on the ground until I could get the keyboard cord wrapped around her wrists."

"Gee, that sounds familiar."

One side of Jett's mouth kicked up. "Not even close to the same thing you and I did, so don't go there."

She couldn't help it; her thoughts were all over the visual of Jett stretched out atop a sexy femme fatale, a woman he'd found appealing, a woman with whom he'd just indulged in ambitious sexual participation.

Jett gave her a chiding frown. "I restrained her so she couldn't bludgeon me to death. It was one hell of a struggle without a single ounce of pleasure involved. By the time I got her immobilized, I had a damned black eye, a cut on the bridge of my nose and a bite on my neck that hurt for a week." He shook his head in self-disgust. "The guys at the station still give me crap over it."

"So let me get this straight. You picked up a complete stranger and then…"

"Did the nasty with her."

She didn't want or need his clarification. "And you were hurt because it didn't work out quite as you'd planned?" Natalie tried to muzzle herself, but failed. "Such a tragic story."

He didn't take offense. "Not tragic, no, but I felt like a damned fool. She threw out bait and I took it, hook, line and sinker. No one likes to be a dupe, honey." He simply held her breast now, his big, warm hand inside her shirt, curved around her possessively.

Not stroking, not playing, just…holding.

As if he now had the right—and she supposed he did.

"One point though—the encounter that night was far from intimate. It was sex, and only sex." He bent to kiss her, deepening the kiss with the lick of his tongue and a hot exploration. He eased back a millimeter. "What you and I do is very intimate. Don't ever confuse the two, okay?"

It always felt like more to her, but she hadn't been sure of Jett's feelings on the matter. "Since you say it was…somehow detached from emotion—"

"Very detached."

"Then it's not at all the same as my bad experience." Dredging up the past always left Natalie hollow. "If you think you felt duped, imagine being in love with someone and thinking he loves you back, only to find out he wants to get in on the inheritance."

The smile faded off Jett's mouth. "You were in love with him?"

Probably not, but at the time… "I thought I was."

Jett's arm around her back curled her in close to his chest, and near her ear, with complete sincerity, he whispered, "Tell me his name and I'll gladly kill the bastard for you."

## CHAPTER FOUR

NATALIE BLINKED AT HIM. "I hope you're kidding."

"Maybe." Jett could tell she didn't take him seriously. True, he wasn't in the habit of killing for personal reasons, but after seeing the hurt in her eyes, he wouldn't mind a little physical retribution against the one who'd caused her pain.

But now that she'd admitted she hadn't loved the ass, maybe he could just beat him up real good. "Want to give me a name?"

"No!" She smacked his shoulder and laughed. "You're outrageous."

Some other guy had broken her heart, hurting her enough to make her wary of commitment. That fact gnawed on Jett. Didn't mean he wanted the bozo to show back up or to make amends. Hell no.

"Pricks like him always have stuff they want to keep hidden." Kissing her throat, Jett breathed in the scent of her skin, the perfume of sensual female. "What do you say, sweetheart? You want me to dredge up all his dark, dirty secrets? Maybe drag the schmuck's name through the mud a little?"

Smiling, Natalie put her fingers to his mouth to hush him. "Not necessary. Believe me, Jett, he stopped being important to me long ago."

If that was true, she wouldn't still have her barriers up. But he was working on that.

Holding her gaze, Jett opened his mouth enough to draw in one fingertip. Natalie's eyes flared, her lips parting.

He licked the tip of her finger, drew it deeper into his mouth, curled his tongue around her.

Her eyelids drooped in carnal awareness.

He knew damn good and well the images she'd have, of him at her breast, sucking gently; him between her soft thighs, eating her toward an orgasm.

His breathing deepened; he loved the taste of Natalie, the intensified scent of her body, how wet she got and how quickly she responded to him.

Needing her again, he released her finger and leaned her back on the couch. Her legs naturally parted for him to settle between them.

Already hard, he growled, "Damn, I want you. Again."

"But…we just—"

In a rush of need, he went to work on the buttons of the flannel. "Doesn't matter." The truth caused him no small measure of alarm. It didn't matter how often or how thoroughly he had her. "I always want you." He worked his jaw. "Every fucking second of every day."

His gravelly tone, bordering on resentment, gave her pause. "That's a…bad thing?"

Forcing himself to stop, to think, Jett closed his eyes and cursed. "No." Two breaths, a third, and he had a meager grasp on his control. "No, it's not bad. It's just…" He didn't have an appropriate word to define the loss of control and pounding need, so he said, "Unsettling."

"You don't want to want me?"

Wanting her wasn't the problem, he could deal with that. Hell, he'd wanted plenty of women throughout his lifetime. Then he had them, one time or a dozen times, and that was it. The wanting ended.

With Natalie, everything was different. Exactly how different, he didn't know. Jett met her gaze.

The pizza guy had impeccable timing.

His knock saved Jett from trying to come up with a plausible reply. "There's dinner." He kissed her then sat up, hauling her up with him. "Stay put. I'll get it."

Natalie clutched shut the front of the flannel. "Jett! You have…" When he looked back at her, she nodded at his lap.

"A boner, I know. Trust me, the pizza guy won't mention it." Jett felt her watching his every move as he got his wallet and went to the door. Always cautious, he looked out the peephole before turning the locks.

The delivery guy wasn't alone. Hunkered down on the floor a few feet behind him sat a very cute, very dirty little gray dog with white markings and anxious eyes.

Jett frowned at the unkempt condition of the animal. With accusation, he sized up the delivery kid. "Your dog looks hungry."

"He's not mine." The young man glanced back at the animal with a worried frown. "He was out front and followed me in." Then hopefully, "I thought maybe he belonged to someone in here."

That got Natalie's attention. Shirt now decently fastened around her voluptuous breasts, she came to the door and leaned around Jett to look out at the cowering dog.

Immediately she said, *"Ohhhh...."* in the softest tone Jett had ever heard from her.

Both he and the delivery boy looked at her with male awareness.

When Jett realized that, he scowled at the kid. "He's not our dog."

The pizza guy started stammering. "Yeah. Sorry about that. I didn't mean to let in a stray. I thought... you know...maybe he was..."

Seeing the guy go all tongue-tied over Natalie spiked Jett's discontent even more. "Here." He shoved a few bills at him.

The young man looked at the money and started to fumble for change.

Jett shook his head. "Keep it."

"But..." Going agog at the hefty tip, he said, "That's twice what you owed."

Reluctantly, because he did want the guy gone, Jett said, "You did good letting the dog in. I appreciate it."

Struggling to keep his gaze off Natalie, the guy swallowed. "You'll take care of him?"

Jett nodded and saw the pizza guy let out a long breath of relief. The young man's concern was enough that Jett felt like giving him another bill or two. "I'll see to him."

"Thanks, man. And good luck." The guy split in haste, anxious to avoid sparking Jett's temper again.

Paying no attention whatsoever to the food or the male delivering it, Natalie smiled at Jett. She had the look a woman gets when she thinks she's seeing something extra sweet in a guy.

Jett frowned. "What?"

"You're going to help the dog."

He didn't want her to see him as a marshmallow. He wanted her to want him, in every way that he wanted her. "Of course I am. Wouldn't anyone?"

She shook her head. "Obviously not, or the dog wouldn't have been out there all alone, abandoned." Still looking ripe with affection, she glanced at the dog. She had heart in her eyes, her soft side on glaring display. "He isn't wearing a collar."

Uneasy with so much attention, the dog lowered his head and tucked his tail. He looked up at Jett sideways, his big brown eyes slightly crossed.

Too cute, Jett thought, but he wouldn't voice that observation aloud. "Looks like a hound mix, probably around a year old."

"How can you tell?"

"I know dogs." The poor animal shivered, his eyes filled with pleading. "It's okay, boy."

"Oh, Jett." Natalie bit her lip, fretting. "He looks cold and hungry."

"Yeah, he does." Jett handed the pizza box to her. "Can you take care of this?"

She automatically accepted the food. "What are you going to do?"

"Try to bring him in."

She all but staggered. "To your apartment?"

"Yeah." When she stood there in what he supposed was silent surprise, Jett asked, "Is that a problem?"

"No! No, of course not." She looked from him to the dog and back again. That soft expression intensified. "I think that's a wonderful idea. Really wonderful. I just didn't…"

Didn't expect him to like animals? Didn't expect him

to be compassionate? Yeah, they had a lot of ground to cover. There was too much that she didn't know about him. But spring break would help with that.

"Thank you." She touched his biceps, her fingers light, caressing. "I don't know any other men who would willingly bring in a stray." Her hand settled on him and her smile went tremulous.

Jett cocked a brow. Why the hell was she thanking him? He was doing it for the dog. But seeing her like this, so…open to him…he was glad he loved animals so much. "It's not a problem."

When Natalie said nothing more, Jett turned back to the dog. "You need a little attention, don't you, buddy?"

The dog's ears perked up in hope.

Jett knelt down and the dog, while still cowering, started thumping his tail in excitement. He seemed friendly enough, but Jett didn't want to take any chances.

He asked Natalie, "Would you mind going in by the dining table, just in case he gets nervous?"

Proving she knew little enough about animals, she said, "You think he might bite?"

"He's scared, honey, of me and of you. A scared animal sometimes reacts defensively. I can handle it as long as I know you're not going to get hurt."

"Oh. All right." Balancing the pizza box in one hand, she stroked Jett's hair with a new level of affection. "Be careful, okay?" She gave him a fond smile and then moved away.

Deep inside Jett, something chaotic and danger-ous settled into a solid, thumping rhythm. Until that moment, he hadn't been sure that he'd be able to reach Natalie. Really reach her.

Now he knew he would.

Huh. He would have gotten a dog weeks ago if he'd known that was all it took to get past her barriers.

After watching Natalie retreat to the other side of the room, Jett turned back to the dog. He loved animals and couldn't abide anyone who didn't share his compassion. Nice to know that Natalie felt the same way.

Holding out a hand, Jett said, "Good boy."

The dog whined in exultant hope and began army-crawling on his belly a few inches closer. Though Jett laughed at the dog's antics, his heart nearly broke. The little fellow badly wanted the attention, but he was afraid to trust it.

Sort of like Natalie.

But in the end, Jett knew that his will would win over them both.

"Natalie, how about grabbing some lunch meat out of my fridge? I think a little food will help earn his trust."

Within seconds she was behind him with not only the packaged meat but a dish of water, too. The dog's ears shot up and his nose quivered as he sniffed the air.

"Thanks. You can set the water inside the door there."

After Natalie had backed up again, Jett tossed a slice of meat to the dog. It landed right under his chin, and still he watched Jett warily as he bent to snatch up the food then wolfed it down in one gulp. The pup sat up straighter, anxious for more.

"You liked that, did you?" Grinning, Jett tossed the next piece a little closer to his door, and the next closer still. Making a trail that led into his apartment, he baited the dog and then waited.

As if starved, the dog chowed down on his way in. Jett could see his ribs sticking out; the thinness of the young dog made his paws look that much bigger.

Sitting down on his ass, Jett again held out a hand. Speaking in an even tone, he said, "Now that you've eaten all my deli meat, how about letting me pet you?"

Tail going like crazy, the little dog sniffed his hand, licked his fingers and came in close to devour the rest of the lunch meat. Jett emptied the entire package. The dog was too busy inhaling the food to object as Jett stroked him along his back.

After the dog finished it all, he sat back in expectation.

Jett shook his head while cautiously scratching near the dog's left ear. "You're a little glutton, aren't you? Well, that's all there is for now. I don't want you barfing all over my floors." He nudged the water bowl closer. "Come get a drink while we let that settle, and then we'll see how you do."

As Jett spoke, the dog's ears twitched this way and that. He did investigate the water and made a sloppy mess lapping it up.

When Jett reached out to pet him again, he didn't seem to mind at all. In fact, he was overjoyed by the sign of acceptance.

Natalie came closer. "He's so adorable, isn't he?"

"If you say so." Mostly floppy ears had tinges of white on the tips. A marbling of white ran down the oversized straight nose, over his chin and throat, and blossomed out in a diamond pattern on his chest. Two paws were white, and the long tail ended with a white streak.

Jett stroked the dog and although he could feel his bones, he didn't find any burrs or noticeable injuries. "He needs a bath, a brushing and a lot more food."

"And he needs someone to love him." Kneeling down, Natalie reached out for the dog.

Surprised by the quaver in her voice, Jett bent to see her face. Dampness spiked her lashes and left her eyes glistening. Feeling very indulgent, he asked, "Hey, are you crying?"

She sniffed and shook her head. "No."

Yes she was, and the purely female reaction had a dual assault on his senses. Her tenderness made him feel like the macho protector; she was so quintessentially female that it stirred him on a basic level. Another part of him ached at seeing her upset, because he suspected the reason.

In so many ways Natalie was an enigma, independent and forceful one minute, vulnerable and achingly sweet the next.

She wanted acceptance, but was afraid to trust— much like the abandoned animal.

Seeing her distress left an ache in his chest. "Ah, baby, he'll be okay."

Her smile wobbled. "Thanks to you."

To shore up that statement, the dog curled up next to Jett. He rested his head on Jett's thigh and let out a lusty sigh.

Natalie reached over to rub his ear. "Poor little guy is exhausted."

Rather than make a big deal out of her teary-eyed

emotion, Jett tried to lighten her mood. "I like his crossed eyes."

Natalie gave a watery laugh. "They're not really crossed. Just close together. And with his nose so big..." When she curled her fingers under the dog's chin, he closed his eyes in bliss.

Making up his mind, Jett said, "You know what? I think I'll keep him."

Excitement brightened her eyes more than the tears had. "Keep him? Seriously?"

Jett rolled one shoulder. "Sure, why not? It's pretty obvious that he's a stray. And I don't have a dog, so..." He said again, "Why not?"

She hurriedly settled herself cross-legged and leaned into his side. Smiling at the dog, continuing to stroke his ears, his neck, she admitted, "I've never had a pet."

"Why not?" Growing up, he and his sisters had always had animals. They'd become members of the family, living into old age with a lot of love and affection.

Looking wistful Natalie shook her head. "Dad didn't allow them when we were younger, and since I've been on my own, I figured I wasn't home enough to give a pet the care and attention it would need." She fidgeted, adding, "Besides, I'm not sure I trust myself to know what to do since I've never had any experience with animals. What if I did something wrong?"

"You wouldn't." Jett instinctively knew that Natalie would do anything and everything necessary to protect those dependent on her, whether it be a pet...or a child.

Thinking of her with a kid did something funny

to him, something disconcerting because it was so pleasing.

"Jett?"

His right eye flinched. Hell, he'd barely gotten her to agree to see him out of bed and already his mind had gotten way off track.

"Caring is the biggest part of the job." He put his hand over hers on the dog's nape. "Because you care, you'd make sure he was fed and clean and healthy, and that he got exercise. That he felt secure. That's all there is to it."

Beneath his hand, hers trembled. She skirted his gaze. "You have more faith in me than I do."

He released her hand to catch her chin, bringing her face around to his. "I'm a damn good judge of character." And Natalie Alexander was golden, through and through.

"That's why you got clocked with a keyboard by a female spy?"

Jett grabbed his chest, as if she'd dealt a lethal blow. Then he laughed and lifted both eyebrows. "That time doesn't count because it wasn't her character I paid attention to."

Natalie shoved him with her shoulder, but her mouth twisted with a repressed laugh. "Jerk."

"You brought it back up." He smiled with her. "You'd be a great pet owner, Natalie. Take my word for it."

"Thanks. But given my lack of experience, I don't think I'll test the validity of that on some poor dog."

Jett could see her yearning, how badly she wanted to believe him. In the normal scheme of things, Natalie was such a confident woman. Seeing her like this twisted him up inside.

He conspired a swift solution that worked twofold; he could give Natalie a chance to accustom herself to the responsibilities of a dog, and at the same time he'd be building one more bond between them. "We'll share him, okay?"

She went still then jerked toward him, her face flushing with warmth. "Share him?"

"Sure." Most would consider that a chore, but Natalie acted as though he'd just given her an amazing gift. Her enthusiasm made him want her. Again.

Of course, he always wanted her. The woman could sneeze and it felt like a come-on to him.

Showing great restraint, he held himself in check.

Puzzling over his offer, she asked, "How would that work?"

"We both have full-time jobs, but between us he'll get plenty of attention. That is, if you're sure that you don't mind helping."

She looked thrilled. "I love the idea." She put her arms around Jett and squeezed him tight. "Thank you!"

The dog caught on to her excitement and jumped up. With his tail going like crazy, he yapped, turned a circle—and lifted his leg to pee.

With a yelp, Natalie lurched back out of range, but Jett wasn't quite so lucky. The bottom of his jeans got sprinkled.

He looked at Natalie's face and knew she was afraid of how he might react. Did she expect anger? Outrage? Abuse against the poor animal for getting excited?

He'd have his work cut out for him, winning her trust.

Jett rubbed the dog's ear. Deadpan, he said to Natalie,

"This might be a good time to mention that there could be some messes until he gets trained."

Relief left her giggling. One hand over her mouth, she scrambled to her feet and headed into the kitchen for paper towels. "He can stay at my place sometimes?"

Damn, but she kept his emotions in turmoil. How the hell could she be so killer-sexy and still be so damned sweet?

"If you don't mind the occasional accident." Maybe with the dog as an incentive, she'd break down and spend the night with him instead of scuttling back to her own apartment even before their breathing had quieted.

Usually he avoided the commitment implicit in spending the night together, but the idea of holding Natalie all night, waking with her in the morning, appealed to him.

Jett tried to take the towels from her so he could clean up the dog's accident himself, but Natalie bent to the task without hesitation. Her hair fell forward, hiding her face, but he knew she was smiling.

Staring down at her, Jett noted the delicate line of her spine, the flare of her hips and her utter lack of squeamishness. He marveled that she'd come from an entitled background.

Not once had he ever seen her put her nose up at anyone. She didn't shy away from hard work. She drove a modest car and dressed conservatively, both in style and cost. She laughed easily, spoke her mind and lived independently of her wealthy father.

In no way did she act like one of the moneyed elite. His family would adore her.

Her family, he assumed, would disdain him. Not that he gave a damn what they thought.

As Natalie threw away the paper towels and washed her hands, Jett picked up the pup so it wouldn't get excited and make more of a mess. He got a big licking-kiss for his trouble.

"That's what we should name you," he told the dog as he wiped his face on a shoulder.

"What?" Natalie asked when she returned.

"Trouble."

She laughed and cuddled close to him to pet the dog. "No way can you saddle such a sweet little dog with that name."

"Sweet, huh? I need to change my jeans, woman. Nothing sweet in that."

Twin dimples showed in her cheeks as she bit back a big grin. "He just lost control, that's all." And then to the dog, "Didn't you, baby?"

The dog wriggled with happiness, and Jett tucked him under his arm for a better grip.

"I am so glad you're keeping him."

Jett heard the unremarked "but" in her statement. Natalie had the wheels turning, drawing conclusions that were probably all wrong.

Did she think his decision to keep the dog excluded him from going with her on vacation?

She didn't know his family. In fact, he had a feeling she didn't understand the idea behind "family" at all.

When the dog started squirming around again, Jett decided it might be a good time to take him out real quick. He snagged a jacket from the coat tree by his door and stepped into his athletic shoes. "Soon as I take this beast out so he can commune with nature, I'm going to call my sister, Connie. She's a vet. She can keep the dog until we get back from the lake. And by then, she'll have him good as new."

Startled by that outpouring, Natalie hustled after him. "You have a sister?"

"Three actually, all of them younger, all of them nosy as hell." He put a kiss to her forehead. The dog tried to do the same, which lifted Natalie's frown. "That pizza is going to be cold before we get to eat it. You want to set things out while I'm gone? I'll just be a few minutes." He walked out the door before she could question him more.

Once outside, a cold breeze washed over Jett. For as nice as the weather had been lately, the temperature seemed to be dipping fast. At least it helped to clear his head. So much had happened in such a short time, much of it because of the dog.

"We need to come up with a name for you."

Ears down and tail tucked, the dog didn't react to his voice.

After setting him in the grass, Jett watched him closely, ready to grab for him if he tried to run off. He didn't. Instead, he hunkered down and stared at Jett as if he'd just been discarded.

Again.

Between Natalie and the dog, his damn heart felt shredded.

"Not happening, buddy." Crouching down in front of him, Jett spoke in a calm, even tone. "I won't budge, I promise. Do what you need to do and we'll go back in together." He stroked the dog's back then held himself very still.

After a few more minutes of worry, the need

apparently became too great and the little dog went to a line of bushes. Jett realized he had nothing for cleanup but he didn't feel too guilty about that. After all, the dog had been a stray only minutes ago. But first thing after they returned from vacation, he'd make a trip to a pet store for supplies.

When the dog finished, he again army-crawled over to Jett, approaching with anxiety.

Damn. "Come here, buddy." Jett held open his arms and the dog crowded in. "Maybe Buddy works as good as any other name." He lifted the dog. "What do you think?"

This time he got the desired response; the little dog's whole body quivered with the furious shaking of his tail.

"Great." Jett had to grin, and he even bent to put his face against the dog's scruff for a moment, giving him the affection he craved. "We'll run it by Natalie for approval."

Jett strode into the apartment, put the dog on the floor and kicked off his shoes. Natalie stood at the small dinette table, setting out napkins and colas in a too-precise way.

It looked right, seeing her there at his table.

In his life.

Shit. Jett rubbed his face then dropped his hands and drew her attention by saying, "I think he likes the name Buddy. That okay with you?"

She looked up in time to see Buddy try to steal one of Jett's shoes, probably for chewing. Jett retrieved it from him and, carrying both shoes, went straight into his bedroom to change his jeans. Twice he almost tripped over the dog as it stayed close underfoot.

Natalie wasn't that far behind, either. He heard a sound and, wearing only boxers, looked up to see her standing in the doorway watching him.

Her gaze stayed south of his waist, and of course his dick made note of her heated interest.

"Something on your mind, honey?"

Her gaze shot up to his. It took her a second to re-group. "I like the name Buddy." The dog's ears flicked forward then back again. "Did you see that? He already knows his name."

"Smart dog."

"So…" Sounding cavalier, she asked, "Did you say that you have three sisters?"

"That's right." Her curiosity amused him. Just a few hours ago she wouldn't have asked him anything at all of a personal nature. "If any of them knew about you, they'd be camped out here right now trying to learn all they could."

"They're that interested in your dates?" As soon as the words left her mouth, she faltered. "Well, not that we're dating, but—"

"We'll be traveling together, sleeping together all night." He tossed his jeans into a laundry basket in the closet floor and pulled on clean ones. "I'd say that constitutes, at the very least, dating, wouldn't you?"

She bypassed his question to say, "I don't know if I want your family judging me."

"They're not like that." But apparently her family was. Even her sister? Jett wondered. Natalie said they were close, so hopefully Molly wasn't the critical type. "They all love me, and they're all smart."

"Meaning?"

"They'll know right off that you're different."

She shook her head in denial and backed up out of the doorway as he approached. "I'm not."

He wrapped a hand around her nape to keep her from retreating more. Her hair, all curly and cool, lay against the back of his hand. A flush heated her skin, amplifying her unique scent. He breathed her in and felt himself stir.

Looking at her mouth, he said, "You are very different."

"How so?"

He coasted his thumb along the column of her throat, over a rapidly tripping pulse. "I've never before finagled an invite to join a woman on her vacation." Knowing he had coerced her nettled him. If she'd had her way, she'd be in her own apartment right now, packed and ready to leave first thing in the morning—without him.

Natalie made a rude sound. "I bet it's usually the women who are trying to finagle more time with you."

Jett smiled. He got his fair share of play, but other women *had* rejected him. It had never bothered him that much, because none of them mattered the way Natalie did.

"There, you see? That proves my point of you being different, because you wanted to go off without me." After a soft, deep kiss, he released her and started them both toward the kitchen.

"I didn't," she admitted. "Not really."

His guts clenched, but he kept things light. "Could have fooled me." Hell, she'd fought him tooth and nail at first.

"Truth is, I didn't think you'd be interested."

Jett shook his head. Yeah, his family would love her. "Lady, you don't know your own appeal."

Licking her lips, she measured her words carefully. "I do in bed." Her cheeks reddened and she stammered, "I mean, we seem to really click there."

"Click?" His mouth twisted. "That's such a cold, unemotional word for how we burn up the sheets."

Her chin lifted. "Well, I'm not as good at verbal sparring as you are. But you know what I mean."

"Yeah, I do. You thought I wanted the convenience of regular sex with no other attachments." Only on rare occasions had he ever had the urge to introduce a woman to his family. It usually involved unavoidable social functions like the marriage of a relative or a holiday party. He always kept things simple, and his family knew not to make too much of it. But a vacation?

Jett had a feeling that his siblings would take one look at Natalie and know she had thrown him for a loop.

"Does your family know…" She gestured lamely. "You know, that we…how we…"

"That you use me for booty calls?"

Her face flamed. "Have you felt used?"

"Wonderfully so, yeah." Trying to hide his smile, Jett held out her chair, but she glared at him, making him laugh. "Come on, Natalie, do you really think I'd deliberately do or say anything to make you uncomfortable?"

Grudgingly, she conceded the point. "I guess not."

"Your vote of confidence warms my heart." After she'd taken her seat, he went to his own. The dog went under the table and rested across his foot.

It occurred to him that Natalie might not know how

family stuff worked. "My sisters and I are close, but my private life is off-limits. All joking aside, what you and I share is definitely private."

Avoiding what he'd said, Natalie picked up her pizza and asked, "Will you tell me about them?"

"Sure." Maybe because her own family was so broken, she couldn't quite conceive of his. He was proud of them all and didn't mind sharing. "Connie's thirty, married, with a four-year-old daughter. Heidi's twenty-eight, a legal secretary, married with two daughters, a one-year-old and a three-year-old. And Betts, only a year younger than you, is a nurse, still single and no kids yet. The brothers-in-law are nice, hard-working guys, and they love my sisters." He shrugged. "Everyone has their differences on occasion, but never anything major."

"There are a lot of girls in your family."

"There's an understatement." It accounted for part of the reason that they all doted on him so much. "The four-year-old is really prissy, and the three-year-old is a tomboy. As Uncle Jett, I get a free pass to spoil them." Soon, he'd introduce Natalie to his boisterous clan. They'd love her and, he hoped, vice versa.

The dog let out a lusty sigh.

Natalie bent to look under the table. "The poor baby is worn out."

Jett peered under the table too, but he paid more attention to Natalie's small feet. They were soft and delicate and very female. She had her toenails painted a funky powder blue. Demure on the outside, a little risqué underneath—that was Natalie.

He thought of how she wrapped her legs around him,

how sometimes her heels pressed into the small of his back, urging him to go deeper, harder…

"Jett?"

God, he was obsessed. "Buddy will get plenty of sleep tonight at Connie's office. She has pens for the dogs."

"He'd be caged up?"

Jett caught her pained expression. "For his own safety, yeah."

Natalie fidgeted for a moment then asked, "Couldn't you take him to see your sister in the morning instead?"

"I could," he told her slowly, wondering if she was again trying to put him off from the vacation. "But I'm going with you."

For only a heartbeat, Natalie thought about what he said. "How early could your sister see him? I don't mind if we leave a little later than I'd first planned. We could even leave the next day if we had to."

Jett sat back in his seat. Natalie would change her vacation plans for an abandoned pup? That told him volumes about her caring nature.

He'd wanted to spend more time with her, but with every minute that passed, he had to wonder how much time would be enough.

Rubbing the back of his neck, he said, "That's okay by me, if you're sure."

"We just got him. If we turn right around and leave him again, he might feel abandoned."

Better odds were that the dog would get attached to his sister while they were away. Jett shrugged. "Possibly."

She again peeked under the table at Buddy. Looking

wistful, she said, "I'm sure your sister would be wonderful to him, but...maybe we could just take him with us?"

Hell, they'd be just like a happy little family. He wasn't sure how he felt about that. "The place you're renting, it allows pets?"

"For a fee. I don't mind paying the extra. It'll be fine."

Looking at her face, Jett didn't have the heart to disappoint her. He finished off another slice of pizza and collected his cell phone. "I'll call Connie right now. We'll see what we can work out."

# CHAPTER FIVE

WHILE PUTTING IN THE call, Jett watched Natalie bite into her pizza with renewed gusto. Had she been fretting about leaving Buddy?

His sister answered on the second ring. Knowing he didn't need to identify himself, Jett said, "Hey Connie, you busy?"

"Putting away dinner dishes. Why? What's up?"

Jett knew that he had to word this just right. "I was going to head off to spring break with Natalie tomorrow."

On the alert, Connie said, "Natalie? Who's Natalie?"

Because Natalie stared at him, listening to his every word, Jett couldn't yet explain to his sister. "The thing is, we found a little dog today. Or more like he found us. He seems okay, not injured or anything. But since Natalie wants to take him with us, I'd like to have him checked over first. Do you think you could see us first thing in the morning?"

There was a pause, and then: "*Us,* as in you and the dog, or you and the girl?"

Pizza held in one hand, her face comically blank, Natalie started shaking her head.

Jett pretended not to see her. "As in me, the dog and the girl."

"I'll make time."

Jett had known his sister would react in just that way. "Great." If only Natalie was as easy to predict.

"How early can you get to my office?"

"As early as you need us. Natalie wanted to take off first thing tomorrow anyway. What time do you go in?"

"Usually eight, but I can get there at seven-thirty to see you before the scheduled appointments."

"That should do. Hang on." He lowered the phone. "Does seven-thirty sound all right to you?"

Like a deer caught in the headlights, Natalie remained frozen.

As if she'd agreed, Jett put the phone back to his ear. "Seven-thirty it is. We'll be there. Thanks."

"Looking forward to it, Jett."

He knew that tone only too well. "You will not embarrass me, Connie. Understand?"

"I have no idea what you're talking about."

Something else occurred to Jett. "And don't round up the troops either."

Connie laughed. "Spoilsport."

After Jett hung up, Natalie pushed to her feet, both hands planted on the tabletop. She got her voice back with a vengeance. "You want *me* to go with you to see your sister?"

"You're taking half responsibility for the dog, right?" That took her aback, but Jett continued anyway. "You need to hear what she has to say. What if Buddy is sick and needs some sort of treatment?"

"I hadn't thought…"

So that she'd know he wasn't shying away from financial obligations, Jett said, "I'll pay for everything, but you should know what's going on."

Her mouth opened twice without her saying anything. She steadied herself. "I will share the costs with you."

"Connie is my sister, so—"

"She's not my sister."

Seeing the mulish set to her mouth, Jett shrugged. No way would Connie charge them anyway. "All right."

At his easy capitulation, her eyes narrowed. "Well... good."

Jett waited.

She clasped her hands together. "Do you actually think he might be sick?"

"I'm not a vet, but he seems healthy to me." Because Jett had her cornered and he knew it, he played it casual. "The thing is, we have no idea yet how he might react in a car." He bit into another slice of pizza, a man without ulterior motives. "In case he gets upset, it'll be easier with us both along for the ride."

Natalie couldn't refute the logic in that. "What did you mean that your sister shouldn't round up the troops?"

"The rest of the family," Jett explained. And then, while watching her, he added, "They're going to want to meet you, Natalie. And if I don't miss my guess, they'll use tomorrow as an excuse to make it sooner rather than later."

NATALIE COULDN'T BELIEVE his cavalier attitude about this. They'd only just agreed to alter their simple sexual relationship into something more social.

And now he expected her to meet his family! That

was…well, wasn't that a monumental thing? Like tipping the scales?

She braced herself for sound arguments. "It's not that I think your family won't be…fine."

Jett took another giant bite of pizza, watching her with an enigmatic expression.

"I'm sure they're very nice people."

He finished off his cola. "I've always thought so."

Natalie heard a gnawing sound and, puzzled, looked under the table. "Oh no!" Buddy was chewing on a chair leg. Aghast, she crawled under the table and retrieved him.

As she backed out with the dog in her arms, she glanced up and saw Jett with a brow cocked.

Oh Lord.

Hugging the dog closer, Natalie said, "He, ah…" She closed her eyes, unable to spit it out. But when she heard Jett shifting, she opened them again.

He leaned down to look under the table, and she knew he'd just seen the gnarled wood. "Damn." He didn't sound all that angry, but he did look resigned.

Natalie waited for him to get mad, and when he didn't, she marveled at him. Buddy had just scarred one chair of a four-chair matching dinette set—but Jett took it in stride. In fact, he seemed more concerned with eating than with the damage to his property.

Such an amazing man—in more ways than she'd ever considered.

For some reason, she felt guilty about the chair. "Can it be repaired, do you think?"

Jett shrugged. "I guess I better get him some chew toys first thing. My sister probably has something at her clinic."

His incredible acceptance of the dog momentarily sidetracked Natalie. Anyone could see that Jett was a man well used to female attention. He had a confidence streak a mile wide. In every situation, he seemed at ease.

He was gorgeous, charming and he had that dreamy rock-hard bod. So he *had* to be a regular lothario, right?

Yet that image seemed in direct odds to a family man, a guy who viewed any meddling from his sisters with warm affection. The freewheeling bachelor persona contrasted sharply with the man who shrugged off destruction of his personal property by a stray dog.

Knowing she was fast sinking past the point of no return, Natalie sighed.

"Is there a reason for that mournful sound?"

She shook her head and continued to watch him. Jett always looked good to her. Better than good. His lean but strong physique was a big turn-on for her. And those eyes...

She shivered. Jett had the most incredible eyes she'd ever seen on anyone. The man could look at her, and she felt seduced.

But now, having unveiled new dimensions to his personality, she found him more tempting than ever. When she thought of spending the next several days with him, butterflies took flight in her stomach.

She wanted and needed time to acclimate before being scrutinized by his family.

Jett's gaze remained on her, intent, watchful, as if awaiting something.

She cleared her throat. "I can go along tomorrow in case Buddy is afraid of the ride. But considering how things really are between us, maybe it'd be better if I waited for you in the car instead of going into the clinic."

He tipped his head just a little, noting how Buddy rested against her. "How are things between us?"

Being honest, Natalie said, "New."

"We've known each other for a while now."

"In bed, yes."

He countered that by saying, "In every intimate way possible."

Oh God, if he talked about all that they'd done together, she'd start to *feel* it, too.

Her entire body flushed under the impact of Jett's potent gaze. But then Buddy rested his chin on her shoulder and let out a loud doggy sigh. Absently, Natalie cuddled him. She hadn't known that holding a pet provided so much pleasurable warmth and affection. Against her cheek, his fur was warm and soft, his whiskers tickling.

Without looking at Jett, she said, "Everything is different now that we're…shifting the way we spend time together."

The seconds ticked by and she couldn't take it. Feeling Jett's unnerving stare, she glanced up.

Very slowly, he left his seat and came to her.

He cupped her face. "You don't come from a big family, so you don't know how this works."

"How what works?"

"I guarantee you that right now Connie is on the phone with one of my other sisters, and between them, they'll make sure the whole family knows about you within minutes."

That idea staggered her. Why would they care? She

was far from the first woman Jett had ever dated, and
she knew she wouldn't be the last. He had more experience than most ten men combined. Knowing what
she did about him now, about his edgy career choices
and daring lifestyle, only emphasized the differences
in their lives.

So why introduce her to his family?

The idea almost panicked her. She knew zip about
big families. As a teacher, she met parents on a purely
professional basis. As a daughter, what she knew of
parents was laughable. She and Molly were close, but
it wasn't like in most families.

Most families didn't include one parent gone and the
other…uncaring.

Natalie squeezed the dog tighter. "You told Connie
not to alert them!"

Concerned, Jett rubbed his thumbs over her cheeks
and said with a strange sort of apology, "She will
anyway."

"But…" Natalie shook her head. "That doesn't make
any sense."

Jett's gaze stayed steady on her face. "Natalie…"

Time to quit while she was ahead.

Bending down, Natalie put Buddy back on the floor.
He'd been totally limp against her, utterly relaxed, and
now he looked startled, filling her with guilt.

He bounced his gaze back and forth between them
with trepidation.

Jett said to him, "It's okay, Buddy."

And just like that, he dropped his butt down to sit.

Bemused, Natalie let out a breath. "You've cast a
spell on him or something." Many times she had wondered why Jett, and Jett alone, could draw such strong

reactions from her, getting her to do things normally considered uncharacteristic to her nature, making her feel things she hadn't known were possible. Now she had evidence that he possessed some strange power.

He tipped her face up to his. "About tomorrow—"

Oh no. She could not discuss this with him right now. She mustered up a cheerful expression. "How long will it take us to get to your sister's clinic?"

The heat of his frustration beat against her. "Fifteen minutes or so."

"I'll be ready in plenty of time." She forced a yawn. "But for now, I'm exhausted. It'll be a long day tomorrow, and I need to finish getting a few things together. I still have to shower, too. And I absolutely have to reach my sister before I go."

"Shh." Jett kissed her, and somehow, after all they'd done, this kiss felt different.

Sweeter.

More…loving.

No. *No, no, no.* Natalie pushed back from him, alarmed, afraid. She could not let herself be convinced of a depth of emotion that probably didn't exist. Jett wanted to spend more time with her. Fine. She could do that.

But simple dating rituals did not equal love.

Before he could say anything more, she started for the door. Buddy jumped up and stared after her. Jett tracked her with a frown.

She blocked both expressions of appeal, determined to escape. When she didn't slow, Buddy plopped down on his butt and whined. Jett put his fists on his hips.

Forcing a smile, Natalie said, "Good night. I'll see you both bright and early tomorrow morning."

And as she went out the door, both males gave her identical expressions—of deep disappointment.

A LONG HOT SHOWER did little to help focus Natalie's jumbled thoughts and conflicting emotions. On the one hand, she was thrilled at the idea of expanding her relationship with Jett; on the other, the thought of setting herself up for heartbreak absolutely terrified her.

No, Jett wouldn't deliberately mislead her. Any hurt feelings or damaged pride would be her fault, not his. He hadn't asked her to commit to him. He only wanted to traditionalize their time together. He wanted them to *date*.

Nothing misleading in that.

But to have to meet his family, too? She shuddered at the thought. Meeting them would imply a sort of emotional intimacy that, to her knowledge, didn't exist for…him.

For her part, knowing him better only sharpened the ache in her heart.

With Jett so wonderful, his family had to be pretty great too. What did she know of interacting with family? Nada. Well, except for Molly—whom she couldn't reach, damn it.

Where was her sister?

She glanced at the clock, but it wasn't so late that she couldn't indulge in a quick phone call. She called her stepmother first, but that was a dead end. Kathi claimed to have no idea where Molly had "gotten off to" and she didn't share Natalie's concern.

"She's probably doing a book signing or touring or something."

Natalie shook her head. "She always tells me first."

Impatient, Kathi laughed. "Don't be absurd, Natalie. Your sister is a grown woman, not a child, and she doesn't have to account for her every moment, not even to you."

Natalie rolled her eyes. "I wasn't saying—"

"You know how Molly is. When she gets involved in research, she often forgets everything and everyone else."

*With you and Father,* Natalie wanted to say, but she held back the snarky reply. Molly worked hard to maintain a relationship with their father because she still cared about those familial ties.

Natalie didn't really give a flip one way or the other.

Striving for a polite tone, she said, "Could you ask Father if maybe he's heard anything—"

"Not tonight I won't." Kathi laughed again in a wholly condescending way. "Natalie, dear, it's late and you know that your father is far too busy to be bothered with this sort of nonsense."

"But Dad might know something."

"I'll mention it to Bishop in the morning and if he does, I'll call you. But really, stop panicking."

Through her teeth, Natalie said, "I am not panicked. I am concerned."

Kathi let out a sigh. "With you, it's hard to tell the difference. Just give your sister a few days before you start bothering Bishop or anyone else. Now I really must go. Good night, dear."

And with that, Kathi hung up. Natalie growled at the dead phone. No, she didn't dislike Kathi just because she'd married her father, or because her father hadn't mourned her mother's death for long, or because

Kathi had effectively distanced her even more from her father.

She disliked Kathi because she was a sanctimonious, uppity, judgmental bitch.

And because, given those traits, she was the perfect woman to be Bishop Alexander's wife.

Making a face, Natalie decided on a long shot and called Molly's ex-fiancé, Adrian.

Being that Adrian ran a bar, this was normal business hours for him. His bartender answered and put her through to Adrian's office.

Surprise sounded in his tone. "Natalie?"

God, how Natalie despised Adrian Wiseman. From the very beginning, she'd known that he wasn't good enough for her sister. It had taken Molly a while to realize it, unfortunately. "Hello, Adrian. I'm sorry to bother you."

Cautiously, because Adrian held out hope of getting back with Molly, he said, "It's fine, fine. What's up?"

"I haven't been able to reach Molly. She's not answering her calls, and...you know how close we are."

Unlike Kathi, Adrian accepted that. "Yes, I do." A new alertness entered his tone. "You're worried?"

"Getting there, yes. Tomorrow I'm leaving for a spring-break vacation, but I hate to go without talking to Molly first."

He cleared his throat. "Ah...you do realize that we're no longer engaged?"

Dolt. "Like I said, Molly and I are close." And she'd cheered for Molly during the breakup. Never, not for a single second, had she ever considered Adrian good enough for her sister. He was an opportunist who saw dollar signs when he looked at Molly, not only because of their father's wealth but because of Molly's fast-growing fame as a bestselling novelist.

"Right." Annoyance sharpened Adrian's tone. "So then you're calling me...why?"

Natalie sighed. "Just a long shot, I guess. I didn't know who else to ask. It's not like her to take off without telling me first."

A heavy pause strained her patience, and then Adrian drew all the wrong conclusions. "You think she might be having regrets?"

"What? No!"

Adrian didn't seem to hear her. "Maybe she's off by herself, rethinking her position, maybe...missing me."

Oh, good grief. "Not likely, Adrian. I thought you might have talked to her, though, and since you haven't, I'll let you go."

"I'll call her too," he rushed to say. "If I get hold of her, I'll let her know that you're concerned."

Lovely. Now Molly would strangle her. "That's okay. I'm sure Kathi's right and Molly is just off researching something. You know her research sometimes takes her to obscure places. Maybe she doesn't have cell reception or something." Natalie rushed through her words, but she wanted off the phone before she said anything else to encourage Adrian. "Gotta go. Take care, Adrian. Bye-bye."

Adrian was in midsentence when she hung up on him, and she winced in guilt. She'd ended up doing the same as Kathi!

Without her sister to talk to, Natalie accepted that she had no one.

Except Jett.

But she couldn't do that to him. In almost every way, Jett was the ideal bachelor. He had the job he wanted, the hours he wanted, the freedom he wanted.

He was good at being single, and he was great at winning female attention. She had to remember that at all times.

So what to do?

It took a few deep breaths for her to make up her mind. Men like Adrian were a dime a dozen; she and her sister had both had their share of shrugging off the jerks, the users, the fakes and phonies. But a man like Jett?

One in a million.

And he wanted her.

She'd be a fool *not* to take everything he offered, and if that meant navigating the uncomfortable social scene, or even meeting his family, so be it.

With her mind made up, Natalie went to the living room where she had everything she'd need for the trip piled up by the door. One tote bag held her beauty supplies—makeup, hair brushes, lotion and the like. She had her laptop case and her camera. Another bag held a few snacks for the road. Yes, she liked to stop often on the long drive, but she also liked to munch while driving.

She dragged her sparsely packed suitcase back to her bedroom, plopped it up on the bed and opened it. Now that Jett would be joining her, she needed to exchange her warm, practical thermal pajamas for something more appealing. After she'd loaded in a thin nightgown, some sexy panties and a negligee she'd never had reason to wear, she closed up the suitcase and put it at the end of the bed.

Standing there in the dim, silent bedroom, alive with expectation for the coming week, Natalie detected the sound of an engine in the parking area.

She was ridiculously attuned to Jett, so she easily distinguished the distinct sound of his SUV. Wherever had he been?

Knowing she'd have a better view of the lot from her dining room, she left her bedroom and went to the patio doors to peek out the curtains. Sure enough, Jett parked his shiny black SUV, and his headlights went dark.

Puzzled, Natalie stood there, wondering where he'd gone and why. For her, it was late, but then she kept a school teacher's hours. Being late March, it still got dark early, and even worse, wind whistled and tree branches bent beneath a gathering storm.

But as a bachelor, Jett often went out late. Before they'd gotten sexually involved, he'd sometimes come home in the wee hours of the morning. Natalie frowned as she watched him open the driver's door and step out. Thanks to the well-lit parking area, she saw him heft an overflowing bag into one arm. Beneath his other arm he carried a big padded item—and she realized it was a doggy bed.

Struck by his caring, she bit her bottom lip.

The cold wind blew Jett's dark hair into his face and parted his unzipped jacket, but he didn't rush. He lifted Buddy from the vehicle and set him on the ground. Buddy now wore a collar attached to a leash that Jett had wrapped around his wrist.

Natalie squinted at the bags he carried. She could just make out a dog dish and a giant chew bone on the top of the stuffed bag.

He'd gone shopping for Buddy.

*Ahhhhh....*

She put a hand to her mouth and tried to fight back the emotions—without success. Knowing what he'd done, and that he probably thought nothing of it, left her staggered by his bighearted nature.

That damned emotion swelled even more, choking her, making her feel both hot and soft. They'd both put in a full day, the weather was turning nasty, and still Jett had gone out of his way to make Buddy comfortable.

Natalie's quickened breathing fogged against the icy window. She rested her forehead there, but it did nothing to cool her.

She couldn't wait to get to Tennessee tomorrow. It wouldn't be summer-warm, but it should be milder than the brisk Ohio weather, especially now with a storm blowing in. She and Jett would be all alone together. She anticipated all the things she'd missed in life, like quiet meals together, maybe a few joint showers, walks in the woods with Buddy, talking, exploring and...growing closer.

When Jett glanced up at her window, Natalie ducked away. With her apartment dark he wouldn't be able to see her anyway, but she didn't want to take a chance. At the same time, she liked it that he'd glanced toward her place, because she always glanced toward his.

And sometimes she saw him in his window, as if he, too, could recognize the sound of her arrival.

It occurred to her that Buddy looked not the least traumatized by the trip in the car, which negated her need to go along with Jett in the morning. But she wanted to go anyway. He'd invited her, the dog was half hers and…she wanted to spend every minute with Jett that she could.

Not that she'd start making assumptions. No. Even if it killed her, she would make this a no-pressure relationship for him. Somehow she would adapt to the social standards of casual dating.

An hour later, despite the pep talk she'd given herself, Natalie went to bed thinking about things she shouldn't, things like a lasting romance, a future and a happily ever after—with Jett.

## CHAPTER SIX

NATALIE FUMED IN SILENCE.

For over an hour now they'd been on the road to Tennessee, and she was *still* rattled. After Jett had loaded all of Buddy's new belongings into the back of his SUV, he'd carried out her bags while she did her best to urge Buddy back into the vehicle.

He may have been fine leaving the vehicle last night, but he was not so keen about getting back into it. In fact, he'd behaved as though she wanted to drag him to his death.

How Jett had managed the night before, on his own, Natalie had no idea.

Finally, after much effort, cajoling and insisting, she had gotten Buddy into the SUV and they'd arrived at Connie's veterinarian clinic bright and early with a fractious, frightened Buddy in tow.

Jett, damn him, hadn't seemed the least bit surprised to find all three of his sisters there. He'd merely shaken his head in fond exasperation while the women wore various expressions of curiosity and offered up differing excuses for the early morning visit, none of them viable or believable.

They were there to meet her, and Natalie knew it.

Feeling shanghaied and on display, she'd stood there, self-conscious and out of her element, watching them in awe. They were the most boisterous, outrageous, out-spoken and *lovely* women she'd ever met.

All laughing and talking at once, the sisters had taken turns hugging Jett, and much to Buddy's delight, they doted on him as if he were the most special dog ever.

The family resemblance between brother and sisters was strong; the woman all had eyes as dark as Jett's, but lighter and much longer brown hair. While they were tall, between five-eight and five-ten, they weren't as tall as Jett. And where Jett was all man, the sisters were ultrafeminine, but no one could deny the similarities in features.

Their open affection and bold teasing had rendered Natalie mute and she'd remained in the doorway like a dolt. She and Molly were close, and sometimes when alone together they would crack up for one reason or another. But this…this demonstrative display was very new to her.

Her father and her stepmother would be appalled by such an animated show of emotion.

Somewhere deep down inside herself, Natalie wished she could be a part of it all. It seemed very natural the way they teased each other, touched and laughed.

Only after harassing their brother wore thin did the sisters finally peer at Natalie with unabashed interest.

Putting his arm around her, Jett had pulled her forward and gone through rather formal introductions.

Connie smiled hugely and, while staring at Natalie, said to her brother, "'Bout damn time."

When he only hugged her closer, Heidi said, "Good grief, Jett, I barely recognize you in territorial mode, but I like the new you!"

And the youngest sister, Betts, had propped her hands on her slim hips. "So *she's* the reason you ran me off the other day, hmm?" She'd eyed Natalie critically until Jett growled at her, and then she'd laughed loudly, elbowed the closest sister and said, "Okay, I get it."

Confused, Natalie asked, "Get what?"

But instead of an answer, she got a giant hug from Betts.

While squeezing Natalie tight, Betts said to Jett, "Since you brought her here, you're off the hook."

Heidi grinned. "I'd say he's totally redeemed himself."

Not long after that, Connie had scooped up Buddy and headed off into a back room with him. Since Jett had the leash around his wrist, he went along to help.

Natalie attempted to follow, but the remaining two sisters intercepted her. As if trying to learn all they could in a short span of time, they fired casual and friendly questions at her. They asked about her work, her hobbies, even her vacation, but they never once crossed the line into prying. Apparently they saved that for Jett.

After remarks about the cooling weather, the talents of teachers, lakes, dogs and other mundane topics, Heidi remarked about Natalie's "beautiful" hair. Ill at ease, Natalie tucked a springy curl behind her ear. Her stepmother had always described her wildly curly hair in none-too-flattering terms. She'd grown accustomed to hearing that she looked tawdry, unkempt, cheap and tangled.

As yet, Natalie wasn't used to flattery from Jett, and now she heard it from his sisters, too.

Heat flooded her face as she stammered her thanks. "You're very kind."

Waving that off, Betts started a new thread on how sweet it was for Natalie to take Buddy along on her vacation. "You've changed his entire life. Dogs are meant to be part of a family, not alone on the street. It's fantastic that you're including him like this."

More heat scalded her neck. "Jett's the one who first thought to keep him. I'm not really used to animals—"

"You'll be great. I can tell." She brushed her hand along Natalie's arm, disturbing clinging dog fur from her sweater. Grinning, Betts said, "Looks like he's already breaking you in."

"And I don't hear you complaining," Heidi added with a wide smile. "I like a woman who doesn't get all fussy over the little things. Shows you're a natural with pets."

The inane chitchat and unending good humor wore on Natalie. "I hope so. But I'm glad I'll have Jett to help me get acclimated."

Both women grinned hugely. "Oh, you definitely have him," Betts said, again poking her elbow at her sister. Heidi chuckled in agreement.

Just when Natalie thought she'd expire from awkwardness, Jett stuck his head out of the back room. He looked at Natalie's drawn expression and then scowled at his siblings.

Having no real clue what had transpired, he said to them, "Mind your own business," and then he held out a hand to Natalie. "Come on in. You can help us with Buddy."

But the sisters didn't take Jett's comment to heart. If

they did, they wouldn't have followed her into the back room and turned Buddy's appointment into a family affair.

There was laughter, warmth and jokes aplenty.

It would have been wonderful—only Natalie wasn't family, didn't know anything about family and had no idea how to take part in the camaraderie they all shared. It wasn't that they excluded her, only that she didn't know where or how to jump in. She answered questions directed at her, laughed quietly at the humor and watched it all in yearning.

She and Jett were at the clinic for almost two hours.

Two hours that felt like ten and left her starkly aware of the vast differences in the components of her family and Jett's.

Not once since they'd gotten on the road had Jett mentioned his family, why they'd all been there waiting, what they had wanted or what he thought about it.

Now, after so much silence, Natalie felt strained to the breaking point. She glanced at Buddy, well-groomed and worn out, settled in his cushy bed on the floor between the seats in the back of the SUV, gnawing on a giant chew bone. He'd really been worked over with a flea bath, shots, ear cleaning, nail trimming, tests for parasites, a good brushing and various other things that had all combined to make him forget his displeasure with riding.

Without the dog's anxiety to occupy her, Natalie had no way to distract her turbulent thoughts.

Trying for subtlety, she shifted her gaze to Jett's profile.

She wasn't subtle enough.

"All right." While still appearing very pleased about something, Jett gave her a quick telling look. "Out with it."

"It?"

"You've been over there stewing about something." He flipped on the wipers to counter the growing accumulation of fat snowflakes on the windshield. "After the onslaught of my loony sisters, I wanted to give you some time, but the silent treatment is making me nuts."

Making *him* nuts? Fine, he wanted to talk about it? She'd talk about it. Natalie turned off the radio and folded her arms to glare at him. "Was that whole scene with your family familiar?"

Laughing, Jett cocked one brow. "In some ways, yeah. Real familiar. My sisters have always been lovable pains in my ass." He grinned at her. "In other ways, hell no. That was about as atypical as it could get."

She didn't understand him. "How was it unfamiliar?"

"I've never seen my sisters so agog. It was downright hilarious. You probably don't realize it, but they were trying hard to rein themselves in—without much success." He reached over to brush the backs of his fingers across her cheek. "It was funny to see them tripping over themselves trying to make you feel welcome."

So he didn't always get those gibes when introducing a woman? Natalie didn't want him to misunderstand. "They were very nice."

"I'll interpret that as your polite way of calling them overwhelming. But yeah, they *are* nice, honey." In the distance, thickening snowfall turned the sky white. The dropping temps fogged the windshield, so Jett turned up the defroster. "I know they liked you."

With that odd yearning still ablaze inside her, Natalie bit her lip. "They told you that?"

"I know my sisters. If they hadn't liked you, I'd have heard all about it." They passed a car that had slid off the road, with a police cruiser already on the scene. Jett scowled in concern.

A second later his car phone rang. He pushed a button on the bottom of the rearview mirror and Heidi said, "Hey, Jett."

First thing, Jett said, "You're on speakerphone, sis."

Natalie narrowed her eyes at him. What did he think his sister would say? Something about her?

Heidi laughed at him. "Thanks for the warning. But no worries. I wasn't going to embarrass you. I just wanted to check on you. The weather reports are showing some unexpected heavy snow. Not just Ohio, but Kentucky and Tennessee, too."

"We're seeing signs of it now." He peered through the windshield. "Starting to look nasty."

"Bummer. It'll be terrible if you two ended up stranded, all alone together, in a cozy little cabin in the woods. Whatever will you do to pass the time?"

Laughing, Jett said, "I'm sure we'll think of something." Then he tacked on, "Brat."

Heidi snickered. "I'm sure you can handle snowy road conditions, Jett. I have complete confidence in you. But why don't you check in every so often anyway, just to keep us from worrying?"

"You're going to worry no matter what, but sure, I'll let you know when we get settled."

"Thanks. You know I love you bunches."

As Jett said, "Back atcha," his gentle, easy smile tugged at Natalie's heart.

"Give Natalie a smooch from me."

"Good*bye,* Heidi." Grinning, Jett disconnected the call on her enthusiastic farewell.

His love for his sisters couldn't be more apparent, and obviously they felt the same. But it boggled Natalie's mind that they'd fret over him. Jett was six-plus feet of solid, capable and in many ways lethal male.

Other than Molly, no one had ever really worried about her. And now she couldn't reach Molly.

Jett reached for her hand. "C'mon, Natalie. Don't look like that. You'll get used to my sisters being mother hens. It's just their way."

Would she be with him long enough to get used to it? She snuffed that thought real fast. "I don't mind. I think it's sort of…endearing, how close you all are."

That seemed to bother him. "Speaking of sisters…" He glanced at her. "Did you ever get hold of yours?"

Natalie shook her head. "She's still not answering her phone, so I emailed her this morning. Hopefully by the time we get to the cabin she'll have replied."

His hand squeezed hers. "You're a little scared for her, aren't you?"

"I don't know." Logic told her that Molly was just involved with her fast-growing career. "She has a movie deal in the works, and deadlines and research, so I know she's busy."

"But not too busy for her sister."

She frowned, because Jett had just pinpointed her problem: she was hurt. "It's not like her to stay out of touch like this." Then she half laughed at herself. "I sound ridiculous, don't I? My stepmother said so, and she didn't even want to bother my dad with it. But I can't help thinking that something might be wrong."

"Not ridiculous at all. You're her sister, and sisters have a way of sensing these things. Did you want me to check into it?"

Natalie's brows shot up in a mix of indignation and curiosity. "Are you offering to investigate my sister?"

Jett shrugged. "I could probably figure out where she went, where she's been—"

"No." Molly wouldn't appreciate anyone snooping through her personal life. But then, because her worry felt real, Natalie added, "At least, not yet. I'll give her a few more days and hopefully it'll become a moot point."

"Fair enough." Jett kissed her knuckles and released her hand. "But I don't want to see you worry. So when you're ready, let me know and I'll find out what I can."

Not only did Jett understand her concern, he was willing to help. And with that, he stole another little piece of her heart.

"Look at that sky," Jett told her. "The snow's turning to frozen slush." Everyone now drove well below the speed limit, and still cars were slipping left and right.

Ice stuck to the wipers, interfering with visibility. Just then, they passed a mild wreck involving two cars that had collided with each other. It didn't amount to much more than a fender bender. But less than half a mile from there they saw a car flipped into the gully, with three other cars stopped nearby to help.

Jett said, "Shit," and leaned a little closer to the steering wheel.

Natalie twisted to look out the window, stunned that

the weather had changed so drastically. "Looks like your sister had good reason to call. It's really coming down out there."

"The last weather report I heard said a storm, but I wasn't expecting this." He concentrated on the road. The accumulated snow had been pushed aside by the traffic and narrowed the lanes. "We're not sliding, but it looks like a lot of other cars are."

"Maybe I should turn on the radio to check the updated weather reports?"

"Yeah. I'd like to know if we're driving into or out of the worst of it."

Natalie switched around the stations until she found the news. It wasn't good. The storm was proving worse than weathermen had predicted and since ice had joined the snow, many smaller roads were already shut down and the interstates were fast becoming congested. Unfortunately, it would be both behind them and ahead of them.

They listened to the weatherman intone the news with ominous warnings.

*"Over three inches have already accumulated throughout Ohio, Kentucky and Tennessee with up to nine inches now expected. Slick road conditions are being blamed for numerous reports of car wrecks. All along Interstate 75 and 71, cars and trucks are off the road with a few serious accidents that have required air support. The mixture of ice and snow should be considered hazardous. Many areas are under a level-three snow emergency. If you don't have to be on the road, stay home."*

Natalie frowned at the admonition. She turned to look out the rear window but couldn't see far with the snowfall so thick. "I guess there's no point in turning around?"

Jett glanced at the odometer and shook his head. "We should be about halfway there." He turned the defroster up even more. "At this point going back wouldn't be any easier than going on."

Guilt assailed her. It was because of her plans that they were now out on the road in a possibly hazardous situation. She stared at Jett's frowning profile. "I didn't hear anything about a snowstorm."

He met her gaze for only an instant and then said with feeling, "As I recall, weather reports held little interest for us last night."

If the heat in his words wasn't enough to scorch her, the memory of what they'd done certainly was. Natalie stared at him, remembering everything.

Voice low, Jett said, "Babe, when you look at me like that, I feel like I'm already inside you."

Oh Lord. And now she felt it too. She tightened her thighs. "Whether we heard the news or not probably wouldn't have mattered. They're saying it wasn't expected to be this bad."

Jett shifted, cleared his throat and allowed her the change of topic. "It's a little snow—no big deal. Don't worry about it."

"Hopefully as we get farther south, it'll lighten up."

"Maybe." He stretched out his left leg, shifting again. "If things start to get too dicey, we might have to stop at a different hotel along the way. You okay with that?"

"Jett, I'm fine with whatever we need to do. Really. But it might be difficult finding a hotel that accepts pets."

"We'll see."

She reached over to touch his biceps. "Your leg is hurting."

His brows came down and again he glanced at her. "I'm fine."

The cross way he said it let her know that he was touchy on the subject. "Why don't you let me drive for a while?"

"Not necessary." He eyed an exit, but it was buried in snow, nearly invisible.

As he passed it, Natalie scowled. "You don't trust me to drive?"

"I trust you plenty." His hands flexed on the wheel. "But I'm driving."

Exasperated, Natalie let out a breath. "Your leg is bothering you, I can tell. You don't have to be so macho about it."

"Macho?" He snorted. "It's not my leg bothering me, honey. It's a boner."

"Oh." Natalie looked at his lap, saw the truth of his words, and elation rolled over her. Even now, in these less-than-ideal circumstances, Jett wanted her. She was so pleased by that, she couldn't help but chuckle. "I see." She started to ask him what she could do to help, but Jett cut her off.

"A change of topic is in order." He shifted again. "Did my sisters grill you? I sort of got caught up in caring for Buddy and didn't really think about leaving you alone with them in the outer room."

Given that his leg wasn't the reason for his restlessness, Natalie decided to let him off the hook about having her drive. After all, they really had nowhere to pull over to make a switch anyway. "We talked, but they weren't intrusive." She wouldn't tell him how the women had complimented her. "In fact, they were very kind."

"I want you for more than convenience, and they know it. Of course they were kind."

Natalie bit her lip at that. Was that how Jett saw most women, as "convenient"? Normally she'd be up in arms on behalf of her sex, but this time, more pressing thoughts took precedence.

How could Jett possibly expect to keep things casual if he involved his entire family this way? Being too direct left Natalie's stomach jumpy, but she *had* to know, so she mentally braced herself, then asked, "How much more?"

His expression sharpened, turned a little grim. Keeping his gaze focused on the slick road ahead, he said, "Now there's the million-dollar question, huh? Especially considering that I had to twist your arm to get anything more at all."

Talk about evasive answers. Well, Natalie refused to put him on the spot. "I have a suggestion."

He speared her with a glare then cursed as the car in front of them fishtailed before regaining control. He held the wheel a little tighter. "I'd love to hear it. Shoot."

"I say we don't get too serious. We both want to have fun, for now…for as long as it lasts."

JETT SQUEEZED THE WHEEL HARD. *For as long as it lasts.* Those carefree words pounded through his brain. Her sentiments mirrored his, because he really didn't know where their relationship was headed, or even where he wanted it to head.

But he did know that once he'd introduced her to his family, things would be trickier. He couldn't even claim that he'd been surprised by his siblings' attendance at the vet clinic. He'd known that Natalie would have them all there. It was a wonder his mom and dad hadn't shown up too.

For years, his family had been on him about settling down. It was payback for all the times he'd played big brother, running off guys he considered not good enough.

But regardless of his siblings' acceptance of Natalie, he still felt free to make up his own mind about their future, free to guide things as he saw fit. Every woman he'd ever dated had wanted more from him, and he'd been the one calling the shots, keeping things casual.

Not Natalie. She left him feeling indecisive and antagonistic and provoked by her lack of interest. Hell, she looked at him and he got hard—and how did that affect her?

She laughed.

Before he could think of a reply to give her, a small car a few yards ahead of him started sliding again, and this time it didn't recover.

"Damn it." Jett did some fancy driving to avoid getting caught as the car swung wildly one way and then swung the other way before going off the road and into the sloping area between the southbound and northbound lanes. It stopped hard, sending up a spray of snow and ice.

Glad that he'd kept so much distance between him and the other drivers, Jett slowed even more.

"Oh my God!" Natalie leaned toward him to look out the driver's door window.

Jett didn't want to take his gaze off the road. "Driver okay?"

"Looks like." Natalie settled back into her seat. Sounding shaken, she said, "I saw a couple of people in the front seat, and the passenger was already on the phone."

Good. They'd be fine—not that he would have endangered Natalie by stopping on the treacherous road anyway. "Cops are patrolling. Someone will be along soon to…" His words trailed off as they both noticed a semi, bent in half, on its side in the gully. The trailer had spilled its load, and now boxes were everywhere.

"This is nuts." Natalie put her hands to her face. "I've never seen so many wrecks."

She no sooner said it than a truck zipped past them at a much higher speed. Jett made a sound of disgust. "I have a feeling we're going to see a whole lot more too, since some drivers don't have enough sense to slow down."

Over the next hour they did indeed see more cars and trucks off the road. And at one exit they even saw an ambulance overturned. The police were out in force, but already they'd spotted at least two cruisers also off the road.

Natalie seemed so concerned, Jett went out of his way to keep her occupied. Together, they sang along with an older song on the radio. He shared a few ribald jokes with her that had her both blushing and laughing out loud. Buddy took turns sleeping, leaning over the seat to lick Natalie's ear and gnawing on his chew toys and bones.

Jett told her more about his family, and she told him

more about her sister's writing career, especially the movie deal in the works.

They went through some of the snacks they'd brought along, so neither of them was overly hungry. They enjoyed a comfortable familiarity, making slow but steady progress toward the cabin. All in all, it was a pleasant trip despite the weather hazards.

And then Buddy stopped being patient. He decided he needed a break and he needed it now.

Natalie did what she could to calm the dog, but he was not only unused to riding in cars, he wasn't used to holding it either. He paced the space available to him, howled and put his paws up against the doors and the back of the seats.

He became so frantic that Natalie looked ready to cry over his upset.

"He's all right, Natalie."

"He doesn't understand." And then, "What if he goes in your car?"

Jett shrugged. "Then I guess I'll be cleaning it. Just keep an eye on him and make sure he doesn't aim for the luggage."

She went mute before snickering.

"What?"

"Ohmigod, can you imagine if that happened?"

Jett grinned. "If it did, we'd be doing laundry right off. Either way, it wouldn't be all that tragic." He felt bad for Buddy too, but at the same time, he appreciated Natalie's empathy, how hard she worked at trying to soothe Buddy.

Seconds later, good fortune shone on them. "I think I see a clear exit. We can get some food and gas too, but I don't see any signs for lodging." He heard her cooing to Buddy, promising him relief, and Jett smiled. "I'm guessing you could use the break, too?"

"Are you kidding? I needed to go hours ago."

Jett carefully veered off on the slick exit. "Why didn't you say anything?"

"What could you do about it? Nothing. You had your hands full just keeping us on the road."

Sensible, considerate, sexy Natalie. Every second with her deepened his feelings.

Jett shook his head and made it off the highway, but just barely. The one and only gas station he saw, attached to a small store of supplies, had a sign offering hot dogs and coffee.

"I'll pull up close to the building to let you out under the overhang, then I'll drive Buddy over to that semi-clear spot behind that big metal garbage bin. Wait inside for me, okay? When Buddy's done, I'll pull back up front and you can wait with him while I run in."

"Sounds like a plan."

He noticed that Natalie had her knees together and bit back another grin. If he'd known things were so dire for her, he could have figured out something. What, he didn't know, but he could be resourceful when it came to her comfort. Pretty soon, if everything went as he planned, she'd be comfortable enough with him to tell him everything she needed, even outside the bedroom.

Buddy again worried that he was being dumped, so Jett had to take extra time to convince him otherwise. He had to crouch down by the dog as Buddy did his business in ten different locations. All the while, Jett talked to him, rubbed his ear or scratched his back.

By the time Buddy finished and Jett had the gas

tank refilled, his own situation was critical. His jeans now snow-covered up to his knees, his ears and nose red from the cold, Jett again pulled up in front of the gas station.

Natalie had her arms laden with hot dogs, chips and colas. While he stowed the food on the floor of the front seat, she crawled over the seat into the back to dig out food and water for Buddy. The dog hadn't yet learned manners and he made a mess, and a racket, refilling his belly.

Shaking his head, Jett told her, "Be right back."

He left the SUV running to keep her warm but locked the doors on his way out. After he finished inside, he asked the cashier about weather reports. Unfortunately, it sounded as if road crews couldn't keep up with the downfall and shops were closing early so workers could avoid being stranded.

When Jett got back out to the SUV, he found Natalie looking dazed. He used the remote to unlock his door and got behind the wheel, relieved that she'd forgotten all about taking a turn driving. No way in hell would he let her behind the wheel. He did trust her driving ability, but she was far jumpier than him.

He frowned at her expression. "What is it, honey? You okay?"

She had her fingertips pressed to her temples and her eyes closed. Jett touched her chin to bring her face around to his.

"Natalie? What is it?"

She groaned as if in pain then covered her face. "I feel like such an idiot."

He had no idea why but said, "Not even close."

Catching her wrists, he pulled down her hands. "Why do you say that?"

Avoiding his gaze, she let out a long shaky breath. "I don't have my suitcase."

Jett pulled back. "How?" He'd carried out everything she had by the door—and it was plenty. "I know I put all your stuff in the back. I even double-checked to make sure I didn't leave anything behind."

"You didn't." She flicked a look at him. "Last night I'd carried my suitcase back into my bedroom to switch out a few things."

"What things?"

"Pajamas that were…nicer." She rolled her eyes. "Since you were coming along with me."

Ah. He opened his hand on the side of her face then bent to see her eyes. "Nicer, as in sexier?"

"Yes."

Well, damn. Sorry that he'd miss it, Jett stroked her cheek with his thumb. *So damn soft.* "You left it in your bedroom?"

She nodded miserably.

He tried not to smile at her woebegone expression. "Honey, when you're sleeping with me, you won't need pajamas of any kind, I promise."

"I get cold at night—" She held up a hand, anticipating his claim that he'd keep her warm. "Seriously, Jett. I'm not at all comfortable with the idea of sleeping in the…"

"Raw?" Hell, just talking about it was stirring him. Again.

Her shoulders drooped. "The only clothes I have with me are the ones I'm wearing."

"Doesn't sound like a major problem from my end."

He pulled her closer. "I wouldn't mind keeping you naked for the entire vacation. In fact, that sounds like one hell of a plan to me."

She groaned. "I'm serious, Jett."

"All right, sorry." He could understand why she was upset, especially after the grueling day fighting the weather. "We'll stop somewhere and you can pick up some stuff."

"Of course we won't." She shook her head in resignation. "It's already getting dark and the roads are terrible. If we finally make it to the stupid cabin, the last thing I'll expect to do is shop."

Trying to bite back his smile, Jett said, "I have extra boxers you can borrow."

She swatted at him. "It's not funny."

"Funny, no. But I promise, you being naked will definitely be fun—for both of us."

"You're incorrigible." She swatted him again. "I can't spend all my time naked—and no, don't insist that I can."

He caught her hands and pulled her close for a kiss that made *him* forget all about the stupid weather. "Until the weather clears enough for us to shop, you can sleep in one of my shirts. It'll fit you like a night-gown anyway."

"That'll help, thank you." She rubbed at her forehead. "But God, this entire trip has been snakebit from the start."

Including his companionship? He let out a breath and touched her downy cheek. He loved the feel of her skin, so warm and fundamentally female. "Why don't you think of it as an adventure?" He went one further, saying without much thought, "Years from now, we'll be laughing about it."

The minute the words left his mouth, she stared at him. Jett stared back. Hell, he hadn't actually meant to say that—but yeah, he could see them on a couch together, reminiscing about the trip from hell.

Even as they sat there, both of them uncertain what to say next, the gas station lights went off. Drawn from profound introspection, Jett turned his head and watched as the lone cashier locked up the place then went to a truck and carefully pulled out of the lot.

"Looks like we got refueled just in time."

Buddy hung his head over the seat, his nose almost touching Natalie's ear. His dour mood reflected hers. Every so often his ears lifted as if he hoped to hear something encouraging.

Natalie's big brown eyes held a lot of uncertainty. And then her phone beeped. She jerked as if pulled from a daze. Scrambling, she located it in her purse and opened it.

"Getting reception now?"

She shook her head. "No, but I did get a message. I guess they can come through even when the calls won't."

"From your sister?" That would cheer her up.

"No." She bit her bottom lip then groaned with dread. "It's from the manager at the cabin rental."

*Now what?* Jett wondered. He watched her face as she perused the message, seeing her dejection grow. "Let me guess. We can't get to the cabin."

"He says the roads are impassable. The best we can do is try to find a hotel for the night and hope things are better tomorrow." She looked out the window. "But how can they be? The roads to the cabin aren't paved, they're gravel, winding through the woods, up and down hills. That's why I chose the place—because it's remote and private."

Damn it, Jett would not let her trip be ruined. He patted her thigh. "I guess we better look for a hotel room, then."

"He said he'll reimburse me the down payment on the cabin." She chewed her bottom lip and finally looked at him. "Jett, I am so sorry you got stuck on this wasted trip."

Stuck? His irritation sharpened because that wasn't how he saw it. Sure, the travel was tense, Natalie more so. But they were together, and for him, that had made it more than worthwhile.

Now, he needed Natalie to admit the same.

## CHAPTER SEVEN

JETT SAT BACK IN HIS SEAT and gave her a remote look. "Do you honestly think I'd have been happier sitting at home, knowing you were out here alone in this fuck-ing mess?"

At his coarse language, her eyes widened and her jaw loosened. *"Jett."*

He ignored her chastising tone. "You were going, Natalie. With or without me, right?" That alone still burned his ass. He'd have missed her, but she'd planned to be away from him with no qualms at all. "Well let me tell you something, lady, given this shit weather, I'm damned glad I'm here, too, even if you aren't."

"Jett." This time she said his name more softly, still in reprimand. She searched his face. "You're actually glad you're here?"

"Damn right. At least this way I can see that you're fine instead of wondering if you were one of the cars stranded off the road."

Her expressive face filled with tender emotion. "I guess I hadn't thought about how that might bother you."

Of course she hadn't, because she thought of their relationship in terms of sex and only sex. He narrowed his eyes. "I've actually enjoyed talking to you while we're both wearing clothes."

Her mouth twitched. "Is that so?"

Knowing he sounded a little unhinged, not at all like his usual self, Jett gave one sharp nod. "But I'm definitely looking forward to having you all alone tonight, too. *All* night." His abdomen clenched at just the thought. "With or without pajamas, Natalie, I'll be keeping you close enough to stay warm, I promise."

Her lips lifted in a slight smile. "I'm looking forward to that, too."

"Then how the hell can you think this is a wasted trip?" The more he tried to reach her, the more annoyed he got. Sometimes it felt as if he was fighting a losing battle. Only he refused to lose. Ever.

But especially with her.

"You're right, and I'm sorry." She touched his shoulder. "I'm very glad you're here, please don't doubt that. Except for worrying about a wreck, you've made the trip…fun."

She took the wind out of his sails, leaving him scowling for no reason at all. "All right then." Left with nothing else to say, Jett put the SUV in Drive and turned out of the parking lot.

As Natalie reached for the food on the floor, she fell silent, prompting him to additional nagging. Never in his life had he nagged, but now, he couldn't seem to stop.

His jaw tightened. "You know, it's damn frustrating how you do that."

Surprised, she lifted her brows at him. "What's that?"

"The way you disconnect from me." It was dicey getting off the roads that hadn't been cleared. Carefully, Jett veered onto the highway. "In bed, you're always crystal clear. I know just what you want, when you want it."

Giving him a heated perusal, she said, "I know."

Her acknowledgement of their sexual compatibility kicked him in the gut, making his blood rush, his skin burn.

But damn it, he had to stay on track. "The thing is, out of bed you're so damn complex. Half the time I can't figure you out."

Natalie tilted her head. "Maybe that's because there's nothing to figure out. My life is boring."

"How can you say that? You're the most fascinating woman I've ever met." Every time she revealed another piece of herself, Jett somehow felt more whole, as if each step closer to her helped to fill up the empty places inside him.

He shook his head at that morbidly poetic thought; damn it, he did not have *empty places*. What bullshit.

"No way."

"You're kidding right?" How could she be so unaware of herself? "Look at you. You're sexy as hell, but you don't seem to know it. You burn me up in bed, but outside of bed you're this perfect little teacher."

Her brows came down as if that someone insulted her. "Perfect little teacher?"

Jett laughed. "So many contrasts with you." Maybe that was it—the contrasts intrigued him. But... "I even enjoyed watching you interact with my family."

She hesitated. "That was actually sort of scary."

"Meeting my sisters?" Yeah, they were outgoing and often outrageous, but they weren't bullies. "Why?"

Busying herself with arranging the food, Natalie

spoke casually, maybe hoping he wouldn't hear the gravity in her words. "Comparisons, I guess."

Jett considered that. From what he'd learned, her family was the exact opposite of his. He had hoped the contrasts would show her how nice things *could* be. But maybe it hadn't worked out like that. "Elaborate on that, will you?"

She took a drink of her cola and set his—with the straw inserted—in the cup holder. "I liked them. A lot. It was confusing but fun to be in the middle of the chaos your sisters create."

Jett hadn't considered things all that chaotic, not like when the whole clan got together. Holidays were especially nuts, but in a terrific way.

Natalie handed him his hot dog, and he ate it in two bites. She lifted his cola for him to take a drink then returned it to the cup holder.

As if they'd been coordinating this sort of thing for years, they worked in complete harmony. On a gut level, Jett had known that it would be like this with her. Hopefully this trip would convince her of the same.

But if he came on too strong, if he got too insistent, she'd bolt. He knew it. It was another of those contrasts he'd mentioned: she had no inhibitions in bed, but outside of sex, he'd never seen a woman so skittish of commitment.

Somewhere in her past, someone had hurt her.

Now, with the distant relationships of her family, she had few people to count on.

For at least the near future, he'd be by her side, protecting her, sharing with her, just being with her.

And with that thought in mind, Jett prompted, "The scary part?"

While gathering her thoughts, she fed him a chip. "Around our house, everything was always solemn and circumspect. After my mother left us, we usually only saw our father when he needed to lecture us on something or when his social affairs required that he trot out the sterling offspring."

Jett felt sick at such an upbringing, but even more than that, the way she'd said her mother "left" them— not that she'd passed away but that she'd *left*—caused him concern.

"There were very few meals with my father," Natalie told him, "but when he was there, it was silent. We were at the table to eat, not to joke, not to bother him. We had to show perfect manners."

Yet she'd eaten pizza at his table with a stray dog under her feet. "That sucks."

She lifted her hot dog in a salute. "For Dad, the idea of eating fast food in a car while traveling would be obscene."

"Fuck it." Fuck *him*. "I'm having a good time."

Natalie laughed as she fed him another chip. "Me too."

She didn't realize he was dead serious. Bad weather and road conditions aside, he was finally getting her to open up. He'd brave hell for that, so what did icy roads matter?

"When we did see Dad at home, it was in passing, as he was on his way out to another appointment. Sometimes he'd be gone for days, even a week or more. He didn't keep us apprised of his itinerary, but when he wasn't around we just assumed he was off on business."

"He sounds like an unfeeling prick."

She laughed again, but this time there wasn't much humor in the sound. "That about covers it." Her laugh faded to a secret little smile.

Enjoying the sight of that, Jett asked, "What?"

"I was thinking of my sister." She shook her head with the memory. "Dad's library was one of the rooms off-limits to us, so of course, that's where Molly liked to go. I told her I didn't care about his stupid library, but the truth was, I didn't dare go in there."

Lethal rage put a stranglehold on Jett. "What would he have done if he'd found you there?"

Natalie stroked his arm in comfort. "He didn't abuse us physically, Jett. Not ever. Dad's idea of punishment was a threat to separate us."

And since they had only each other, that threat would be worse than anything else. "Separate you how?"

"Boarding school, summer camp, things like that. Looking back, I realize those were idle threats because Dad never spent money on things like that for us. He says that he wanted us to grow up independent of his wealth and social standing. He wanted us to make our own way."

"So you attended public school?"

"Yes. We aced classes and we were always well dressed, because anything less would have reflected on him. But the extracurricular stuff that helps you bond with peers, like band or dance or drama...no way. I think that's why Molly turned to books."

"As an escape?"

"Yes. And it turned out well since she's now a very popular writer."

Jett could hear the pride whenever Natalie talked of her sister, but he knew that Natalie must have been equally influenced by the conditions of her life. "Why'd you become a teacher?"

The defroster ran on high, and still it could barely keep the ice off the windshield. More and more cars and trucks were showing up in ditches and over the median. Buddy now treated them to the resonance of a doggy snore. The weather outside the SUV served to blanket them in a unique form of intimacy. Jett could almost hear his own heartbeat, and hers.

For only a moment she looked out the side window, but then she turned her gaze back to Jett, searching for understanding, for things he desperately wanted to give her.

"I always remembered how it felt," she whispered. "All though school, I was different when I shouldn't have been. Unlike the kids who had real issues, my life was charmed."

Would she always be so hard on herself? "Your issues were real."

Natalie shook her head, and her hands fisted. "Not really, not like the kid who's being physically abused at home, or the child with a physical or mental deformity. Even compared to the kids who were just unpopular because they weren't as pretty or as well-to-do as some of the others, I was better off." She stared at Jett. "Kids can be so damn cruel, when being a kid is hard enough."

That bothered Jett because for him, life had been pretty fantastic. He couldn't remember ever being singled out for any unfavorable reason. Usually just the opposite.

His classmates had liked him; he'd been one of the popular kids.

He'd done his fair share to combat bullies, and

whenever possible he'd gone out of his way to befriend the kids who were ostracized. But then, he'd had parents who taught him sympathy and compassion in the same way that they'd encouraged him in everything from sports to education to…any damn thing he'd ever wanted to do.

"So like my sister, I'm glad for what my upbringing brought me. It's taught me how to recognize the kids who are really troubled, and now I'm in a position to help. At least most of the time."

"Most of the time?"

"There was one boy…he was so withdrawn, so antagonistic. I knew something was wrong, but I didn't realize how bad it was. He wouldn't confide in me, and I couldn't reach his mother on the phone." She squeezed her eyes shut. "He was homeless, Jett. His dad had passed away and his mother took off on her own, and he had…no one."

Despite the treacherous conditions of the icy road, Jett reached for her hand. "You can't know everything about everybody, honey. Kids are good at hiding things, especially when they feel shamed by their circumstances."

Natalie nodded without conviction. "Only a few days after I went to the administration to request that they somehow get hold of his parents, they found his body in an alley. Accidental overdose, they said."

Jett cursed softly, hurting for Natalie and for the boy who'd been neglected. "Nothing hits you like the death of a kid."

Her hand clutched his hard. "You say that like a man with personal experience."

"Yeah." He shifted, uncomfortable with some

memories. "I've been hired to find plenty of runaways." And those were always the most urgent cases for him. "Sometimes the end result is good, sometimes not."

To let her know that he did understand, Jett expounded on one experience. "There was this mom who hired me to locate her thirteen-year-old daughter. The girl had left home and was missing for three weeks."

"You found her?"

He'd found her all right—and thank God that he had. "She wanted no part of going home. Turns out, her stepdaddy was a sick fuck."

"Oh God." Natalie curled a fist to her mouth. "That poor girl."

"Yeah. When I told the mother, she refused to believe it. She even accused the girl of just wanting to ruin her happiness." It sickened Jett to remember how incredulous the mother had been, how she'd accused her daughter of lying.

Stupid bitch.

Head turned in suspicion, Natalie asked, "What did you do?"

"I wanted to do exactly what you're thinking I did."

"Beat him to a pulp?"

"Yeah. But that wouldn't have helped the kid any, so instead, hard as it was, I followed the law to the letter. I went to the authorities—and I took her with me."

Natalie let out a breath. "I'm so glad you didn't leave her there."

"That wasn't an option. I told her if she came with me, I wouldn't let anyone hurt her—and I meant it." Even with the proper people who handled such things, he hadn't wanted to let her out of his sight. "She was placed in foster care, but she kept my card with my number in case shit went south again."

Arrested, Natalie stared at him in near awe. "She's okay now?"

"Yeah." He couldn't help but smile. "She's…let's see. Almost fifteen now. So she's been with these foster parents for over a year. They love her and she adores them. She still has some issues." He glanced at Natalie with meaning. "You know, you don't just get over stuff that bad. But she's doing great."

"You still talk with her?"

Jett shrugged. "Sure. She keeps in touch, and I do the same." He'd sent her a card on her birthday, and sometimes he sent her cards just for the hell of it, those goofy cards meant to give a smile.

"You're amazing, Jett."

"What?" Blustering at the compliment, he shook his head. "No, don't go that route. That's not the point I was trying to make. I was showing what a difference it can mean to kids if someone cares the way you do."

"Thanks. But you're still amazing." She smiled and seemed to draw her thoughts together. "Your sisters are amazing, too. Confident and beautiful and fun. They're happy, anyone can see that."

He spoke with utter sincerity, saying, "You're all those things too."

Her silly smile told him that she didn't believe him. "My father is so…staid, that around our house we never had the unrestrained conversation and laughter that happened today at the clinic. I enjoyed it. I would have taken part if I'd known how."

Deciding that he'd make it so, Jett said, "You'll learn how, I promise."

"And then what?" She watched him in that curious way of hers, her gaze wary and hopeful at once. "I get used to your wonderful family, I get used to *you,* and then if things don't work out…" She lifted her shoulders in question.

Back to square one, damn it. Jett squeezed the steering wheel. "I would never hurt you, Natalie."

"Not on purpose, no. I believe that." She sounded so reasonable, so detached that it made him nuts and made him want her. "I meant what I said, Jett. You're wonderful. In so many ways."

Because he knew she drew unfavorable comparisons, it put his teeth on edge. "You're wonderful too, damn it."

Instead of replying to that, she said, "The differences in our families are pretty stark." She wadded up the garbage from their meal and stuffed it all into one bag. "I assume you know that already, being you're a sleuth and all that."

He cocked an eyebrow. "You're on thin ice, lady. One more crack about me snooping—"

Her mood lightened at his feigned temper. "You did snoop!"

"Smartass." He grinned at her. "I don't know everything about you, not by a long shot. But even with what I do know, I'd still like to hear details from you."

She sobered. "So…you don't know about my mother?"

The new tension in her tone felt like a fist closing around his heart. "I know she died when you were young. That's all." He'd seen no reason to delve beyond that, seeing it as grave enough, awful enough, without added details.

Natalie sat silent for so long that Jett hurt for her. "I was nine the first time my mother tried to kill herself."

Jett caught his breath on a wave of pain. How hard would that be for a sensitive little girl? "Damn, Natalie. I'm sorry."

"She threw herself off a bridge. Twice, actually. The first time she failed because there was a rescue team doing drills in the river below her." Natalie's mouth twisted with pain and sarcasm. "Perfect timing, right? They fished her out, ruining her dramatic display."

Oh God. "Honey…"

"I think she was pretty miserable. At least, that's what Molly has always told me, that Mom didn't hate us, but that she was an unhappy woman who didn't know how to make herself happy." She frowned a little. "Living with my father could make anyone miserable, I'm sure."

He gave silent thanks she'd had Molly to help diffuse some of the hurt. Though her sister couldn't have been much older herself, he knew they'd comforted each other.

When he finally got to meet her sister, he planned to give her a big hug of gratitude.

"But I don't blame Dad entirely." Natalie's words were filled with contempt, but her expression was wounded. "I mean, if Mom did hate him so much, why would she leave her daughters with him, you know? Why didn't she just divorce him and take us with her?"

"I don't know." Damn, he needed to get to a hotel so he could hold her. Highway lamps flickered on, and headlights barely cut through the growing darkness. The six-hour trip had turned into eight, and they needed to get settled, to eat real food, to stretch. "Everyone is different, baby. Some people aren't as strong as others."

"Molly thinks I'm strong. She always says that, so I guess she really believes it."

"I'd agree." It definitely took great inner strength to survive so much unhappiness and still have her tender heart and gentle understanding intact.

"Back when Mom died, Molly seemed so much older, and I really relied on her. But there's only three years separating us." She stared off into the distance. "She's more than my sister. She's my best friend, too."

"I'm glad the two of you are so close."

She didn't seem to hear him. "After Mom jumped off that bridge, she spent a long time in a really exclusive hospital. You know the type, where you pay through the nose to be pampered, and they cater to your every wish."

Jett didn't know what to say, so he nodded.

"I hated visiting her there, especially since Dad would be the one to take us. The entire day would be ruined with friction, condescension and strained civility. At home, Mom and Dad barely talked, but while she was in the hospital he spent all his time telling her that she was being selfish and weak and that she'd embarrassed him." Natalie laughed in that humorless, sad way again. "Nurses overheard him but said nothing since he was paying the bills, and that embarrassed me. It still embarrasses me."

"It shouldn't. Your parents are not you."

"But that's pretty much what my family is, you know? Awkward and ugly and cold."

He understood now why she avoided talking about them. "That had to be hell on a kid."

She drew a slow deep breath. "After Mom came home again, Molly kept saying that she'd be okay. I don't know if she believed that or if she was just trying to protect me. Or maybe she wanted to convince herself."

Jett had wanted her to open up to him, but now he almost couldn't bear it. "She wasn't okay."

"Far from it. And regardless of what Molly had said, neither of us was real surprised when she took another jump off a bridge, this time over a highway."

Jett cursed low.

"There was no fishing her out that time." She stared down at her hands. "It was a gory, headline-worthy scandal, and that's what Dad was mostly put out over. Not once did I see him cry or get emotional over any of it. I honestly don't think any woman—or maybe even any person—has ever meant that much to him."

Not even his daughters. The idea left Jett furious. "Parents should be there for their kids."

She nodded. "Being a teacher, I see mostly good parents who really love their children. They're not perfect and they make mistakes, but not because they don't care—just because they're human."

"Making mistakes is the biggest part of being in a family. But when you love each other, a few mistakes are easily forgiven." Even as he said it, he wondered about her relationship with her sister. "Have you and Molly had any differences?"

"I really despised Adrian." She winced, as if guilty. "Molly said that I didn't think anyone was good enough for her, but that's not true. I want her to be happy, and if she'd married Adrian, I'd have made the best of it."

"Sometimes people in love wear blinders."

"That's just it, though. Adrian was convenient, but I don't think Molly really loved him." Natalie waved a hand. "Anyway, it all worked out when Adrian finally showed his true colors. Molly dumped him, and she wasn't all that broken up about it, so I say good riddance."

"What about your stepmother? Do you both like her?"

"Kathi." She wrinkled her nose. "She's perfect for my father. And I have to give her credit for trying to make us into some sort of family, as impossible as that seems."

Jett hated how she said that, as if she'd almost given up on the idea of family.

In the next second, his thoughts shattered as a semi tried to pass them and lost control. Everything happened fast.

Horns blared as the semi swerved across the lanes, forcing two cars to crash into each other as another slid wildly and almost hit them. Jett had just winged past that collision when another car fishtailed in front of him.

For a split second, Jett lost control of the SUV and they went sliding sideways. Natalie never made a sound and neither did he. Then the tires gained traction in the thick snow on the perimeter of the lane and Jett again righted the vehicle. Ice and snow pelted the windshield, leaving him temporarily blind before the wipers managed to shove aside the slush.

And then he saw it, that damned semi now sideways in the road. When Jett touched his brakes, he slid over the icy roadway.

"Damn." Squeezing the wheel in a death grip, he tapped the brakes again, more gently this time, and steered toward the berm. The truck's trailer flipped over and dragged the cab toward the median.

Behind them, Jett heard the impact of steel on steel as two other cars reacted to the sight of the semi and lost control.

The semi flipped over into the median, finally *out* of Jett's path but too late for him to continue on. The SUV made contact with a high pile of snow and ice on the side of the road.

The impact jarred them hard; Buddy yelped as he rolled out of his doggy bed.

Jett went still, his heart in his throat and fury burning his blood. For a heartbeat of time, he didn't move. Buddy jarred him by barking and jumping up to look over the seat.

Jett glanced at Natalie. She had a death grip on the padded door handle, her other hand at her heart. Hand shaking, he reached over and touched her. "Natalie?"

"I'm fine." She sounded calm. "Are you okay?"

No, he was not okay. In rapid succession a dozen scenarios had played out in his brain, all of them involving injury to her. Out of pure terror, he'd pictured the SUV wrecking, the semi crushing her, her soft flesh bleeding...

He was a man of control, but for one of the few times in his life, he knew he was rattled. God, the thought of anything happening to her left him devastated. Weak, shaken, sick.

*What would he do without her?*

That's when it struck him.

"Jett?" She covered his hand with her own. "Say something."

He locked gazes with her, and got blasted with reality. Oh hell.

Like a ton of bricks landing on his chest, crushing out all his air, he realized that he loved her.

*Really* loved her, like the forever kind. Like marriage, kids, picket fences and all the fanfare.

His eyes burned and his throat felt tight. He didn't just want more time with Natalie. Hell no.

He wanted everything.

He turned his head to stare straight ahead. Less than a quarter of a mile up, an exit had been cleared. Jett put the SUV back in gear and, bless the fates, backed out of the snow and ice without a problem. "Buddy needs you."

Natalie gave him another worried look, but she did comfort the dog as she looked out the rearview window. "Everyone looks okay."

He didn't want to look back. He couldn't. "People are out of their cars?"

"Yes. The truck driver, too. There are at least…" She did a quick count. "Looks like six cars and the truck, all stopped, with the road blocked. Those poor people. They'll be stuck for a while."

Working his jaw, Jett took the exit, and right there, bludgeoned by the blizzard, a hotel came into view. "We're going there." Natalie didn't reply, but that didn't stop him from talking. "I'm getting us off the road, right now."

In an attempt to calm him, she said, "Okay, Jett."

He glanced at her with new awareness. Ah hell, now

she wanted to placate him—because he was behaving like an ass.

New emotions rushed through him, all but obliterating his logic. He needed something to do so that he didn't crush her close and declare himself.

"I'm calling my sister." He used the speed dial in his car.

The second she answered, Jett gave her the name of the hotel and the location. "The roads are shit. We won't make it to the cabin, so we're staying here for the night. Got it?"

Heidi said, "Sure. But Jett? You okay?"

"Fine. Perfect, in fact. But I gotta go. The parking lot hasn't been cleared yet, so I need to be alert. Bye." He hung up on her.

Natalie watched him the same way she'd watch a lunatic. "Jett, it's okay. *We're* okay."

"Not yet." He wouldn't be okay until he'd found a way to bind her to him. "But we will be just as soon as I set you straight on a few things."

Disgruntlement laced her tone when she said, "Just what is that supposed to mean?"

"After I have you and Buddy settled." His SUV pushed through the thick snow in the parking lot of the hotel. Luckily they had a covered entry and he pulled up there. "Stay put while I sign us in." He looked at her and couldn't believe he'd been so blind. She would have made this trip on her own. She could easily have been one of the people forced off the road, or worse.

Hating that thought, Jett caught the back of her neck to drag her close for a hot, hungry kiss. Gentler now, he said, "Okay?"

She looked dazed. "All right."

Realizing that they were now stopped, Buddy got excited. He came over the seat in one bound and landed on Natalie. She laughed as she caught his collar so he couldn't follow Jett out.

His heart in his throat, his libido raging, Jett jogged into the building. The hotel was nice enough to give them a room even though their usual policy denied pets. He paid a hefty extra fee for the privilege of bringing Buddy in, promised to clean up his messes and got room keys for their one and only suite.

Within twenty minutes he had them and their belongings inside. While Natalie ran a hot bath, Jett took Buddy out a side door to do his business. Not a single speck of ground could be seen through the thick snow, so Jett let the dog go where the opened door had cleared a spot. Buddy still got a little snow-covered, but he no longer seemed so panicked or afraid.

"We'll be all right, Buddy. You'll see."

Buddy bounded around in agreement, burning off some energy before Jett took him back inside. To keep the dog occupied, Jet set up his doggy bed, his water and food dish and gave him a big juicy chew toy.

Buddy looked to be in doggy heaven.

With that done, Jett went into the bathroom and found Natalie resting in a steamy tub, her curly hair piled atop her head, her eyes closed and her luscious body lax. The water lapped at her chin and had already turned her toes pink.

She looked exhausted.

Jett stood there, no longer so stunned by his revelation. Of course he loved her. How could he not?

And it had nothing to do with her being elusive, as he'd first thought. Sure, that had first enhanced his interest, after her incredible body and sexual daring had caught his attention.

But it was Natalie herself who kept his thoughts in turmoil and made him feel those remarkable, unrecognizable, profound emotions. By being herself, a kind, intelligent and sexy woman, she had completely stolen his heart.

Life had taken her to hell and back, but she remained generous and open, honest and accepting. She used her childhood hardships as a learning tool to help other children now. He had no doubt she could be stern when necessary, but she would always be fair.

"Natalie?"

She looked up at him, her lashes spiked, her cheeks dewy. She sounded slumberous. "I didn't hear you come in."

She didn't bother to cover herself or act shy about her body. From the beginning, she'd been an uninhibited lover. It was only in sharing her heart that she became shy.

But he'd get her over that. "Have you washed up?"

"Mmm." She closed her eyes again. "I did that first, because I knew once I got warm, I'd get sleepy."

"Not too sleepy, I hope." As he scooped her out of the tub, her eyes flashed open again.

"Jett!"

Water sluiced down their bodies and onto the floor. He didn't care.

"I need you, Natalie." Such an understatement. Now that he knew he loved her, he wanted to hear a similar declaration from her. But he didn't mind going first.

"I thought you'd be tired from all that tense driving."

"Especially after that, I need you." While carrying her to the bed, he kissed her nose, her forehead, her temple and ear. "I'll always need you, you know."

Her breath caught at the weighty meaning of those words. "What?"

Jett stood her beside the bed. He touched her cheek, brushed the corner of her mouth with his thumb. "Damn, but the things you make me feel are…powerful."

"Powerful?"

He held out a hand, showing her. "You make me shake."

"Oh, Jett." She closed both her hands around his. "That's just reaction from a near wreck."

"No, honey. That's reaction to knowing you could have been hurt. I wouldn't be able to bear that." Smiling was beyond him, so instead he kissed her. "Don't move."

He was back in seconds with a towel and he went about drying her. Going down to his knees in front of her, he took his time, being quite thorough. "God, Natalie, I love your body."

She laughed nervously, her hand in his hair. "I don't understand you tonight."

Jett looked up at her. "I love your laugh, too."

Her voice trembled. "Jett, really…"

"And the way you shrug off compliments." He stood and cupped her face. "You're tired, aren't you?"

After slowly licking her lips, she ventured, "Well, not *too* tired, not now, not after you've just been touching me."

He made a sound between a growl and a groan. "I

especially love how sexual you are." Knowing his repeated use of the *L* word had thrown her, Jett gently lowered her to the bed and knelt over her. "Just relax and let me do everything."

"But…" Her beautiful eyes searched his. "You have to be tired, too."

He shook his head and cupped her breasts in both hands. "I'm in love. Now hush."

She went perfectly still, frozen, stiff—but Jett didn't let that stop him. He caressed her breasts, teased her nipples.

"Jett, wait." Natalie tried to catch his arm. "What did you say?"

"I said for you to hush."

"No, before—"

He drew her nipple into his mouth, stealing her breath.

But her fingers clenched tight in his hair. "Damn it, Jett."

Laughing a little, he said, "I even love it when you're bossy."

She breathed hard and fast, her gaze intent. He watched her throat as she swallowed. "You said…you said you love me."

He could understand her confusion. "I've been battling with myself, pissed off one minute, jealous the next. And so damn turned on I couldn't stand it, but it was never enough." He shook his head. "You've turned me inside out, woman."

Natalie searched his face a moment, then frowned. "Good."

"Good?"

"You've turned me inside out, too." Tears burned her eyes. "You love me?"

"Why else would I let you torture me like this?" He pushed her hair from her face. "When I lost control of the car... God, I've faced a lot of shit in my life, and I just sort of roll with it. But thinking you could have been hurt? It shook me. Bad. And I knew I had to stop being a chickenshit and just 'fess up."

Slow to accept his declaration, she asked uncertainly, "By saying you love me?"

"Yeah." He gave her a lopsided grin and shook her a little. "And if you love me, too, you need to put me out of my damned misery and tell me so."

She launched herself close to him. "I love you. I've loved you for a long time now. I didn't want to admit it because if I did, and you didn't feel the same—"

"I feel it. Trust me, I've got it bad." Lowering them both to the bed, Jett kissed her parted lips. "Say it again."

Her hands opened on his chest. She stroked him then slowly slid her arms around his neck. "I love you, too."

Thank God. But she was so skittish about family and relationships, he had to make sure she understood. Braced on his elbows over her, he gave her his most intent stare. "I need more than just sex, Natalie."

Her gaze was soft, her voice more so. "How much more?"

In comparison, he sounded harsh and demanding. "Everything. The whole shebang." The more he talked about it, the more he needed it. The more he needed her. Of course, she looked so happy and so accepting that his thoughts had already skipped ahead to being inside her, to hearing her cry out, feeling her squeezing him… *Stay on track, Jett.*

"The whole shebang, huh?"

"Commitment, marriage, fidelity." As her legs wound around him, it became more difficult to explain. "You haven't known the best relationships, honey, but I swear to you, we'll be good together. We'll be fucking *amazing* together."

"I know."

"We'll have the forever kind—" Her smile finally reached him. Jett straightened his arms, staring at her in bemusement. "What do you mean, you know?"

She laughed with affection. "Jett, I already told you that you're wonderful. I meant it. So a lifetime with you would be wonderful."

"You'll marry me?"

"Yes." The smile remained but was now more subdued. "I might need time to get used to things. I mean, your family is the exact opposite of mine."

"We'll work on your family."

"No." She shuddered. "I don't want to do that. And trust me, once you meet my father and stepmother, you'll feel the same."

"Whatever makes you happy." If that meant winning over her ass of a father, he'd do it. Somehow.

But if she truly wanted to cut him out, that was fine with Jett.

Big tears welled in her eyes, and her smile trembled. "The thing is, I always knew my family was…abnormal. I always believed there could be love and friendship and happiness."

"You'll have that with me, I swear."

"I know, because today, through that long trip from hell…I realized I already had it. You made the whole thing fun. Well, except for that business there at the very end—"

"Don't." Jett closed his eyes, unable to think about that and how easily he could have lost her. "I'm not perfect, Natalie."

"I know that too."

Jett cocked a brow. So now she was laughing at him? He grinned. "For you, I'll try to be perfect."

"For me, if you'd just go on being you, I'll be a very happy woman."

Her complete and utter acceptance of him put him over the edge. Within half a minute he had stripped his clothes away. Seconds after that, he was over her again, kissing her, touching her.

Entering her in one long, smooth thrust.

Everything was different now. More potent.

More satisfying.

They had one moment of shock when, just after they came together, Buddy tried to jump up onto the bed.

Natalie screeched, and that made Buddy howl.

Still in a fog, it took Jett a second to realize what had happened. Luckily the dog was too short to make the leap, though he was certainly trying. "Down, Buddy." Jett jerked the comforter around them both.

Natalie started giggling, and once she started, she couldn't stop.

Chagrined, Jett felt his own smile crack. Yeah, everything was different.

And damn, it couldn't be more perfect.

THREE DAYS LATER, STILL snowed in, Buddy came to the bed and barked. Natalie didn't hesitate. She nudged Jett.

"Hmm?"

They were both naked. Again. Or maybe still. Jett had dressed to get them food and to take Buddy out, but so far she'd only been partially clothed at any given time.

She hadn't been out of the room once—and hadn't minded in the least.

"Jett?"

"Mmm…Natalie." He tried to pull her closer, already kissing her shoulder, his hand sliding around to her stomach.

The man was insatiable.

She was *so* lucky.

"Buddy has to go out."

Letting out a sigh, Jett turned to his back and managed to get his eyes open. He yawned, stretched and lifted up on an elbow to look at her. "Hey, beautiful."

Very softly, Natalie said, "Hey."

He lifted one brow then smoothed the sheet away from her breasts. "Didn't I tell you that you wouldn't need clothes?"

"You were mostly right." Natalie swatted the sheet back down. "But if I had clothes, I could offer to take a turn with Buddy."

"I don't mind." Jett patted her hip and rolled out of the bed. "Be back in a few."

Skipping boxers and a shirt, he pulled on jeans, stepped into his shoes and grabbed his coat. Buddy, already well used to their routine, danced around him.

Jett hooked the leash to his collar. "He looks energetic

this morning, so I'm going to walk him around the halls a little after he takes care of his business."

"Want me to order room service while you do that?"

"Naked?" He gave her a mock frown. "Hell no. I'll bring something back with me."

And so it went. Natalie did little to nothing while Jett pampered her in the most outrageous ways. She was still in the shower when he returned. She heard him and started to turn off the water, but then the shower curtain moved and he stepped in behind her.

He kissed the nape of her neck and wrapped his strong arms around her. "Natalie?"

She put her head on his shoulder. "Hmm?"

"This is the best damn vacation I've ever been on."

Shaking her head, she laughed and said, "You're easy."

Slowly, the grin slipped over his face. "I've had you all to myself all this time. It's been perfect." He set her back from him again. "But the damned snow has finally stopped and the roads are getting cleared. No way could we make it to the cabin. The side roads are going to be screwed for a while. But it looks like we could head back tomorrow morning, if that's what you want to do."

Only one more day alone with him. Natalie sighed. "I've loved every second here with you."

"But you're worried about your sister, right?"

"Yes." Before getting in the shower, she'd checked her email account. "I got an email from her."

"And? You don't look happy about it."

Far from happy, she was now more concerned than

ever. "There was something wrong with the message."

"What kind of wrong?"

"It was too brief, and far too cryptic to be from Molly."

"What did it say?"

"Just that she'd be gone for a while, off having some fun for a change, and that she'd get in touch when she could." Natalie shook her head. "That's not her. She'd have told me where she was going, given me a way to get in touch with her." Natalie chewed her lip. "If she was going to have fun, she'd want me to know about it."

"The way you want her to know that you're having fun now?"

Natalie nodded. It was so frustrating that she couldn't reach Molly. And deep down inside herself, she knew something wasn't right. "If you're sure you don't mind, I think we should head back."

"Of course I don't mind. If it was one of my sisters, I'd be the same." His sexy mouth lifted into a grin. "Speaking of my sisters, they're going to go even more nuts for you once they know we're getting married."

Natalie touched the middle of his chest then dragged her finger ever so slowly downward. Life was ready to intrude, but she still had today. "Guess I better make the most of our remaining time, then."

"Sounds like one hell of a plan." Jett closed his eyes when she circled her hand around him. "As long as you remember that our remaining time is forever."

\* \* \* \* \*

*What kind of trouble is Natalie's sister,*
*Molly Alexander, in?*
*Find out in WHEN YOU DARE,*
*the first of a sizzling new trilogy*
*from Lori Foster*
*and HQN Books.*
*Coming soon!*

# GAIL'S GONE WILD

## Susan Donovan

\* \* \* \*

This book is dedicated to all the
bangin'-sick teenagers I'm blessed to have in my life.
I won't embarrass you by printing your names.

Dear Reader,

*"Rule number one is never, ever fall in love with a guy you meet on spring break...."*

Gail Chapman may be the chaperone for her teenage daughter and friend, but after meeting Key West neighbor Jesse Batista—a sultry, sexy, earring-wearing sea captain with a big secret—Gail is the girl who's gone wild.

This novella was inspired by a real-life trip with my teenagers to Key West. But hold off on those plane tickets. The only place you'll find Jesse is right here in these pages.

Happy reading!

Susan Donovan

# CHAPTER ONE

"But, Mom! How can you do this to me?"

Gail Chapman looked up from her morning newspaper and into the angry face of her seventeen-year-old daughter, Holly. "The answer is no," she said again. "There is no way on earth I am letting you go to Florida alone for spring break. Do you think I don't know what kind of trouble a girl can get into down there?"

"But I'll have Hannah with me!"

Gail tried to keep a straight face, but the idea that Holly's best friend, the voluptuous Hannah Marko, would somehow provide a barrier between her daughter and disaster was laughable. The two of them were Thelma and Louise without a lick of life experience or a decent map. "I said no, and that's my final decision."

"*God!*" Holly stomped her feet like an enraged toddler. "I can't believe you'd mess up my entire senior year like this! You're ruining my whole life!"

"Actually, I'm helping you avoid that very thing."

"*Aaauuuggghh!*" Holly balled up her fists. The veins and tendons stood out from her neck so much that Gail thought she looked like the Incredible Hulkette in size-three skinny jeans.

"The answer is no, Holly."

"But you don't understand—"

"Sure I do," Gail said, calmly removing her reading

glasses and folding her hands on the kitchen table in front of her. "I am not a shut-in, sweetheart. I know all the temptations the world has to offer."

Her daughter made some kind of dismissive clicking sound at the back of her tongue before she said, "What-*evs*."

Gail sighed.

"But Daytona Beach is perfectly safe, Mom!" Holly twirled around on her Uggs and flopped into the other kitchen chair. "There's lifeguards, like, every ten feet down the sand! And police everywhere! And, you know, their whole economy depends on tourism, so, like, they have to make sure nothing bad ever happens to the spring-break kids because that would be bad PR and totally negatively affect their economy!"

Gail was impressed by her daughter's logic, but it was all a load of bull and they both knew it. "The answer is no," she said again, standing up and clearing away her breakfast dishes. As she rinsed them out in the sink, she felt Holly press close behind her.

"Please, Mommy?" Holly made the plea in her cutest, sweetest, little-girl voice.

"No."

"Dad would say yes!" Holly's voice had magically regained its full measure of teenage torment. "If I lived with Dad, he'd let me go!"

Gail nearly choked as she placed her bowl and spoon in the dishwasher. Holly was right. Her dad would likely endorse any vacation that included alcohol poisoning, random disrobing and waking up in a stranger's hotel room, since that was pretty much his preferred getaway. It was all a moot point, of course. Holly couldn't move in with her dad anytime soon, since Curtis Chapman would be a guest of the federal prison system for another four years. And that was contingent upon good behavior, which had never been his strong suit.

"No, Holly. That's my final answer."

"You're being unreasonable! Give me one good reason why I shouldn't be allowed to go!"

Gail turned. She put her hands on Holly's upper arms and held her firmly. She looked right into her daughter's big, beautiful brown eyes—a move that now required her to look up instead of down because her baby was about an inch taller than her. She spoke slowly and seriously.

"A terrible disease. An unplanned pregnancy. An auto accident. Being hit by a bus. Drowning. A shark attack. An unintentional starring role in the *Sluts of Spring Break* DVD available for $19.95 on the Internet."

Holly's mouth fell open.

"What?" Gail asked. "Did you think I'm some nerdy small-town English professor with no idea of what goes on outside of Beaverdale, Pennsylvania?"

Holly blinked. "Well...*yeah.*"

Gail kissed her daughter's cheek, keeping her smile hidden. "I need to get ready for my nine o'clock class. You've got five minutes until the bus gets here."

"But, *Mom*—"

"We'll talk about it more this evening," Gail said, heading toward her bedroom. "Maybe we can come up with some kind of alternative plan, okay? Maybe you and Hannah can do something fun a little closer to home."

"Oh, right," Holly said, grabbing her backpack and

heading for the front door. "I can see it now—spring break in Amish Country! We could make cheese and go on buggy rides! Hey—you could be our chaperone, Mom! I can't wait to tell Hannah! This spring break is gonna totally *rock!*"

"Bye, honey." Gail got the words out just before Holly slammed the door behind her. She chuckled to herself as she pulled out a brown skirt and beige blouse from her closet, thinking that it wasn't all that long ago that she'd tried the same thing with her own mom. And lost. Gail ended up spending her senior-year spring break in the backseat of Tommy Brancovicci's beater 1981 Gran Torino, which, come to think of it, was nothing but a shark attack on dry land.

As she dressed, Gail ran through the day's schedule in her mind. She taught her Intro to American Lit class at nine and her Honors Hemingway Seminar at two, with student conferences from ten-thirty to noon. She was meeting Kim for lunch—it had been far too long since she'd seen her best friend. And she had a department meeting at four and had to pick up the dry cleaning on the way home. Oh! And she should swing by the campus print shop for her new business cards, so she could proudly tell the world who she'd become: Gail Chapman, PhD.

She shook her head at the irony of it. The heck with Holly and Hannah! What did two impossibly young and free girls need with a vacation? Gail was the one who'd earned a spring break!

She froze. Holly's sarcastic proposal began echoing in her head.

*Chaperone?*

Maybe her daughter was onto something.

GAIL PICKED AT HER CAESAR salad with a fork, trying to summon the courage to answer Kim's question. "Well, it's kind of embarrassing…"

Her best friend laughed. "Come on, Gail. I've known you for thirty of your thirty-six years on the planet. There's nothing left to be embarrassed about. We've gone through sex, love, money, heartbreak, divorce, parenting, various career crises and Curtis's embezzlement trial. How could your choice of vacation destination be embarrassing?"

Gail looked up at Kim and shrugged. "We're talking my dream vacation, right?"

Kim nodded. "Right."

Gail took a deep breath. "Well, the one place I've always wanted to go—you know, like my ultimate fantasy getaway—is Key West. And I figure now is the perfect time. The girls get their spring break and I get my trip of a lifetime."

It took exactly one second for Kim's face to go from excitement to stone-cold disappointment. She shook her head back and forth and closed her eyes. After taking a moment to compose herself she said, "Is this a Hemingway thing? Because if this is a Hemingway thing, I swear to God I'll—"

"Not completely."

Kim put her hand on Gail's arm. "Key West is wild, honey. It's the home of street parties and dangerous smugglers and all-you-can-drink booze cruises."

"I realize that, but the girls would have restrictions and a curfew," Gail said. "They'll be heading off to college soon, anyway, and I figured this will give them a taste of freedom but with adult supervision."

Kim looked dumbfounded.

"What?" she asked.

"I was referring to *you,* Gail."

She waved Kim off. "Oh, you know I'd never let anything happen to me."

Kim roared with laughter, drawing the stares of some of the other diners at their favorite lunch spot near campus. "That's what I'm worried about, Gail—that you wouldn't let anything happen to you, that a trip to Margaritaville would be completely wasted on you, that you're going there solely for some kind of Ernest Hemingway geek-fest!"

It was Gail's turn to laugh, and it felt good to laugh that hard. Kim's reaction didn't surprise her, and Gail couldn't fault her friend. The whole idea did sound suspiciously work-related. But it was the truth—for as long as she could remember she'd been fascinated by the lore of Key West, the city's wild and romantic history and, yes, its connection to the romantic Papa Hemingway legend. He'd written some of his best work there, after all.

"If I went to Key West I'd find a way to relax a little," Gail assured her.

Kim sighed. The waiter came by to refill their iced teas, which gave her a chance to study Gail carefully until he was out of range. "I know what your version of relaxation is," she said, a note of accusation in her voice. "Books. Reading. And if you're feeling like a really naughty girl, you'll write notes in the margins."

Gail giggled.

"That wasn't intended to be funny."

Gail rolled her eyes. She knew Kim meant well, and there was certainly a seed of truth to what she was saying, but this was all fantasy anyway. She had no idea if she could get a hotel room for herself and the girls at this late a date. She had no idea how much it would set her back. She had no idea if the girls would even agree to this plan. Most of all, she wasn't exactly the world's most spontaneous person, so this whole flight of fancy was way out of her comfort zone.

Yet, despite all that, Gail hadn't been able to get the idea out of her head since getting dressed that morning. Something about it felt right. Maybe it was time she did something out of her comfort zone. Maybe it was time to live a little.

"You need to get out, Gail." Kim took a gulp of her tea, as if fortifying herself to finish her thought. "You're the poster child for deprived women everywhere. You need to go out and get funky on the dance floor. Have a couple cocktails with umbrellas in them. You need to enjoy the company of a handsome man of dubious character who makes your legs weak."

Gail shook her head. "You know I'm only interested in someone who's honest and loving. The rest of that stuff isn't important."

"Whatever you say," Kim said, displaying the same doubtful look Gail got every time she swore off chocolate forever. Again.

"Perhaps I need to refresh your memory," Gail said, stabbing at her salad with a little too much wrist action. "The last time I fell for a handsome man of mystery I got pregnant and ended up pledging my troth to Bernie Madoff Jr."

Kim's giggle turned into a sigh. "Fair enough," she

said, "but life isn't over for you, Gail. Don't cheat your-self like that. You're still young. There's a whole world out there. A whole world of *men*."

Gail pretended to be fascinated with her romaine lettuce.

"How long's it been since you had any fun?" Kim asked.

Gail looked up and answered matter-of-factly. "I went out for a beer with some of the other professors a couple of weeks ago."

"Uh-huh."

She groaned, realizing that Kim wasn't going to let her off easy today. Her friend was well aware that it had been two years since she'd had any kind of sex and six years since she'd had decent, meaningful sex, or at least what she'd told herself at the time was decent and meaningful. A few days afterward, Curtis admit-ted to his multiple fidelity "slip-ups" and expressed his desire to become her ex-husband. Soon after that, he was arrested for embezzling nearly two million of his investment clients' dollars.

"Besides," Gail told Kim. "I'm not sure how much weak-kneed dancing I'd be able to do. If I went to Key West I'd have Holly and Hannah with me, remember?"

Kim shrugged. "You could find a way. All you've done for the last five years is teach, work on your dis-sertation, raise Holly, worry about money and fall into bed exhausted at night, only to do it all over again the next day. You deserve to cut loose a little."

Gail rolled her eyes. "Fine. Maybe you're right."

"Hell *yes,* I'm right!" Kim smiled, as though it was all settled. "Go have your spring fling in Key West, then. And I'm truly sorry I can't get away from work to go with you. Do you think you can handle those two girls by yourself?"

"Of course I can," Gail said. "The three of us will have a blast together."

JESSE DOMINIC BATISTA cradled the cordless phone under his chin while he made his morning patrol of the cottage grounds. As he listened to his agent's long-distance lecture on the importance of meeting deadlines at this crucial comeback point in his career, he scanned the small yard that fronted Margaret Street. In his left hand he clutched a plastic trash bag and a paper sack for recycling. He used his Playtex-Living-Glove-encased right hand to snag the empty beer bottles from the grass. As usual, they'd been tossed over his privacy wall during someone's late-night stroll home from the Duval Street bars. Jesse opened the wrought-iron gate to scan the sidewalk for any trash, cigarette butts or the occasional condom wrapper.

It was official. Spring break had come to Key West.

Jesse straightened, using the latex glove to shield his eyes from the bright morning sun. He repeated his position to his agent. "Tell them I need two more weeks, Beverly," he said into the phone. "Tell them it's real simple—if they want a manuscript, they can have it today. If they want a *good* manuscript, they'll have to wait two weeks."

Jesse heard Beverly produce another heartfelt sigh before she updated him on his latest mediocre sales figures and a movie studio's bid for his screenplay.

"I'll get back to you in a couple of days about

everything. Promise." Jesse said his goodbyes and hung up, shoving the phone into his pocket.

Since he was already on the sidewalk, he decided to pick up the trash in front of his absentee neighbor's house, a cute craftsman bungalow rental shaded by two old palmetto trees. Being Saturday morning, he knew the current invading horde would soon be heading out. Then the cleaners would swoop in to do their magic—scrubbing bathrooms, hosing down porches, cleaning the pool and wiping down the inside of the fridge. By late afternoon, a new group would move in, thrilled by the charm and comfort of their temporary island home, excited that their vacation stretched out before them, days of azure skies and eternal ocean followed by nights of booze, music, food and laughter.

Jesse didn't begrudge them their good time. Most of the renters were polite and responsible. Every once in a while, he'd meet someone truly interesting. And a couple of times, he'd lucked out with a group of beautiful women escaping their minivans and office cubicles for an all-girls week of mischief.

Jesse swallowed hard, thinking of Cammy. She'd seemed so sweet and real. And yet, she was neither. To this day, it still amazed him how months of pain had been the price he paid for a few nights of pleasure. Jesse shook his head. Never again would he do something so profoundly stupid. If he wanted to remain sane and solvent, Renter Chicks would be forever off-limits—no matter how pretty they were. No matter how sweet and real they seemed.

Jesse returned to the cool shade of his own little private oasis and locked the gate behind him. He couldn't help but smile. Yes, the steady stream of tourists was part of life in Key West, but it was worth it. He got to call the most unique city in the United States his home.

Though he'd been in the cottage for two years now, it still gave him a rush of pride every time he stood here, on the walkway, looking up at the original Batista homestead. He'd put a huge chunk of money into the place and poured his heart and soul into returning it to its original beauty, and now it suited him perfectly.

Of course, he hadn't always been thrilled with the prospect of owning the place. When grandmother Ella left it to him five years before, he felt put-upon. He didn't want the hassle or the responsibility. Just because he was a well-known author didn't mean he was filthy rich, and it was obvious that restoring the dilapidated house and grounds would be an enormous undertaking.

But the cottage was his family legacy, and if he didn't take it on, who would? His brother who lived on a ranch in Wyoming? His brother's chronically broke ex-wife, Lelinda, who hustled a living off the tourists? His unemployed cousins in Miami?

So Jesse set out to save what he could—the bathroom's original vintage tile and claw-foot tub, some of the exterior clapboard and all the Dade County pine flooring, the rosewood fireplace mantel, the carved front door and the ornate wrought iron from the upstairs back veranda. Everything else was gutted and rebuilt, and as soon as work was completed, he sold his condo.

Though the Queen Anne cottage was now a historic landmark and part of most of the city's architectural walking tours, to Jesse it was simply home. It was where he let his imagination run free, where he slept with the windows open to the sea breeze whispering in the banyan tree and where he wrote. It was his retreat. His heart. The cottage was his place in the world.

Jesse went to the side of the house to ditch the trash and recyclables and check on a hurricane shutter that was coming off its hinges, making a mental note of what tools he'd need to repair it. He went back around to the front and climbed the porch steps, opening the door to a view of gleaming floors and an elegant center staircase. It never ceased to amaze him that his great-great-grandparents came from Cuba with nothing, yet within a generation the Batistas had become one of the most influential families in the Southern Keys.

And to think—Jesse was the last local descendant of the original clan. He was the proverbial end of the road.

The phone in his pants pocket began to ring. It was Fred Luna's number on the caller ID. Jesse knew what this meant, and his heart sank in sadness—Fred's wife, Yvette, was probably back in the hospital and he needed Jesse to captain the boat. Of course he'd do it. Spending an evening as "Captain J.D." on the sunset cruise was the least he could do for his lifelong friend. As a bonus, a night in the company of drunken tourists almost always gave him an idea for a future fictional character. Between the occasional captain gig on Fred's party boat and helping Lelinda with her walking tours—one of which, unfortunately, he'd long ago promised to do first thing tomorrow morning—Jesse was never hurting for inspiration.

"No problem, man. Of course I will," he told Fred.

"I'll be at the dock at four. Give Yvette my love, and let me know if there's anything else I can do."

HOLLY HAD DECIDED SHE'D make the best of it. It wasn't as if she had much of a choice. The way her mom had put it, it was either spring break in Key West, with her coming along as chaperone, or spring break in Beaverdale, also with her as chaperone. *Duh!* Holly and Hannah talked about it and decided they could work with that first option.

A guy they knew in Honors Biology knew a guy at the college who could get fake Pennsylvania IDs custom made for fifty bucks a pop. Holly and Hannah scrounged up the cash and were quite pleased with the results. (Holly's claimed she was twenty-three years old and a resident of Philadelphia.) They had the IDs packed in their suitcases, along with their new bikinis, anklets, suntan lotion with body glitter already added and all kinds of cute outfits and sandals.

At first, Holly's best friend was really worried the trip wouldn't be any fun. Hannah had all kinds of questions, but Holly had convinced her to give it a try. What if Key West didn't have the same all-out party scene as Daytona or South Beach? she'd asked. (Then they'd make their own party scene.) What if the guys were older? (That might be a nice change of pace—older guys tended to have more money anyway, right?) And how would they possibly be able to slip under the Mom Radar to have any fun?

That one had been the easiest for Holly to deal with.

First off, Holly assured her friend that her mom

wasn't the worrywart type. "She trusts me completely. I've never given her any reason not to."

Hannah laughed. "You just haven't been caught."

"Exactly. And anyway, you know my mom's asleep by nine every night. As long as we're home by sunrise, she'll be clueless."

So at that moment, as the plane descended onto what already looked like a tropical paradise surrounded by a neverending blue-green sea, Holly and Hannah gave each other a wink and a thumbs up.

Let the partying begin.

## CHAPTER TWO

OH, YESSSS.

Gail pulled the chain on the ceiling fan, and the wide rattan blades began to whir. She placed her glass of lemonade on the wicker table, along with the stack of brochures she'd collected at the airport, then settled into the porch rocker. She pulled the cotton sundress down over her thighs and wiggled her toes in the shade provided by the big palm tree. This was hard to believe. For ten glorious days she and the girls would be relaxing in this adorable, tidy little house on Margaret Street. What luck it was to find this place at the last minute—and right in the heart of historic Old Town! The rental agent said a family called to cancel only six hours before Gail made her inquiry.

"It must be fate," the woman had said.

Whatever it was, the place was idyllic. They had their own inground pool out back, where the girls were already swimming, reggae music pumping out of a pair of outdoor speakers. They had a gas grill, a big-screen TV with cable and DVR, and in Gail's master bath she had a Jacuzzi tub *and* a shower stall! It was heaven on earth! Now all she had to do was decide which activities they'd do when they weren't relaxing at the house. They could choose from snorkeling, water scooters, sailing trips, deep-sea fishing, swimming with dolphins and all kinds of historical tours.

Sure, this vacation was pricey, but it had been a snap to justify the expense. Since this was the first vacation Gail had taken in six years, she'd calculated that she'd spent only $447 per year on vacations during that time. If that wasn't thrifty, she didn't know what was.

Gail took a sip of the ice-cold lemonade, savoring the complexity of the sharp sweetness as it slid down her throat. As she rested her head against the rocker, she felt a lock of hair stick to her damp neck. She was perspiring. Already. This was fabulous! Thanks to the miracle of flight, she'd been picked up in a bone-chilling Philadelphia rain and dropped off in the subtropics.

Gail let go with a sigh of relief, the stress falling away like a shell, her dry winter skin sucking in the humidity like a sponge. Her chest and bare arms were gently tickled by the ceiling fan's breeze.

Oh, how she'd needed this chance to unwind. Kim had been absolutely right.

*"What the goddammed fucking hell?"*

Gail's head popped up and her ears perked. The man's voice was so close it sounded as if he was right on top of her.

"Shit, shit, *shit!*"

She swiveled her head to her right. She saw movement on the other side of the thick screen of foliage separating her yard from the house next door. Then she heard a few banging sounds, like someone taking a hammer to metal.

"This is patently absurd," said the baritone voice in the next yard. "I pay twenty-five bucks each for historically accurate reproduction shutter hinges, and this is the kind of substandard crap I get? In less than two years? Does no one have a sense of pride in their artistry anymore?"

Gail leaned forward on the edge of the rocker and peeked between two large flowering bushes, looking to see if the man was speaking to anyone. She determined that he was alone over there, which made her even more curious. What kind of man would buy historically accurate reproduction shutter hinges and then talk to them? Curse at them? While using words like "patently" and "substandard," no less?

She craned her neck. She could almost see him. If only he'd turn to his left a bit…almost there…now just a little bit more…

Gail's eyes widened in comprehension.

*Oh.*

So *that's* what George Clooney would look like after a month on the beach—all sun-roasted and sexy, salt-and-pepper scruff on his face and threadbare jeans hanging low on his chiseled hips.

Gail watched her foulmouthed neighbor examine what was obviously the offending hinge. He moved it back and forth in his hand, his scowl deepening, the muscles undulating in his hands, wrists and forearms.

She couldn't take her eyes from him. A hot heaviness started low in her belly, and the longer she stared, the more intense the heat became, spreading, rising, causing her breath to become jagged. Despite the warm air, full-on goose bumps broke out on Gail's arms.

She blinked. She licked her lips. The dark-haired hinge examiner wore a tiny silver hoop that glinted in the dappled sunlight. Maybe he was a pirate, one of those dangerous smugglers Kim had mentioned, a pirate smuggler with a rippling layer of muscle beneath the tanned skin of his abdomen. A pirate with defined biceps and strong shoulders. A pirate with an English degree.

Without warning, he looked up. His piercing blue eyes flashed at Gail, first with surprise, then with irritation. She gasped. She slammed herself into the back of the rocker, eyes straight ahead, hands gripping the armrests while she held her breath. How embarrassing. She shouldn't have done that. Now her neighbor would think she was nosy.

"Oh, *great.*" An instant after the scholarly pirate made that sarcastic comment, Gail heard his sandaled feet clomp up his porch steps. Then she heard his door opening and closing.

Well, that had been awkward. Apparently, Gail didn't even remember how to behave around extremely attractive men. Kim had been right. She really should've gotten out more.

"DID YOU SEE THE WAY THAT dude looked at us?" Hannah spread herself out on her stomach at poolside, dangling her fingers in the shallow end while Holly floated nearby in the warm water. "I swear he was undressing us with his eyes."

Holly laughed. "All guys do that. They can't help themselves."

"Yeah, but that dude was *sick* hot."

"You need to slow down," Holly said, paddling over to where Hannah lay. "Pace yourself, girlfriend. We've been here, like, two hours. He was just the cabdriver."

"I know, but he was hard-core exotic!" Hannah lowered her forehead to her arms and sighed.

Holly swam to the pool edge and propped herself on her elbows, kicking her feet lazily in the water behind her. "I've got a feeling this place is going to be crawling with sick-hot guys, and we've got ten whole days to meet every one of them, right?"

Hannah lifted her eyes, her expression now serious. "Your mom's sweet and this place is totally tight. I kinda feel bad in a way, you know? We're going to be having such a ballin' time and she's just going to be sitting around reading on the porch. It's sad."

Holly laughed. "But that's her idea of fun! She's not much of a partier. She can't dance or anything. So I wouldn't worry too much about my mom." Holly wagged an eyebrow and was careful to lower her voice—not that her mom could hear anything while that Shaggy tune was pumping out into the courtyard:

> Who da man dat love to make you moist and wet—uh?
> Who da man dat love to make you moan and sweat—uh?

"If you say so," Hannah said with a shrug.

"So what do you want to do tonight? Should we sneak out to the main party area? What's it called again?"

"Duval Street?"

"Right."

Hannah ratcheted her neck back in response. "What are you, wack or something? Of course we should sneak out to Duval Street!"

"All right, then," Holly whispered. "We're going to need a plan."

SHE SMELLED HIM BEFORE she saw him, catching a whiff of clean male skin and fabric starch in the breeze. He stood on the sidewalk, head covered in a bright white captain's cap with a navy blue bill, the barest hint of a smile spreading across his clean-shaven face. For some reason, he'd gotten rid of the salt-and-pepper scruff and the hoop earring. Why? Why would he do that? It was a tragedy!

Equally tragic was the fact that he was now fully clothed, wearing a pair of pressed white slacks and a pale blue golf shirt embroidered with the words "Luna Cruises, Captain J.D." He knocked playfully on the front gate, though it was unnecessary. Gail had been staring at him, openmouthed, for a good three seconds.

She flew to her feet, a brochure for therapeutic massage skidding across the porch floor.

"Good afternoon. My name is Jesse," he said in the same baritone voice he'd used to curse the shutter hinge about an hour before. "I'm your neighbor. Just thought I'd introduce myself and welcome you to Key West."

Gail's throat had seized shut. She couldn't speak. She felt like an idiot—a mute idiot. "Guh," she finally croaked out. "Guh-ail. From Pennsylvania."

The man approached the porch, stopping on the bottom step, careful not to invade her space. He held out his big, browned hand.

Gail shoved her damp palm toward him. After an instant of contact, he withdrew, hiding his hand in his trouser pocket. It was almost as if he couldn't stand the idea of touching her, even though he'd initiated it.

"Well," he said, looking down toward the porch floor uneasily. "Here. You dropped this." He scanned the cover of the brochure before he returned it to Gail. "So you're thinking of getting a massage?"

Gail blinked several times and continued to stare. She couldn't help it. He wasn't George Clooney. He was better. And he wasn't a pirate. He was a legitimate boat captain! And all she could think of was how the clean-shaven captain's big hands would feel rubbing her naked flesh, some type of aromatic tropical oil providing a friction-free slide from her heels to her hairline, and everywhere in between.

"Oh, yeah, that would be so great," she whispered.

He studied her for a moment, then his dark eyebrows drew together in a scowl. She thought he had the sultriest deep blue eyes she'd ever seen in her life—even with the grimace.

"Okay, then. Enjoy your visit."

Just then the front door flew open, and Hannah and Holly literally stumbled onto the porch, laughing loudly and dripping pool water at their feet. They stopped in their tracks, backs straightening. Holly's gaze went from the man to her mother, eyes wide in wonder.

"Girls, this is our neighbor, Jesse," Gail said, somehow regaining the ability to speak in full sentences. "Jesse, this is my daughter, Holly, and her best friend, Hannah."

"Hi," Holly said.

"Hey there," Hannah said, shifting her weight and sliding a hand along the slope of her well-rounded hip.

"Hello," Jesse said, averting his gaze.

Gail rubbed the back of her damp neck, anxiety coursing through her. She'd never seen that bikini on her daughter before. The garment—if you could call two partially shredded strips of fabric a garment—was not appropriate for a high school student, or anyone who didn't make their living thrusting her pelvis onto a pole. However, Holly's swimsuit was a burka compared with the three triangles Hannah was sporting, and Hannah was far more endowed than her daughter.

"Excuse me, but I need to get to work. Enjoy your stay." Jesse smiled politely and tipped his cap to the ladies before he left. They watched him walk from the house, out the gate and down the sidewalk.

No one said anything for many long seconds.

Hannah broke the silence. "Who knew Cap'n Crunch was such a bangin' hottie?"

The girls broke out into an attack of the giggles. Gail continued to stare down the sidewalk, awash in some kind of stunned awareness, long after the bangin' hot captain had disappeared.

JESSE REVIEWED THE manifest with the crew chief. There'd be forty-four passengers on board Fred's customized sixty-foot motor yacht tonight, sixteen of whom had made a vegetarian meal selection and one who needed handicapped access and seating. Once he completed the yacht's safety check with the first mate, Jesse grabbed a cold drink and watched the crew carry on the necessities—containers of fresh shrimp, grouper and red snapper, hamburgers, barbecued chicken and pork, and veggie burgers. There were vats of several varieties of salads, sandwich fixings, guacamole and salsa. There were several varieties of chips and pretzels. Sodas. Fruit juices. Bottled water. Liquor and more liquor. Mixers. Enough beer for a football stadium.

Jesse knew that every passenger who'd forked over

$175 to Luna Cruises had specific expectations for their six-hour ocean excursion. They expected to have a blast. They planned to eat and drink to their heart's content. They would dance and flirt. The music would be thumping and nonstop. They would get the stunning Key West sunset promised in the brochures and, if the weather held out, their magical night on the water and under the stars. Once they'd returned to Sunset Marina at midnight, the passengers would thank Captain J.D. profusely, maybe sliding a folded ten-dollar bill into his palm, which he'd pass on to the hardworking crew. A woman or two might slip him their hotel room information and a cell phone number. Those went into the trash.

Jesse wasn't a kid—he was a thirty-eight-year-old man who'd learned a lot of hard lessons. The way he saw it, he'd rather have no woman at all than the wrong woman, and, unfortunately, the hotel and cell phone types were almost always of the latter category. He hadn't been as lucky as his friend Fred, who'd spotted Yvette in the ninth grade and had never looked back. These days, all any of them could do was hope that love and modern medicine would be enough to save her.

In Jesse's world, even the women who seemed normal often weren't. Cammy had been so elegant and understated. He'd been fascinated by her from the moment they met. By her second night in the rental house next door, Jesse had been smitten by her laugh, her intelligence and her fun-loving nature.

Soon after, Jesse was the villain in a crazy woman's make-believe drama of domestic violence charges, paternity accusations and restraining orders—a complex fiction worthy of one of his bestselling suspense novels. It had been nothing but a setup. Cammy had never wanted Jesse. She'd just wanted a bundle of his money and her fifteen minutes of fame, both of which she got. And after the public relations disaster, sales of Jesse's latest hardcover release were down by twenty percent.

All of which made his current dilemma not much of a dilemma at all. Yes, there might be many things that intrigued him about the pretty *mami* who'd just unpacked next door. Like the intelligent curiosity in her light brown eyes. The fall of all that thick blond hair. The modest and simple cotton sundress that revealed little and yet hinted at everything. And the fact that she didn't wear a wedding ring. But what he found especially appealing was how embarrassed the woman named Gail had been when he'd caught her staring at him, and how tongue-tied she'd seemed when he introduced himself.

It was as if the woman had no game whatsoever. And that was the most refreshing thing of all.

But he wouldn't fall for it. He wouldn't think of her again. He knew better.

Besides, even if this Gail chick were his one true love, his soul mate, a perfect match delivered to his doorstep, nothing would ever come of it. Jesse already knew that Gail from Pennsylvania wouldn't have much time for herself on this vacation. Not with those two teenage girls to look after—especially the brunette with the hellacious curves and the video-ho bikini. Unfortunately, he'd seen this same story unfold before, right in the same rental house. Pretty little Gail was in for a rough go in paradise.

GAIL CAREFULLY SPREAD out the brochures upon the recently cleared dining table, the open-air Conch Republic Seafood Company buzzing around them. All things considered—and the mysterious captain next door was one of the things she was considering—this vacation was already shaping up to be full of interesting possibilities.

"The first Hemingway walking tour starts at 8:00 a.m.," she said, scanning the schedule on the flier's inside flap. "Is that too early? Would you rather do the 10:00 a.m. tour? Or we can do the Pirate Museum tomorrow instead and save the Hemingway stuff for Monday, when it will probably be less crowded."

When Gail got no response, she looked up from her brochure. She was greeted by bug-eyed stares of horror.

"Uh," Hannah said, averting her eyes and obviously kicking Holly under the table.

"Yeah, about the whole vacation schedule thing, Mom," Holly said, clearing her throat. "We were thinking that it would be better if we kind of split into two groups, you know, according to our age range and interests. Don't you think that's a great idea?"

Gail shoved the Hemingway brochure and all the other full-color fliers into the big straw bag at her feet. She didn't intend to pout, but she truly wanted the girls to have a well-rounded experience here in Key West. Was that so terrible?

"It's just that we already have plans, Ms. Chapman," Hannah offered, smiling sweetly. "And we thought it would be nice for you to have some time to yourself for a change, you know? Just think—you could browse the art galleries, sip your lattes, hang out in bookstores."

Despite herself, Gail chuckled under her breath. "I see. And while I'm doing all this sipping and browsing, you'd be doing what, exactly?"

Hannah was about to answer that question but Holly cut her off. "We'd be playing volleyball on the beach. Riding our rental bikes. Shopping. Getting ice cream. You know, just having fun."

Gail folded her arms across her chest, not falling for a word of it. Although she'd gone over the rules with the girls before she even purchased the air tickets, it was clearly time for a refresher.

"You're good kids. I know you want your freedom. I know you believe you're mature enough to make wise decisions and stay safe."

"But?" Holly fell back against her chair and pursed her lips, waiting for the rest.

"But I am responsible for you," Gail said. She turned her attention to her daughter's friend. "And Hannah, I swore on my life to your mom and dad that I'd keep you out of harm's way and bring you back in one piece. You understand that your parents have entrusted me with the most precious thing in their lives, right?"

Hannah rolled her eyes.

"So let's review, shall we?" Gail leaned in on her forearms, speaking softly enough that other diners wouldn't hear her morph into the world's most boring human being. "No sex. No alcohol. No pot. No getting into or onto anything on or near the water without my prior permission. No getting into cars or onto motorcycles or mopeds with anyone other than me, period. No flirting with bouncers at bars to get them to let you in without ID. You will use your cell phones to check in with me, and you will answer if I call. There will be no violating curfew—you will both be home by midnight every night, no exceptions."

Since neither girl said a word, Gail decided to wrap it up.

"And if you don't follow these basic rules, you'll both be on the first thing smokin' out of Key West. End of vacation. And, Holly, I'm sorry to say that for you it would be the end of life as you know it."

Their mouths dropped open from the force of the insult Gail had delivered. Then Holly's tongue made that clicking sound of disbelief before she squealed, "We just wanted to go to the beach, Mom! *God!*"

Gail relaxed into her chair, her blood pressure returning to normal. "So we're in agreement on the rules?"

Their nods were slow and lacking in enthusiasm, but they were nods, nonetheless.

"Fabulous," Gail said. "The beach sounds great, then."

Holly and Hannah looked at each other quickly. "Are you coming with?" Holly asked.

Gail laughed. "No. You've agreed to the rules, so I trust you. You don't have to spend your vacation hanging around with old, boring me."

"Thank God," Hannah whispered.

"But there's one condition—you can't wear those skimpy swimsuits out in public. They're pornographic."

The waiter appeared at tableside, and Gail watched the girls' sullen frowns turn to sparkling grins the instant the handsome young man looked their way. Gail knew what it felt like to be Holly and Hannah. It wasn't all that long ago that she and Kim had been seventeen, running around with all the same boy-crazy hormones coursing through their veins, with grand plans of their own. Gail only wanted Holly and Hannah to find a happy medium. She wanted them to enjoy the adventure of this vacation without losing their heads.

Gail suddenly had a sobering thought. She couldn't even remember what it felt like to lose her head, over anything or anyone. In fact, self-denial had been her field of expertise lately, hadn't it? Maybe she should order a second set of business cards from the campus print shop: *Gail Chapman, Doctor of Chastity.*

"Dessert, ladies?"

*My God…* Gail stared off into space. *I really am the most boring human being on the planet!*

Suddenly, she thought of the brown-skinned, sexy-as-hell captain next door and for a moment—just a moment—she wondered what it would be like to let go with a man like that. Completely. Holding nothing back.

That was a ridiculous fantasy. She could never do that. *Could she?*

Gail sighed heavily. It was a sigh of longing and deprivation.

The smiling waiter glanced her way, pen poised. "So you've decided?"

"Decided?" Gail snapped. "What do you mean by that?"

"Uh," the waiter said, his eyes big. "Dessert?"

"Oh! Of course." Gail ignored the girls' questioning stares and reviewed the dessert menu. She didn't want anything, but she felt she had to provide a cover for that embarrassing sigh. She picked the first item that caught her eye. "Just give me this double-fudge chocolate multiple or—" Her voice failed her. Her face went numb in embarrassment.

The waiter laughed. "So you're up for a multiple orgasm tonight?" he asked.

Holly gasped then hid her face in her hands. "Shoot me now," she mumbled.

All Gail could do was nod.

## CHAPTER THREE

SHE WAITED AT THE TALL wrought-iron gate in front of the Hemingway Home & Museum, checking her watch again. The brochure said to be there at precisely 8:00 a.m., with cash or credit card, wearing comfortable shoes. It said not to be late. Gail had done all those things, yet she was alone on the sidewalk and it was now 8:04.

The airport cab driver had warned them that Key West operated on Margaritaville time. Apparently, he wasn't joking. Now it was 8:05.

She heard laughter from the other side of Whitehead Street and turned. Gail squinted through the soft morning light, not quite sure she could trust her eyes. An elderly couple was making slow progress along the crosswalk, with the sexy captain at the woman's elbow, gently guiding her toward the gate. He wasn't wearing his jaunty cap that morning, and his thick black hair curled around his ears. The earring was back. And so was a hint of the salt-and-pepper fuzz. And he was smiling—a big, glorious, white-toothed smile she was seeing for the first time.

Gail gulped in air. She pressed her butt against the high stone wall that surrounded Hemingway's house and hoped she could fade into the background. She held her breath. But Jesse looked up, and Gail could see that he recognized her instantly. She watched surprise flash in his eyes, followed by irritation, just like when he'd caught her staring at him the day before. Clearly, Captain Jesse might have big, bright smiles for little old ladies, but only a suspicious frown for her.

"I'm just here for the tour!" Gail busted out with that pronouncement before he'd even reached the curb, as though she needed to explain herself. Which was silly. She had nothing to apologize for. She might have fantasized about her gorgeous neighbor just a tiny bit the night before, in the privacy of her bedroom, with the blinds drawn, but it wasn't like she was *stalking* him or anything.

"You're here for the 8:00 a.m. walking tour?" Jesse dropped the old woman's elbow and stared at Gail warily. "The 'In Hemingway's Footsteps' tour?"

"Well, yeah." Gail clutched her straw shoulder bag to the front of her body, as if protecting herself. "What's it to you?"

That's when she heard it for the first time—Jesse's laugh. Its rich resonance penetrated her flesh and bone, causing her to shudder with pleasure. The intensity of that reaction startled Gail. Why did this guy affect her like this? How did he reduce her to a fool while setting her on fire inside? She didn't like it much. It made her feel as if she wasn't in control of herself.

Jesse shook his head, letting go with a deep sigh. "Then the gang's all here, I suppose." He gestured to the elderly couple. "This is Pete and Lana Purdy of Little Rock, who are celebrating their sixtieth wedding anniversary, and this is—" Jesse stopped in midsentence, his scowl deepening. "I'm sorry, Gail, but I didn't get your last name."

"Chapman." Gail released the grip she had on her shoulder bag and shook the couple's hands. "Dr. Gail Chapman from Beaverdale, Pennsylvania."

Jesse exploded with a strange sound somewhere in between coughing and laughing. It figured, Gail thought. Deep down, the erudite captain was just another eighth-grade boy who thought anything with the word "beaver" in it was absolutely hilarious. She ignored him.

"Oh, how marvelous!" Lana Purdy said, beaming. "Pete here had a GP practice for fifty-five years. Delivered nearly six hundred babies, didn't you, dear? And what is your specialty?"

This happened a lot. Gail smiled down on the pudgy little lady with short white curls. "I have my PhD in literature. I'm an associate professor at a small liberal arts college."

Lana smiled. "How perfectly lovely!"

*"Just great,"* Jesse said under his breath.

That was it. Gail had reached the limit of her patience with this guy. He might be sexy as hell, but that had already been canceled out by the fact that he cursed at inanimate objects, had the emotional maturity of a Little Leaguer, scoffed at her profession and walked around sporting a near-permanent scowl. The man couldn't be much older than Gail, but somewhere along the line he'd become a curmudgeon. How sad for him.

Gail cocked her head to the side and glared at Jesse, and he met her gaze straight on, unabashed. She scrutinized his face for flaws—there were none—while he studied her, one dark brow arched over one of his dusky blue eyes. The two of them remained in this standoff for several seconds, while Gail wondered about a few

# YOUR PARTICIPATION IS REQUESTED!

Dear Reader,

Since you are a lover of romance fiction – we would like to get to know you!

Inside you will find a short Reader's Survey. Sharing your answers with us will help our editorial staff understand who you are and what activities you enjoy.

To thank you for your participation, we would like to send you 2 books and 2 gifts – **ABSOLUTELY FREE**!

Enjoy your gifts with our appreciation,

*Pam Powers*

**SEE INSIDE FOR READER'S SURVEY**

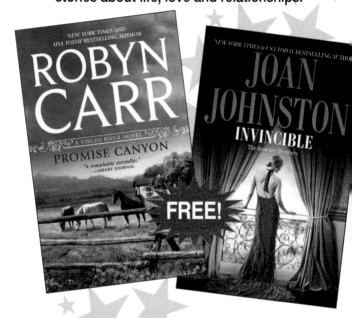

# YOUR READER'S SURVEY
## "THANK YOU" FREE GIFTS INCLUDE:
▶ 2 Romance books
▶ 2 lovely surprise gifts

**PLEASE FILL IN THE CIRCLES COMPLETELY TO RESPOND**

1) What type of fiction books do you enjoy reading? (Check all that apply)
   ○ Suspense/Thrillers    ○ Action/Adventure    ○ Modern-day Romances
   ○ Historical Romance    ○ Humour              ○ Paranormal Romance

2) What attracted you most to the last fiction book you purchased on impulse?
   ○ The Title    ○ The Cover    ○ The Author    ○ The Story

3) What is usually the greatest influencer when you <u>plan</u> to buy a book?
   ○ Advertising          ○ Referral          ○ Book Review

4) How often do you access the internet?
   ○ Daily ○ Weekly ○ Monthly ○ Rarely or never.

5) How many NEW paperback fiction novels have you purchased in the
   past 3 months?
   ○ 0 - 2              ○ 3 - 6              ○ 7 or more
   **FDH2**            **FDJE**             **FDJQ**

## YES!
I have completed the Reader's Survey. Please send me the 2 FREE books and 2 FREE gifts (gifts are worth about $10) for which I qualify. I understand that I am under no obligation to purchase any books, as explained on the back of this card.

### 194/394 MDL

| | |
|---|---|
| FIRST NAME | LAST NAME |

ADDRESS

| | |
|---|---|
| APT.# | CITY |

| | |
|---|---|
| STATE/PROV. | ZIP/POSTAL CODE |

(SUR-ROM-11)
© 2010 HARLEQUIN ENTERPRISES LIMITED
® and ™ are trademarks owned and used by the trademark owner and/or its licensee. Printed in the U.S.A.

## The Reader Service — Here's How It Works:

things. Why was Jesse here, anyway? Why did he feel the need to introduce everyone? Did he fancy himself some kind of rude one-man island-greeting committee? And where was the tour guide?

Suddenly, Jesse's expression changed. The curiosity disappeared, replaced by a calm determination. Gail knew he was going to say something to her. She had a feeling it would be something important.

"Cash or credit?" he asked.

*HOLY HELL, WHAT A MESS this was shaping up to be.*

Beaverdale Gail knew far more about Hemingway than he did, which wasn't much of a shocker considering she had a PhD in American Literature and Jesse's only qualification was that he was a nautical-suspense author filling in for a flighty ex-sister-in-law who'd once again been summoned to traffic court.

It occurred to Jesse that if he had any hope of making that extended deadline in two weeks, he'd have to find a way to stop anyone else from asking for more favors. Maybe it was time for one of his deadline lockdowns: disconnect the phone, unplug the DSL and lock all his doors and windows.

The little tour group had come to one of their designated stops, 328 Greene Street, the site of the original Sloppy Joe's Bar and Grill. Jesse explained that it was once a ramshackle establishment run by Ernest Hemingway's fishing and carousing pal, Joe Russell, and went into his summary of Hemingway's legendary drinking. "He had a tendency to get into trouble when he'd had a few too many," Jesse said. "He had his famous fistfight with the poet Wallace Stevens here."

"Actually," Gail cut in, speaking more to the Purdys

than him, "Hemingway was at home that evening, completely sober, when his sister told him that Stevens was at a house party claiming that Hemingway was a horrible writer. Ernest was so angry he drove to the house on Waddell Street and pummeled Stevens into a bloody heap on the floor. The poet was hospitalized and had to be fed through a straw for days."

"Fascinating," Lana Purdy said.

Jesse stared at the professor in wonder. Clearly, she had a lot of free time on her hands back in Beaverdale. But Jesse was the local. He was the tour guide here. He may have gotten that one detail wrong, but he had a whole arsenal of useless Hemingway minutiae at his disposal and he wasn't afraid to use it.

He turned to Lana Purdy, who seemed to be legitimately interested in all this garbage, bless her soul. "Intriguingly enough," Jesse began, the sarcasm dripping from his tone, "Wallace Stevens wasn't even a famous poet at the time. He was still making his living—"

"Selling insurance," Gail said. She slowly raised her gentle brown eyes to Jesse's. "But you were right about Ernest often getting into trouble here. He met up with his third wife on a barstool at Sloppy Joe's." She smiled a smile so slight that he could have missed it if he weren't paying close attention. "It was love at first sight for both of them," she added.

Jesse laughed hard at her typical female delusion. Gail had romanticized what was essentially a sexual sting operation, not unlike the one that had snagged him. "I'm not sure about that, Professor Gail," he said, still chuckling. "It was garden-variety entrapment. The chick ambushed him, actually paying the bartender twenty bucks to introduce her to the very married Hemingway."

Gail raised her chin. "I take it you don't believe in love at first sight?"

Jesse smiled kindly at her. "I believe in criminal background checks, Professor. And credit reports and not chucking the God-given capacities of my frontal lobe just to get me some—" Jesse stopped himself, suddenly remembering that Dr. and Mrs. Purdy were hanging on his every word. "Just to spend time with a pretty woman."

Gail made a dismissive clicking sound at the back of her tongue and rolled her eyes. It reminded Jesse of a thirteen-year-old being told to clean her room. She turned on her heel and started walking.

They continued their stroll through Old Town at senior-citizen speed, passing French pastry shops and sidewalk eateries and art galleries. Jesse didn't mind the slow pace because it gave him plenty of time to watch Dr. Gail walk. As he spoke about the publishing projects Hemingway worked on while living in Key West, Jesse studied Gail's appearance and tried to decide why, exactly, he found the woman so damn alluring. She wore a preppy cotton skirt that hit just above her cute knees, a simple tailored sleeveless blouse and a pair of sensible sandals. Her hair was back in a ponytail. She wore very little makeup. And she was lugging around a shoulder bag big enough to stuff a corpse in.

For the life of him, Jesse couldn't figure out why he found that unremarkable getup so provocative. Maybe living here most of his life had made him immune to tight spandex minis and cleavage-enhancing halter tops. Maybe his imagination was getting the best of him again, deciding that beneath the professor's old-school exterior was something untamed, something deliciously and thoroughly…well…*wild*.

"Actually," Gail said, correcting what had apparently been yet another of his tour-related inaccuracies, "*To Have and Have Not* was a character study of Key West locals, but it was also a commentary on the distribution of wealth in this country during the Depression."

"Fascinating!" Lana said.

"I'll tell you what's fascinating," Dr. Purdy said, marking the first time he'd opened his mouth since the tour began. "How the hell could a man as pickled as Hemingway write his own name, let alone a whole slew of novels?"

Jesse decided it was the perfect time to discuss Hemingway's creative process, but Gail beat him to it.

"He did most of his work in the first half of the day, between eight and one, when the air was at its coolest—and before he started drinking," she said.

Jesse jumped in. "He usually wrote in the studio he kept on the second floor of the pool house, which we'll see when we get back to the Hemingway House in just a few minutes."

Gail's warm brown eyes flashed at him. Obviously, she was enjoying their little battle of trivia as much as he was. Without warning, Jesse's mind traveled to that small liberal arts college she mentioned, where she stood at the front of a lecture room, skirt slit up to here and blouse unbuttoned down to there, her loose blond hair swinging as she turned her back to write something on the board. In the fantasy, Jesse's mouth began to water as he stared at the professor's gorgeous bottom cradled in the tight skirt. In reality, he was focused on her smooth legs and small sandaled feet, and his walking shorts were starting to tent.

He was in a heap of trouble. No way had he intended to hit on the temporary *mami* from next door. What the hell was going on here?

Dr. Gail was behaving like a snooty academic and he was, he knew, acting like an ass. But it didn't seem to dampen a damn thing. Every time they looked at each other, his skin sizzled and his blood pounded. Gail was a brown-eyed, blond, buttoned-up package of female smarts and sensuality, and he was captivated. Simple as that. And though every working synapse in his brain was telling him to back away, he couldn't help but nudge closer every opportunity he got. It was crazy. It was stupid. He knew better.

The very last thing he needed was to get involved with another woman who wanted a piece of his money and fame.

"By the way, Jesse, are there any other jobs of yours I should know about?" Gail smiled sweetly when she asked that question—no sign of sarcasm whatsoever. "Because I'm headed to the Pirate Museum tomorrow and I'm half expecting to see you employed there, too."

Jesse's heart stopped. She had no idea who he was. Well, of course she didn't. He hadn't told her, after all. They hadn't met at a book signing. Sure, he was famous enough, but it was entirely possible that a brainiac like her didn't read popular fiction. She might not have ever heard of J. D. Batista, author of the blockbuster "Dark Blue" suspense series set in the Florida Keys.

As if on cue, Jesse's gaze wandered two doors down and he knew he had to act fast. He lodged himself between Gail and the huge display window of Island Books, where his face and latest release were prominently displayed.

"Shall we cross here?" he asked, placing a hand at the small of Gail's back and pushing her toward the busy street. "Dr. and Mrs. Purdy? Would you come along, please?"

Though Gail frowned at him as though he was a madman, Jesse got the group across Duval and away from his poster-sized publicity photo. If pretty Gail didn't know who he was, that meant all the electricity being generated between them was real. He wanted to keep it that way. Jesse couldn't remember the last time he'd been attracted to a woman who wasn't aware he was a local celebrity. This was too interesting to ruin now.

"Well?" Gail asked him. "Aren't you going to tell me?"

Jesse smiled at her and shrugged, making sure his body blocked her view of the bookstore as they walked. "Like most locals, I piece together a living doing a little here and a little there, but I can assure you I don't work at the Pirate Museum."

Gail tipped her head just a little and inspected him from stem to stern. "Hmm," she said. "That's a shame. I think you'd fit right in."

Just then, Lana Purdy giggled. "I must say, this has been the perfect way to celebrate our sixtieth anniversary."

"I'm glad," Jesse said.

"The two of you just crack me up," she continued,

hooking her arm in her husband's. "Watching you two flirt so outrageously reminds me of our courtship so long ago." Lana squeezed her husband close to her side and gave him a playful kiss on the cheek. "That was such an exciting time, wasn't it, dear? We couldn't get enough of each other back then!"

They still had a block to go to get back to the Hemingway House, but Gail stopped walking. Jesse watched her pull the giant carryall to the front of her body and stare at Mrs. Purdy in shock. Okay, fine. The old lady was a little off base, but did Gail have to look *that* horrified?

*"Courtship?"* Gail asked, her eyes widening.

Jesse laughed. "I think you're mistaken about that," he told the cute old woman. "Gail and I hardly know each other."

Lana smiled and patted Jesse's arm. "Oooh!" she said, shimmying her shoulders daringly. "That makes it even better!"

GAIL STOOD BEHIND THE red-velvet rope that dissected Ernest Hemingway's bedroom. She stared down at the double bed that he'd shared with his wife. Or wives. Or, technically, his mistresses prior to becoming his wives. She studied the simple white chenille bedspread and matching pillow shams, picturing what the scene would have looked like all those years ago, the covers rumpled up and soaked with sweat from unbridled— and possibly even illicit—lovemaking.

She immediately straightened, looking around the room to make sure no one had witnessed her mental debauchery. What in the world was her *problem?* When had she become such a slattern? Why did she have sex on the brain?

One quick glance at Jesse, and she had her answer. He stood so close to her side that the skin of her arm felt hot. Technically, she felt hot all over. She needed to get a grip. She needed a cool glass of water.

"That's a damn small bed if you ask me," Dr. Purdy said, the second statement he'd made all morning. "Can't get too creative in a bed that small."

"Oh, you!" Lana said, giggling.

Gail could see the corner of Jesse's mouth curl up in a faint smile, and he looked everywhere but at her.

"As I was saying," he continued. "Hemingway had a ramp installed from the bedroom to his pool house studio, so he didn't even have to…"

Gail wasn't paying attention to Jesse's words. She couldn't hear much anyway because the seductive sound of the man's baritone had caused the inside of her skull to hum. She decided to look at anything but the bed. Her eyes traveled to the way Jesse's shirtsleeve had been rolled up on his muscled forearm. Then they strayed to the front of Jesse's shorts. That had been a mistake.

She dabbed at her damp forehead, praying that no one in any of the tour groups converging in the Hemingway House could sense her private struggle. Of course they couldn't. To everyone gathered near the velvet rope, Gail was just another visitor strolling through Hemingway's bedroom. No one had any idea that she, Gail Chapman, PhD, was having a life-altering crisis.

Suddenly, the room began to reel. It felt as if her world was coming off its axis. Hemingway's bed mocked her. It was nothing but a monument to uncontrollable desire and wild sex and everything she'd been doing without for too long, and it was all she could do not to start panting and howling like some kind of rabid animal.

She didn't dare look at Jesse again. She didn't have the courage. She kept her eyes down and her bag clutched tight as people moved around her.

"Gail." Jesse's deep voice had become a whisper, just for her, so close to her ear that she could feel the heat of his breath.

Slowly, cautiously, she looked up at him, and his sultry blue eyes wrinkled in a smile. Gail found herself counting the short silvery hairs sprinkled through the dark stubble on his chin and cheeks, and wondered if the barely there beard would feel rough to her fingertips.

"Gail?" he repeated.

"Yes?" Her focus lingered briefly on his wide, sumptuous mouth before she looked into those remarkable eyes once more.

"The group is moving on to the pool house," he said, nodding his head toward the crowd clomping down the outside steps. "Would you like to come along?"

She couldn't speak. All she could do was surrender to those dark blue pools of wantonness. Oh, God, she was going under.

"Are you all right?" Jesse's trademark frown had reappeared, but it was fainter this time, and it seemed to be born of genuine concern rather than disapproval. "You look a little flushed, Professor."

She nodded. Maybe she should say something. Maybe she should tell him that the whole morning had been too much for her repressed libido to handle—the taunting bed, the sultry heat, the witty repartee, the references to Hemingway's sexual bravado and Jesse's god-awful good looks. Maybe she should just tell Jesse the truth—that everything about him was so mesmerizingly masculine that she couldn't trust herself. She was on the verge of doing something completely out of character.

That's when Jesse reached up and brushed a loose strand of hair from the side of her face. That barest tickle of his touch sent an electric rush through her.

"I…" That was all she could get out. Gail swallowed hard. If only she'd rented a house that happened to be next door to a cute little retired couple like the Purdys, or, better yet, a group of vacationing Buddhist monks. Then maybe she wouldn't be coming unglued like this.

"Yes?" Jesse asked.

It was the small hoop earring that sent her over the edge. It caught the sunlight and zapped her like a laser. Later, she would convince herself that the bright flash had short-circuited her brain.

"I haven't had sex in two years," she blurted out, breathing hard. "I'm a wreck. I came here hoping to meet a man of dubious character who could make my knees weak. I'm sorry, but it's the truth. I'm unstable, and very, very deprived. You should probably stay away from me."

Jesse's eyes widened significantly. Gail held her breath. Would he laugh at her audacity? Would he be offended? Sickened? Would he call for museum security?

He did none of those things. Instead, Jesse's eyes mellowed, then he helped himself to a languid visual journey of all things Gail, from the crown of her hair to the tips of her toes. When he was done, he leaned in close.

And kissed her.

## CHAPTER FOUR

"YO. PRETTY GIRLIES."

Hannah tossed her hair and groaned, ignoring the man's comment as she and Holly walked toward the water's edge. Once they were out of earshot, Hannah leaned in toward her friend. "Did you see that dude? It should be against the law for someone so totally old to wear a Speedo! He was, like, almost as old as your Mom!"

"I think I'm going to dry-heave," Holly replied.

Hannah suddenly perked to attention. "Hi!" she said, swiveling her head to catch the eye of a much younger and hotter dude who was making his way across the sand.

The man just barely raised his chin in acknowledgment.

"Damn," Hannah said, sticking her toe into the gentle waves of the Gulf of Mexico. "The guys here are totally stuck-up, unless they're old and desperate and wearing gold chains. Then they're just plain creepy."

"I got some breaking news for you, Hannah." Holly couldn't help but laugh at her friend's naiveté. "Remember what I told you? That some of the best-looking guys here are gay?"

Her friend's eyes widened behind her sunglasses.

"Him? But, I mean, I realize there are a lot of gay men in Key West, but he was so…I don't know…"

"Perfect?" Holly asked.

Hannah nodded and sighed. "I guess that should have been my first hint, huh?"

"You girls aren't afraid of getting burned?"

The girls looked up into the faces of two incredibly good-looking guys who'd approached them unnoticed. They were maybe just a few years older. Both had dark, dark brown hair and dark, dark brown eyes and big, white smiles. And the way they were checking them out indicated there wasn't a gay bone in either of their totally buff bodies.

"Your skin looks delicate," one of them said, touching Hannah's shoulder with his fingers. "You should probably put on some sunscreen."

The girls turned to each other with open mouths.

*Hot twins?* Holly couldn't believe it. *How freakin' epic is this?*

"So, have you had lunch?" one of them asked.

Holly watched her friend smile and straighten her spine, as if the boys weren't already aware of her 36Ds—as though anyone south of the Everglades wasn't aware of them.

"No," Hannah answered. "And I'm suddenly starving."

THE KISS ALONE WAS SO unexpectedly delicious that Jesse was nearing sensory overload. So when Gail's cell phone began to vibrate somewhere inside the Sherpa-sized straw bag now wedged between their bodies, the direct buzz to his crotch was almost too much to bear.

He hated to do it, but he pulled his lips away from hers. Gail stared at him with eyes as big as sand dollars.

"I should probably get that," she said.

He nodded, pressed his fingers to his lips as if to seal in the sensation and backed away. Jesse headed out through the set of French doors to the museum veranda, gulping down the fresh air. *I just made out with one of Lelinda's paying customers,* he thought to himself. *I just kissed the woman staying next door, a woman I barely know.* He heard loud giggling and turned to see that apparently he'd done it in front of a dozen Chinese visitors, to boot.

Jesse waved to them sheepishly. "Welcome to Key West," he muttered, leaning his elbows on the railing. Even through the tourists' snickering, Jesse could hear Gail on the phone with her daughter. He turned his head to look at her.

"That sounds fun, honey," she was saying, her eyes darting toward Jesse every few seconds. Gail tried to smooth down her hair. "Sure, that's fine. I appreciate your asking for permission. Wear life jackets and call me when you get back to the dock. Don't forget to reapply your sunscreen. Remind Hannah, too."

Jesse watched her turn off her cell phone and tug awkwardly on her skirt. Then Gail took a deep breath and squared her shoulders before she headed his way.

"I apologize," she said in what was obviously her professor's voice. The wanton strumpet who'd revealed herself only moments before was nowhere to be seen. "I think I better walk home."

"I'll go with you," Jesse said.

"No, that's not necessary."

"Oh, yes it is."

Jesse followed her down the back steps to the Spanish-tile courtyard and past Hemingway's exotic inground pool. He gave a quick wave and shouted a thank-you to the Purdys, who were seated on a bench under a large eucalyptus tree. Jesse jogged to keep up with Gail before she'd made it to the front yard and out the gate.

"Hold on, Gail."

She shook her ponytail, not looking back.

"Look, I have a moped parked right around the corner. I'll give you a lift back to the house." Jesse had reached her side, but she hadn't slowed her march. It was impressive that Gail was at least five inches shorter than his six-one frame but her stride could cover some serious territory. "Talk to me, Professor."

She turned to face him. He wasn't prepared for what he saw—profound embarrassment. Guilt. Desire. Tears streamed down her cheeks.

It was then that Jesse knew his first impression of his neighbor had been accurate. She had no game. She was out here in the world without pretense. And that kiss had affected her deeply. It was clear that Gail Chapman was a vulnerable and attention-starved woman, and Jesse shouldn't be messing with her. If he were smart, he'd let her walk on home by herself the way she'd insisted. He was about to tell her as much when she looked up at him and smiled sadly.

"You're an exceptionally smart and handsome man." Gail's brown eyes were unflinching. "I'm sure you have a wife or girlfriend—or maybe several of them. But that's none of my business. What I'm trying to say is that I shouldn't have thrown myself at you. That's not like me at all. And I'm sorry."

"You don't need to—"

The professor pressed the palm of her small hand against his chest to stop him from saying more. "I've been divorced for six years, Jesse, and I haven't dated much. My ex-husband was a philanderer and a white-collar criminal, and I admit I basically shut down after the divorce. I'm no good at this sort of thing. Casual sex, I mean."

Jesse blinked, dumbstruck. Never in his thirty-eight years had he heard a woman cut to the chase the way Gail just had. Her raw honesty was startling.

"Thanks for the tour. You really know your Hemingway, Captain." She gave his shirt an affectionate pat. "Goodbye."

"You've got it all wrong," he said.

Gail spun around, a small frown between her pale brows.

"I've never been married and I am not seeing anyone."

"Oh."

"And that was the most incredible first kiss I've had since Myra Castillo planted one on me in sixth grade." Jesse couldn't figure out why, but it gave him a rush of pleasure to see Gail's shy smile return.

"I have an idea." Suddenly, Jesse was feeling protective of her. He wanted to salvage her day. "Let me give you a private tour of Key West. Just you and me—" Jesse stopped himself, tipping his head toward her purse. "And your very large straw bag."

Gail sniffed, trying to act offended but already starting to laugh.

"What in God's name do you have in there, any-way?"

"Nothing. Yet," she said. "But I wanted to have it with me so I could carry any treasures I might find while I'm in town—artwork, cute T-shirts, a good book."

Jesse grinned, making a mental note to circumvent Duval between Angela and Petronia until he could get Chago to dismantle the permanent J.D. Batista shrine in the window of Island Books. His buddy owed him a favor.

"I'm at your service," Jesse said, extending his hand to the lovely professor.

She accepted it. Jesse didn't understand why or how, but the way her hand slipped into his felt like an answer to a question, a question he hadn't even planned on asking.

"SO WHERE ARE YOU STAYING?"

Though the girls had been hanging out with Luis and Nestor for only a couple of hours, they already felt comfortable, as if they'd known each other for years. Hannah laughed at most everything that came out of Nestor's mouth. Luis seemed to be the more serious of the two and, in Holly's opinion, the most handsome. The two local community college students seemed really polite and sweet.

Then again, the brothers thought Holly and Hannah were twenty-one-year-old juniors at Drexel University on their spring break, but those were just details.

"On a little street off Truman Avenue," Holly an-swered. "I forget the name, but we always manage to find it."

Luis took another bite from his grilled sandwich and cocked his head as he listened. "So you're in a house, not a hotel?"

"Oh, yeah!" Hannah said. "It's a really pretty cottage with a private pool and everything!"

Neither girl missed it when Luis and Nestor's eyes connected over the lunch table.

"But my mom is with us," Holly felt compelled to add. As much fun as a few beers and a little what-what in the pool sounded, she thought she should let them know it wasn't going to happen. Not unless they could get her mom out of the house for several hours, and that was about as likely as five feet of snow accumulating in the Florida Keys. Holly looked around the table, embarrassed. No one knew that she'd called her mom from the ladies' room just a few minutes before to get permission to go out on the boys' water scooters. *God, did it ever suck being seventeen!* "My mom just earned her doctorate and needed a vacation, so we asked her to join us," Holly said.

"Cool," Nestor said.

"No problem," Luis said.

The group was about to leave their outdoor table and head to the dock when Holly suddenly snapped to attention. Rolling toward the stop sign on Front Street was her mom. On the back of a moped. Her arms were wrapped around the hottie captain from next door. Her skirt was jacked up high enough for her to put the guy in an upper-thigh death grip.

She couldn't freakin' believe it.

Hannah began smacking Holly's arm. "No way!" she said, pointing to the moped. "Do you see that?"

Holly nodded, speechless.

The boys laughed. "Oh, so you're J.D. fans? That figures," Luis sent a knowing smile to his brother. "Our dad owns Island Books. We've known Uncle Jesse all our lives. He's like family."

Holly frowned at Luis. Why was he suddenly putting on the swagger? Why did he think that knowing their neighbor dude would impress them?

"That's nice," Holly said, turning just in time to see her mother rip the ponytail holder from her hair and tilt her face back into the sun. The moped took off down the street and Holly heard her mom laugh, her blond hair flying out behind her in the wind.

"Who's the babe with Uncle Jesse?" Nestor asked.

"No idea," Luis said. "Just another party girl, I guess."

## CHAPTER FIVE

TRUTH BE TOLD, GAIL DIDN'T want to get off the moped.
Ever. Driving around for the last couple of hours had not
only given her a complete understanding of the layout
of Key West—from its historic Old Town to the strip
malls—but it had given her an excuse to plaster herself
up against Jesse's back and spread her fingers over his
muscular chest and stomach. She'd never before touched
a man so powerfully built. She liked it. She didn't want
it to end.

However, staying on the moped forever was imprac-
tical, and Jesse had just asked her if she was hungry.
Gail had to admit she was. So Jesse swung the moped
around and headed to what she figured was a restaurant
on the eastern end of Duval Street. Instead, he pulled
up in front of what looked like a very exclusive yacht
club and turned off the bike. A beefy man in an ivory
linen suit looked over the top of his sunglasses and had
begun to bark at Jesse for pulling into a no-parking zone
when he suddenly broke out into a wide grin.

"Jesse! Where you been, man?"

"Mook!" Jesse helped Gail off the moped and then
gave the man a big hug. "It's been a while."

"Things going good for you these days?" Mook made
the inquiry of Jesse, but his eyes had fallen on Gail.

She hoped her hair didn't look too wild or her face too flushed.

"Couldn't be better. This is my friend Gail."

The three of them chatted for a bit, long enough for Gail to decide that Jesse did, in fact, know every local person on the island. As they'd tooled around town, he'd beeped and waved at what seemed like hundreds of friendly faces—guys at the marina, women who ran health food restaurants, jewelry galleries or ice cream shops. He'd stopped briefly to chat with a man at a gas station and one of the caretakers at Key West cemetery, who'd taken them on a quick tour of graves dated all the way back to the late 1700s.

Jesse had grown up here, he'd explained to her, and many of his childhood friends remained in town. He'd told her that the Conchs were a close-knit community.

"The who?" she'd asked.

Jesse had explained that anyone born here called themselves a "Conch," and the city itself was nick-named the "The Conch Republic," for the large-shelled sea snails that were once plentiful in the surrounding waters.

Gail wandered away from the laughing and chatting friends, drawn to the dramatic ocean vista that lay beyond the pier. Jesse had mentioned that Key West was where the Atlantic met up with the warm waters of the Gulf of Mexico. All Gail knew was that the startling blue-green sea looked smooth, clean and infinite. Seagulls and pelicans swooped through the clear sky. Dozens of tiny islands dotted the waters beyond. Gail wondered to herself what it would be like to live somewhere so outrageously beautiful.

"Shall we?" Jesse reached for her hand and Mook let them through a locked iron gate, gesturing them on.

"Enjoy your lunch," Mook said, smiling big.

But instead of leading Gail to one of the white-linen-covered tables at the resort's busy waterside restaurant, Jesse pulled her in the opposite direction. They walked down a long pier, boats of every description bobbing along on each side.

"Where are we going?" Suddenly, Gail felt the slightest twinge of discomfort. Was she putting herself in danger? She liked Jesse, obviously. He seemed like a great guy. And there was no question that he was sexy and gorgeous. But it sure looked to Gail as though he was about to escort her off the end of a pier.

"Do you trust me?" he asked, his eyes smiling behind his sunglasses.

"No offense," Gail said, "but I don't know you well enough to trust you." Immediately, she wished she'd chosen a more diplomatic answer.

Jesse only laughed. "I hear you, Professor. No offense taken. Have a seat."

They'd reached the very edge of the dock and, obviously, there were no chairs in which to sit. Jesse gestured to the weathered wood planks beneath their feet. "Okay, why not?" Gail said, giving him a tentative smile as she lowered herself to the dock. She took off her sandals and let her bare toes dangle over the ocean.

Jesse plopped down next to her, his leg touching hers from hip to knee. Slowly, he turned his head and looked down at her.

The only sounds were the faint bustle of the yacht club's restaurant behind them, the water licking at the pilings and the occasional screech of seabirds. The pressure of his body against hers made her feel safe, alive. Jesse and Gail simply looked at each other, Jesse's expression relaxed and kind, his dark hair gently fluffing in the breeze. An understanding was passing between them, Gail realized. The moment was important. It was intimate. Suddenly, the most pressing need in Gail's world was kissing him again.

Jesse leaned in close.

"So, do you know a lot about the ocean?" No sooner had those words escaped her mouth than Gail began laughing at herself in embarrassment. A beautiful man brought her to a beautiful place to kiss her—exactly what she wanted—and she goes and asks about the marine ecosystem? She squeezed her eyes shut and shook her head.

"I do, but mostly by osmosis," Jesse answered, as if he saw nothing strange in her inquiry. "A lot of my family and friends have been fishermen or made their living off the ocean in some way." Jesse brushed Gail's cheek with his fingertips. "You seem embarrassed, but it's not an odd question—I mean, look around. The ocean is kind of hard to ignore in these parts."

Gail laughed. "Thanks," she said, grateful he made her feel so at ease. She really should try to relax. She should try to just accept herself, awkwardness and all. Gail knew who she was—she was a woman who'd spent her life with her nose in a book—and, at thirty-six, a personality transplant probably wasn't in her future. So what if she wasn't smooth? She wasn't used to this kind of attention, from this kind of man. There was no shame in that.

Gail took a deep breath. "Jesse…" She gazed out toward the horizon line before she turned to look him in the eye. "You've probably noticed by now that I'm not much of a seductress."

He chuckled.

"I'm a nerdy intellectual. I'm not used to hanging out with, uh, men like you."

"Tour guides?"

Gail laughed again. "Actually, I was referring to extremely good-looking men with earrings and muscles. It's a little nerve-racking for me. Plus, I really suck at small talk."

"It's not my favorite, either."

That's when Jesse gently bumped his shoulder against hers, a gesture of solidarity so tender it shocked Gail. Clearly, he was trying his best to let her know he understood her. She liked that. A lot. She grinned up at him.

"The truth is, I prefer to talk about things that are real and matter to me," Jesse said, his voice a little wistful. "Protecting the ocean is certainly one of those things."

"What are some others?"

He cocked his head thoughtfully. "My house. Giving everything I can to my work. My friends." He glanced down at her. "Then there's diving, sailing, good food and salsa dancing—and enjoying the company of an intelligent, funny and beautiful woman when that rare opportunity arises."

Gail felt herself blush. She looked away.

"You're a lot more than a nerdy intellectual, Gail." She felt Jesse reach for her hand. Was it really only yesterday that her scowling neighbor could barely stand the idea of shaking hands? "And I'd like to hear the details—where you grew up, what you teach, what life is like back home, oh, and, of course, how long you've been burdened by an unhealthy obsession with Ernest Hemingway."

Gail laughed again, thinking to herself that Kim would love this guy. She reminded herself to call Kim that evening. Gail would probably start the conversation with *"You're not going to believe this..."*

Gail began to tell Jesse about her life. She mentioned that she was up for tenure. She talked about the long process of earning her PhD, and her students at Beaverdale College. She'd only just started on the Curtis years when she felt footsteps clomping on the dock behind them. Gail whipped her head around to see a parade of six men in white waiters' jackets, looking as if they were about to set up camp. Two men carried a rolled-up canopy of some kind. Another guy had a rug. The others had a table, chairs and a dolly stacked with large containers.

*"What in the world?"*

Jesse pulled her to her feet and motioned for her to stand with him on the side of the dock, giving the entourage room to pass. Gail stood in stunned silence as a private dining room took shape before their eyes. The canopy went up first, and Gail could tell by the way its aluminum poles slipped into slots that it had been custom made for the spot. A small sisal rug was spread out and the table and chairs arranged upon it. Linens were placed on the table. Silver, glassware and plates came out of containers. A small vase of fresh flowers was placed in the middle of everything. One of the waiters opened a bottle of white wine and shoved it in ice to keep it cold.

The whole process took no more than five minutes.

Then they all smiled and headed back down the dock, leaving a single cooler next to the table.

Gail emerged from her shock soon enough to shout several thank-yous to the waiters, then looked up at Jesse. He seemed quite pleased with himself.

"Do you do this for every nerdy woman who rents the house next door?"

Jesse laughed. "Uh, no. Shall we?" He placed his hand at the small of her back and guided her to her seat. He pulled out the chair for her and took his place across the table. Jesse poured them both a glass of wine and offered a toast. "Here's to a vacation you'll always remember."

HOURS AFTER THEY'D finished their yellowfin ceviche and green salads, and long after they'd drained the bottle of crisp pinot grigio, they were still talking. Mook probably thought they'd fallen off the dock at this point. When Jesse glanced to his right, he was surprised to see the sun low in the sky. It had been years since he'd had this much fun getting to know someone, and he couldn't remember any instance when it had been this easy.

They'd covered a lot of ground in just a few hours. He'd learned that Gail was passionate about literature, art and classical music, but that she hadn't had much in the way of leisure time. She had a quick mind and a quicker wit, and he'd laughed his ass off more than once. She told him that she'd had the same best friend since elementary school, like Jesse. And Gail had been through a lot with her ex-husband. Though she was discreet and kind when she talked about her ex, the basic story was enough for Jesse to comfortably stick Curtis Chapman in the "Grade-A Douche Bag" column. It was no mystery why Gail had kept her distance from men since.

He'd noticed how Gail's eyes lit up whenever she mentioned her daughter, an honors student waiting to hear whether she'd been accepted to the University of Pennsylvania. It had been just the two of them for many years now, and Jesse was impressed with how Gail had juggled everything.

He'd discovered that Gail's laughter had a roller-coaster lilt to it, starting low, then building, then softening again. He'd enjoyed the ride every time.

And Jesse had figured out why he'd been so damn attracted to her from the start. He *liked* her. He'd liked her the first time they spoke and he'd gone on liking her. And all that was before he even touched on how enjoyable it was just to look at her.

Gail was beautiful, certainly. He loved that she'd let her hair down and it fell in soft waves around her face. He thought her eyes were stunning—a kind and warm café au lait that sparkled when she smiled, and that she'd accented with a single stroke of eyeliner on her upper lid. Those eyes were framed in long lashes and delicate, light eyebrows. He liked her little nose. And that silky peach-pink mouth—surely she'd noticed him staring at her lips. The truth was, he wanted to kiss her again. He hadn't gotten nearly enough kissing.

The rest of Gail Chapman was, in a word, lovely. She had firm, delicate arms and soft, small hands. She was probably about a size eight, with a shapely bottom, nice but not overly large breasts, great legs and cute feet. A lot of women would have chosen to strut that kind of stuff in skintight Dolce and Gabbana. Not Professor

Gail. Her choice was breathable cotton from the L.L. Bean catalog.

The idea made him hard enough to cut glass.

"Am I keeping you from anything?" Gail asked. "We've been here a long time. I didn't mean to monopolize your day."

"Me?" Jesse was shaken from his stupor. "No. I'm enjoying myself immensely."

She sent him a sweet smile, then lowered her eyes.

By this point, Jesse believed he had a decent working knowledge of Gail Chapman, and he knew his hunch had been more than wishful thinking. Beneath that mild-mannered exterior lurked a wild woman just *dying* to escape. She knew it, too. She'd basically admitted it back at the Hemingway house. *"I'm unstable, and very, very deprived."*

But Gail was still fighting it. She was still afraid of it. And Jesse decided that he was the man to facilitate her release. He'd provide her a safe and comfortable place where she could let it all go.

"How about you?" he asked. "Am I keeping you from anything?"

She thought that was funny. "Nope." She looked right in his eyes and pursed her lips. "So tell me more about your day-to-day life."

Jesse had been telling her his story all afternoon. Most of it, anyway. Sometime after his second glass of wine, he'd made a decision. Bottom line—he wouldn't lie to her. Should Gail or her daughter ask if he was J. D. Batista, the author, he'd say yes, he was. Gail would probably be angry with him and think she'd been misled somehow, but he'd deal with that when it happened. In the meantime, Jesse's plan was to tell her enough of the truth that he could sleep at night, but not enough to alter the sweet and uncomplicated connection growing between them.

"Well, in addition to working on Fred's boat and helping with the walking tours, I usually write every day."

Gail's eyes flew wide. "Seriously? You're a writer?"

"I try to be," he said, watching carefully for any flicker of recognition in her eyes. There was none.

"Wow! That's so exciting! What do you write?"

"Mostly fiction," he said. "I also do a little poetry, and lately I've been trying my hand at a screenplay, which is a lot tougher than I imagined."

Gail's brows knit together. "Do you think you'll be published one day?"

Jesse froze. Answering this question honestly without giving himself away was going to be a challenge. He was an author with eight *New York Times* bestsellers under his belt, but, as every writer knew, that was no guarantee of future success.

"There's always hope," was Jesse's answer.

Gail let go with a laugh. "I knew it all along, of course," she said, a knowing look on her face. Jesse thought his charade was over until Gail finished her thought. "I knew you had to be a writer or an English teacher."

Jesse smiled. "Yeah? What tipped you off?"

"Your vocabulary," she said, folding her arms under her breasts. "You cursed your shutter hinge using words like *artistry* and *substandard* along with the usual *shits* and *fucks.*"

Jesse choked. Hearing those words come out of professor Gail's mouth was as jarring as it was hilarious.

"Sorry you were subjected to that," he said. "I get a little uptight about my house sometimes. It means a lot to me."

Gail raked her fingers through her hair and studied Jesse for a moment, her brown eyes focused on him. "I need to ask you a personal question, Jesse," she said. "If you don't want to answer me, just tell me to go to hell."

He couldn't imagine ever needing to do that, but he agreed.

"How can you afford your place?" She looked repentant the instant the words tumbled from her mouth. "What I mean is, that's a really expensive house and you're a man with a couple of part-time jobs—you know, the starving artist type. I don't get it."

"Ah," Jesse said.

"Are you a drug smuggler? A member of organized crime?" She leaned closer and her expression became quite serious. "Have you embezzled millions from those who trusted you?"

He laughed hard. When he'd gained his composure, he answered her. "I assure you, I am none of those things. And I'm not starving."

She shook her head. "Sorry, but I had to ask. We're living right next door to you. You've kissed me. I'm having a romantic lunch with you and I'm wildly attracted to you. It's something I needed to know because…" Gail stopped speaking and rubbed a hand over her mouth anxiously. "Here's the deal, Jesse. I learned my lesson with Curtis. I have no interest in wasting my time with a man who's not on the up-and-up. Honesty is more important to me than anything else. *Period*."

Jesse didn't know whether to laugh or cry at the

irony. He was interested in a woman with trust issues rivaling his own, yet he couldn't give her what she wanted—complete honesty—because of his own trust issues. Not yet, anyway.

"No apology necessary, Professor," he said. "I inherited the house from my grandmother a few years ago along with part of her estate. I'm the last one of my family who still lives in Key West."

"Oh."

It got quiet between them for a long moment. Gail turned to look out on the water, and Jesse was struck by the elegant curve of her neck, the perfect angle of her jawline. He wanted to kiss her there. He wanted to kiss her everywhere.

Without turning back around, Gail flashed her eyes at him, catching him in midgawk. She smiled.

Jesse smiled back.

"This is my first vacation in six years, Jesse. Did I tell you that?"

"No."

Gail faced front in her chair again, her hands folded in her lap. "You offered up a toast today, a toast to a vacation I'd always remember."

"I did."

"Well, that's what I want. Can you help me with that? Do you have time in your schedule?"

From the depths of his brain, he felt the monster stir. It had somehow managed to stay dormant all day, but the honeymoon was over.

What about his deadline?

Jesse had less than two weeks to get his manuscript in shape. Normally, this would mean twelve to fourteen hours a day at his laptop, breaking only for the necessities of caffeine, food, a punishing workout and sleep when he could calm his mind enough to allow it.

Yet, in Gail's company, he'd forgotten all about his deadline. Not only that, he'd forgotten how getting involved with Cammy had nearly ruined his life, and that he was attempting to forge a comeback with this book.

Did he have time for Gail? That was a good question. But the real question was this: *What the hell am I doing? Am I nuts?*

Jesse swallowed hard. "How many days do you have left on this vacation?"

"Eight nights, nine days."

"And what exactly do you want to do?"

Apparently, Gail had already given this a great deal of thought, because the list tumbled out fast and furious. "I want to learn to scuba dive. I want to go on one of those booze cruises under the stars. I want a naked therapeutic massage. I want to swim with the dolphins and learn to dance the salsa. I want to eat all kinds of exotic delicacies I can't get back in Beaverdale. And I want to go skinny-dipping."

Gail paused. She closed her eyes for an instant, and to Jesse it looked like she was summoning the courage to continue. Suddenly, her eyes flew open. "And I want you to make wild, unrestrained love to me, Jesse."

He sat with that last request for a moment, narrowing his eyes, working the logistics out in his head. "Do we have to tackle everything in that particular order?"

"Not necessarily."

"All right. Good to know." Jesse's heart pounded in his chest. Gail's bluntness was amusing. It was damn hot, too. "So," he said, trying to keep a straight face. "Would you mind if we combined a couple of those activities, you know, in the interest of time?"

A wicked smile had crept onto her pretty little mouth. "Like going skinny-dipping with dolphins?"

"That could work." Jesse reached across the table for her hand, and she slid it into place without hesitation. "Or I could feed you exotic foods while demonstrating the salsa and massaging your naked body under a canopy of stars."

"That sounds like an efficient use of everyone's time," she said.

It was at that moment that Jesse told his deadline monster to fuck off. He told the memory of Cammy to fuck off. The woman sitting across the table from him was one in a million. He'd never met anyone like her. He didn't think women like her existed, except in the pages of his books. So what if he had to ask for another two-week extension? It wouldn't be the end of the world.

"All right, then." Jesse rose from his chair and helped Gail to a stand. As soon as he got hold of her, he yanked her close and kissed her hard. He wanted to make a statement with the kiss. He wanted Gail to know she'd found the right man for the job, that she was in very capable hands. Jesse slid his palm down the curve of her back to the globes of her L.L. Bean-covered ass, where he gave her a firm squeeze.

She jumped. Jesse ended the kiss. "We'd better get going." He grabbed the straw bag and hooked it over Gail's shoulder before guiding her back toward land. "We've got a lot on our schedule."

# CHAPTER SIX

"HELLO? MOM?"

"Hi, honey. What are you up to?"

Holly rolled her eyes. What are *we* up to? She couldn't believe this. What are *you* up to was the issue.

"We're still hanging with the friends we met this morning. We're down near Mallory Square and want to stay for the sunset celebration then go for pizza. Would that be okay?"

"Sure. That sounds fun. Just remember your midnight curfew."

"Right."

Just then, Hannah got all up in Holly's face and started asking questions. *"Is she with him? What are they doing?"* Holly shushed her friend and shooed her away.

"So, what have you been doing today, Mom?" Holly hoped she sounded casual enough.

"Oh, a little of everything," was her answer. "I took the Hemingway tour then wandered around the island to get my bearings. I talked to some of the locals then had lunch. I'm getting ready to jump in the pool."

*And? And?*

It looked like there wasn't going to be any *and*. Holly realized her mom wasn't going to say a word about the hottie captain, which pissed her off because her mom always got so *parentnoid* on her about the importance of honesty, but here she was—not one word about how she'd shamed herself zooming around town with her skirt yanked up to her granny panties!

Just then, her mom began to confess.

"I suppose I should mention that I spent most of the day with our neighbor, Jesse. Turns out he's a very nice man."

Holly nodded her head dramatically and gave Hannah a thumbs up, their prearranged signal that her mom was coming clean.

"Wow, that's cool, Mom. Sounds like you had fun."

Her mom was silent for a moment. "Yep," was all she said. "Well, I better go. Call me when you're on your way back to the house so I know when to expect you."

"Sure."

Holly felt somewhat calmer. So what if her mom was having a little fun with the dreamy old dude from next door? It was her vacation, too. It was all perfectly innocent.

"See you then, honey," her mom said. "Thanks for checking in."

"No prob. Hey, wait." Holly stopped herself from hanging up. "Mom?"

"Yes?"

"Be careful out there."

WHAT KIND OF HIDEOUS, despicable mother was she? When Holly called to check in, Gail had just finished stuffing herself into her daughter's bikini, the one Gail had only yesterday deemed pornographic and unfit for public display.

Yet she was about to head downstairs to put herself on display for Jesse, the guy from next door.

*Ohmigod, ohmigod, ohmigod...*

Gail examined herself one last time in the floor-to-ceiling mirror. She had to admit that her body looked pretty good for her age, but the suit was slut city. What kind of skanky shops had found berth in the Beaverdale Mall, for goodness' sake? Gail only thanked God she'd shaved her bikini area that day, because there was no room for error in this thing.

But seriously. She couldn't really go through with this. *Could she?*

She heard the clank of the back gate and ran to the upstairs window. Jesse had just let himself in. He wore only a towel, which was angled low to one side and knotted at the hip. He carried a bottle of wine and two glasses in his hands, which he placed on a table. Gail watched him move in the glow of the setting sun, his brown skin gleaming, the light casting shadows on his ripped stomach and cut arms.

Suddenly, he turned. He must have felt the heat of her stare. This time, Gail wasn't ashamed to be caught ogling, so she smiled and gave him a little wave.

Jesse tilted his head and brought one muscled arm across his body, rubbing the skin low on his abdomen. It was impossible not to notice that he was already getting aroused—the thin terry cloth was no match for the bulge taking shape beneath it. Gail watched in fascination as the ends of the towel began to open like a curtain.

Holy shit. He was naked under there. The most gorgeous hunk of man she'd ever seen in her life was naked underneath his towel! And he was waiting for her, ready to give her the kind of vacation memories a girl just couldn't get at, say, Disney World.

Deep down, Gail knew it was now or never.

Before she could change her mind, she raced down the steps and through the downstairs, sliding open the patio doors. She stepped onto the pool deck, shaking her hair and posing for him the best she could, thinking that she felt like a woman possessed. The pre-spring-break Gail would never have had the guts to do something like this.

Jesse said nothing. He appeared to be frozen where he stood.

"This isn't my usual kind of swimsuit," Gail said, stating the obvious. "I don't usually wear a two-piece."

Jesse's eyes went wide. "Two pieces of what?" he asked, chuckling. "Sweetheart, that's barely enough thread to floss my teeth."

Gail laughed—the man made her laugh! She figured if his fiction was as funny and colorful as he was in person, he might really be able to make it as a writer someday. "Should I take it off?" she asked.

Jesse shook his head very slowly. "Nope. That's my job. Where are the girls?"

"Not coming home until later tonight. I just spoke to Holly."

"Good. C'mere."

"Wait. How about some music?" Gail turned and scurried over to the outdoor bar, where she'd seen the girls fiddle with the sound system. She hit the "on" button, and the ground began to pound.

*Give it to me, baby, nice and slow.*
*Climb on top like you ride in the rodeo...*

"Or not," she said, flipping it off.

She heard Jesse laugh. "What's wrong with a little mood music?" He'd begun to walk his way over to her, tented towel and all. The smile on his face was almost as wide as the gap in the terry cloth.

Gail let out a squeak of anxiety. Her breathing accelerated. Her mouth became parched.

Was she really going through with this? Was this really happening?

Jesse walked right past her, brushing against her hip on his way to the sound system. The music was on again, but at a much lower volume.

He stood right in front of her. "Gail."

"Yes?"

Jesse slid his fingers up into her hair and pulled her head back ever so gently, stopping when she had no choice but to look up into his dark blue eyes. He placed a string of hot kisses along the side of her face, her jawline, her exposed throat. Her knees began to wobble.

"If you want to stop, just say so," he whispered, still kissing. "I'm only the tour guide here. This is your vacation."

Gail giggled and nodded at the same time. She was giddy. Drunk. Her skin was on fire everywhere his lips landed. She had the feeling of being lost, gone, out of her mind with lust for him. The volume might have been reduced, but she could still hear the overtly sexual lyrics of that song, words rhyming in subliminal seduction— behind, grind, thong, gone, zipper, quicker…

Jesse nibbled on her earlobe and his hands began to slide down her back to her butt, hips, thighs. Suddenly he grabbed her and pulled her tight against the front of his body. She felt his large erection poke into her belly. "You're really something, Professor, do you know that?"

She shook her head. If he didn't kiss her soon she was certain something inside her would snap out of place, never to function properly again.

"You're the perfect combination of brains and beauty, such achingly sweet beauty." As Jesse whispered these words, his tongue flicked her earlobe, then behind her ear, then at the tender skin of her throat. She couldn't stand this. She could hardly breathe.

Jesse had the manual dexterity of a pickpocket. In lightning speed, he'd moved one hand up to her bikini top and deftly pushed one of the triangles of fabric aside so that her whole breast was exposed. She gasped.

He tweaked her nipple—harder than she might have expected from a man she'd only just met—and brought his mouth to hers. *Finally.*

She opened up to him. Jesse's tongue was sweet and hot and skilled as it explored her. She heard a desperate moan and realized it had come out of her. She was losing her mind!

Suddenly, she felt the fingers of his other hand brush against the tiny crotch of the bikini. His touch was light. He didn't poke or prod.

Jesse pulled his mouth from hers. He looked her directly in the eye. "You're soaking wet."

She moaned again. She was coming apart in his hands, with his words.

*"Fuck me."*

Oh, yes she did. She said it.

"I thought you'd never ask." Jesse grabbed her under the thighs and picked her up. Within seconds they were inside the house, up the stairs and in her bedroom, where he laid her on the bed.

"Don't move," he said. "I'll be right back."

As if she'd be capable of movement! Yet, surprisingly, as Gail watched Jesse walk from the room, her hands immediately began to wander of their own volition, approaching the vee of her bikini bottoms. She just wanted to see if Jesse had been exaggerating about the state of her arousal. That's all. So she dipped her fingers inside, and discovered that, if anything, he'd been downright genteel in his description.

She had no control over herself. Gail closed her eyes and continued touching, stroking, sliding her fingers in her own wetness. She'd never been so turned on in her life. When she heard Jesse at the bedroom door she sat up, eyes wide, ashamed that she'd been caught.

His hands were holding the wine, the glasses and a string of condoms so long it reminded Gail of a party pack of lollipops. She swallowed hard.

"One condition," Jesse said, placing the items on the bedside table and closing the drapes. "No shame. No embarrassment. Just pleasure. Deal?"

Gail found herself nodding.

Jesse was in front of her. He pushed her legs open where they draped over the side of the bed, forcing his way close. She couldn't help but notice that his erection was directly lined up with her mouth.

He grabbed her hand, the hand that had just been down inside her swimsuit. Jesse raised it to his lips and licked the juice from her fingertips. Gail gasped. When he was done, he bent at the waist. They were eye-to-eye.

"Now, that's my idea of an exotic delicacy, Professor.

And I plan on treating myself to a lot of it this week. Will that be all right with you?"

Gail nodded, speechless.

"Then tell me again," Jesse said. "I need to be absolutely sure this is what you want."

"Fuck me. *Right now.*"

With one flick of his wrist, the towel fell to the floor. Gail's eyes nearly popped from her head.

"There will be plenty of time for you to explore me, sweetheart. I'm not going anywhere. But right now, I have to get inside you. I just have to be inside your body."

She grabbed his face with both her hands and pulled him down to her mouth. Gail felt his fingers deftly untie the swimsuit. His hands began to travel everywhere on her body—her neck, her breasts, her belly, her legs, all while he kissed her, took her over and over again with his tongue.

They rolled together. Gail was on top of him, her fists full of his dark hair and her legs spread over him. She felt like a she-devil, like some kind of animal just released from a cage, like a stranger who'd been living inside her all this time had finally been given permission to come out to play.

Gail reached behind her and grabbed a condom. She handed it to Jesse, who looked up at her with as much wild desire in his eyes as she must have had in hers. Who was this man who'd been thrown into her world and her bed? What was happening to her?

She scooted down then lowered her mouth to his hard cock, gently and slowly tasting what he'd so kindly unveiled for her pleasure. He was thick and long and he tasted salty and clean. She dragged her tongue along the underside of him then closed her lips down on the head, taking as much as she could into her mouth.

"Whoa." Jesse had his hands in her hair. "Hold up, wild woman."

Gail raised her head, afraid she'd done something he didn't like.

"It's been a while for me, Gail," he said, his eyes filled with a tender honesty. "Not quite as long as you, but long enough, and the way you're going at me you're going to make me come."

She nodded. "We wouldn't want that, now would we?"

He gave her a crooked grin then ripped open the foil wrapper.

GAIL WAS A WILD WOMAN all right, but she was also intensely erotic, fluid in the way she moved her body, and so ethereally beautiful that he felt as if he were looking into the face of an angel.

She was spread beneath him, and he was poised to enter her. She was so wet and open from his hand and his tongue that she'd started to pant. This was good.

He grabbed two handfuls of her luscious bottom and pulled her up to him. With one agonizingly pleasurable push, he got the head of his cock inside her. She was tight, slick and already pulsing around him.

With slow determination, Jesse got all the way in her. Her body was trembling. Her eyes looked up at him, pleading for more. So he gave it to her, in, out, his hands clutching her ass, her breasts rolling in rhythm with his thrusts.

"Oh, hell, *yesssss*," Gail hissed.

Jesse smiled through the waves of intense pleasure

now rippling through him. He watched her face. She was lost in her own onslaught of bliss. She moaned, and her head rolled back and forth on her lovely neck.

Suddenly her eyes shot open. Her lips parted. And she clutched at his arms and shoulders. "I'm coming."

He lowered his face near hers. "Come for me, Gail. That's what I'm here for."

"Oh, God." Her eyes went blank. She was hanging on the edge.

*"Do it, you sexy little mami,"* he whispered, just before he crushed her mouth with his. She exploded in his arms, beneath his body, her raucous scream absorbed by his kiss. It was all he could do to stop himself from coming right along with her. But he managed. He wasn't anywhere near ready to wrap up their first go-around together.

Jesse slowed his pace, pulling his lips from hers so that he could see her. Gail's expression was one of utter satisfaction, complete with rosy cheeks and a drunken little smile. Her eyelids hung heavy over her soft brown eyes.

"Worth waiting for?" he asked.

Gail let go with a giddy chuckle. "Yeah," she breathed.

Jesse gathered her tightly in his right arm. "Wrap your legs around me," he said. She did. Then he pushed himself up and turned around to sit on the edge of the bed, his cock still embedded in the heat of her body. She placed her arms loosely around his neck, smiling down at him.

"You know, I have to admit something, Gail," he said, his fingers kneading her back and buttocks.

"Yeah?"

"I saw it right away," Jesse continued. "I could tell

that underneath your good-girl packaging you were a sexual beast."

She giggled softly and began to stroke his hair. Jesse closed his eyes and had just begun to luxuriate in the moment when he felt Gail do something wonderful—an unmistakably bad-girl trick—with the lower half of her body.

He opened one eye to see her smile as she squeezed him, wiggled on him, slowly raised and lowered herself on him.

"You bring it out in me, I guess," Gail said, throwing her head back in pleasure as her inner muscles pulsed around him. She began a slow and intense grind, her soft little groans coming in rhythm with the undulations of her body.

Jesse knew he wouldn't last three seconds if she kept this up.

"Gail?"

She let her head fall forward and looked down into his face. Her eyes were half closed in ecstasy and her beautiful blond hair tumbled down next to her cheeks. She never stopped wiggling on him and never stopped squeezing.

"Yeah?" she whispered, distracted.

Jesse had to laugh. It was clear to him now that Professor Gail was a single-minded sexpot when in pursuit of pleasure. He fuckin' *loved* it.

She began to ride him faster. "I'm going to come all over you again," she breathed. "Oh, God, it feels so good."

That was it. Jesse shuddered and he clutched at her, pulling her body closer as he rode out the searing heat of his orgasm. It took several moments for him to catch his breath. While he waited, he ran his hands all over the silky skin of her back, bottom and hips.

"Damn," he whispered, pulling away from Gail and cradling her face in his hands. As he kissed her cheeks and chin, he thought about how lucky he'd been to be saddled with Lelinda's Hemingway tour that morning.

It had turned out to be one of the most outstanding days of his life.

"WHAT THE—"

Holly stood in the open sliding door, staring at the sexy old dude from next door and her mom, romping around in the lit-up pool like teenagers. What were they doing? What music were they listening to? Why was her mom laughing so hard?

*Please, God. Don't let them be naked.*

"I thought your mom hated hip-hop," Hannah whispered into Holly's ear.

"With a passion."

"You said she goes to bed every night around nine."

"Like clockwork."

"Hey girls!" Her mom waved enthusiastically, a huge smile on her face. It was then that Holly noticed the familiar straps of her mom's fugly one-piece aqua-blue swimsuit and knew it was safe to start breathing again.

"Hey!" Hannah answered for both of them. "Here we are, home by curfew, just like we promised!"

"That's great, girls. I really appreciate it."

Her mom paddled over to the pool's edge while the captain dove underwater. Holly watched him glide to the pool wall, all sleek and dark muscles in the Day-Glo green water.

She didn't trust him. He was probably a player. And her mom was clueless. It was like watching an Animal Planet episode on lions and gazelles on the Serengeti. She wanted to cover her eyes.

"I was just getting ready to head home." Jesse propelled himself straight out of the water then smoothed back his hair. Hannah made a little squeak of appreciation as he turned his back to them and bent over to grab his towel. At least his swim trunks were the normal kind and not an old-pervert Speedo.

"Did you guys have fun tonight?" her mother asked, looking up at them with that big smile still on her face. Holly decided she looked totally blissed-out.

Oh, God.

"A great time," Holly said, not wanting to be outdone by her mom. "We met these awesome local boys who were really nice and showed us around."

Her mom just nodded, but the comment caught Jesse's attention, and he spun toward them while he toweled off his hair. "Oh yeah? What are their names?"

"Luis and Nestor," Hannah answered. "They said you were like family to them."

Jesse's arm stopped in midair. It was only for a split second and he went on as though nothing happened, but Holly noticed the reaction.

"Do you know them?" her mom asked Jesse. "Are they good kids?"

"Absolutely," Jesse said, smiling a smile that Holly thought looked genuine. "Their dad's one of my best friends. No worries."

That seemed to make her mom happy.

"Just tell them I said to behave."

Hannah thought that Jesse's comment was funny, but Holly detected a real nervousness in the way Jesse was moving and speaking. Now she knew for sure the guy couldn't be trusted.

Just then her mom jumped from the pool and began to dry off, asking if the girls had eaten and inviting them to join her and Jesse tomorrow. He was taking her to swim with the dolphins, she said.

"Thanks, but we have plans." Holly answered while keeping an eye on the captain.

"Oh. Okay, then." Her mom gave both the girls a kiss on the cheek. "I'm headed off to bed—I'm completely exhausted."

*I just bet you are,* Holly thought.

Then she watched her mother smile at Jesse. "I'll see you tomorrow. Thanks for a wonderful day."

The captain smiled back at her. "Sleep tight."

Hannah and her mom had already stepped through the back sliding door, and the captain was headed to the pool gate.

"Um, Jesse?"

He turned around, the smile he had for her mom still hanging around on his face. "Yes?"

"She's not, you know—" Holly checked to make sure her mother was out of earshot. "My mom, I mean. She's not all that experienced with men. She's kind of naive."

Jesse tugged the towel tight around his waist and looked at Holly with kind eyes. He nodded slowly, as if he was thinking about what she'd said.

"Mom's only been with my dad, and she got pretty hurt."

"She's told me everything."

That was a surprise. Holly took a step closer to him. He really was very handsome—for an old guy. "Don't hurt her. Just don't. It wouldn't be good."

A smile spread across Jesse's face, and he looked away, almost like he was embarrassed. He laughed softly before he looked at Holly again. "Your mom is a very perceptive and smart woman. I wouldn't worry too much about her."

She shrugged, not wanting to admit that was what was going on here—she was *worried* about her mom.

Jesse took a step closer to her and gently placed a hand on her shoulder. "Believe me, Holly. The last thing I'd ever want to do is cause your mom pain. She's a very special lady, and she deserves the best."

Holly crossed her arms over her chest and studied him. He seemed like a decent enough guy. And he liked her mom. That was obvious.

"Well, okay," Holly said tentatively. "But I'll be keeping my eye on the two of you, just in case."

## CHAPTER SEVEN

"CHAGO. YOU UP?"

His friend yawned into the phone. "I am now, man. What's going on?"

"Your boys home yet?"

"Oh, shit. What'd they do now?"

Jesse laughed. "Nothing. I just have a favor to ask you. Are you awake enough for this conversation?"

"Hold up, man."

Jesse heard him rustle out of bed and take the phone in another room so he wouldn't wake his wife.

"Okay. What's goin' on?"

Jesse took a breath. "Listen, I know this is going to sound strange, but hear me out. I need you to take down the 'Dark Blue' series display for a few days, and put my books in the back room where no one can see them."

The phone went quiet for a moment. "Say *what?*"

"Please."

"What the hell for, man?"

"As a personal favor to me."

Chago laughed. "Sure. No problem. That'll leave me with *Pat the Bunny* and the cookbooks. I'll have to beat the customers away with a stick."

Jesse felt horrible, but he pressed on. "Please, Chago."

"Look, you'll have to tell me what this is about,

because you and I both know that J. D. Batista is the only marketing hook I got. That new chain store on Roosevelt is killing me, man."

"I know. And I'm sorry."

"So what's this got to do with my boys?"

Jesse gave him a basic summary of the situation, describing Gail in only the most general terms, explaining that he was asking only that Nestor and Luis not mention anything about his writing career to the girls. Jesse emphasized that he wasn't asking them to lie, but he would appreciate it if they didn't bring up the topic in conversation.

Chago said nothing at first, then Jesse heard him chuckling into the phone. "Okay. Sure. I'll tell the boys," he said. The chuckling started up again.

"Thanks."

"You sure about this, man?"

Jesse sighed. The truth was, he'd never attempted anything like this charade. He'd never needed to, but Cammy's con game had made him damn near paranoid. "Look, I can see something happening with Gail, okay? She's that great. I just need a couple days before I tell her everything."

"This is about Cammy, isn't it?"

"In a roundabout way, yes."

"So you're testing her, is that it? You want to make sure she's not gonna sell your ass to *The National Enquirer?* Is that what's going on?"

"Yeah."

Chago whistled low and soft. "Whatever you say, man, but I think you're making a mistake. If this Gail is as great as you say she is, she's not gonna like it when she finds out you've been lying to her. I don't know too many women who'd stand for that kind of shit."

"I'm not lying. I'm *postponing*."

"Right," Chago said. "So that's it? You just want me to move my only moneymaker to the stockroom? You sure I can't interest you in a quart of my blood? My bone marrow? My fuckin' kidney?"

Jesse laughed. "You're a good friend, man. I appreciate it. It's just for a few days."

"Consider it done," Chago said. "I guess it's the least I can do. You've single-handedly kept me in business all these years."

"I appreciate it."

"I just hope you know what you're doing, man. From where I sit, it looks like a train wreck in the making."

NOT THAT GAIL WAS AN OLD hand at this sort of thing, but she recognized what was happening with Jesse. She was being swept away. The hours in his company were running together in a blur of sunshine, ocean, laughter, discovery and pleasure. She treasured every moment of it, too, even as a tiny ball of panic began to form in her stomach, warning her that it was all temporary, an illusion, and that it was building up to nothing but a wistful memory.

And she let it happen anyway.

On Monday, Jesse took Gail out on his sailboat to where the dolphins played. Since Jesse was a friend of a marine biologist who'd studied Key West dolphins for over a decade, he got a heads-up on where to find them. Jesse followed his friend's directions to a spot about six miles from land, where currents had swept schools of fish that were attracting one of the dolphin pods for feeding.

Gail gasped when she saw her first two bottlenose dolphins, so graceful and shiny in the water. She and Jesse lay down on their bellies on deck to watch. That first dolphin couple was soon followed by another, then at least a dozen more animals. They swooped, dived, circled and talked to each other in clicks and chirps. One couple even jumped out of the water with fish in their mouths, as if showing off.

Gail was in awe. "This is one of the most incredible things I've ever seen," she whispered to Jesse.

"I'm really glad," he said, leaning close to kiss her softly.

Jesse and Gail eventually slipped into the water, treading softly as they waited for the dolphins' curiosity to pique. It wasn't long before they ventured close. Gail was so exhilarated to be in the water with the beautiful creatures that her hands trembled. One dolphin brushed up against her leg. Another swam by and rolled over on its back, slowing just enough for her to touch the silky skin of its underbelly.

It wasn't long before they swam away, but as Jesse helped her back into the boat Gail knew she'd been forever changed by the experience. Her spirit felt bigger and wiser for it.

They sailed toward the coral reef for snorkeling. When they'd started off that morning, Jesse had explained to Gail that her interest in scuba diving was admirable, but certification classes would eat up much of her vacation. He suggested she save that for another time, and offered to arrange it for her.

"Another friend of yours?" she asked, smiling.

"Yep. He runs the best dive shop on the island. He'll take very good care of you." Jesse had been at the helm of the sailboat when he said this, and he'd paused for a moment, turning to study her. Gail remembered how powerful his gaze felt, how beautiful he was in the early light, his hair whipping in the wind.

"The next time you come to visit me, I'll hook you up."

Gail hadn't known what to say. It surprised her that Jesse might want to see her again. She felt the same, of course, but it was a shock that it was mutual. She let the comment slide.

Snorkeling was the second mind-blowing thrill of the day for Gail. Jesse said the Key West Marine Sanctuary included the world's third-largest living barrier reef. They slipped into the warm tropical waters and, after Jesse gave Gail a quick lesson in how not to swallow gallons of seawater, they were off.

Gail decided right away that the world she'd entered was like an underwater garden, bursting with color and movement. Her eyes bugged out behind her mask.

She saw what she recognized immediately as a stingray, and pointed it out excitedly to Jesse. Later, Jesse would tell her they'd seen dozens of varieties of tropical fish, including blue tangs, sergeant majors and parrotfish.

Eventually, they swam back to the boat for lunch. Jesse had packed cucumber and cream cheese sandwiches, fruit and chocolate, which nearly melted in the time it took to pluck it from the cooler and unwrap it. Jesse fed Gail small pieces, and she licked the sweetness off his fingers.

They returned to Margaret Street late in the afternoon, and it was then that Jesse introduced Gail to his home. She was awestruck by how rich and shiny it was inside, all the dark wood, the off-white plaster walls filled with art.

Jesse led her through the downstairs to his backyard, a shady and private oasis lush with flowering bushes, palms and a mighty tree that twisted around itself before it exploded into a giant canopy protecting the whole property. Jesse told her it was a 150-year-old banyan tree that he'd always thought of as the guardian of his family's homestead. He led her to the hammock beneath the tree, where they snuggled together. The peaceful joy she felt in his arms—combined with the day's salt air, sun and water—sent Gail almost immediately to sleep. She woke up when her cell phone went off, opening her eyes to see Jesse gazing down at her with a smile. She prayed she hadn't been drooling.

Later that night, Gail was put at ease about Luis and Nestor when they picked up the girls in person. They seemed like well-mannered young men, and though they looked like identical twins, they told Gail they were a year apart. Holly and Hannah rushed them out the door before Gail could ask too many questions, but Jesse assured her that their father had laid down the law with them—they were to remain on their best behavior, or else.

It was then that Gail realized just how fortunate she and the girls had been. They'd arrived just days ago as tourists and strangers, but Jesse had brought them into his circle, making their vacation feel more like a homecoming. She didn't know how she'd ever express to him how much that meant to her.

While Holly and Hannah spent Tuesday with the

boys at Bahia Honda State Park beach, Jesse took Gail to art galleries and out to lunch. They returned to Gail's cottage for a nap, a swim and a roll on the king-size bed. Jesse continued to surprise her with how generous and patient he was as a lover and how he managed to combine excitement with tenderness.

That was the first time that Gail worried she was getting too attached.

Gail spent Wednesday with the girls, joining them for an all-day water sports adventure on a catamaran. She invited Jesse but he declined, saying he had some work to catch up on and that they'd hook up for dinner. She missed him. She admitted that the idea of missing someone she'd just met was silly, but it felt strange to be in Key West without him. Gail started to think about how difficult it was going to be when she had to leave.

That was the second time she worried about getting too attached.

Gail had a blast with Holly and Hannah, parasailing, snorkeling, jet skiing and kayaking. Watching the girls ineptly race their kayaks had her doubled over in laughter. At lunch, Holly asked her mom if everything was going okay with the hottie captain. Gail put down her sandwich.

"It's going just fine," she said, smiling. "I'm having a lot of fun."

When Hannah excused herself to go to the boat's ladies' room, Gail knew this conversation was pre-planned.

"Is everything going well with Luis and Nestor?" Gail asked.

Holly shrugged. "They're cool. I mean, it's not like

anything serious will happen between any of us, but it's nice to get the inside treatment here, you know? They know all the best places and can get us in free everywhere and everything."

Gail smiled at her. "It's the same with Jesse."

Holly didn't say anything for moment and tapped a fingernail on the side of her water bottle. Eventually she looked up, and Gail could see she was upset.

"Holly, is something wrong?" She reached for her daughter's forearm, now brown as a berry and covered in a sun-whitened fuzz. "Has something happened?"

Holly gave her a smirk. "I don't know. You tell *me*."

Gail nodded, patting Holly's arm until her daughter yanked it away. "So you're angry that I'm spending so much time with Jesse?"

"No. Not angry." Holly scowled at her, the wind tossing around her daughter's soft blond hair. "Just concerned that you don't know what you're doing."

Gail bit her bottom lip to stop from laughing. "I see."

"You're not very experienced, Mom, and you've been out with Jesse at all hours, doing God only knows what, and I just don't want you to do something you'll regret."

Gail smiled at her daughter. She was touched that Holly saw her as needing guidance when it came to men. "What are you worried might happen, honey?"

Holly made that clicking sound of disbelief with her tongue. "Hello? I'm worried that you're going to get totally sprung over this guy that you hardly know, Mom!"

Gail didn't want to sound tragically unhip, but she had no choice. "Sprung?" she asked.

Holly shook her head in disbelief. "You know, crushing on him, falling in lust with him, when it'll never amount to anything. Seriously, Mom, rule number one is you never, *ever* fall in love with a guy you meet on spring break—it'll only bring you pain."

Gail took a big gulp of her water, stalling. She couldn't deny that Holly had a point, but the fact still remained that Gail was the thirty-six-year-old woman in this conversation, and Holly was the child.

"I appreciate your concern, but I can take care of myself just fine," she said eventually. "Jesse and I are adults and we know what we're doing, and that's enjoying each other's company."

"What-*evs!*"

Suddenly, Gail understood what the conversation was really about. She smiled at her tenderhearted daughter. It had been just the two of them for so long that Holly must feel a little possessive of Gail.

"Do you want me to spend more time with you, honey? Do you feel like I've abandoned you or something?"

Holly's mouth dropped open. "Uh, not hardly, Mom."

Gail had begun to frown in consternation when the lightbulb suddenly went off in her head. This time, she was certain she'd gotten to the bottom of things. "Am I embarrassing you, Holl? Is that it?"

"Duh!" Holly said, smacking her palms on the table. She lowered her voice to a whisper. "Think about it, Mom—it's *my* spring break, but it's my *mother* who's letting herself go totally wild with some hot guy, riding

through town on a moped with her thighs on display!
It's absolutely humiliating!"

Gail was stunned. "You saw me?"

"Yeah. Me and everyone else. Luis called you a party
girl."

Gail sat up straighter. "He did? Really?"

"That's not a compliment, Mother."

Gail tried not to smile too much, because she knew
she needed to address the cause of her daughter's discomfort, but she was secretly thrilled with her new
reputation. She'd been a lot of things in her life—book-
worm, mommy, trusting wife—but never a party girl.

"Holly," she said as gently as she could. "I appreciate
your looking out for me. I really do."

Her daughter shrugged.

Gail knew that Holly had never seen her mother
as a sexual creature, because her mother hadn't seen
*herself* that way. Not for a very long time. It had to
be disconcerting for her daughter, and maybe a little
threatening.

"You know that you will always be the most important person in my life, don't you?" Gail asked.

Holly picked at the paper label on her water bottle.
"I know, Mom."

"You need to be absolutely clear about that, honey,
because it turns out I really like this dating thing."

Holly looked up and blinked in surprise. Gail touched
her daughter's hand.

"Something's happened to me here, Holly. I think
I'll be going back to Beaverdale ready to start living
again. My life is going to be different, and I hope Jesse
will be part of it. I want you to be okay with that."

"Did I miss anything?" Hannah returned from the

restroom, and she plopped back onto her spot on the bench. Holly glanced at Gail one last time and lowered her eyes. "Not a thing," she said.

JESSE HAD A STRING OF surprises lined up for Gail, and he couldn't remember the last time he'd had so much fun in the pursuit of someone else's happiness.

His buddy with the little house on a private beach up in Pirates Cove told him he was out of town but the house key was in the usual place. "Knock yourself out," he'd said. "Beer's in the fridge." Lelinda had hooked Jesse up with her friend who ran the dress boutique, who helped Jesse pick out something he thought Gail would love: a deep red halter dress made of the softest cotton, with a full skirt that would hit her right above the knee—perfect for a night of salsa lessons. He'd booked her a ninety-minute massage, as well. And he'd reserved his favorite table at the Grand Café for her last night in town, an event he chose not to think too much about.

It gave Jesse pleasure to see Gail stagger out of her massage, a look of ecstasy on her face. Then he took her home and gave her cause for a few more. Their nighttime skinny-dip in Pirates Cove was a sensual heaven of warm water, soft touches and wet kisses. Later, on blankets spread out near the beach campfire, Jesse rolled with Gail, held her close and buried his face into the side of her neck when he pushed inside her. That's when the realization went through him like an electric current—in a couple of days she'd be gone, the smell of her skin would be gone, her laugh would be gone. It seemed impossible.

Gail cried when she opened the box and found the

red dress. She held it up to herself and twirled for him, trying hard to fight back her tears.

"I feel as though I'm in a dream," she told him. "Thank you, Jesse. Thank you for being so kind, for making me feel so special."

He'd taken her by the shoulders then and set her straight. "This isn't about kindness, Gail. Meeting you is one of the loveliest surprises of my life. You are special to me. You are special, period. Don't ever forget that."

When he took her dancing at the open-air Latin music club, she became a focused and serious student, doggedly repeating dance steps until she got them right. With some encouragement—and a few mojitos—Gail managed to loosen up enough to simply enjoy moving to the music. Jesse thought she was more beautiful that night than he'd ever seen her—radiant, relaxed, her eyes shining with happiness.

It was hard to believe that the confident, booty-shaking party girl in his arms was the same woman he'd encountered on her porch only a week ago, tongue-tied, stiff as a board and self-conscious.

During a slow song, Jesse held Gail close, swaying slowly with her in a sea of dancing couples. He kissed her fragrant hair and nibbled on her bare shoulder. He could barely make out the words she whispered into his ear.

*"I think I'm falling in love with you."*

Jesse pulled her tighter, fear and longing coursing through him simultaneously. He moved her body in rhythm with his own until he was ready to respond.

"I feel the same," he said. "You're very easy to love, Professor."

That night, after Gail checked to make sure the girls were home safe, she returned to his house. She stripped off her simple robe and joined him in his bed, kissing him from head to toe. Jesse felt the love pouring out of her and into him. Her love felt like a blessing, and the most intimate gift anyone had ever given him.

"I want you to come back to Key West soon," he said. "As soon as you can."

Gail sat up, letting one leg dangle over the edge of his bed. She tipped her head and smiled at him tenderly. "I appreciate your saying that. But I'm worried that after a while you might forget me. It would be perfectly natural." She gestured at their naked bodies in the moonlight. "This sort of thing usually turns into nothing more than a nice memory."

Jesse sat up, too, and grabbed her face in his hands. "That's not going to happen, and you know it." She tried to look away, but he wouldn't let her. "Gail, what I've had with you has been special. Unique. And I don't want it to end with your vacation."

Her smile spread.

"But there's something you need to know about me first. Please hear me out."

A tiny crease formed between her brows. "Okay," she said, her voice tentative.

He took a deep breath, knowing there was no way to do this but push through it. Jesse owed her the truth, and it couldn't be *postponed* another second.

"Something happened to me last year," he said softly. "A woman came to stay in the house next door—your house—and she seemed really great at first. I'd never allowed myself to fall for a tourist before her."

Gail gently pulled at his wrists until his hands fell

away from her face. The look of confusion in her eyes nearly killed Jesse.

"Go ahead. I'm listening," she said.

"It was nothing but a setup, Gail. She basically blackmailed me, almost ruined my life."

"But…" Gail shook her head as if trying to sort through her thoughts. "She didn't succeed, right? She didn't hurt you, did she?"

"She sure as hell tried."

Gail blinked, remaining silent. Slowly, she began to scoot back on the bed, never taking her eyes from his face. She brought the sheet to the front of her body, that beautiful body she'd become comfortable sharing with him. It was painful to watch.

"I'm not sure I understand," she said, resorting to her tightly wound professor voice. "I always assumed I wasn't the first tourist you've been involved with. Are you just reminding me of that reality?"

He'd made a mistake. He should have told her up front. Chago had been right—this was the train wreck he'd seen coming.

"Not at all," he said.

Gail suddenly laughed. "Wait a minute—you know what?" She smiled and held up her hand, palm out. "We've had a wonderful time together. Let's not ruin it. You don't owe me an explanation about anything." She began to stand up. "I should probably go home and pack."

"Please don't." Jesse placed his hand on her shoulder. "Please." She stayed but angled her body away from him. "Don't shut down on me, okay? I'm telling you this because you deserve the truth."

She lifted her chin. "Then just say it."

"The woman hired a smarmy lawyer and spread gossip about me." Jesse watched as Gail's eyes went huge. "She spun a fantasy about how I smacked her around, got her pregnant and then kicked her to the curb. She took me to court and filed a fictional paternity suit against me. The whole mess was picked up in the tabloids and the celebrity magazines."

Gail reared her head back and frowned. "Was any of it *true?*"

Jesse laughed. "No! Of course not! It took a ton of money and a few years off my life span, but I got everything thrown out. She was a nut job."

Gail nodded very slowly. "I'd like to say I'm sorry for the pain she caused you." Her eyes were earnest, hurt. "But why did you pick this moment to tell me about her? You wanted me to know there was another spring-break slut before me, is that it? That you've done this kind of thing before?"

"Oh, God, no," Jesse said, his heart breaking. This was a nightmare. "You are nothing like her, Gail. There's no comparison."

"Then why are you telling me this?" Gail's voice was ominously flat. "And better yet—why would celebrity magazines give a rat's ass about what happened between a tourist and a part-time tour guide? And where did that 'ton of money' come from?"

Jesse automatically tried to touch her but she recoiled. Clearly, she wasn't interested in his touch.

"Did you teach her to salsa?" Gail's lips began to quiver. "How about skinny-dipping at a private beach? Did she get the VIP treatment like I did, with the dolphins and the private lunches and the fancy dresses and everything else you did to make me feel so special?"

Jesse raked his fingers through his hair. This was worse than he imagined it would be, and he hadn't even gotten to the good part. "Please hear me out."

"I thought I already had." Gail stood, reaching for her robe. She whipped it off the floor and onto her body, yanking hard on the sash around her waist. "You just said you were falling in love with me and you wanted me to come back soon, but this—" Gail waved her arm around. "It's like you're giving me a warning not to get my hopes up, that I'm not all that special after all, that you did this before and you've always regretted it."

She turned away from him. Jesse leaped from the bed. "Gail, don't. That's not why I'm telling you."

"Then why?" she asked, spinning around.

"Because I need to explain to you who I am. She targeted me because I'm sort of famous. She wanted my money and her fifteen minutes on TV."

Even in the low light, Jesse could see Gail's face drain of color. *"Sort of famous?"*

Jesse grabbed his own robe from the bedpost and hastily wrapped it around himself. He flicked on the bedside lamp.

"You know how I told you I was a writer?"

She nodded, frowning.

"I'm J. D. Batista. I'm a bestselling suspense writer. Have you ever heard of the 'Dark Blue' series set in the Keys?"

Gail turned her head to the left and stared off into space, as if she was trying to conjure up a distant memory. "Vaguely," she said, looking at him again, her eyes suddenly devoid of emotion. "Then again, I've never really cared for that kind of trash."

Her words stung. "Okay. I deserved that."

Gail laughed. "This is hilarious," she said, the sarcasm oozing from her voice. She put a shaking hand to her mouth before she went on. "So let me see if I got this straight—you lied to me about your writing, telling me that you *hoped* to be published one day when you already had a major career? And you did this because you thought I was another psycho tourist out to get you?" The tendons in Gail's neck stuck out like guitar strings. "Is that what this is all about?"

Jesse couldn't help but see the irony of the situation. Gail Chapman was the only woman whose opinion mattered to him, and she was sickened by his deceit and thought his work was trash.

This hadn't turned out the way he'd hoped.

"Gail, please listen. I only wanted to be sure you liked me for who I was as a person before you knew I had money and fame." Jesse's legs felt weak. He'd blown it with her. He knew it. "I always planned to tell you."

Gail laughed bitterly. "Really? When? When I was already home? When I came upon your books in some Walmart somewhere?" She flapped her arms in agitation. "Or maybe you wanted to wait until after I'd fallen completely, totally in love with you! Oh, wait—that's already happened!"

"Please forgive me. I made an awful mistake."

"You know what the worst part is?" Gail's cheeks had become red and blotchy with anger. "You *knew* how important honesty was to me! I told you, Jesse. I told you that I'd been burned by a lying, cheating, embezzling asshole, and that honesty was the only thing I absolutely had to have from a man."

Jesse's head felt as if it would explode. In trying to

protect himself, he'd hurt her. "I am so sorry," was all he could say.

Gail wasn't finished. She poked a finger in his chest. "But think about this—however bad that girl hurt you, Curtis hurt me more. It was my *husband* who betrayed me, not some tramp from the vacation house next door. Yet I still opened up to you, Jesse! I had the courage to be myself with you!"

He'd never felt this low in his life.

Gail spun around. She headed out his bedroom door and made a beeline directly toward his office, the door to which he'd intentionally left closed whenever she came to the house. Jesse watched her flip on the light and stand in the doorway, nodding.

He came up behind her and leaned an arm on the doorjamb. He'd never before felt queasy with embarrassment at the sight of his framed book covers and rave reviews.

Gail spun around to find that his arm blocked her way out. She stared at him with cold, hard eyes. "The tragedy is that I *did* love you for who you are—who I *thought* you were, anyway—and if I'd known from the start that you were some famous mystery writer I would have found a way to love you *in spite of it!*"

"It's really more suspense than mystery," he couldn't stop himself from saying.

She shook her head in disbelief. "You're a total dipshit, J. D. Batista. Hey, that must be what the 'D' stands for! Dipshit!" She ducked under his outstretched arm and raced down the stairs in her bare feet. He ran after her.

"Gail, wait! You can't just walk out. We need to talk!"

"I don't want to talk to you right now," she said, reaching for the front doorknob and looking over her shoulder. "I'll let you know when and *if* I ever feel like talking to you again."

Jesse placed his hand on her back, but she jerked away from his touch. Those soft brown eyes burned.

"Oh, I almost forgot!" she said, preparing to slam the door behind her. "Thanks for the vacation memories!"

## CHAPTER EIGHT

JESSE SAT AT HIS DESK. He stared out the window at the banyan tree, his first cup of morning coffee in his hand, still reeling from what had happened with Gail the night before. What his agent just told him hadn't improved his mood any, either.

His publisher had said no on the two-week extension request. They wanted the manuscript by 10:00 a.m. the next day. But for good reason, Beverly told him in an excited voice. They'd moved up the pub date of that book by six whole months. And they'd decided to send him out on tour with his summer release.

"This is a sure sign that they believe in you, Jesse, that they're certain you can turn those numbers around." Beverly waited for some type of enthusiastic response from him, but when she didn't get one, she continued on. "I'm not sure you realize how big this is. Authors aren't getting this kind of support right now, Jesse, not in this economy. And they're behind you even though your numbers are down."

He didn't say anything.

"Jesse? Do you hear what I'm saying? Isn't this *fabulous?*"

Not exactly.

Gail was leaving in twenty-four hours, the exact same time his publisher expected to have his completed manuscript in hand. How was he supposed to send in a halfway decent manuscript and win Gail back at the same time?

Jesse got up from his chair and began to pace. "So I guess this isn't a good time to tell you that I was about to ask for a two-week extension on top of the two-week extension they just nixed?"

Beverly didn't answer right away. "No," she eventually said. "That wouldn't be smart."

He walked back and forth in front of the eight custom-framed book covers hanging at precise intervals on his office wall, knowing in his heart that Gail had been right. He was a dipshit.

His agent had one more point to make, apparently. "I have to ask you, Jesse, what's going on in your life that's more important than your career? You seem quite distracted. You're not having more problems with that crazy tourist, are you?"

He stopped pacing and leaned a hip up against the windowsill. For some reason, all he could think of was the moment Gail first slipped her hand into his, just before he took her on the moped tour. Before that day had ended, she would have revealed her heart to him, made him laugh and pranced around in a dental floss bikini for him.

Jesse stood straight, the truth of it suddenly hitting him like a boat anchor upside his head. When he'd told Gail he was falling for her, he'd meant it. But it was more than that. Gail Chapman was the only woman he wanted. She was the one he'd been looking for. And it was as simple as that.

"Did I lose you, Jesse?"

"Nope," he told his agent. "Still here."

"Is everything all right in your world?"

Jesse laughed. He could never tell Beverly what was going on. If he told her that a really special woman was staying in the rental house next door and he'd fallen in love with her, his agent would dump his ass as a client. Then she'd send an emissary to Key West to track him down and shoot him where he stood. And Jesse wouldn't blame her one bit.

"Everything's fine," he said.

"Then get the manuscript to them by tomorrow morning."

He shook his head, disgusted with himself. How had he gotten into this mess? He had to finish a book and win Gail back—at the same time. "Fine. Tell them it's on the way."

He hung up. He sat down at his desk once more, knowing he wouldn't be getting up anytime soon.

HOLLY SCOOTED THE CHAIR closer to the desktop computer and signed in to her Internet account, warning everyone that her typing might not be up to snuff on a strange keyboard.

"Then let me do it," Hannah said, pulling up the chair to her right.

"Oh, no you don't." Holly shook her head. "This is my mother's heartache, so it's only right I should get the honors."

Gail took the seat to the left of her daughter, cautiously sipping at the hot cup of coffee in her hand. It had taken some convincing, but she'd agreed to accompany the girls to the Internet café in Old Town to do a little research on J. D. Batista, master of fiction, in both his books and his life.

She had nothing else to do. They were leaving the next morning. Besides, she'd cried so much that they were out of tissues at the house.

"Okay, girls!" Holly said in what Gail thought was a voice far too perky for the occasion. "Get on Google and let's search the living crap out of him!"

A couple of clicks on the keyboard, and there he was. That sure didn't take long. Gail had to admit that Jesse looked exceptionally handsome in his publicity shot, and that yes, the picture did look familiar. She'd probably seen his face and his books in a dozen bookstores over the years, but since she didn't read that stuff, it never registered with her. She peered closer to the photo, deciding something looked off about him. He wasn't wearing his little silver earring, for starters. He was clean-shaven. And his eyes seemed friendly but empty somehow. Flat.

Gail sat up straight. Her chest pulled tight. The reason Jesse's publicity picture looked strange to her was that it wasn't the Jesse she knew. What she was looking at was his public face, and she'd seen him only on his home turf. Gail had become accustomed to Jesse's eyes when he looked at *her*—when they made love, danced, laughed together, or walked hand in hand. Maybe he'd been himself with her that week, after all.

"Check this out!" Holly pulled up several articles about Jesse's legal troubles. Gail had to admit the woman who made the charges was easy on the eyes. She looked elegant. She looked *believable*. But when Holly read aloud some of the ugly details, Gail felt nauseous.

The woman's claims made Jesse sound like a monster. Granted, Gail had known him only for nine days, but never once had she seen any of the traits his accuser described. Gail had seen only generosity, tenderness and passion. Until last night, that is, when he dropped the "full disclosure" bomb on her.

"I don't like spying on him like this," Gail suddenly announced, rising from her seat near the computer. "I've seen enough to know that Jesse told me the truth about who he is and what happened with that woman. I don't need to know anymore."

"Ah, c'mon, Ms. Chapman!" Hannah said, smiling. "If you're getting back into the dating scene, you're definitely going to need to know how to do this!"

That sure buoyed her spirits. "I'll be over by the window. Let me know if anything really bad comes up."

Holly looked at her as if she was crazy. "This isn't bad enough for you?"

Gail took a deep breath. How was she going to explain this to her daughter? She never wanted Holly to think it was all right for a man to deceive a woman, because it never was. That had been the central lesson in Gail's catastrophic marriage to Curtis.

But Gail knew that the older a person got—and the more complicated their history became—the less black and white the world was. Jesse hadn't told her the truth about his career. Fine. But if she'd been in his position, would she have done things any differently? Perhaps not. And he'd shared everything else with her, hadn't he—his home, his city…his heart?

"Look," she told the girls. "Jesse fell for that woman there on the computer. She trapped him, blackmailed him and tried her best to destroy his career." Gail shrugged and turned toward the window table, speaking more to herself now than Holly and Hannah. "The whole thing made him wary. So when I showed up, he did what he had to do to protect himself. Unfortunately I got hurt in the process. But unlike the woman who set out to destroy him, Jesse didn't hurt me intentionally. He just didn't think of the consequences of his actions."

"Thanks for that teachable moment, Mom," Holly said.

Gail collapsed into a chair in the sunshine. She stared out the window of the café, remembering the talk she and Jesse had their first day together, when he'd arranged for their private luncheon. She'd asked him how he could afford his lifestyle, her worst fears being drug smuggling, embezzlement and the mafia. She'd never even thought to ask him about popular fiction.

She sat quietly, drinking her coffee, while Holly and Hannah continued their cyberinvestigation. When they believed they were sufficiently informed, Gail said she was going to take a walk to the bookstore. Curiosity had gotten the better of her. "Do you want to come with?"

"Sure," Holly said, smiling. "Nestor and Luis are working today. We were going to stop in anyway."

"May I help you?"

A short, round man with a friendly face wandered over to Gail as she perused the aisles. It seemed odd to her that the books were spaced so far apart on the shelves, as if the bookstore owner had depleted his inventory or was preparing to go out of business.

"Yes, hi," Gail said. "I was looking for J. D. Batista's novels, and I assumed that you'd carry them, since he's a local author. Do you know if the other bookstore in town has them in stock?"

The man's eyes bugged out, but he said nothing, which Gail found odder still. Just then, Luis and Nestor spotted the girls and strolled over, trying to look cool when they were clearly thrilled that they had visitors.

"Hey," Hannah said, playfully grabbing at Nestor's arm. "Why didn't you guys tell us who Jesse was?"

Nestor shrugged. "Because Dad told us he'd kick our asses to Cuba if we—"

"That's enough." Obviously, the man was the boys' father and Jesse's friend. It was all starting to make sense to Gail.

"Get outta here. Take the day," he said to his sons, and they were happy to oblige.

"Bye, Mom, we'll check in later!" Holly said, heading for the front door of the bookstore. Suddenly, she stopped and turned. "You'll be okay?"

"Absolutely," Gail answered her.

Once the group had gone outside, the man sighed deeply and extended his hand to Gail. "My name is Santiago, but my friends call me Chago," he said, smiling. He motioned for Gail to walk with him. "This is my store."

"I'm Gail," she said.

"Yep, I figured as much," he said with a chuckle. "Jesse said you were beautiful, and he was right."

She smiled tightly. "How sweet of him."

"So, he finally told you everything, huh?"

Gail nodded. "What a dipshit," she mumbled.

Chago laughed so hard she feared the few remaining books would come tumbling off the shelves. "Yeah, my friend wasn't thinking straight, unfortunately. He was determined to wait a few days until he told you who he was."

She nodded. "So it seems."

He led her to the stockroom, warning her to stand back. The room was packed floor to ceiling with books. Chago cleared his throat before he spoke again. "If it helps at all, Jesse told me that you were really special, that he could see something happening with the two of you, something long-term."

She nodded, acknowledging Chago's loyalty to his friend. It was sweet. Then she looked around the stockroom and laughed out loud. "Let me see if I get the picture here," she said. "Jesse actually told you to hide all his books? So I wouldn't see them on display?"

Chago chuckled again then pointed behind Gail's back. She turned to see a huge poster-sized version of his publicity photo propped against the wall.

"That ugly mug would've been pretty hard to miss," Chago said with a shrug. "Be careful where you step, Miss Gail. Maybe you should tell me which book you want and I'll get it for you. Probably safer that way."

"I have no idea what I want," Gail said, immediately aware of the appropriateness of that statement.

"Ever read any of his stuff before?" Chago asked.

"Nope."

"You should probably give him a chance, you know," Chago said.

"I'm here to buy his books, aren't I?"

A frown marred Chago's pleasant face as he looked up at Gail. "I meant him as a person, not his books. There are plenty of assholes out there who write good books. Trust me on that."

Gail laughed.

"Jesse is a real decent guy, though," he said. "He always has been. He has his eccentricities and all that, sure, and he locks himself away like a monk when he's on deadline, which takes some getting used to, but he treats everyone in his life real good. If he doesn't deserve another shot, I don't know who does."

Gail swallowed hard. Suddenly, it was all she could do not to cry. How could something so wonderful have gotten so messed up, so fast? "All right, then," she said, trying to sound sprightly. "Which book do you recommend?"

Chago smiled. "Start with his first one so you can familiarize yourself with the characters." He reached over and grabbed a hardcover book with a dramatic dust jacket, the image of a menacing storm bearing down on a small boat.

Gail held it in her hand then flipped it over, finding the same publicity photo. She couldn't help but smile seeing his face. "How many books are there in the series?" she asked.

"Eight, and number nine is set for release later this summer. He's writing number ten now."

Chago nodded toward a dozen cartons stacked near the back fire exit. "I'm not allowed to put the new one out yet."

"I'll take all eight," Gail said.

Chago's eyes went big again. "You sure? You need some help getting them home?"

Gail shook her head, showing him her large straw bag. "Fill 'er up," she said.

By 4:00 P.M., HE'D LEFT six messages on her cell phone and sent flowers and chocolates to the house, but she wasn't ready to talk to him. She wasn't entirely sure how to proceed.

Would tomorrow be the end of something fun but foolish, or the start of something with potential?

Gail did what she always did in times of indecision. She called Kim and laid out the whole story for her, edited for modesty's sake, of course.

"Holy shit," Kim said after hearing everything that had happened in the last few days. "I love that guy's books!"

Gail rolled her eyes.

"And you said you wouldn't let anything happen to you down there," Kim added. "Boy, were you wrong!"

She laughed softly. "Kind of looks that way."

Kim had some logical advice, as always. She told Gail that giving Jesse an opportunity to redeem himself wasn't a sign of her own weakness or gullibility. "The man made a bad call, but that doesn't necessarily mean he's a Curtis Chapman clone," Kim said. "He's already apologized, right? He knows he screwed up. So whatever you do, don't get on that plane without talking to him. Hear him out."

"All right," Gail said.

"What kind of chocolates? What kind of flowers? You didn't say."

Gail laughed at her friend again. "Three dozen yellow tulips and a dozen truffles from a local *chocolatier*."

Kim didn't say anything. Gail couldn't even hear her breathe. For a moment, she thought she'd lost cell phone reception. "Kim?" she asked. "Are you there?"

*"Not Curtis Chapman, not Curtis Chapman..."* Kim

said in monotone. "Just keep repeating that phrase over and over to yourself."

When they hung up, Gail leaned her head back against the comfortable poolside lounge chair. The sun was hanging low in the sky. She'd be flying back to Philly in eighteen hours.

Gail's eyes dropped to the hardback book in her lap. As it turned out, Jesse's first novel was extremely well written. The story was full of double crosses and characters the reader didn't know if they should trust. It had great sex and witty dialogue and a plotline that made Gail never want to leave the world she'd entered.

In other words, Jesse's first novel was a lot like the week she'd just spent in his company.

She sighed, twisting around to look up and behind her, trying to see through the thick foliage to Jesse's house. It looked as if the lights had just come on upstairs.

Kim had been right—he wasn't Curtis. And Chago had been right—he was a decent guy who deserved another shot.

Besides, there was no point in denying the most important reality of all. Gail had broken the number one rule for any spring breaker. She'd gone and fallen in love.

She was totally sprung.

A LOUD BANGING JARRED Jesse out of his writing stupor. For a moment, he wasn't sure if the sound was real or if it had happened in his head, where an entire city block had just gone up in a cloud of black smoke as part of the climactic action sequence.

No. The sound was real, he decided. Someone was banging on his front door loud enough to wake the dead.

"Shit, shit, *shit*," he said to no one. He glanced at his computer to check the time. He was almost going to make it. He'd designated eight hours of his day to rush through one last edit, then he would be emailing the manuscript to New York. He didn't give a damn how much work it still needed, which was unlike him. Jesse had always prided himself on the fact that he turned in near-perfect manuscripts that hardly ever needed revisions. It was his trademark.

But not this time. If they wanted his manuscript, they could have it. He'd do revisions later. It didn't matter. He had a life to live.

The woman he loved was getting on a plane in the morning, and there was still a lot to be settled between them. He had a whole lot of apologizing to do. They had plans to make for their future.

The banging continued. "What the fuck do you want from me?" he asked the gods, raising his arms over his head. He couldn't break now! He'd built in just enough time for a quick shower before he went over there and professed his love to Gail. If he stopped now, there would be no shower, and therefore a much-reduced chance at winning her back.

The truth was, she hadn't returned his calls or acknowledged the flowers or candy. She might have decided to go out for dinner, ruining his plans for the night, or she might have even taken an earlier flight, ruining his future. But the last time he looked, she was still over there at poolside, her back to him, reading or sleeping, he couldn't tell which, but obviously not too distraught over their argument. So he simply couldn't stop now, no matter who was at the door. He was minutes away from finishing. He was minutes away from emailing this sucker to New York and getting his ass back to Gail.

The banging continued.

"What is wrong with people?" he muttered, getting up from his chair for the first time in at least three hours, shaking his legs to get the blood back in his limbs. "Have you never heard of the sanctity of a man's home? Do you not realize that some people have fucking contractual obligations? What the fuck is wrong with the world?"

Jesse grabbed the door handle and was about to fling it open and continue his diatribe when he was shocked to his senses. It was Gail. She had a thoughtful smile on her face. She stood on his porch in that same conservative cotton sundress she'd worn the day he met her. But she'd accessorized differently today. His first "Dark Blue" novel was clutched to her chest.

"You're a very good writer," she said.

Jesse couldn't breathe.

"You're still a dipshit, but I'm going to give you another chance, because I know you had your reasons."

Jesse's eyes widened. He must look like hell.

"In fact, you're quite talented."

She opened the book and began to read a paragraph from the second chapter, using her now-familiar English professor voice. When she was done with her recitation, she closed the book and looked him square in the eye.

"This is beautifully economic use of the language," she said. "You don't resort to flowery descriptions or melodramatic dialogue. It's real. It's raw, and your sentences have a driving power to them."

For an instant, Jesse worried he might be hallucinating. Maybe he'd gotten himself dehydrated again. It happened sometimes when he was on deadline.

"It almost reminds me of Hemingway."

Jesse laughed.

"And I apologize for calling your books trash when I hadn't even bothered to read them. My thesis committee board would cringe if they knew I'd committed such a sin."

Jesse smiled. "Apology accepted."

"Are you okay?" Gail asked. "You look pretty awful."

*Talk about economic use of the language.*

"Yeah," Jesse said, rubbing a hand over his rough beard. "I'd hoped to be better groomed when I got down on the ground and groveled before you."

She nodded, giving him a once-over. He was still in the robe he'd worn during their fight the night before.

"I love you, Gail," he said.

She looked up at him, her eyes clear and smiling.

"And I'm truly sorry for not telling you everything about me from the start." The moment the words left him, Jesse felt the weight of exhaustion and relief press down on him. He had to laugh at how ridiculous he was about to sound. "But here's the kicker—my publisher just moved up my deadline to tomorrow morning. I was racing through my manuscript so I could spend time with you before you go."

She cocked her head politely.

"And I don't want you to go, Gail. I really don't want you to go."

She stepped through his doorway and placed herself directly in his embrace. He pulled her tight, smelling her, feeling her heat and the beat of her heart, never wanting the moment to end.

"I accept your apology," Gail said, the words muffled by his robe. "Why don't you shower while I make you something to eat? Then you can finish up."

"Seriously?" he asked her, stunned.

"Sure," Gail said, easing out of his embrace. "You're on deadline. I understand."

Jesse stood in shock for a few seconds. "You do?"

She grinned. "Of course. I love you, too, Jesse."

Jesse gripped her by the shoulders and kissed her hard and fast. "A half hour, tops," he said, already heading up the steps. "And you don't have to cook. I have an eight o'clock reservation for us at the Grand Café. I wanted your last night here to be special. If I hurry, we can just make it."

"That sounds even better." Gail grinned at him from the foyer. "I have a good book to keep me company in the meantime."

## *EPILOGUE*

WHEN THE SMALL PLANE began to descend, Gail's stomach dropped with it. Goose bumps broke out all over her body, just like that first time she'd laid eyes on him, naked from the waist up and yelling at his shutter hinge. It seemed like a lifetime ago.

Within minutes she'd be in Jesse's arms again, where she belonged.

The six weeks had gone quickly, just as Jesse had assured her they would. The days rushed by as they took care of life's business 1,347 miles away from each other. Gail had been swamped finishing the semester and getting Holly's admissions paperwork completed for her freshman year at Penn. For Jesse the focus was a two-week book tour and manuscript revisions. After all the deadline drama, his publisher was thrilled with the finished product, calling it his best novel yet.

Jesse had kept his word. Although the rapid-fire texting of the first few days got old real quick, he kept up with a steady stream of emails and phone calls. And even while he was on tour, he managed to mail her a handwritten love letter once a week, in cursive as flowing and elegant as the words on the page. Gail always saved those letters for nighttime, to read once she was in bed and the house was quiet. She would savor his words, letting the rich cadence of the language fall over her like a velvet blanket. On letter nights, Gail took Jesse with her into sleep, and into her dreams.

Interestingly enough, Gail had decided the separation had been good for them. It had forced them to get to know each other on a deeper level, relying on communication alone to keep the spark alive.

But boy, oh *boy,* had she missed the sex. Since her adventures with Jesse, there was no such thing as being chaste and sane at the same time. Those days were over.

Kim had joked that if she'd known all the good that would come from it, she'd have forced Gail to release her inner harlot years ago. But Gail knew that wasn't how it worked. Gail had met Jesse at just at the right time in both their lives, under the right circumstances and in just the right place.

She tucked her straw bag under the seat in front of her and took a deep breath to calm her nerves as the plane's landing gear touched down. Gail then was put through the hell of waiting for other passengers to gather their crap and get out of the plane. She began bouncing around in her sandals, picturing in her mind how far she'd have to walk from the gate to the unsecured waiting area, and Jesse.

Forget walking. Gail ran. Within seconds she saw him standing beyond the security scanner, a huge bouquet of flowers in his hand and the biggest, widest grin on his face. His earring flashed in the fluorescent lights.

She jumped on him. He crushed her body to his and spun around, kissing her hair, her cheek, her neck, while Gail kept repeating, "I missed you so much. I missed you so much…" The feel of his stubble on her skin made her cry. She was with him. Finally.

Jesse let her slide down the front of his body until her sandaled feet returned to the floor. He grabbed her face in his hands and studied her.

"You're real."

Gail laughed. "Of course I am."

When the tears began to form in Jesse's blue eyes, she felt a tidal wave of tenderness and love for him. It had been a rough go, but he was sure about her and she was sure about him. There were no more doubts. Now, all their focus was on the future.

Their plan was for Gail to spend a month in Key West, while Holly stayed with Hannah's family and got ready for school. Then Jesse would return with her to Pennsylvania, where they'd all spend the autumn together. Beyond that, who knew? Gail was even looking into positions at the community college in Key West. Jesse was willing to live part of the year in Beaverdale. Anything could happen. Everything was possible.

He kissed her quickly then retrieved her bag and the bouquet from the tile floor, where they'd been tossed in the heat of the moment. Jesse slid his arm around Gail's waist as they walked to baggage claim.

"Holly sends her love," Gail said, looking up at him.

Jesse laughed. "Tell me about it. She's been texting me all day, warning me to be on my best behavior."

"No!" Gail said, surprised. "What did she say?"

"Well, I believe her exact words were—" Jesse pulled his phone from his pocket and clicked to his messages— *"Try not to be such an asshat this time."*

Gail gasped. "I don't even know what that means!"

Jesse laughed as he shoved the phone back in his pocket. "I get the general drift."

"She thinks you're great, you know," Gail said, grinning at him. "She told all her friends that I'm dating a famous writer."

"A famous asshat," he said, and they both laughed.

After they waited for her luggage, they walked out to the parking lot together. Gail felt the heat slam into her.

"It's so good to be back!" she said, stretching her arms out in the humid air.

"Have you thought about what you'd like to do while you're visiting Key West?" Jesse's eyes were full of humor as he tossed her suitcase into the trunk of his car.

"Of course. I made a list," Gail answered.

"Is it a long list?"

"Very. An entire month's worth of activities."

Jesse came toward her, his grin getting bigger as the distance between them disappeared. He nudged her until her butt hit the side of the car then pressed his hard and strong body against hers.

"Do we have to do them in any particular order?" he asked.

"That won't be a concern."

"Oh? And why's that?"

Gail gazed up into his dark blue eyes, wagging her eyebrow teasingly. "Because there's only one item on my list, but I want to do it over and over again."

Jesse laughed, moving in for the kiss. "I'm sure that can be arranged, my wild one."

\* \* \* \* \*

# JUST ONE TASTE

## Victoria Dahl

* * * *

This story is for Tara.
Thanks for bringing me back to Boulder.

Dear Reader,

Welcome back to Colorado! The first time I saw Boulder I couldn't believe it was a real place. For a girl who grew up on the plains, Boulder looked like a magical town plucked from a television show. (Specifically, *Mork & Mindy*. It was set here.) But the real town is even better than anything you'd see on film. Boulder is a stunningly beautiful place. There are mountain peaks, aspen groves, ice-cold creeks and gorgeous neighborhoods. And there are the people of Boulder, who are smart and creative and take pride in being a local.

I hope they don't mind that I've added a few more locals to the mix with the Donovan family. This family of three siblings runs Donovan Brothers Brewery right in the heart of Boulder. Tessa is the youngest of the family and the only sister, but she keeps her brothers wrapped around her little finger…while she keeps them in the dark about her extracurricular life. Jamie runs the front room at the brewery with ruthless charm and a devastating smile, though he can't manage to get control of his love life. And then there's the oldest brother, Eric...

Eric Donovan took charge of the family and the brewery at the age of twenty-three, and he doesn't have a rebellious bone in his body. He's the soul of responsibility...until the night he meets Beth Cantrell in a hotel hallway and decides there's something to be said for an occasional walk on the wild side. Even the most straitlaced guy needs to loosen up once in a while, and Beth is a woman experienced in small-town discretion.

I hope you come to love Boulder and the Donovan family as much as I do. Happy reading! And I'll see you back in Boulder soon!

All my best,

Victoria

# CHAPTER ONE

ERIC DONOVAN DIDN'T often fantasize about strangling his younger brother. But this time, Jamie had outdone himself, and Eric was glad his brother wasn't within arm's reach.

The roar of the convention hall assaulted Eric's ears, the noise ratcheting his tension to a whole new level as he handed out samples of Donovan Brothers beer to the crowds. Their booth was one of the most popular at the Boulder Business Expo, which was exactly why Jamie was supposed to be handling beer duty. Jamie was the face of Donovan Brothers, after all. Eric worked behind the scenes.

When his phone buzzed in his pocket, he shoved the tray of Flatiron Amber Ale toward the reaching hands and watched half the miniglasses disappear into the feeding frenzy.

"Well?" he snapped into the phone.

"I'm sorry," Jamie said. "I can't track him down. I'm going to have to stay at the brewery to cover his shift."

"Shit," Eric growled, closing his eyes in an attempt to focus his thoughts. "Jamie, this is…less than ideal."

"I'm sorry, man."

"I warned you that it's never a good idea to hire a friend. And that goes doubly for you and the kind of slackers you hang around with. What the hell am I supposed to do now?"

"I sent Henry over. He'll be there in ten minutes."

"Henry is a dishwasher!"

"He can hand out samples as well as anyone else."

Eric wiped a hand over his face and shook his head. "All right. I'll handle it." As usual.

"I'll try to get—"

"Yeah, we'll talk later." The samples of ale were already gone. Eric snapped the phone shut and rushed to play bartender, checking the faces again to be sure they were all middle-aged. No problem there. The expo wasn't exactly bubbling with teenagers.

Eric didn't have his brother's charm or easy way, but he could at least draw a few samples and get them out to the crowds. Unfortunately, he couldn't hand out samples *and* strike a new distribution deal at the same time. Given the choice, he would've pulled out of this local conference altogether rather than miss the chance to negotiate with the owner of High West Air.

The airline was based in Denver and designed to compete with the newer, high-quality airlines. High West offered more legroom, no luggage fees and warm brownies on every flight. And Eric was *this* close to closing a deal to make Donovan Bothers Brewery the only beer on the menu. High West wanted something hipper than a big name brand, and Eric was determined to fill that need. It was a perfect partnership, but the owner of the airline was an arrogant pain in the ass and took pride in never being available for a meeting.

This time, Eric had him cornered. Roland Kendall was at the expo, and Eric was going to nail him down.

Fifteen minutes later, he saw Henry hurrying toward

the booth, and he felt his blood pressure drop a notch or two. This day could still be salvaged from the ruins, regardless of Jamie's screwup. Henry, thankfully, had been outfitted in a brand-new Donovan Brothers polo shirt, so he looked almost like an actual bartender. He also looked closer to seventeen than twenty-one, so Eric could only pray the kid had brought his ID in case the authorities stopped by.

"Mr. Donovan," he panted. "Jamie said—."

"Can you draw a beer?"

"Yes, sir."

"Okay, keep the samples going out. Be polite. Smile. Ask for ID if anyone looks under thirty-five. And direct any questions to me. All right?"

"Sure. No problem."

Keeping one eye on Henry to be sure he could handle the task, Eric pulled out his phone and placed a call to Roland Kendall. "Yeah?" a harsh voice answered.

"Mr. Kendall, this is Eric Donovan. I'm hoping to take you to lunch today."

The man grunted in response. He was a grouch, no question about it, and he loved being the one with the upper hand. "I can't do lunch," he barked. "I'm getting together with a supplier."

A *real* supplier, he meant. Eric ground his teeth together, hard. He'd been working this bastard for six months. "Dinner then?"

"Not tonight."

He tempered his voice, hoping to hide his frustration. "How about tomorrow? Mr. Kendall, you know how determined I am to secure this contract. Give me one chance to tell you what we have to offer."

Another grunt. Eric rolled his eyes.

"We'll talk tomorrow," Kendall said just before the line went dead.

Christ, this guy was killing him. The bastard clearly wanted Eric to do a little more begging. Fine. He was strong enough to handle that if it meant taking the brewery to the next level. Getting his beer into the hands of national travelers would create new demand for the product. And new demand meant new territory.

He snapped the phone shut and rubbed his forehead.

"Mr. Donovan?" Henry called.

Eric took a deep breath. When he looked up, he saw that Henry was scrambling with the glasses but still keeping up. Then Henry tipped his head toward the far edge of the table, and Eric saw a familiar face and found himself smiling for real.

"Donovan!" Andrés Villanueva called with a wave. He was the top chef in Boulder and had just opened another restaurant that the critics were going nuts for. Eric grabbed two samples and headed over.

"Congratulations on all the buzz," he said, handing Andrés a glass. They clicked glasses and downed the ale, and Eric felt marginally more relaxed as the bitter coolness soothed his nerves.

"Hey, we got your new summer wheat on tap," Andrés said. "Really nice. A little hoppier than last year's. I like it. Give my compliments to your brewmaster."

"I will, thanks."

"We're having a tasting dinner tonight in the Evergreen suite. Come by. Seven o'clock."

"I hope you're serious, because I haven't managed to sit down to one of your meals in months."

"Absolutely. Bring Jamie, too."

"He's covering the bar today."

"Damn," Andrés said with a grin. "I was hoping he'd bring a beautiful date I could steal out from under his nose. I swear to God, I almost succeeded with that blonde he brought in last fall."

Eric could only laugh, because he'd be damned if he could figure out which blonde it might've been. "I'll see you at seven."

By the time Andrés moved on to the next booth, Eric's mood was considerably lighter. He wanted to get out from behind the table and mix it up himself, but until his brother got the staffing mess straightened out back at the brewery, Eric was going to be stuck here. He'd better make the most of it.

The brewery was in a unique position. Sure, they needed all the friends he could garner in the food and beverage industry in Colorado, but contacts outside the industry were important too. Donovan Brothers wasn't a restaurant-style business. It was strictly the brewery and tasting room. So to keep their name in the public eye, they sponsored marathons and charity events. They threw parties at the finish line of bike races and worked with up-and-coming art galleries on openings. Eric had worked damn hard to saturate the Colorado market of restaurants and bars, and now it was time to expand.

He worked the crowd until the lunchtime lull then stepped back to return a call from his glassware supplier. Halfway through the conversation, he caught sight of a woman a few booths down. She wore a straight brown skirt that stopped at a respectable length, just a millimeter below her knees, but the fabric cradled her tight ass like a glove. His words slowed to a stop.

"Eric?" the salesman prompted.

"Right. Sorry. Yeah, Wednesday will be fine. I'll see you then." He disconnected, his eyes still locked on the brunette as she laughed and shook her head at a man visiting her table. Her dark hair was pinned up in some sort of professional-looking twist, and she wore a white button-down blouse with her brown skirt. Totally conservative, yet something about her radiated sensuality. Maybe it was the small waist offset by that round little ass. Maybe it was the long neck. Or maybe it was the pair of four-inch dark green heels he glimpsed when she walked to the far end of her booth.

Yeah. It was definitely the heels.

Eric cleared his throat and got busy unpacking more of the souvenir glasses. He stacked them within easy reach of the tap, gathered up the used glasses people had left behind and stowed them in the empty box. Then he glanced toward the other booth again. This time, she was on the phone, looking serious now, nibbling on a fingernail while she listened. Eric watched as her lips closed over the tip of one finger before she shook her head and started talking. He knew he was only imagining the tiny glint of wetness on her nail, but he narrowed his eyes anyway.

She probably wasn't as sexy as he thought she was. He was just stressed. And she had a sweet face that seemed a warning against thinking dirty thoughts. He spared one more look for her curves then put his head down and finished packing. But when he stood and hoisted the box to his shoulder, his eyes swept by her again, and he realized she was watching.

His double take was less than subtle. There was no covering it up. Her eyes slid away, but they touched on him again a second later. Her lips quirked in the briefest of smiles.

With the box on his shoulder, Eric couldn't just stand there staring, so he turned and walked out of the booth, his head buzzing with awareness. He couldn't quite tell her age—somewhere between twenty-five and thirty-five, maybe. Old enough that she wasn't just some pretty face hired to be a marketing bunny.

"I'll be back in five," he called to Henry before heading toward the loading area. He didn't need to walk by her booth, but on the return trip, loaded down with a box of clean glassware, Eric took the long way around, just out of curiosity. He was still fifty feet away when it became clear the woman was no longer at her station.

He was in the middle of a mental shrug when the booth branding became visible. The stylized letters of the sign became words. The words registered in his brain and took on meaning. Eric's mental shrug became a psychic flailing.

Ho-ly *shit*.

No wonder she oozed sensuality. The woman worked for a sex shop. Oh, the sign said "erotic boutique," but a sex shop by any other name was…

Good God.

His pulse sped as he walked by, trying not to stare. But that was probably conspicuous as hell. Every other red-blooded man in the vicinity was staring.

The White Orchid. Hell, even the name was sexy-class, just like the woman. He knew of the place, of course. It was infamous and only a half mile away from the brewery. He'd never been inside, but the art deco-style building appeared completely benign, offering no hint at the naughty wares sold inside. The displays in the large windows were tasteful. High-heeled boots and cute little hats, not a sex toy to be seen. Not in the window, anyway.

Eric's heart pounded as if a bullet had just zipped past his ear, but as he slipped back into the comfort of his safe, unsexy booth, he wasn't sure why. Had his pulse picked up because he'd just avoided a bullet? Or because he'd come so close to an amazing explosion?

Whatever the reason, he kept his eyes straight ahead for the next half hour. Still, his brain spun to a blur with thoughts of what a woman like her might be like if someone got a chance to get close to her.

"BETH," CAIRO GROANED, "I can't take another minute here with these people. It's geek city."

Beth Cantrell nodded as if she understood, but she was occupied with staring at the hunky geek serving beer a few stalls over. She'd taken her lunch when he'd disappeared earlier, hoping she might accidentally run into him in the hall, but no such luck. She was back now though, and enjoying the show.

"Actually, you know what?" Cairo said. "They're not geeks. Geeks can be hot. These guys are just…dweebs. Preppy dweebs."

"Mmm-hmm," Beth agreed. Preppy dweebs were the horror of her friends' existence, but they were Beth's secret, shameful craving. A secret she'd carry to her grave. All the women in her world dated edgy guys. Men with tattoos and piercings. Men who lived alternative lifestyles that matched up perfectly with the alternative girls who worked at The White Orchid. Unfortunately, Beth's image was a bit like a mirage in a desolate sexual desert.

She eyed the dark-haired guy in the blue polo shirt again. She'd caught him looking a couple of times....

Cairo gave a long-suffering sigh. "I told you this was a stupid idea, Beth. A *business* convention? We don't belong here."

That snapped her out of her distraction. "Excuse me? We're a legitimate, profitable local business. How do we not belong at the business expo? I've already arranged a meeting with that cute little slipper company—"

"Oh, right. The kitten heels!"

"And I'm very interested in the tea shop. The owner says there are several tea blends that are supposed to enhance female sexual experience, and she'd love to have a feature in the store. Next winter, we could do a front table with the teas and those white-fur panties. I think we still have that Russian fur cap..." That would be spectacular, now that she thought of it. A mannequin wearing faux-fur bikini bottoms, a little bustier top and the Russian hat, standing next to a table with an array of female aphrodisiac teas. Not with the kitten-heeled slippers, though. Furry snow boots would be perfect. Maybe they could even prop a little teacup in the mannequin's hand...

"Cairo," she said, "do you want to try out one of the teas?"

"Sure, but maybe you should try it instead. When was the last time you had any action?"

No way was Beth going to reveal that answer. "The point is not to torture anyone. I want to know if the teas really increase blood flow to the sex organs. And if they work, you have the perfect outlet—or two—to help alleviate the effects."

Cairo grinned, her gorgeous face brightening to

nuclear levels of pretty. No wonder she had two boy-friends. Two edgy, energetic boyfriends who were happy to entertain Cairo at the same time if that was what she was in the mood for. And she usually was.

Beth was thrilled for Cairo, and a tiny bit envious, but in all honesty, the idea of sleeping with two guys left Beth shaky with anxiety. Still, she hid her nervous thoughts behind a smile. "So will you try the tea?"

"I absolutely will. I'll call you as soon as I know the results."

"Well…take a few minutes to regain your strength first. Or a few hours."

Cairo winked before heading back to the table to pass out more White Orchid magnets and pinup-girl pens. Things had quieted down, but a few men in business suits still hovered nearby. Cairo was adorable with her black pixie cut and sexy '50s outfits. Her little red wrap dress managed to look innocent even as it showed off her fantastic rack and quite a bit of thigh.

The men looked either self-consciously amused when accepting one of the magnets, or they approached Cairo with a lascivious smile. Either way, Cairo could handle them. But Beth was more interested in the women. Women made up ninety-five percent of their clientele, just as Annabelle Mendez had planned when she'd opened The White Orchid fifteen years earlier.

Now Annabelle was off on a "soul-cleansing world tour," and Beth was in charge of everything. Payroll, taxes, purchasing, human resources. Everything. And it felt good. She loved her job. She loved her employees. She loved that she spent her days helping women get closer to their sexual dreams. Too bad Beth couldn't seem to get a handle on her own fantasies.

She glanced toward the guy in the polo shirt one more time and caught him looking again. Sparks zinged through her belly, and she smoothed a hand down the front of her fitted blouse.

God, he was cute. Square, clean-shaven jaw. Dark brown hair cut boardroom short. When he'd picked up that box, his biceps had flexed, stretching the armband of his shirt as if he were in one of those exercise-machine commercials.

He was Beth's preppy fetish come to life. She didn't even want to look at his ass in those khakis. It would drive her mad.

"Focus," she scolded herself. She wasn't here to drool after grown-up frat boys. She was here to make connections with other female-oriented business owners.

"I'm going to take a look at those two jewelry designers I scoped out earlier," Beth said. "When I get back, you can take your lunch."

Beth grabbed her phone so she could take notes and pictures then slipped out of the booth. She knew she'd have to walk past him, but she tried not to think about it. Still, she couldn't stop her hips from swinging a little more fiercely as she approached. She knew the moment his eyes found her. She felt his stare like a stream of light sneaking through pine trees. As she drew even with his booth, her skin warmed.

Part of embracing your sexuality was loving your body, and Beth wasn't modest about her ass. It was her best feature. She loved the shape of it, and this skirt loved it, too.

So she didn't bother lying to herself. She had no doubt he was checking out her ass, and her whole body tingled as she glanced toward the booth. Donovan Brothers

Brewery, the sign read. Air rushed out of her lungs. She knew that place. It was less than a mile away from The White Orchid. She dared a second look toward the table. *Jamie Donovan, proprietor,* read the little cardboard stand on the table.

When she let her eyes rise to him, their gazes met, and she felt her cheeks turn hot as she looked away. He was watching her as she moved on, she knew it, and she could barely hear the echoing noise of the place as she continued down the row of booths.

Jamie Donovan. The name turned through her brain for a moment. She'd heard of him, hadn't she? He was…a bartender. Of course. A notoriously flirtatious bartender who sometimes wore a kilt. Even the girls in the shop had mentioned him on occasion, so he must be something special. But maybe those were just rumors. He didn't strike her as a playful ladies' man. His face was serious and his eyes were cool, and he was obviously an owner of the brewery.

But if he *was* a ladies' man…

An idea took form. A ridiculous thought that she immediately dismissed. But the idea was sticky and sweet and it stuck in her head despite her attempts to bat it away.

She could have a fling. With him. She'd be just one fling among his many, after all. She'd mean nothing to him, and he might be worth the risk.

Still, he lived in her town and worked only a few minutes away from her. "Bad idea," she murmured to herself. If her coworkers found out, she'd never live it down.

Squaring her shoulders, Beth headed toward the first jeweler she'd noticed. But thoughts of Jamie Donovan persisted. Her brain, which was normally cool and logical, was preforming excuses in anticipation of her arguments.

Yes, Boulder was a small town, but it wasn't *that* small. They'd never run into each other before, after all. And Jamie Donovan clearly knew how to navigate these treacherous waters. She'd heard him called cute, funny, sexy and adorable. She'd also heard some serious compliments about what he had going on under his kilt. But she'd never heard him called a dog.

A flush took her face as she honestly considered the idea of flirting with him, testing the waters. But that felt dangerous. Anytime it got beyond flirting, Beth was lost. When you worked at an erotic boutique, men expected something more. Something *better.* And there was nothing more or better about Beth the way there was about Cairo or Annabelle or any of the other bold women she worked with.

Beth was just…regular.

But if it was a fling, it wouldn't matter if he ended up disappointed, not as it did during real dating. There'd be no awkwardness. No breakup. No painful winding down until they "decided to see other people." It would happen and it would be done.

And maybe, just maybe, it would be the sexual adventure she'd been waiting her whole life for.

But surely that was a lot to pin on one poor preppy bartender. Her smile widened with amusement as she waved at the designer she'd come to hunt down. A little sexual fantasy was good for a woman's soul. At least Beth knew her soul would be getting some great fortification tonight.

## CHAPTER TWO

ERIC WAS STUFFED FROM the ten courses of so-called small-bite plates he'd been served at the tasting dinner, but he made himself finish the salted caramel torte that had been set in front him. One, because it was only polite, and two, because it was the most delicious damn thing he'd ever tasted. The only thing missing from the meal had been a good lager, but wine had been a nice change. Not that he'd ever admit that to the person who'd invited him.

"Thank you, Andrés," he said, standing to shake his friend's hand. "Amazing. But next time, don't forget the beer."

"Beer is for peasants," Andrés replied with a wide smile. Eric might have taken offense if he hadn't raised so many pints with him.

"I'll remind you of that next time you stop by the tasting room."

Andrés handed him a little box wrapped with a gold bow. "A torte for your brother. I know how much he enjoys sweets."

"Thanks. Stop by the brewery in a week. We've got an apricot hefeweizen that's almost ready."

"That's a deal, my friend."

Andrés moved on to the next table, and Eric took a last look around. He'd already schmoozed with everyone at the dinner, and he still had a younger brother to yell at, not to mention invoices to review back at his office. So he said his goodbyes and escaped to the quiet of the hallway. He was scrolling through his BlackBerry when he walked around the corner, sparing a glance down the hallway as he did. This part of the hotel was packed with meeting rooms and suites, and the hall was a jumble of corners and alcoves. The hallway jagged to the right about twenty feet ahead, and beyond the corner of the wall, Eric caught a glimpse of one green high-heeled shoe.

The tip of the dark green shoe tapped the floor in a languid rhythm. He watched it closely. His pace slowed.

As he drew closer, Eric saw a delicate ankle, then the curve of a smooth calf. And then he caught sight of the brown skirt.

It was her.

Despite his certainty, he was still surprised when he passed the corner and saw her profile. Her hair was down now, a sexy fall of sable brown that shone beneath the floodlight above her.

She leaned against a glass railing, staring down into the hotel atrium. Her arms rested on the railing, and one knee was bent, the foot still tapping out a secret rhythm against the floor.

Christ, those heels.

She turned her head then, and her gaze met his. For a moment, she looked just as shocked as he felt. Her lips parted. Her brown eyes went wide.

Eric's focus fell to her red lipstick as she recovered herself and smiled.

"Hi," she said, her voice just slightly husky at the edges. "You're Jamie Donovan, right?"

"I—" His fingers twitched as he started to reach out to her. "Actually—"

"I'm Beth," she continued. "Beth Cantrell." Her hand slid into his, distracting him from correcting her.

"Nice to meet you, Beth."

She laughed a little, and his stomach tightened at the sound. "In case you're wondering if I'm a stalker, I saw the sign on your table. That's how I know your name. And you're a little notorious."

"I am?"

She raised one shoulder in a shrug, and her fingers tightened for just a second before she drew her hand away. "Just a *little,*" she answered, her eyes twinkling.

She thought he was Jamie, which was kind of a surprise. He would've expected Jamie to be well-known at a place like The White Orchid. Still, she'd heard about his brother, and her grin was for Jamie, not Eric.

He meant to correct her. He really did. But he hesitated. Eric wouldn't flirt with a woman who worked at a sex shop. He was responsible, careful and risk-averse. But Jamie? Jamie would do way more than flirt with her.

A door opened behind him, and she darted a nervous glance past his shoulder. He followed her gaze, but the man who stepped out of the room moved on down the hallway.

A peek at her ring finger revealed bare skin. "Are you waiting for someone?"

"Oh, no. I just finished a marketing session. I need

to waste a few minutes before the next presentation. It's on tax prep. Are you going?"

"No, I was at a dinner." He gestured down the hallway.

"The Andrés Villanueva dinner? Wow, you are lucky."

"Are you a fan?"

"Who isn't?"

Eric rubbed a thumb over the box in his hand, considering. It was meant for Jamie, but Jamie sure as hell didn't deserve it. If he'd been at the expo as he was supposed to have been, he would've had his damn torte. "You're not one of those women who doesn't eat, are you?"

"No, I am definitely not one of those women."

Offering a wolfish smile, Eric held up the box. "Want a little taste?"

Her dark brown eyes went wide. "What is that?" she demanded.

"It's manna from heaven, also known as salted caramel torte."

"Shut up," she gasped.

He gave the box a little wiggle. "Want it?"

"Yes!"

The lustful anticipation on her face shot heat into Eric's veins. She stared at the box as if it held something naughty. What were the chances that he'd be presenting *her* with a naughty gift?

"Wait here for one second," he said before rushing back the way he'd come. He snuck into the room and snatched a clean fork and a napkin from a wheeled tray.

Still, he hesitated before stepping back into the hallway. He could just hand her the box and the fork and be on his way. Or he could watch her eat it.

Yeah, he was totally going to watch her eat it.

When he walked around the corner, she grinned in delight.

Eric held the fork just past her reach. "I noticed a seating area just past the elevators when I was lost earlier. You've got a few minutes?"

"I do. And if the dessert is everything you say it is, I might even chance being late to the tax seminar."

"A risk taker."

A laugh bubbled from her throat and she pressed a hand to her lips to stifle it. "Not really."

He found that seriously hard to believe. "No?"

"Well…" Her gaze slid toward him and she gave him a quick once-over as they walked. "Maybe tonight I am."

At that moment, Eric decided he was fully committed to taking this just as far as Jamie would. He deserved some fun just as much as the next Donovan Brother, didn't he?

NERVOUS EXCITEMENT SHIMMERED along Beth's skin as she followed the man around a corner and found herself in a small alcove with a coffee table and four chairs. Despite her anxiety, she took a moment to appreciate the picture he presented. He'd changed into dark slacks and a crisp blue button-down shirt. The pants fit him perfectly, showing off his narrow hips and tight ass. Nice.

She had yet to see his infamous kilt, but she didn't mind. In fact, she'd much rather ogle his business attire.

He waved her into a chair before taking the one beside it. Then he handed over the prize.

"I should've grabbed you a glass of wine, too," he said as she tugged at the elaborate gold ribbon.

"Oh, no. Wine before a tax seminar? I'd wake up two hours from now, sprawled across a whole row of chairs."

The ribbon finally sprang free, and Beth made an effort not to tear the cardboard as she yanked it open. Buttery sweetness drifted upward and she sighed. "Oh, man."

"Taste it," he urged.

She crossed her legs, aware that a few inches of her thighs were exposed as the skirt snuck up. She didn't bother easing it back down. Instead, she took the fork he offered and dug in.

"Oh, my God," she moaned as the first bite of salty sweetness hit her tongue.

"Told you."

She swallowed, fighting the urge to moan like a woman being pleasured. But she *was* being pleasured. By caramel and buttery crust and sea salt and chocolate. "Oh, good Lord."

She might sleep with this man just to reward him for the torte.

His eyes watched her mouth. She licked a crumb from her lip and watched his own lips part in response. For a brief moment, she was *that* woman. The woman she pretended to be for her coworkers and customers alike. The woman who *knew* all, because she'd lived all.

Maybe Jamie Donovan's gift was making a woman feel like a sensual goddess. She didn't even mind if this was his standard act, as long as she could push her way onto the stage.

She cleared her throat and looked down at her plate, still afraid to turn the flirtation into something else. Instead, she concentrated on cutting off a perfect bite of torte and savoring every second of flavor as she chewed.

"So," he said slowly, "I passed your booth."

"Oh?" She wished she'd asked for wine now. She'd had a vague hope that he hadn't checked out her booth. That he'd talked her into dessert without any of the complications that came along with a man's awareness of her work.

"Your job must be pretty interesting." He was staying neutral. That was a good sign. People had varied reactions to The White Orchid, but oftentimes men fell into the sly and smarmy camp.

And her job *was* interesting.

Beth let herself smile. "There's never a dull moment."

"I bet. How did you end up working there? Or do you own the shop?"

"No. I interned there almost ten years ago, working for the owner, Annabelle Mendez. Somehow I never left."

He coughed, choking on incredulity, it seemed. "You interned there? Like, as a *kid?*"

"As a *college* student. I was all grown up and legal, I promise."

"But…what did you major in?"

"At first, anthropology, but I just happened upon a class in Cultural Sexuality, and it was fascinating. Then I took a higher-level course in Women's Sexuality Through Western History, and…"

"And *what?*"

"And…suddenly, I found myself transferring to women's studies with a minor in anthropology. I interned at The White Orchid as part of a course, and…here I am. It's my passion."

His eyebrows rose. "I had no idea that kind of passion could be so…scholarly."

"Oh, yeah? How did you think I fell into this?"

"I don't…" An honest-to-goodness blush crept over his cheeks.

Beth couldn't quite believe it. Oh, she saw plenty of blushing customers at the store, but men never blushed because of *her.*

Something like liquid electricity zinged down her spine. Beth studied his face. He had a square jaw and a strong, straight nose. His eyes were smoky blue, almost gray, and his eyebrows were dark slashes above them.

As for his mouth…she could spend hours imagining the feel of those sculpted lips against hers.

"I wasn't thinking anything," he finally offered, his smile both chagrined and charming.

He looked as if he would smell good. Like starch and shampoo. She decided to let him off the hook. "I'll drop it."

"Okay, great." Relief chased across his face.

Beth ate her dessert and weighed her options. He was cute. Hot. Sexy. And well-known for flirtation, though he didn't seem particularly forward. If she was brave enough to indulge her fetish for preppy guys, he might just be the perfect candidate for the job. He wouldn't want anything more from her than she wanted from him. And how would her friends ever find out?

She took another bite to buy herself some time. His

eyes watched as she raised the fork to her mouth. As soon as she swallowed, she shook her head. "I'm sorry. Have a bite."

"No way. It's all yours. I'm just enjoying watching."

"Oh, yeah?" She couldn't help but grin. "Interesting."

His head dropped as he laughed.

Lust spun through her like a vicious flock of butterflies. She wanted this man. She wanted to touch him. Taste him. Feel his skin beneath her hands.

"Jamie—"

"Um, listen. Beth…"

"Yes?"

His lips parted as if he were about to speak, but he shook his head before saying a word. Was he nervous, or was this part of his shtick? If it was, it was totally working for her.

He cleared his throat. "I'd still like to get you a glass of wine. Can I buy you a drink?"

Uh-oh. This was do-or-die time. She'd flirted with him. She was interested in more. But that "more" had nothing to do with being seen in public with him. "You mean at the bar?"

"Actually, there's a wine bar across the street. It's a little less hectic."

Her hands tightened around the box until the ends bowed. "I don't think I can. I've got the seminar. But thank you." Even as the words left her mouth, she felt a surge of disappointment. In herself.

She stood up so quickly that she swayed on her heels. He stood too and reached out to steady her with a respectful hand under her arm. God, he was so cute that it hurt.

"Right," he said. "The seminar. Afterward then?"

"I…"

His mouth looked serious now. He was waiting for her to say no. She was waiting for it too. But that wasn't the word that escaped her lips.

"Okay," she said so softly that he leaned forward.

"Sorry?"

She cleared the fear from her throat. "Okay. I'll meet you there."

"I could walk you—"

"No. I'll be fine. It's just across the street, right? Next to the bridge?"

"That's it. So around nine-thirty? Does that work?"

Beth's muscles were tightening up as her heart began to pound, as if flirting with this man was sending her into fight-or-flight mode. "Sure. Nine-thirty. That sounds great."

The elevator dinged and a crowd of voices suddenly filled the hallway.

Crap. What if someone saw her here, cozied up in this small space with Jamie Donovan and chocolate? It would look just as sinful as it was. Beth's heart beat so hard, she wondered if he could hear it. Certainly his smile was slipping. Probably because she was just standing there, staring wide-eyed at him.

"I've got to go," she finally stammered. "I don't want to be late."

"Of course—" he started, but she cut him off.

"Thank you for the torte. It was so good." She thrust

the box into his hands, mourning the last few bites she hadn't eaten.

"So—"

"I'll see you in a little while," she interrupted then whispered, "Nine-thirty," as she backed away from him.

He looked more than a little confused as she turned and rushed for the corridor. She wanted to reassure him, but she was panicking. Just a little. She told herself there was no reason. They'd arranged to have a glass of wine, not a make-out session. But she was shaking as she rushed past the crowd at the elevators.

She'd done it. Maybe. Certainly, there now existed the possibility of sex with Jamie Donovan.

Wow.

The tax seminar was in the same room her earlier session had been in, so Beth had no trouble finding it, even in her ridiculous state. She burst in, startling the four people who'd already taken their seats.

And when Beth found a seat for herself, she clenched her hands in her lap and looked down to see that she was still holding the fork in one white-knuckled fist. There was no pretending to be the smooth, cool sex-store manager now. He'd gotten a glimpse of the real Beth. He might not even show up for that glass of wine.

*Right,* she told herself. No need to get too excited. He might not show. And if he did, that didn't mean they were going to have sex. And even if they did have sex, there was no guarantee it would be great. Probably it would be just like the other disastrous times she'd tried to expand her sexual horizons.

Beth took a deep breath, filling every single cell of her lungs. Then she let it slowly out, willing all the anxiety from her muscles. Annabelle always said that a woman determined the course of her life with her expectations. If Beth expected disastrous sex, she'd get it in spades. So tonight, she'd expect good things. Great things. Lovely, sexy-bartender things.

She raised the fork to her mouth and licked the last of the sticky caramel from the tines. And Beth thought she just might be tasting heaven.

## CHAPTER THREE

THE LINE OF FERMENTATION tanks gleamed behind the glass wall like works of art. Despite his nervousness, Eric spared the vats an affectionate glance as he walked through the utilitarian kitchen. Given a choice, he'd rather be the brewmaster than the business manager, but somebody had to take care of the business.

His sister, Tessa, was great at the accounting side of things and the paperwork involved with human resources. Jamie took care of the front room and most of the duties that called for time with the public. That left Eric with supervising…everything else.

At least he'd resisted the countless suggestions that they turn the brewery into a restaurant and take on all the extra work that would entail. He wanted nothing to do with that side of the business. Donovan Brothers was a true artisan brewery, focused solely on their product. They brewed in small batches and then bottled and kegged for distribution to restaurants, grocery stores, bars and liquor stores. The front was a tasting room, and the only food they served was pretzels and peanuts. Still, they needed a kitchen to prep for catered parties.

Eric dropped off a box of glasses next to the dishwashing station and headed for the front. He didn't bother pausing to take a deep breath before he pushed open the swinging door. He'd learned from long experience that it would do nothing to temper his irritation with Jamie.

Unsurprisingly, Jamie was delivering a round of beers to a table of attractive women. Also unsurprisingly, the women were laughing and chatting him up while they checked out his legs. Jamie usually wore a kilt while working, claiming that it honored their Scots-Irish heritage. But more likely than not, it was solely about the attention it drew.

Eric shook his head and checked the sales on the register. They were good even for a Friday night. It was spring break at the university, but the exodus had little effect on sales at the brewery. They'd designed the tasting room as an alternative to the other bars in town. It was quiet and comfortable. Celtic rock played over the speakers, and they hosted the occasional band. But the tasting room closed at eight, nine on the weekends, so they didn't draw much of a party crowd. Their customers were grown-ups who just wanted to grab a beer with friends or play a round of pool before heading home.

And strangely enough, more than half their customers were women, not quite the norm for a brewery. Strange, yes, but no mystery.

The women at the table all burst into laughter at something Jamie said, and they made friendly protests when he started back toward the bar with a wave.

Jamie might be irresponsible and laissez-faire, but he was damn good at making the tasting room a place people wanted to be. That was a skill Eric would never acquire.

"Hey," Jamie said as he came around the bar. "How'd it go today?"

He didn't hesitate over the lie. "Nothing unusual. But that bastard Kendall is still leading me on. Maybe dinner tomorrow. Maybe not."

Jamie grunted in answer and began washing pint glasses.

"And you?" Eric asked. "Any luck getting in touch with your friend?"

Jamie didn't look at him. "No. But I talked to his roommate. Apparently Anthony was invited along on a spring-break trip to Cancun and decided he couldn't resist."

"Shit," Eric snapped, grabbing a towel off Jamie's shoulder to wipe down the bar. Not that it needed wiping down. Jamie was meticulous about that, at least.

"Unfortunately, my backup bartender is out of town, too. But Tessa is going to try to help tomorrow, so I can—"

"No. She's been busy enough with tax season. Let her do her job."

Jamie grabbed the towel back and dried his hands. "Look, I'm sorry. Shit happens, man."

Eric met his brother's eyes. Jamie's green eyes looked nothing like Eric's. That reminder was enough to make Eric look away, out over the tables of happy customers. It also threw cold water on his anger. "Yeah. It's all right. We'll deal with it."

"I'd still like to come to the dinner. Maybe I can get away."

Eric shook his head. "I'm telling you, it's not a good idea. He's not going to like you."

"Everyone likes me," Jamie said with a smile.

"God, you're obnoxious. Which is exactly why this guy won't like you. He wants to be the center of attention. He won't appreciate it when the waitress flirts with you and not him."

"We'll see."

"No, we won't see. You hold down the fort. I'll take care of the distribution."

For a moment, Jamie looked as if he might protest. His mouth tightened, his eyes narrowed. Eric was curious what he was about to say, but then Jamie just ran a hand through his hair and shook his head. "Did Henry work out?"

"Yeah, he was great."

"I'll take over the dish-washing while he's working with you then."

"Thank you. That'd be great." A customer raised a hand at the far end of the bar, so Eric slapped Jamie on the back. "I'll be in my office for a few minutes before I head out again. Are you okay here? You need a break?"

"I'm good."

Eric was relieved he wouldn't have to stand in at the tap. He'd had his share of socializing for the day, aside from one very specific person he wanted to see. He told himself he'd chosen the wine bar because it was quiet and they wouldn't have to deal with the crowds at the hotel. The real reason was that it was quiet and they wouldn't be *seen* by the crowds at the hotel.

And if he was really going to use Jamie's name to pursue an unwise affair, the fewer people around, the better.

But was he truly going to do it? At this point, it would be more than awkward to correct her. But it would be irresponsible not to, and Eric was always responsible.

He was also always boring, serious and stressed out.

Jamie, on the other hand, seemed to have found the secret to eternal satisfaction: do what feels good.

Eric had no doubt in the world that Beth Cantrell would feel good.

He glanced at his watch. Just past eight-thirty. He had time to get a little work done before he headed out. He also had time to change his mind and tell her the truth.

For the next five minutes, Eric stared at the computer and brooded. Not quite the same as working.

He'd meant to tell her his real name. He really had. He was Eric, after all. The brother who always did the right thing. The brother who would never use falsehood as a seduction. Then again, Eric didn't really engage in seduction at all. He dated. Sometimes. But with Beth it wasn't about a date. He wasn't hoping for the beginning of a relationship. There was something hotter than that between them. Something urgent. Wasn't there?

Maybe if he hadn't watched her eat that torte, he could've just let it go. But he *had* watched her eat it. She'd savored it. Moaned over it. Her eyelashes had fluttered and closed. Her lips had parted on a pleased sigh. Her tongue had darted out to moisten her mouth and capture his attention.

There'd been nothing good or clean about her then. Not one single thing. And she made Eric want to be dirty, too.

Maybe it was the wrongness of what he was doing that caused vivid excitement to awaken every nerve in his body. He felt…alive. Intrigued. Guilty and righteous all at once.

He rubbed both hands over his face and forced himself to open his email window. He deleted some messages and scrolled through a few more. He reviewed a few invoices and signed off on the larger checks that needed two signatures.

By the time he finished up, it was nine. As he stood and grabbed a jacket, Eric knew he wasn't going to tell Beth his real name. What the hell did it matter? Jamie was just a name to her, a reputation. Eric was real flesh and blood, and he wasn't going to lie to her about that. No, that he could offer her with complete and utter honesty.

BETH HADN'T BEEN IN DANGER of falling asleep during the seminar, at least. She'd been wide awake and anticipating this walk across the street.

As usual, a few steps down the path toward living out a fantasy and Beth was a nervous wreck. She paused on the sidewalk to close her eyes and visualize sexual success.

She believed with every fiber of her being that women needed physical fulfillment as much as men did. That women should feel free to seek out their pleasure as earnestly as men did, whatever that pleasure might entail. But she couldn't seem to *discover* what hers was. She had trouble relaxing enough during sex to get off. She had no interest in group sex or spanking or other women. She wasn't turned on by whips or latex or leather. Her only *kink* was preppy boys, for God's sake, a desire so vanilla it couldn't even be called a kink. There had to be something else that would get her engine running, something more interesting, something hot enough to distract her from her own thoughts.

But maybe it wasn't some*thing,* but some*one*. Because Jamie Donovan made her warm in very special places. And when she walked into the bar and saw him, those special places ratcheted from warm to hot.

Hands in his pockets, he leaned against a red-velvet banquette toward the back of the bar. She couldn't see his expression in the dim lighting, but somehow she already knew the shape of his wide shoulders and the line of his bent head as he stared at the floor. His sleeves were rolled up, and his hair was mussed as if he'd run a hand through it more than once.

She was only five feet away when he looked up. His blue-gray eyes sent sparks down her spine. When the sparks reached low enough, lust exploded like fireworks inside her. The man looked for all the world like a furious, determined, *sexy* stockbroker forced to work overtime to address a financial crisis.

He looked like a preppy *god*.

And Beth was the troublesome financial crisis. Oh, wow.

A waitress brushed past her, but Beth was stuck, held to the ground as his frown edged up into a smile.

"Hello," he said.

"Hi."

"I got a booth…" He stepped back and gestured toward the deep circular booth. The only light provided was a flickering candle in a beaded lamp. As if he were reading her mind.

She slid into one side, and he slid in opposite, and they were cocooned in dark red velvet. Beth could just see the edge of the bar and a dark hallway beyond it.

"I forgot to get your number," he said, flipping open his phone.

"Oh, right." She scrambled to get her own phone out of her purse. Was this the point at which she told him she wasn't looking for a relationship? Should she type BOOTY CALL next to his name so he'd get the idea? She typed in a simple "Jamie Donovan" and tried to think of a diplomatic way to say "please don't use my number after tonight."

Her mind worked frantically as they exchanged numbers. Her hand trembled as he handed her the wine list. She had to say something, right? Or should she just let things take their natural course? "Jamie…" she finally blurted out—and a waitress appeared as if by magic.

"What would you like this evening?" the girl asked.

Good question.

He smiled. "Do you have any recommendations?"

*Yes,* Beth thought. *How about the hottest sex I've ever had and not a peep out of you afterward?*

The server rattled on, but Beth couldn't concentrate. He had spread his hand out on the table, and she could only stare at it. That hand might be touching her later.

"Beth?" he prompted.

"Oh! What are you going to have?"

"The Shiraz, but I'm no wine expert. You might want to—"

"I'll have that, too."

He gave her a helpless smile and shrugged. "Okay, two glasses of the Shiraz." When the waitress disappeared, he leaned closer. "We should've gone somewhere with beer. I'd feel much more confident and manly while ordering."

Beth couldn't keep up her worried monologue when he was smiling so close to her. And she'd been right about him. He did smell good. Like starched cotton and soap. As though he should be on the cover of a Polo catalog. Beth's heart shook with nervous joy. "You seem manly enough."

"Oh, manly *enough?*"

"Maybe," she answered with a grin. "Notice I qualified it with 'seem.'"

"Ouch. I didn't know you were into sadism."

She laughed, but his smile slipped a little.

"Um, you're *not* into sadism, are you?"

"Oh, God," she laughed, tears springing to her eyes in amused relief. He looked so *worried.* Did he only want her to be a normal girl? What a nice change. "No," she finally said. "I am not a sadist. Or a masochist, if that's your next question."

"Good. I didn't think you looked—I mean, not that people look a certain way. Or that I thought this was leading to a… That we would… Ah, shit."

He leaned his head back against the cushion as Beth laughed until she couldn't breathe.

"I'm sorry," she gasped.

"Oh, no. I'm pretty sure I'm sorry."

The waitress delivered their wine and he snatched his up with a muttered, "Thank God."

If he was nervous, then maybe this was okay. Maybe she wasn't a failure. Maybe this kind of sexual tension was *supposed* to make you nervous.

She suddenly felt so much better that she scooted a little closer while he wasn't looking and clicked her glass against his. "Cheers."

He opened his eyes and his gaze dipped to her mouth as she put the glass to her lips. "Cheers," he murmured back.

"Mmm. It's good. Your manhood is safe with me."

He tasted the wine and his eyebrows rose. "That is good. How could you ever have doubted me?"

"I didn't really. In fact, I've heard amazing things about you."

"Oh." A pink flush rose up his face.

"I'm sorry. Was that rude? It's just that…"

"Beth—"

"Listen," she interrupted. "I just…" She leaned even closer. Her arm brushed his, and the crisp hair on his forearm sent pleasure sizzling through her. "Jamie," she whispered, "can I be completely honest with you?"

## CHAPTER FOUR

ERIC WAS FILLED WITH a strange and arousing mixture of lust and guilt. Her arm slid along his, and a very interesting amount of cleavage was exposed when she leaned so close to him. She was the sexiest woman he'd ever met, and every time she said "Jamie" it was rubbing his conscience raw. Now she was offering complete honesty?

He would have stopped her if he hadn't been so intent on hearing her thoughts.

"You know where I work."

He nodded and watched her pink lips touch the edge of her glass. She drank, and when she lowered the wine, her lips were even pinker. Ruby-red and touched with dampness. Eric's mouth went dry.

He felt hypnotized, and when her knee brushed his, he reached automatically to touch it. Beth inhaled sharply, and those ruby lips parted just the tiniest bit.

"Because of my job," she continued, the words slightly breathless. "You might think…"

Fascinated by her response and drawn in by her soft skin, Eric rubbed his little finger along the inside of her knee. She edged her leg closer to his, parting her knees, giving him space. His mind tumbled over in a primal surge of victory.

"What I'm trying to say," she whispered, "is that I don't usually do this."

"This?" he repeated. Her skin was so hot. He spread his fingers wider, edging them past her knee to her thigh.

"Yes," she breathed. "This." And her hand pressed atop his.

This was wrong. Because she didn't know who he was. Because they were virtually strangers. Because they were in public. But wrong felt better than he'd imagined it could.

Wrong felt like the silky heat of her thigh as she dragged his hand higher. It felt like her skirt easing up as he slid beneath it. And it felt like her muscles trembling as she edged her legs farther apart.

Eric suddenly regretted that he'd spent his life doing the right thing. Instead, he wanted to do...*this*.

His fingers brushed the satiny fabric between her legs. Her breath caught in her throat, and Eric ceased breathing altogether. Her muscles tightened as she tried to spread her knees farther, but the material of the skirt was too narrow around her thighs.

Eric didn't mind. He didn't plan to go further than this. This place, where he could slip his fingers between her thighs and rub just there.

Beth bit back a little whimper, cutting it off before it became a moan. She let go of his wrist and put her hand on his thigh instead. He held still, settling in to the idea that he was really doing this, giving himself just a few seconds to decide that he was.

He pressed circles against her clit, feeling the satin grow wet under his touch, feeling her thighs tremble.

He didn't pause even when a group of people passed by, their voices filling the booth for a moment.

She choked on a gasp, but no one could see past the front of the table. Eric had made sure of that, in the interest of privacy, but he hadn't anticipated they'd need it quite this much.

As her breathing grew more ragged, her fingers dug into his thigh. She stared straight ahead, her expression caught somewhere between pleasure and worry.

Was she an exhibitionist? Was that her thing? Eric didn't give a damn as long as she kept making those soft, whimpering sounds. As long as she clutched his thigh as if he was anchoring her to the earth.

"Oh, my God," she whispered.

He didn't move in to kiss her. He didn't dare get any closer. As it was, if the waitress reappeared, she would see nothing more than a man turned slightly toward a woman as they talked. So instead of kissing her, Eric watched her face closely. Redness touched her cheeks like rouge. Her pulse beat hard in her throat. He increased the pressure against her clit, and the skin around her eyes tightened as her pupils went wider.

Someone spoke loudly in the booth next to theirs. Laughter echoed through the booth.

"Oh, God," she moaned. "I…"

Her hips twitched, pushing up against his hand. Her thighs shook around him as her muscles spasmed. She was coming. Right here. Right now. His other hand tightened into a fist that he pressed mercilessly against the table. His cock grew so hard that it hurt.

She bowed her head and he could barely hear her strangled cry as she jerked against him.

Eric stared at the fall of her hair, utterly shocked at

what he'd just done. He'd made this woman come. He'd stroked her to climax in a public place and he hadn't even kissed her yet.

He was going to have to be bad more often.

THIS WAS SEXUAL LIBERATION. This was embracing a fantasy. This was also a little bit awkward as he eased his hand out from between her thighs.

Beth raised her head. She didn't look at him, but she could see that his wineglass wasn't quite steady as he raised it for a drink. She pressed her thighs together and savored the last little spasms of pleasure that took her.

Were they supposed to talk now? Discuss the latest movies? Beth couldn't begin to think at this point.

"Will you excuse me for a moment?" she whispered before smoothing down her skirt and sliding out of the booth.

"Of course," he said, his words following her toward the dark hallway.

She found the women's room and pushed through the door, immediately meeting her own eyes in the mirror. She looked dazed. And flushed. She looked like a woman who'd just done something wicked.

Covering her mouth, she whispered, "Wow." She pressed her hand harder, trying to stop the grin that was starting. But she couldn't stop it. She'd just done something totally insane. In public. "Oh, wow," she said again, the words dissolving into laughter.

Her panties were soaking wet. Her thighs weak and shaky. And he was still at the table, waiting for her.

The door whooshed open behind her, and Beth pressed her lips together to stifle her grin as she reached for the faucet so she'd look less conspicuous. She couldn't just stand there grinning at herself, even if she was the most awesome woman in the building.

As soon as she heard the stall door close behind her, Beth smiled at herself again. She dried her hands and smoothed her hair. She didn't need to touch up her makeup. Her lips were flushed deep red and her eyes sparkled. Hell, yeah.

Beth undid one more button on her shirt and opened the door. She was going to take this man home tonight. Preferably within the next quarter hour.

Three steps outside of the bathroom she ran straight into disaster.

"Beth!" Cairo squealed as she reached out to grab Beth's shoulders. "What are you doing here?"

"Oh!" Beth yelped. "Cairo! I…" She looked past Cairo's head and saw Jamie watching their little reunion. Crap. "I'm meeting with a, um, an accountant. From the accounting seminar. About tax…strategy."

"Well, come here. I want you to meet Harrison."

"Who?" Beth asked, dumbfounded by shock.

"Harrison, my boyfriend. He's a bartender here."

Oh, Jesus. Why hadn't she paid closer attention to Cairo's stories? Harrison was the newer of her two boyfriends, and Beth belatedly remembered that he worked nearby. Unfortunately, she hadn't registered the useful details. "I can't, I need to finish this meeting."

Cairo tugged on her arm. "Come on. It'll only take a second."

Beth had to follow her, but she threw a wide-eyed look at Jamie over her shoulder. She held up one finger in the hopes he'd take the message and stay put. Though he frowned, he leaned back in his seat. Thank God.

"That's him," Cairo whispered, waving toward a young man at the other side of the room. He was slim and of average height, but that was the only average thing about him. His hair was a close buzz cut, bleached so blond it was nearly white. It offered a stark contrast against his bronze skin and black tattoos. He was pierced and studded in multiple places on his face, and Beth knew for a fact that the ornamentation continued down his body.

He stopped before them with a wide, welcoming smile.

"This is Beth," Cairo said. "My boss."

"I'm Harrison. Nice to meet you." He reached across the bar to shake her hand and slid a wine list toward her with the other. "Let me buy you a drink."

"Oh. I'd better…" She darted a look toward the booth.

"No, stay!" Cairo said. "It'll be fun. You said you were almost done with the meeting, right? We never hang out anymore."

Beth couldn't believe this was happening. She thought of Jamie waiting in the booth like some clean-cut sex god. She looked at Cairo's bleach-blond alternative toy with a sense of hopelessness.

"Wait a minute," Cairo said. "Are you sure you're only here for a business meeting?"

"What? Of course, it's just a meeting. Ha! I'll go finish up and I'll be right back. You order for me, Harrison."

She was being ridiculous. She had nothing to be ashamed of. Yes, Jamie looked a lot like an off-duty stockbroker, but Beth didn't have anything to prove. She should just stand up and take it like a woman.

Still, she'd taken a big step today. Best to put off any more growth until tomorrow. Anything more might break her.

She slid into the booth next to Jamie and grabbed her purse. "I'm really, really sorry, but you have to go," she said in rush.

"Excuse me?" Jamie asked, still relaxed against the seat back.

"I know it's awful. Unforgivable really, leaving you like this. After you... But there's somebody here, and—"

He sat straight up. "Do you have a boyfriend?"

"No! It's not that, it's just…"

His confused frown darkened to suspicion. "What?"

"This is hard to explain. And after what we…um… There's someone here from my shop. One of my employees, and…"

"And?"

"And I have an image to maintain."

"I'll sit on the other side of the table. We'll be perfectly respectable."

Heat burned in her face. "That's not what I mean."

"Beth." He raised his hands in helpless question. "I'm trying hard to understand, but I'm missing something here."

She snuck a look around the banquette to be sure Cairo was still at the bar before offering a longer explanation. "Okay, listen. The White Orchid is Annabelle Mendez's dream. It's an extension of *her*. Sophisticated, edgy, daring. Cool and hip and modern. The shop *is* Annabelle, and I'm committed to maintaining everything she is. Every single person I hire is open-minded and forward-thinking. Invested in women's sexual freedom. And I am too. It's just that…"

He leaned forward.

"On occasion, I find myself attracted to a man like you."

"Like me?" He sounded caught halfway between insult and pride.

"Traditional. Sort of…old-fashioned."

*"Old-fashioned?"*

She waved a hand, her mind searching desperately for a better descriptor. "You've got a country-club vibe, you know?"

His mouth opened as if he meant to repeat her words again, but then he only shook his head. He looked… traumatized? "I run a brewery," he rasped.

Beth pressed her hands to her eyes to give herself a chance to gather up the courage she'd sat down with. "I'm sorry." When she opened her eyes, he looked a little less confused, but maybe she'd only pressed her eyeballs too hard. "I'm sorry," she repeated. "I'd heard of you and I kind of thought… Well, considering your reputation, I thought maybe you were a no-strings-attached kind of guy. And, obviously, I'd want a no-strings-attached kind of, um, encounter. Not a date. Not in public."

"You mean you…? You'd want to…"

"Oh, God. I'm sorry. This is so wrong, especially after what just happened. Jamie, I really like you, but I don't know what I was thinking. I can't get involved with a guy like you."

He took a deep breath. "You… Jesus. 'A guy like me?' All this talk about being open-minded, but you seem pretty damn narrow-minded about *me*."

"Oh, there you go," she said, relieved that her ridiculousness had removed any chance he'd like her. "Yet another problem! I've exposed myself as a hypocrite, another good reason not to get involved." She was nodding, but Jamie was shaking his head in what appeared to be utter shock.

Beth's courage was gone. She'd taken control and been honest. She'd embraced her sexual desires. But now that she'd managed that big step, it was time to run away and regroup.

"Okay!" she said brightly. He jumped as if he'd been lost in thought. "I'm sorry about…" She gestured toward his lap. "And thank you. Just… I'm sorry."

She started to slide out of the booth, but he put a hand on her wrist to stop her. "Wait."

She froze.

"You're not exactly the kind of woman I usually date, either."

Beth stiffened. "From what I've heard, you date all kinds of women."

He blinked as if she'd surprised him, then he shook his head. "Regardless, I meant to say that I'll leave, and we can still see each other. Later. Tomorrow. No one needs to know."

Her heart stopped beating for a painful moment. She thought of his hands, his scent, the gorgeous mouth she wanted so badly to taste. And then she thought of the childish panic she'd felt at the sight of Cairo. She clearly wasn't ready for this.

"I don't think it's a good idea," she sighed.

"Think about it."

She shouldn't. But she knew she'd spend all night

thinking about it regardless, so Beth nodded. "Okay. I'll think about it. But no promises."

This time when she slid away, he let her go.

Beth walked away from him as if it were easy. As if everything was back to normal. But inside, she was changed. She could feel it.

## CHAPTER FIVE

TWELVE HOURS LATER, Eric's brain hadn't stopped spinning. He kept staring at the horizon, trying to steady himself, but the horizon was a convention hall filled with milling people, so that didn't help. Still, it kept him from gawking at The White Orchid's booth. Mostly.

Today she wore a black skirt. Just as conservative and businesslike. Just as fantastically cupped over her ass as the brown skirt had been. But this one had a little pleat at the back of her knees that flipped out when she walked.

And the heels. The heels were deep red. How was he supposed to keep his eyes off her for more than a minute?

He let his gaze slip up from her shoes to her calves then over that magnificent ass. The rest of the way up her body, he was telling himself to look away, look away... He should've taken his own advice, because when he reached her face, he realized she was staring back. He held her gaze until she closed her eyes, then he cursed as he turned back to the stacks of promo coasters he was unpacking.

How the hell did she consider *Eric* the inappropriate half of this puzzle? As if he could be seen with *Beth Cantrell,* for God's sake. He was a business owner trying to promote his place as a respectable brewery, not a party bar. And he was, for all intents and purposes, the head of his family. He had an innocent little sister to think of. My God, what would Tessa think if she found out Eric had dated a woman like Beth? What would she *imagine?*

Not that Beth could know any of that. She thought he was a man primed for meaningless sex.

Christ, he'd been crazy even to flirt with her.

But when he turned around to grab another box, his peripheral vision hinted that Beth was looking again. Tension swept through his body, painful at first, but as the tension faded, it left behind a warmth that haunted him like a ghost.

When was the last time he'd felt true physical anticipation? The kind of suspense inspired by the mystery of a stranger's body? But it didn't matter. He wasn't a detective. He wasn't an adventurer. The mystery of Beth Cantrell had nothing to do with him.

But the ghostly warmth stayed with him. He couldn't shake it.

And how was he supposed to when he'd touched her that way? When he'd watched her face as she came apart in his hands?

"Henry," he barked. "I'm going to make the rounds. Hold down the fort."

They wouldn't start serving samples until eleven, so he didn't anticipate that Henry would have any trouble handing out coasters and hats and brochures. But Eric didn't use the chance to pass Beth's booth again. He headed resolutely in the other direction.

The booth he wanted was about halfway across the room. A local roasting company had offered to make a bid on supplying him with barroom snacks like cashews

and peanuts. Eric had promised to hear the owner out.
He liked the idea of organic ingredients and imported
salt, but it would likely prove too pricey.

He was only a few booths from his target when he
spotted Kendall and veered toward the right so he'd be
sure to intersect the man's path.

"Mr. Kendall," he said simply, holding out his hand
as a trap.

"Donovan." The man's hand was just like his face,
big, meaty and unhappy, if the overly strong grip was
any indication.

"It's great to see you again. I was hoping I'd find you
today. You enjoying the expo?"

"A lot of new faces," Kendall muttered with an arrogant look around.

*Yes,* Eric wanted to say, *that's the point.* But Kendall
probably wouldn't appreciate that. "About lunch today.
I hoped we could—"

"Can't do it, Donovan."

Eric felt a surge of anger, but he forced a smile. "All
right. But I hope you've set aside time this evening."

Kendall sighed, his eyes shifting past Eric as if he
couldn't wait to get away. His attitude made Eric want
to growl. He could make this guy a decent amount of
money given a chance.

Eric held his tongue and waited patiently. Finally,
Kendall cleared his throat. "The chamber of com-
merce is holding a reception tonight. Are you going to
be there?"

"Absolutely."

"Fine. We can talk then."

Okay. This was good. It had taken Eric nearly a
year of wrangling to get Kendall to meet him the first

time. This second meeting had taken only a few weeks. Though maybe "meeting" was a bit of an exaggeration. "I'll see you there," he called as Kendall walked off with an impatient wave.

Eric allowed himself one small smile before he headed toward his original destination. This was what he'd come to the expo for, not a secret encounter with a fantasy woman.

Maybe if he told himself that a few dozen more times, he'd stop thinking about Beth Cantrell. But he didn't hold out much hope.

LEATHER, FEATHERS, METAL and lace. Beth scowled at the display that had popped up next to the register at The White Orchid. She had five minutes to fix this before she had to run back to the conference hall for the reception.

"Well," she said carefully to her newest employee. "You've got a really good idea here, Penelope."

"Thanks!"

"But I think it might be a bit too…crowded." More like tacky as all hell and likely to scare off any new customers who might come in. "The handcuffs are good. They're playful. But when you pair them with the flogger and the, um, oversized toy, it startles people. That's why we keep the toys behind the curtain."

"Oh, okay!" Penelope said brightly.

"And I like the way you've paired the lace and the leather. That's classic, right? But maybe we should take the feathered-crotch panties out of the mix."

"Sure. That makes sense."

"Great. I'm really happy with your taking the initiative. Why don't you try one more shot at this, and I'll have Cairo check it out in the morning. Is there anything else going on?"

"Nah, it's slow today. Though we did have a bachelorette group in this afternoon. Guess what their total was?"

"How many women were there?"

"Seven."

Beth tapped her chin, thinking. "How old was the bride?"

"Twenty-three."

"Oh, that's a young group. They're not serious about their vibrators yet. I'll guess $250."

"$525!" Penelope squealed.

"Wow. Early learners."

"I know!"

Beth was laughing as she hurried to her office to fix her makeup and hair. She slipped off her heels and stretched her toes in relief. Heels were standard wear for her, but these expo days were a little long, and there was never any chance to sit down.

But she hadn't noticed the ache in her feet during the day. She'd been consumed with alternating between staring at Jamie Donovan and trying not to stare at him. He had the most gorgeous ass. And then there were those magic fingers. And she *had* promised to think about it.

Sighing, Beth let her eyes wander to the box of samples that had arrived that morning. She usually set out the box in the supply room for any employees who wanted to try them out, but this week maybe she'd take them all home herself. She needed them more than the other girls anyway. She put the top back on the box and slipped it under her desk just in case.

When her cell phone rang, she jumped in guilty shock, knocking a knee into her desk. "Oh!"

The line screamed static as soon as she answered it. "Hello?"

The static roughened before breaking apart for a moment. "Beth! It's…"

It was Annabelle. Somewhere in Asia, if Beth recalled correctly. Thailand, maybe? "I'm here!" she yelled.

The static swelled again. "I've got…can't wait…"

"What?"

"So thrilled! …soon…be a big…" Her voice edged up at the end of every word.

"Annabelle. I can't hear anything you're saying! What are you so excited about?"

"…idea to…" The static finally went quiet. The line dropped dead.

"Well, crap," Beth said, collapsing into her chair. Annabelle called only once a month, and she'd never sounded quite so excited. Beth tried to call her back, but the phone just beeped unhelpfully in her ear. There was nothing she could do except get ready for the reception.

After touching up her makeup, Beth took down her conservative updo and brushed out her hair. She stared wearily at the heels for a long time, wondering if she should put on some flats instead. But she slipped the heels back on, knowing exactly why she did it. There was an excellent chance that Jamie Donovan would be at the reception tonight, and she wanted him to notice her.

Stupid. She told herself she wasn't going to sleep with

him, but damn it, she wanted him to think she was sexy anyway.

Actually… Beth touched the red beaded necklace at her throat and looked down at her shiny red heels. Then she looked at the little closet in the corner of her office, considering the outfits she'd hung there after various store events. Perhaps a little black dress would be better suited for an evening affair.

Or maybe that would just be asking for trouble. Trouble she so desperately needed a taste of in her life.

Oh, what the heck. Maybe she could superimpose a new image over the crazy-eyed Beth she'd left him with yesterday. But the tense arousal that tightened her belly had nothing to do with repairing her image and everything to do with wanting him.

She'd made an awful mistake last night, giving in to her familiar fears. A stupid mistake that she'd spent the past hours regretting. But maybe the perfect opportunity to rectify that mistake would arise. Or maybe the perfect opportunity could be conjured with the right dress.

# CHAPTER SIX

ERIC COULDN'T QUITE believe his eyes when he turned to see the woman walking straight toward him across the crowded reception. "Tessa?" Confusion made him dizzy as his sister rushed in for a hug.

"Hey, big brother. I feel like I haven't seen you in weeks. You work too hard."

He kissed her cheek automatically. "What are you doing here?"

"Jamie and I talked. He needs to cover the bar tonight, but we both agreed I should come help you out."

"It's just a reception."

"But all of this..." she said with a vague gesture. "You shouldn't be the only one working on it. We're all part of Donovan Brothers. We've got to share the burden."

"Of course," Eric said. "But tonight's no big deal. You don't need to hang around here. I'm just going to stalk Kendall for an hour or two. You worked too much last month."

She rolled her eyes and tossed her dark blond hair back. "We're all working overtime. That's the price we pay as business owners, right?"

Eric considered for a moment then shrugged. "You're right. And Kendall is going to love you."

"Why? Does he have a thing for blondes?"

Eric felt his face twist in horror. "Jesus, Tessa. As if I'd let you around him if he did. No, I meant you're the perfect all-American little sister. We'll present a great image."

"Oh. Okay. Good."

"Just, uh…button up your shirt a little more."

She glanced down to her silky gray shirt. "Eric, it's already buttoned to my collarbone."

He narrowed his eyes in doubt but decided to let it go. Tessa was twenty-eight now. He had to stop playing the role of overprotective big brother, but it was tough to let it go. After all, he'd also been a parent to her for nearly fifteen years.

"So give me the lowdown," she murmured as she looked over the crowd. "What's up with this guy?"

"He's arrogant and rich. He's not young and hip like the image they've developed for High West Air. The airline is just one of many high-capital ventures he owns. But he's not a typical high roller. He's been married to the same woman his whole life. They have six grown children and every one of them works for him. He's not a big believer in women's lib, but he finally let his daughter have a chance at moving up. She's the VP of High West Air. His five sons have been executives at his companies for years now."

"Oh? Are any of them single?"

Eric ignored her. "He likes people scraping and bowing, so you'd better limber up."

"Got it," she said with a wink. "Anything else interesting going on?"

"Uh, no." He thought his voice sounded odd instead

of casual, so he cleared his throat and tried again. "Nothing. No."

"Any new contacts?"

He glanced around as if Beth Cantrell might be making her way toward him, but he hadn't spotted her at this reception. Thank God. Probably she was at the web-design seminar. If she showed up and heard Tessa call him by his real name… "Nothing too promising this year. And there he is."

Eric inclined his head toward the doorway where Kendall was comfortably ensconced within a herd of four gentlemen in suits.

"Great! Let's go talk to him."

"Wait," he started, but Tessa was already striding across the room on her spike-heeled sandals. Spike-heeled sandals? What the hell?

Scowling, Eric followed behind his sister, catching up just as she infiltrated the group of men. "Mr. Kendall," she said, "What a pleasure to finally meet you."

Kendall narrowed his eyes at her, his gaze dipping down her body with a hint of scorn, as if Tessa was too young and too female to merit his respect. "Who are you?"

"She's my sister," Eric snapped. In that moment, he didn't give a shit who Kendall was or what he could do for the brewery. In that moment, the bastard was just a sexist ass.

Every eye in their group was on Eric, but Tessa just smiled and cleared her throat. "I'm Tessa Donovan. I'm afraid we haven't had the chance to meet before."

Kendall took the hand she offered and gave it a limp shake. She beamed up at him, and he finally deigned to crack a smile. "You have a lovely sister, Donovan."

"I agree. My sister is a priceless asset to the company. She handles finance and accounting, so you'll be dealing with her when we finally reach an agreement."

"And she's cute as a button," Kendall added.

Eric scowled, but Tessa just gave a little giggle. What a faker. But Eric may as well follow her lead and take advantage of it.

"I was just about to get a drink for Tessa. Would you like to join us? Whiskey, right?" Before Kendall could decline, Eric headed for the bar. He was almost there when he spotted her. *Her.* Beth. She turned away from the bar to look over the room.

Her hair was down again, and she wore those fantastic red heels, but she'd changed into a hip-hugging dress that nearly made him swallow his own tongue. Like everything else he'd seen her in, it was modest, showing only a hint of cleavage and a respectable amount of leg. But the way it wrapped around her hips rocked his world.

It made him want to rock her in return.

"Hello, Jamie," she said in that incredible voice.

He glanced over his shoulder, sure that everyone in the room, including his sister and Kendall, must be watching. Shouldn't everyone's eyes be on Beth? But his sister was occupied with laughing too hard at some joke Kendall had made, and the rest of the room seemed oblivious.

"Beth," he finally said, his eyes sweeping down her body even though he tried hard not to look again. "Are you having a good evening?"

"I am, thank you. Don't let me interrupt your path to the bar, though. You'll never survive this kind of gathering without a drink."

"Oh, I… Yeah, I'm getting a drink for my sister. Can I get you anything?" His mind was racing. What if she said yes? What if Tessa saw him handing this woman a drink and wanted to know who she was? What if she came over to talk?

But Beth cut off his worries by picking up a glass of wine. "I'm good, thanks," she said. "So how do you know Roland Kendall?"

Eric was damn glad he didn't have a drink in his hand yet, because he would've dropped it without question. "I'm sorry?" He leaned an inch closer, hoping he'd misheard her the first time.

"Roland Kendall. He's not getting into the beer business now, is he?"

"No, I… We're trying to get our product onto High West Airlines. You know Kendall?"

She arched an amused eyebrow at his words. Even Eric could hear the incredulous worry in his voice. "He's not a big customer at the shop, if that's what you're wondering. I went to school with his daughter."

"Oh." So Kendall knew exactly who Beth was. Shit. He didn't look over his shoulder, worried he'd look guilty if he did.

"Mr. Kendall is a tough nut to crack," Beth said.

"He is."

"Well, good luck with that." She was walking away before he could say another word. He felt a stark sense of relief that she was moving away from him, but that relief was sharply offset by the pleasure of watching her curves sway as she left.

His mouth watered at the sight, but he told himself it was a good thing she'd called off their flirtation. She'd been right. Their social circles weren't as far apart as he'd thought they were.

This thing between them wasn't meant to be. Still, Eric had given it a hell of a shot the night before. And his body seemed confident that it was the perfect candidate for the job. Too bad he wouldn't get to finish it.

BETH WATCHED JAMIE DONOVAN chat up the group of businessmen who surrounded Roland Kendall. She still didn't see anything of the kilt-wearing bartender in Jamie. Tonight he wore a dark business suit and a pale green tie. He looked every inch the sharp-eyed businessman. Good God, why did he have to be so serious and hot? Her fingers itched to grab that silk tie and pull him out of the room for a quick make-out session in the hallway.

Beth shivered. It was her own fault. She'd primed herself for this by slipping into something decadent and naughty. The fabric of the dress had felt so good under her hands that Beth had gone one step further. A new shipment of lingerie had come in the day before. Beth hadn't put it out on the floor yet, but when she'd opened the box, she'd sighed in reverence.

The silk of the bra and panties was such a pale and delicate gold that it looked like aged ivory. The matching garter was made of soft braids of the same silk and paired perfectly with nude stockings. Beth had had to have the whole set. She'd dug through for her size and left a note to remind herself to pay for them in the morning before anyone else came in.

The lingerie had been well worth the exorbitant price tag. She could feel the expensive material against her skin as she moved. More than that, she could feel the wicked knowledge of what she wore as if it was tattooed onto her. No one else could see it, but she felt daring and sensual and ready.

And maybe he could feel it, too. Their eyes met as she raised her wineglass to her lips, and energy arced between them. This was chemistry like she'd never felt. If she passed it up, she'd regret it for the rest of her life. She knew she would, because she'd felt grief-stricken as soon as she'd opened her eyes this morning.

"Hey there, gorgeous," a man said from just over her shoulder.

Beth turned with a slight smile, thinking he must be someone she knew, but her smile dropped when she saw a stranger. "Pardon me?"

"I'm Will. Will Heston."

She warily took the hand he offered. "Beth."

He kept his fingers wrapped around hers and aimed a glaringly white grin at her. "I saw you at your booth earlier."

Oh, great. One of those guys. Beth tugged on her hand until he let it go.

"You're an incredibly sexy woman," he said, clearly unable to read every "go away" signal she was blasting at him.

"Thank you," she snapped, turning slightly away to look out over the crowd. He didn't take that hint, either. Instead of excusing himself, he edged closer. His chest brushed her arm when he leaned toward her ear as if they were sharing an intimate conversation.

"I'd love to buy you a drink. Somewhere a little more lively, maybe? There's a club over near the university that—"

She stepped a foot away. "No, thank you."

"Are you sure?"

He held out a business card, and Beth glared down at it. Without reaching for the card, she could see the title President and Owner, along with the logo of a local luxury car dealership.

"Oh, I'm sure," she muttered just as her phone began to ring. "Pardon me."

She heard his snort of disbelief as she walked off, but she was too busy juggling her wine and phone to bother to look in his direction. "Hello?"

"It's Cairo!" a cheerful voice sang. "I finally got the boys over here so I could try that tea."

"Oh? And?"

"Aaaand…" Cairo's giggle made Beth grin in response.

"I take it the tea worked?"

"Well, I'm feeling darn good right now." The sound of a loud smack echoed through the phone, followed by Cairo's eardrum-piercing squeal. A male voice rumbled in the background.

"They're still there?" Beth put a hand over her eyes in chagrin.

"Oh, I made sure they won't be moving for a while. Seriously though, the tea had a subtle effect, but I do think it worked. I'm gonna try it again tomorrow when I'm by myself. I think if I don't have so much *visual* stimulation it'll be easier to gauge whether I really feel different."

"Oh, right. Good idea. Thanks, Cairo."

"Jeez, it was my pleasure. Hey, Harrison says *hi*."

As Beth hung up the phone she spotted the tea shop owner, a plump older woman wearing Birkenstocks with her black knit dress. The woman probably didn't carry samples with her, but Beth briefly considered asking, just in case.

Then again, she didn't really need any help. She certainly hadn't needed any last night. She'd come faster than she'd thought possible. Just the memory was enough to make her pulse quicken and her skin sparkle with sensitivity. That kind of chemistry shouldn't be ignored, even if they weren't right for each other in any other way. It was too rare a phenomenon, at least for Beth.

Screw it. She needed this whether she was ready or not.

But… She couldn't approach him in front of his sister and Mr. Kendall, not if they wanted to keep this on the down-low. Beth slipped out the side door of the room and found herself in a dead-end hallway that led to two other banquet rooms. Excitement skittered through her body as she pulled up his number and called. This was who she'd always felt she *should* be. A sexy, daring woman.

"Hello?" he answered in a low voice.

"Hi. It's Beth."

There was a pause. She pictured him moving away from the group. "Are you still here?" he finally asked.

"I'm just outside the room, actually." She drew a deep, quiet breath, and then she took the plunge. "I've been thinking about our conversation yesterday. Maybe we could…" While she tried to think of the exact right words, he stayed silent. She tried again. "I know you're busy, but do you have a moment to talk?"

The line grew muffled for a moment before he

cleared his throat. "Can you give me one minute? Maybe two?"

"Of course. I'll meet you in the hallway next to the side door."

Beth spotted a big mirror at the end of the corridor and walked over to check her makeup. The dress slid against her hips. The ties of the garter belt stretched across her thighs. Her nipples tightened beneath the warm silk of the bra. And when she met her own eyes in the mirror, she saw a sexual goddess on the prowl. Wow. Where had *she* come from?

Who the heck cared? She ran her hands through her hair and watched a slow smile stretch across her face. It didn't matter where the sexual goddess had come from. It only mattered that she was finally here.

Thank God.

A door opened. The sound of the party swelled into the hall. Beth turned and walked toward him.

There was no missing the way his eyes devoured her body. He liked her hips. No question about it. She suppressed her grin in favor of a sexy smirk.

"Fancy meeting you here," he said.

"Thanks for sneaking away." She stopped too close to him then leaned her back casually against the wall, as if she hadn't invaded his personal space.

"So, you changed your mind about being seen with a guy like me?"

She glanced around. "Obviously not. I'm still worried you'll ruin my rep." She tempered her joke with a smile.

"I probably will. And you'd return the favor if anyone saw us."

"We'd better be careful. I don't want to damage your wholesome-brewery image."

His smile faded. His pale eyes narrowed with intensity as he shifted, putting his hand to the wall next to her shoulder. "So what are we doing here?"

She took a deep breath and tilted her face toward his ear. "No one needs to know," she murmured.

His pupils dilated as she felt a flush rise up her cheeks. She'd used his own words to lay it out as simply as she could. *Let's have a secret affair. No one will ever know.*

"I'm in the middle of an important negotiation," he said, his voice taking on a husky edge. "And my sister is here."

"I know." She left it at that. She would've held her breath if she hadn't been so eager to draw in his scent. Afraid that panting aloud would be less than sexy, she inhaled slowly.

"Yet here I am," he murmured. "With you."

He eased a tiny bit closer. If he lowered his head, they'd kiss. Her pulse beat so hard she could hear it in her ears.

"This is not a good idea," he said softly. "You said it yourself. So why are you willing to do this?"

*Honesty,* she told herself. A woman's desires were nothing to be ashamed of. She raised her gaze from his mouth to his eyes. "Because I want you," she admitted. "A lot. It's that simple."

One side of his mouth curved slowly up in a wicked smile. "I get the feeling you're not a fan of complication."

A montage of encounters played through her brain, as if her life were flashing before her eyes. The

uncomfortable blind dates. The brief, failed relationships. The men she'd tried to love, and the men she'd
wanted. Her constant, simmering sexual anxiety.
"You're right," she murmured. "I'm a simple girl."

A door opened farther down the hall. He glanced up,
a brief moment of worry chasing over his face before
he looked back to her. "Simple? I don't believe that for
a second." His eyes lowered to her mouth.

"And I owe you," she whispered. "Don't I?"

"You don't owe me anything. It was my pleasure."

She licked her lips and watched his pupils tighten as
she lifted her chin. He leaned closer, closer…

When the door behind them clicked open, he stepped
smoothly away from her, shoving his hands into his
pockets. By the time they realized it was only a banquet
server, the moment was lost. Or she thought it was.

His jaw had gone tense, after all, as if he were angry.
But apparently the determination in his eyes had nothing to do with saying *no* and everything to do with
pursuing this madness. "Can you meet me in half an
hour?"

"Where?" she whispered.

He met her gaze, his eyes darkening with emotion.
"I'll get a room."

Beth blinked once. Shock hit her in the chest, but
she tried not to let it show. As far as Jamie Donovan
knew, she was good at this. Experienced. After all, she'd
encouraged him to feel her up in a bar.

She didn't have to fake her arousal, at least. That was
charging hard through her veins, heating her skin. "Call
me," she heard herself say. "I'll meet you there." And
then she headed straight downstairs to get a drink.

## CHAPTER SEVEN

SHE WAS REALLY DOING this. Beth couldn't believe it. She stared at the gold mirror of the elevator doors, watching the people in the lobby move behind her in wavy streaks. Could anybody tell what she was doing? She felt as if she was wearing a neon sign on her head advertising her unseemly intentions.

Her hand still tingled where the phone had vibrated against her palm when he'd called. "Room 421," he'd said. That was it. No niceties or polite chitchat. Beth had said okay and hung up before hurrying toward the lobby. Unfortunately the elevator didn't seem to be in as much of a hurry as she was.

When the Up arrow finally lit with a faint chime, she slumped in relief. Then she heard Roland Kendall call her name.

Her mouth made a comical *O* of alarm in the elevator door before it slid open. For a brief moment, she considered sprinting into the elevator and slamming her hand against the Door Close button, but that could possibly be seen as suspicious. So she pasted a numb smile onto her face and turned.

"Hello, Mr. Kendall. How's Monica?" She spoke way too fast, but he didn't seem to notice.

"She's wonderful. I'm still waiting for her to get married and give me some grandchildren, but she can't seem to settle down."

Beth couldn't imagine Monica as a mom. She'd always struck Beth as self-absorbed and manipulative, though she was also smart as hell. Still, if they hadn't been suitemates in college, Beth would never have exchanged two words with the woman.

"So, Beth, are you still running that unfortunate store? You're one of the savviest young ladies I've ever met and it's a shame that you're involved with that place."

Oh, Jesus. Every time she'd seen Roland Kendall in the past few years he brought this up. She wished she could simply excuse herself, but what could she say? *Sorry, I need to get upstairs to have sex with a man I hardly know. Nothing to do with my unfortunate store, though.*

Kendall raised an eyebrow, waiting for an answer. "Well?" His tone suggested that she was answerable to him in some way.

"Um. Still there, yes. Say, I heard you were talking to Donovan Brothers about beer for High West."

"Pardon me? How'd you hear that?"

Oops. In her panic to change the subject, she'd latched on to the one thing she *didn't* want to talk about. "Oh, you know. Small-town talk. But I hear the Donovan family is great." *Don't say any more,* her brain frantically ordered. *Zip it.*

Kendall grunted. "I'm not convinced. I like their product, but the brewery's been around for almost twenty-five years. I need a name that's a little more fresh, I think."

Beth looked at the negativity written so clearly on

his face. Roland Kendall was a successful businessman, but he worked from the gut and had rigid ideas about his businesses. Clearly, he wasn't interested in giving Jamie Donovan a chance.

It shouldn't matter to her. She shouldn't get involved. But Jamie was smart and good-hearted and she didn't like to see him so easily dismissed. "I've met Jamie Donovan," she blurted out, even as she tried to stop herself.

"Oh?"

"I was impressed. You should at least give them a chance. It's a company run by young people, right? How stale could it be?"

"Well—"

"And it's a beloved local company. That could be some great publicity."

"Hmm." He crossed his arms and glared down at the floor.

"Think about it, at least."

"I will."

"Well," she prompted. "It was nice seeing you."

Thankfully, he'd already lost interest in her, and he simply waved a hand and walked away. Beth counted to ten then punched the button with her finger. The doors slid open and she jumped inside.

She put Roland Kendall from her mind, but that left room for the anxiety she'd been feeling before. *Oh, God,* her brain repeated as the elevator rose. *Oh, God, I'm really doing this.* Was he waiting? Was he wondering where she was?

When she stepped out, her heels clicked too loudly against the tile floor outside the elevator before they were muffled by the carpet of the hallway. A sign pointed her in the direction of room 421, and Beth forced herself not to slow as she turned down the hallway and headed closer to Jamie Donovan.

What would happen when she got there? Would they just…*start?* My God, what if he was already undressed?

Her toe scraped the carpet and Beth stumbled to a halt before forcing herself to walk on. No, he was not going to be standing there in black socks and what the Lord gave him. And if he was, she'd simply turn around and run, no question.

But she had to assume everything would go well. If she didn't go into this with a positive attitude, the night would turn out badly. She'd think too much. She'd worry that he wasn't enjoying himself. Then she'd worry that she wasn't enjoying herself, because she so desperately wanted to be the kind of woman who threw herself into sex and devoured every second of it. She wanted to be good in bed, for her own sake. She wanted to love it as much as she loved the *idea* of it.

And Jamie had certainly proved that they worked well together. She had every reason to think happy thoughts.

Beth forced herself to take a deep breath as she approached the next door: 421. The numbers were smaller than she'd expected. Innocuous. They didn't loom or glow. They didn't pulse with red menace.

"Okay," she whispered. Before she could lose her nerve, Beth straightened her dress, smoothed down her hair and knocked.

He opened the door too fast and had to catch it before it slammed into the wall. The startled look on his face drew a shocked laugh from Beth. And the humor wasn't the only thing that prompted relief to well up inside her. He was still fully clothed. And he was holding a tumbler of something bubbly.

"Champagne?" he asked as she stepped past him.

"Thank you!"

"I'm sorry, there weren't any wineglasses."

"No, this is perfect." She took a grateful sip and then sipped again, faced with the horror that she didn't know what else to say. The door closed hard behind her. They were standing alone together in a room with a dresser, a bed and not much else.

Something swelled beneath her breastbone, pressing into her throat. Suddenly, she couldn't breathe. Couldn't swallow. Heat rose up her neck.

"There's a beautiful view," he said quietly, moving toward the window.

A view. There was a beautiful view. The tightness in her chest loosened by small degrees as she realized she'd have a few moments to compose herself.

His pants were still on, after all. He hadn't jumped her. Hell, she was here to have sex with him, and Jamie was behaving with a lot more restraint than that asshole at the reception earlier.

When he reached the window and turned toward her, a frown tugged his eyebrows low. And a realization hit her. Hard.

Beth finally knew what her fantasy was. What buttons she'd always wanted pushed. All those years of wondering, hoping, waiting…and here it was in the stormy eyes of this man.

She didn't want to be the seductress. She didn't want to be the experienced one. She wanted to be overwhelmed. Persuaded. *Coaxed.*

No wonder she'd been such a failure at this. The men who asked her out were looking for a sexual savant. And deep in her heart, Beth wanted to be *seduced*.

She was an old-school-feminist failure.

He tilted his head, and the hard line of his mouth softened. "Are you all right?"

"Yes!" she answered too brightly as she hurried the last few feet to join him.

He slid the window open, and a cool, crisp breeze swept over them. The sky glowed violet behind the black silhouette of Longs Peak.

"You're right," she whispered. "It is beautiful. It's a gorgeous night." Beyond the faint traffic, she could hear the occasional coo of mourning doves. The wind touched her again, licking over her skin like cool hands. She closed her eyes.

"Beth," he murmured. "If you've changed your mind…"

She breathed in the scent of fresh leaves and icy water. "No." Opening her eyes, she met his gaze. "No, I haven't changed my mind." She set her purse on the chair, and then Jamie took the glass from her hand and set it down on the sill.

"Would it be an exaggeration if I said I've spent days thinking of kissing you?"

Adrenaline shot through her. "I don't know. Would it be?"

"Two whole days. Almost. That counts…" His hand rose to frame her cheek. "Doesn't it?"

"Yes," she whispered against his thumb as he touched it to her lower lip. "It does."

The nerves of her lips buzzed as if they were about to go numb, but Beth pushed thoughts of numbness away.

She wanted to feel everything, and he was lowering his head, slowly, as if he didn't want to startle her. As if she had to be eased into this.

The thought tightened her clit and made her hands shake. His lips touched her as if she were fragile.

*Oh, God. Oh, God, yesss.*

He brushed his mouth against hers one more time, and then ever so gently caught her lower lip between his teeth.

Perfect.

Beth sighed against him and raised her hands to his shoulders to steady herself against the rush of sensation. His lips, his teeth, the slow slide of his hands up her back...

What they'd done in the bar last night hadn't made him less of a stranger, and alarm rushed through her brain as he eased closer. But this was the kind of alarm that had fed one-night stands for centuries. The kind of alarm that pushed your blood harder into pulse points and erogenous zones. The fear that made it feel as if every cell in your body was pulling toward your skin.

When their tongues finally touched, he tasted of champagne, and Beth let the sweetness go to her head and overwhelm her worries.

She tasted more deeply, aware that his fingers pressed into her hips when she sucked at his tongue. This wasn't just a first kiss, after all. This was the prelude to illicit sex, and she didn't want to forget that for one moment. So when he slanted his mouth over hers, Beth slid her fingers into his hair and clutched him tight.

*Yes, yes, yes,* her mind sang as they pressed closer. His looks might easily have turned out to be the best thing about him, but they weren't. Not by a long shot.

He smelled good and he tasted better, and he didn't grab her ass or get impatient. No, Jamie Donovan did everything with slow deliberation.

He had experience, after all. He knew what he was doing.

His tongue swept against hers. His hand slid lower on her hip, fingers spreading out until they edged along the swell of her ass. Then he eased his hips close enough that her belly pressed snug against his erection. Unlike some men she'd dated, he didn't hump her like a ninth-grade boy at summer camp. Instead, he just held her there, deliberate and patient. Beth would've melted into a puddle if she hadn't been so intent on staying right where she was.

She didn't know how long they kissed—one minute or twenty—but by the time he reached for the back of her strappy black dress, Beth nearly wept with relief.

The biting sound of the zipper sang through the room. His knuckles brushed down her skin. Finally, just at the base of her spine, the zipper caught. She expected him to pull her dress off immediately, and when he didn't, anticipation buzzed just under her skin, so sharp it was nearly pain. He trailed his fingers down her naked spine, and she gasped against his tongue, spiking coolness into their kiss. She was surrounded by him. His cock pressed to her belly, his arms warming her ribs. His hands teasing her back.

He flattened his palm at the base of her spine, easing her even tighter into him. Heat spread through her like a craving, squeezing everything tight.

She needed to draw more air into her lungs, so she slid her mouth from his, and Jamie kissed along her jaw until he reached her arching neck.

A whimper snuck from her throat. In response to that soft sound, he growled. That low rumble told her everything she needed to know. He wanted her. He liked this. His hips pressed closer, and she rolled into his shaft in encouragement.

He seemed encouraged. A shudder ran through him and he scraped his teeth over the curve of her shoulder.

Urgency overtook her in a sudden wave. She clutched his hair in her fists, and when she guided his mouth back to hers, they kissed hard, like they were fucking already and vicious with it. Jamie gave up his campaign of slowness and pushed her dress down her body.

Her nerves were sent conflicting signals. His hands held her hips in a hot grip, his suit brushed cool against her naked skin. She shivered at the delicious sensation, but she wanted his heat all over, so Beth pushed his coat off his shoulders. He had to let her go to drop the coat, and when he took a step back and his gaze dropped…

His body froze. The coat fell to the floor.

He looked stunned as his gaze swept down her body. Appreciative, certainly, but dumbstruck, as well. His hungry shock gave her just the courage she needed to stand tall and let him look his fill. She knew the pale silk flattered her olive-toned skin. She knew her dark nipples pressed visibly against the thin bra. Her nipples beaded more tightly under his attention.

By the time his gaze worked its slow way back to her face, Beth's cheeks felt flushed with pink arousal.

Slowly, he slid his hand behind her neck and lifted her face for one more kiss. "You're breathtaking, Beth. Way past beautiful."

Tonight, she was. She could feel it in the way his

other hand shaped her waist before sliding down the curve of her hip. Tonight she was a woman who wore red heels and stockings and worked every inch of the outfit.

He nudged her toward the bed and she backed up. It wasn't until her legs touched the mattress that Beth realized how weak her knees were. She lowered herself slowly as he reached for his tie. He pulled the silk knot free and slid the tie off. Five seconds later, his shirt was off, as well.

She wanted to ask for more time to look over his wide chest, but he was leaning over her, and Beth lay back hoping he'd follow. He did. Finally, the heat she'd been chasing all night slammed through her. Stomach to stomach. Chest to chest. Mouth to mouth.

Starving, she dug her nails into his back.

She *needed* this. Now.

She was panting by the time he reached for the front clasp of her bra. She arched into his touch as the fabric slid free, exposing her breasts.

"Oh, God," she gasped as he bent his head and drew her nipple hard against his tongue. Pleasure shot through her, trailing through her belly. Her clit tightened, already so hard she could feel her pulse beating there.

When he scraped his teeth over her, Beth wanted to squeeze her eyes shut and feel everything as deeply as she could, but that desire warred with the need to watch. So she tipped her head up and watched as he licked at the dark, tight bud. When he dragged his teeth over her again, goose bumps exploded across her skin. Her nipple glistened with wetness when he lifted his head and turned his attention to the other breast. Again, he sent painful need spiraling through her.

When he glanced up at her, the irises of his eyes were shockingly pale, like icy silver, as if he got cooler with passion, rather than hot. He slowly sucked her nipple between his teeth as he watched her. And when he pressed his hips tight to hers, she came so close to an orgasm that she threw her head back with a cry.

"Oh, God," she gasped. "Now. *Please,* Jamie. Now."

## CHAPTER EIGHT

ERIC SURGED UP, SO DAMN startled by hearing his brother's name that he nearly leaped from the bed. Beth cried out again, rolling her hips against his.

The pressure against his cock warred with his guilt. Jesus, what if she screamed Jamie's name as she came? He'd have nightmares about that for years. And it was wrong. It was immoral and dishonest and... Beth arched her back, and her nipples were tight, wet buds, flushed a deep red from his rough attention. *His* attentions, wrong name or not.

When he rose from the bed, it wasn't to walk away from her. It was to reach for his belt buckle. He'd deal with the guilt later.

Once he'd stripped, Beth eyed him with such greedy lust that he convinced himself that names didn't matter. She wanted *him*. And he'd never needed a woman more than he needed her.

She eased farther onto the bed. Eric took her heels off before sliding both hands up the warm silk of her stockings. Should he strip her bare? She looked amazing in lingerie, but the idea of seeing her totally naked made his heart pound even harder.

He feathered his thumbs over the naked skin of her thighs, still trying to formulate a plan. But it was so damn hard to think. And then Beth reached for the little ribbons on the sides of her panties. She pulled the ties loose, the fabric slid free, and Eric couldn't think anymore.

He'd imagined her the night before. He'd wondered if she might be waxed nearly bare or pierced or…hell, she might've been on the cutting edge with some sort of adornment he'd never suspect. But she was a simple beauty. Dark curls and wet sex, and Jesus, he thought he might die of hot pleasure as he slipped his fingers along the seam of her body.

She cried out at that small touch, pushing her toes into the mattress, arching up. God, she was perfect, plump heat beneath his fingers. He rubbed her own wetness along her, circling her clit as she sobbed.

Eric's cock throbbed, telling him she was ready, ready, ready. And she was. Before he could explore further, Beth was twisting around, reaching toward the side table where he'd tossed the condoms. He should help her. Be a gentleman and get the protection himself, but his body was beyond his control now. She'd turned over onto her stomach and her spectacular ass was laid out before him.

Good God, her body was a fantasy of smooth skin and round hips and tight muscle. He reached for her, helpless to stop from smoothing his hands down the perfect globes of her ass. He curved his hand over one glorious hip and eased his other hand between her legs. When he sunk two fingers deep into her pussy, Beth gasped and lifted her hips to take him deeper. Her slick folds and tight muscles squeezed against him as he slowly pushed his fingers into her.

She rose to her knees, breathing, "Oh, God," over and over again.

He wanted his cock inside her as she prayed, and apparently she felt the same, because she thrust her arm back and pressed a condom into his hand.

As he slid it on, Beth raised both her hands to the top of the headboard and eased her knees farther apart.

She wanted it like this. Just like this. Nothing romantic or soft about it. His hands nearly shook with the violence of his need as he pressed his palm flat to the small of her back.

Silence stretched between them. They both held their breath. Then he took his cock in hand and slid it along the folds of her sex, rubbing her wetness along her until she squirmed. Finally, his head notched against her, and he pushed inside.

"Ah," she breathed, her hands gripping the headboard tighter. "Ah, God." He eased farther in, watching his shaft push slowly into her body. He'd never felt anything so hot or so tight. Nothing. His muscles had never shaken with the need to set all control aside and simply *take*.

He held himself still, his breath racing from his throat. His fingers brushed the soft fabric of her garter belt, and he was suddenly glad she'd left it on. She looked wicked as sin as she arched her back.

Her muscles eased the slightest bit around him, and finally, his hips were flush against her ass. He tightened his grip and began to move.

"Yes," she urged as he thrust slow and deep inside her. Every stroke rubbed a thousand of his nerves at once. A million. And every tiny whimper from her throat made him want to fuck her harder.

She pushed against his hands, tilting her hips. That tiny little movement pulled him deeper. Eric couldn't stop from taking her faster, rougher. Now instead of easing, her muscles tightened, squeezing his cock in bands of pleasure.

He thrust too hard. Beth cried out and rose higher, but before he could gentle his movements, she reached a hand down her own stomach. He felt her fingers brush the base of his shaft as she rubbed her clit. She moaned at her own touch, and Eric had to close his eyes. He couldn't watch and listen and feel all at once, or he was going to come right then. He imagined how it must feel to her, to touch the soft heat of her sex as his shaft slid deep inside her.

He ground his teeth together and held his pace. Her muscles got so tight he felt as if he was growing thicker inside her.

"Jesus," he rasped.

"Oh, God," she groaned. "That's so…"

When her thighs began to shake, he lost any semblance of smoothness. Now he just fucked her hard, and finally, he felt her begin to spasm around him.

"No," she keened, but she was gone. She groaned and bucked against him, and he barely managed to hold on through her climax. She was still shaking when he let his thin thread of control snap. He came so hard it was closer to torture than pleasure, and he shouted in desperate release.

He was left weak and numb, with no way to support his own weight. Eric leaned forward to grasp the headboard beside each of Beth's hands. His chest touched her back and he pressed his mouth to her shoulder. "Christ, you're amazing," he breathed into her sweat-slick skin. "Amazing."

They rested like that for a long moment, both of

them panting. He wondered if she was as stunned as he. Probably not. She was sensuality personified.

His body insisted he collapse to the mattress and pass out, but he made himself slide from her body with slow deliberation before he eased down next to her. He wanted to impress her with his strength and virility and all-around manliness. He wanted her to know he was totally capable of doing this again. And again. As soon as humanly possible.

THE SOUND OF THEIR PANTING filled the room. Cool air from the open window touched Beth's feet.

Time returned to her. She stared wide-eyed at the bedside lamp.

Good Lord above, had that really happened? Was that what her friends felt every time? No wonder they never stopped thinking and talking and tittering about it. Not that she hadn't climaxed a hundred times over, but to feel that kind of overwhelming physical connection… Yeah, that was brand-new.

She became aware, in slow degrees, of where her body touched his. One calf. The backs of both thighs. Her ass. Nearly her whole back. It felt good, being pressed to this man she hardly knew. It didn't seem possible that she could feel so comfortable with a stranger, but she did. Apparently the best orgasm of a girl's life could work wonders on intimacy issues.

She pressed a careful hand to her belly, amazed at the way her muscles still twitched.

"Sorry," he murmured near her ear, as his arm stretched past her. "I need to…" He reached for the box of tissues on the table.

Beth hid her smile. He was so polite. No wonder so

many women liked him. He was even cuter now than he had been *before* he'd rocked her world.

The man was a god.

She was just starting to close her eyes when the familiar sound of her phone filled the room. Beth disentangled herself and sat up with a guilty lurch to dive for her purse. If it was Annabelle, she had to answer it, didn't she? Annabelle had obviously had something important to say when she'd called earlier. And God only knew when she'd get through again.

When Beth finally found her phone, the display showed exactly the name she didn't want to see. Damn it. "I'm sorry. I have to take this. I'll just…"

"Of course."

She hurried toward the bathroom, opening her phone as she closed the door.

"Annabelle," she said as softly as she could without whispering.

"Beth! Oh, it's so good to hear your voice! *Namaste.*"

"Yes. Hi. *Namaste.*"

"I finally got a clear line."

Beth caught a glimpse of herself and her garter belt in the mirror and stammered. "Uh-huh. Yes."

"Is everything okay? You sound strange."

"Everything's fine." She shot a look at the bathroom door. "It's late here."

"Hmm. I don't know, Beth. You sound decidedly odd. Regardless, I have the most amazing news! You're going to be so excited."

Through the thin door, Beth heard Jamie's phone ringing, too. If he started talking, would Annabelle hear?

"Um, Annabelle… Can I call you back in a few

minutes? I'm not…I'm leaving a dinner and I can't talk. Just don't move, okay?"

"Beth—"

She snapped the phone shut just as Jamie answered his phone. His indistinct words rumbled through the closed door, and just the sound of his voice made her melt. She still wanted him. Even now. Even while she was completely spent and satisfied.

But now she was stuck in the bathroom and didn't know what to do. She frowned at the girl standing in the mirror. A girl in a hotel bathroom in stockings and a garter belt, her sex still wet and aching. It felt way too vulnerable to simply waltz back in there and lie down in the bed. What if he wanted her to leave?

She should leave. He probably didn't want to cuddle and spoon.

The door clicked softly when she opened it, and his voice became crisp and clear. For some reason, she felt shocked that he was standing there still naked with the phone pressed to his ear. He glanced up and she fought the urge to cover herself with her hands. Ridiculous. They'd just had insanely good sex. And he was totally exposed. Her eyes tried to wander down his body, as if she were a man faced with a plunging neckline. *Eyes up,* she chanted to herself. *Eyes up.* His gaze didn't leave her face, which only made her feel more like a caveman.

*Sorry,* she mouthed, tiptoeing toward her clothes. He shook his head, but she ignored him and reached for her bra. The breeze from the open window curled around her and she shivered. She felt better about herself when he finally lost his hold on his gaze and it dipped to her breasts.

"Absolutely," he said into the phone, but when she pointed toward the door, he shook his head again.

She dropped down to snatch up her dress then looked up without realizing how close she was to him. She stumbled back from the nudity so close at hand and yanked her dress on before twisting and turning to get the zipper up.

"Villanueva has a new restaurant on 8th," he was saying as Beth slipped on her heels and grabbed her purse.

"Sorry," she whispered, giving him a little wave.

*Wait,* he mouthed, but she pointed at her phone and gave a helpless shrug as if the call to Annabelle couldn't possibly wait another few minutes. In reality, she needed to get out of here. She couldn't get too attached to him. Not because she'd be embarrassed to date him. Not truly. Jamie had a sizzling reputation even among her friends. He was one preppy guy she might be able to pull off.

No, it wasn't that. The truth was that, all doubts about her own sexuality aside, Beth knew she'd be even worse at love than she was at lust. She'd been working toward a more satisfying sex life for years. But love…oh, she couldn't even look in that direction without wincing. And any more sex like that and she'd be in serious danger of getting attached.

She'd already turned away when she registered that he was reaching toward her. She stuttered to a stop, but when she turned back, he'd dropped his hand.

"Morton's in Denver," he said into the phone, his face tight with frustration as she backed away. "Yes, I know where it is. Absolutely, Mr. Kendall."

*Mr. Kendall!*

She was out the door before she realized she'd been holding her breath long enough to get light-headed. She was on the elevator when she realized she'd forgotten her panties. And she was already on the phone with Annabelle when she was hit with the most shocking realization of all.

She'd just walked away from a great thing. And that was her single, solitary regret about what she'd just done, forgotten panties and all. Hell, she'd even convinced Kendall to give Donovan Brothers a chance.

A smile tugged at her mouth as she heard the phone line open up, feeding sound in from the other side of the world. But her boss's rush of excited words tamped down both Beth's urge to smile, not to mention her feeling of accomplishment.

Her nervous triumph evaporated.

Beth had thought she'd been forced to fake her way through her career for years, but Annabelle's new idea for the store made clear that Beth's charade had only just begun. This was going to take her to a whole new level of faking it. What an awful end to a fabulous night.

## CHAPTER NINE

"EIGHT SHARP," KENDALL was saying while Eric stared at the room door as if it had just punched him in the gut. "And be sure you bring your brother."

"What? I'm not sure that's a good—"

"My daughter, Monica, will attend the meeting, as well. She's handling day-to-day operations for High West. What was your sister's name again?"

"My sister?" His mind wasn't keeping up. He shook his head and forced himself to concentrate on this conversation. "Tessa."

"Tessa," Kendall repeated. "That's right. She's welcome, too, if she can make it. I liked her. She's not one of those ball-busting women."

"Yeah, she's great," Eric muttered. Jesus Christ, he was standing here, still buck naked, and Beth was *gone*. "So, tomorrow at eight," he managed to say.

Kendall grunted what sounded like an affirmative before hanging up, and Eric found himself standing with a dead phone pressed to his ear, his mind still quaking with shock.

She was gone. Just as quickly as she'd arrived. They'd spent one hour together. He glanced at the clock. Jesus, not even an hour. So how did he feel so changed?

Spent, empty, exhausted. But not hollow.

She'd used him, just as he'd used her, and somehow

he was buoyed by that. He'd spent his whole life giving everything to his family. Love and duty. His past, present and future. And he'd given it gladly. But tonight he'd given *himself*. There was no history with Beth, no obligation. They'd offered only what they'd each wanted to give.

Still, he'd expected that Beth would spend the night so they could slake their thirst. The sex had been spectacular. So damn hot he was still seeing stars at the edges of his vision. And it hadn't been nearly enough.

A car pulled out of the parking lot and he watched its lights fade far below, wondering if it was her.

She'd left so quickly, and… He hadn't asked her to stay.

"Shit," he muttered, running a hand through his hair. Had he committed a one-night-stand faux pas? He'd rented the room. He'd invited her up. Maybe conventional wisdom called for her to scramble into her clothes and hit the door unless he stopped her.

Damn it, he'd never done this before.

He turned to face the bed. It was rumpled, but they hadn't even pulled the covers back. It looked almost as if Beth had never happened.

But she damn sure had. His chest still felt strained and tight, as if his lungs weren't quite working yet.

Just yesterday, the first moment he'd glimpsed her, Beth Cantrell had struck him as a fantasy. His opinion hadn't changed after tonight. She was a fantasy. Her curvy softness. Her wet, eager body. Her honest desire.

Staring at the bed, he briefly considered staying. He could stretch out on the mattress and reminisce. Hold on to the fantasy a little while longer.

But right now, the room didn't look like remembered sex. It looked sad and lonely.

With a sigh of deep regret, he picked up his clothes from the floor and dressed. He had work to do tonight and more important things to think about than sex.

But, Jesus, she'd been tight with need, and soaking wet. Eric would've given her anything. Anything she'd wanted. As it'd turned out, she'd wanted exactly what he had. A hot, needful connection. A moment of truth.

He closed his eyes for a moment, letting the memories sink in. Then he reached for his shoes—and paused at a flash of pale gold.

Narrowing his eyes, he reached across his shoe for the delicate material just hidden beside it. "Oh," he said as he closed his fingers over Beth Cantrell's underwear. They were featherlight in his hand, but they added considerable weight to his shoulders.

What the hell was he supposed to do with her panties? His first thought was to return them, but that immediately struck him as creepy. *Hey, little lady, look what I found.* Nudge, nudge.

Weird. But what if she asked about them? It seemed unlikely, but Eric wasn't interested in stammering over a lie. And it seemed a crime to blithely toss out the delicate fabric that had just lain against her skin.

Instead of throwing the underwear in the trash, Eric stuffed them into his pants pocket, suspicious of his own motivation. It wasn't like him to sleep with a stranger. It wasn't like him to have sex based on a lie. And it wasn't like him to walk around with a pair of panties in his pocket. Eric had a sudden fear that this night would turn him into a pervert who got off on fondling used underwear in his darkened living room.

He drew his hand out of his pocket with a curse and snatched up his shoes and socks. One minute later and he was done, buttoned up and tied, cell phone and keys in hand. As he walked out and let the door slam behind him, Beth seemed more a dream than ever.

But reality awaited him in the lobby. She was still there, standing just to the side of the lobby doors, frowning as she spoke into her cell phone.

Eric froze. His hand went immediately to the pocket of his slacks. His fingers touched silk. Should he approach her? Not to thrust the panties at her, but at least to walk her to her car. Shit, he should've thought of that to begin with.

Eric stepped forward. He was within five feet of her when she turned toward him. She shook her head, but he took one more step—

"Eric!"

He whirled toward his sister's voice, heart pounding in panic, and something flew from his hand. His eyes darted after the blur of motion.

"God," Tessa said. "Are you okay?"

His phone landed with a thunk and slid across the carpet. His phone. *Not* Beth's panties.

"Oh, thank God," he breathed, but his panic wasn't quite gone. He started to turn toward Beth to see if she'd heard his name. But his sister's hand touched his arm.

"Hey. Are you all right? I didn't mean to startle you."

Shaking his head, Eric lurched a few steps forward and grabbed his errant phone. "You did startle me. I thought you'd gone home."

"I started to, but I decided to stay for a drink."

That stopped Eric from worrying about himself. "What? Tessa, do you know how dangerous it is to hang around in a bar?"

Tessa gave an obvious look around the brightly lit lobby. "What can I say? I like dark alleys and taking crazy risks."

"Just…" He slid a glance toward the front doors and found an empty spot where Beth had been. His heart sank even as relief loosened the tightness in his throat. Without looking at his sister, he asked how much she'd had to drink.

"Two drinks over the past two hours, Eric. I'm fine."

"I'll drive you home anyway. That way I'll know."

Tessa gave a long-suffering sigh. "Look, *Dad,* I'm fine. I swear. One of those drinks was that awful white wine spritzer you got me."

He cringed as he always did when she called him Dad, but Tessa just laughed and kissed his cheek. "Come on. I'm fine. But you can tuck me into my car."

He walked her out to her car, as he would've done on any evening, but this time he kept his eyes peeled for another woman. But Beth Cantrell had disappeared into the night.

It was over. He told himself he should be glad. He'd landed the meeting with Kendall and lived out a fantasy with Beth, all in one night. But somehow he still felt hungry.

## CHAPTER TEN

DÉJÀ VU. HERE THEY WERE again at the expo, pretending not to stare at each other.

Eric pressed the phone harder to his ear and glared down at the souvenir glasses lined up in rows on the table. "Come on," he growled at his sister. "You can make it. You've got two hours to find someone to work the bar."

"There's nobody else, okay? And I've got a headache anyway. I wouldn't be any use to you."

"Maybe you drank too much last night."

"I had two drinks!"

Eric gripped the back of his neck, hard. "Have Jamie work the damn bar, all right? I want you there."

She muttered a curse under her breath. "Kendall specifically asked for Jamie. Don't be an idiot."

And what the hell was that about? Kendall had never even met Jamie. Maybe he wanted to meet all the owners of Donovan Brothers before he made a decision.

"Eric, come on. We all want this. Not just me or you. Jamie wants to be involved, too."

He squeezed his eyes shut and nodded. "Right." It wasn't that he thought Jamie and Tessa shouldn't be involved. It was just that…Eric took care of things. That was his role. He took care of *them*. He owed them that.

"I know you two are as responsible for the business as I am, it's just…I'm not sure Jamie is right for this job."

"Oh, come on. He's great. What could go wrong?"

"Seriously? Kendall's daughter is coming."

"Jamie's smarter than you give him credit for. And Kendall's daughter will probably like him more than she'll like me."

"That's my point. Look, of course Jamie's smart, but I want you there. Please?"

"He'll be good for this deal. You'll see."

Eric glared blindly out at the crowd, then realized a man who'd been headed toward the booth veered away. Eric tried to school his features into something less fierce.

"I'll handle it on my own," he snapped. "Tell Jamie to take the night off. We'll talk about it tomorrow."

"Eric—"

He snapped the phone shut and hoped to God Jamie didn't show up. The deal was sitting right there in Eric's palm. All he had to do was close his fingers slowly enough that he didn't startle Kendall. Jamie never did anything slowly, especially if there was a woman involved.

Speaking of slowly… Reinforcing his sense of déjà vu, Eric stole a look across the booths to find that Beth was still there. Just like that first day. Today she wore a dark blue dress and heels that reminded him of cream in coffee.

The difference was that now he knew what she looked like under her beautiful clothes. He knew how round that ass was, and how it flexed under his hands when she pushed against him. Her knew that her breasts were high and full and the nipples nearly brown against her skin.

Was she wearing stockings again? Was she thinking about him? Or had she already moved on?

For the briefest of moments, their eyes met. When she looked away, pink climbed up her cheeks, and he marveled that he had the power to make a woman like her blush.

A sweet ache filled his chest as he watched her tape up a box and set it aside.

The hall was clearing out. The convention was over. This thing between them was over. But Eric had a bitter taste over how it had ended. It didn't sit well. Hell, in his work, he knew damn well that half the satisfaction of any experience was the last taste it left on the tongue. She'd left so quickly, and he was still struggling with the lie he'd let grow between them.

She packed up one last box and added it to the pile before she gathered up a sweater and her purse.

"Henry," he said without looking at the kid packing up their own booth. "I'll be back in a few."

She stepped out into the flow of people, moving away without a farewell glance. Eric followed her. He tried to keep a distance. She didn't want anyone to know about him, and he didn't want anyone to know about her. For him, the secret had started from his lie, but now he just wanted to keep the night for himself. He didn't want it cheapened by others' thoughts. Yes, it had been a casual encounter, but it hadn't been meaningless.

Beth headed toward the wall of doors at the front of the conference center. Eric picked up the pace. She moved damn fast in those shoes. He told himself not to get distracted by the tiny bows on the backs of the heels. He told himself not to think about running his hand from her ankle to her calf, up past the sensitive skin behind her knee until he got to the hot, sweet skin of her thigh…

Beth reached a hand out, only feet away from a glass door. Eric took two more steps and wrapped his fingers around her wrist.

"Oh!" she yelped, eyes flying wide as she spun toward him. He used her momentum to turn her to the side and tug her toward a solid metal door that hid the emergency stairwell.

Maybe it was shock, but she followed him through the door with no resistance.

"Jamie. I—"

He had to tell her. He *meant* to tell her. But as soon as the door closed behind them, he covered her mouth with a kiss. Her lips parted immediately. Her tongue slid against his in hunger. Just as desperate a hunger as he felt, surely. Her hands clung to his shoulders as she raised a knee to rub it between his.

Eric was immediately, painfully hard. His body didn't think this was over, not by far. She was live heat beneath his hands, just as she had been last night. Warm skin and slippery fabric and hair that slid over his forearms. He could kiss her forever. She was perfect.

But metal banged somewhere from above them, and the sound was still echoing through the stairwell when Beth pulled away and set a hand to the wall. Her fingers spread wide, going white at the knuckles.

"We can't," she panted.

"I know. Jesus, I know. I only meant to stop you and make sure you're all right. You left so quickly."

Beth put a hand to her chest and licked her lips

nervously. He had an almost overwhelming urge to lean in and taste her again, so he shoved his hands into his pockets and took a step back.

"I'm sorry," she finally said. "I had to take that call. It was my boss. She wants me to start teaching classes. At the shop."

He felt his eyebrows fly toward his hairline. "Classes? On sex?"

"I know." She waved a hand before pressing it to her closed eyes. "I know, it's—"

"Impressive?" Classes. Wow. He'd had a fling with a woman who taught sex classes. He didn't know whether to be freaked out or proud.

Her brow crumpled into lines of worry. "No, it's ridiculous."

Yes, it was that, too. He didn't think Beth would mention him in a class, but shit. What if she did? He definitely couldn't tell her his real name now. Anyway, Jamie would probably love being the subject of a sex-class discussion.

"Jamie," she whispered. "Listen. I'm not really…" Whatever she'd been about to say, she snapped her mouth shut when a voice passed close to the doorway. Her eyes stayed on the door until the voice faded. Then she took a deep breath.

"What?" he asked.

She shook her head. Her gaze slipped to the floor. "Nothing. It's just that I'm going to be really busy for a while." The words excused her from any further contact with him. He could see that plain as day. Disappointment passed over him in waves equal to his relief. Sex classes. Maybe their connection was best left as an amazing memory.

"It's fine," he said slowly. "I just wanted to say goodbye."

"Oh." The tension faded from her face, and she met his eyes again.

"I don't want this to be awkward," he said.

She tilted her head and studied him before reaching up to put her hand to his cheek. "There's nothing awkward here. Or complicated. Nothing we need to explain. Last night was a wonder. So thank you."

"Beth—"

She snuck close again, wrapping her arms around his neck for a hug. The faint scent of her skin was a beacon, drawing him near. He forgot his guilt over not telling her the truth. She was right. It would be awful to ruin that night with awkwardness now. He pressed his mouth to her neck and whispered, "I think the wrong person is saying thank you."

"Oh, no. You have my eternal gratitude."

He was smiling when she kissed him, and it seemed appropriate for such a gentle press of her lips. And in that moment, all his conflicting emotions smoothed out into a long, easy line of happy satisfaction. Last night had been a great idea, and he wasn't going to have another moment of regret over it.

"You were just what I needed," she said.

"An embarrassingly preppy one-night stand?"

She ran a hand over the collar of his polo shirt. "An embarrassingly preppy one-night stand who rocked my world. But don't tell. You'll ruin my reputation."

"It'll be our secret," he said, a hot thrill circling his chest at the words.

They didn't bother with any polite offers of future phone calls or friendly promises to be in touch. Beth whispered, "Good luck with Kendall," against his cheek. He kissed her one last time. She slipped away. And he let her go.

He had to learn how to let things go, after all. He'd start with Beth Cantrell. Maybe in a few months, he'd work on loosening his iron grip on the Donovan family business. Maybe.

But the memory of last night? That was a secret he'd never give up. He'd never share. And no one would ever find out.

\* \* \* \* \*

*They thought their one-night stand*
*would never be found out.*
*But an attraction like this* can't *go unnoticed....*
*Watch for Victoria Dahl's hot new trilogy,*
*coming soon.*

*GOOD GIRLS DON'T*
*BAD BOYS DO*
*REAL MEN WILL*

# PRESENTING…THE SEVENTH ANNUAL
## *MORE THAN WORDS*™ ANTHOLOGY

### *Five bestselling authors*
### *Five real-life heroines*

This year's Harlequin
More Than Words award
recipients have changed lives,
one good deed at a time. To
celebrate these real-life heroines,
some of Harlequin's most
acclaimed authors have honored
the winners by writing stories
inspired by these dedicated
women. Within the pages
of *More Than Words Volume 7*,
you will find novellas written
by Carly Phillips, Donna Hill
and Jill Shalvis—and online at
www.HarlequinMoreThanWords.com
you can also access stories by
Pamela Morsi and Meryl Sawyer.

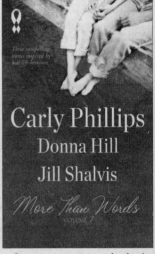

*Coming soon in print and online!*

### Visit
# www.HarlequinMoreThanWords.com
to access your FREE ebooks and to nominate
a real-life heroine in your community.

Proceeds from the sale of this book will be
reinvested in Harlequin's charitable initiatives.

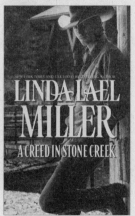

# REQUEST YOUR
# FREE BOOKS!

## 2 FREE NOVELS
## FROM THE ROMANCE COLLECTION
## PLUS 2 FREE GIFTS!

**YES!** Please send me 2 FREE novels from the Romance Collection and my 2 FREE gifts (gifts are worth about $10). After receiving them, if I don't wish to receive any more books, I can return the shipping statement marked "cancel." If I don't cancel, I will receive 4 brand-new novels every month and be billed just $5.74 per book in the U.S. or $6.24 per book in Canada. That's a saving of at least 28% off the cover price. It's quite a bargain! Shipping and handling is just 50¢ per book in the U.S. and 75¢ per book in Canada.* I understand that accepting the 2 free books and gifts places me under no obligation to buy anything. I can always return a shipment and cancel at any time. Even if I never buy another book, the two free books and gifts are mine to keep forever.

194/394 MDN FDC5

| Name | (PLEASE PRINT) | |
|------|------|------|

| Address | | Apt. # |
|------|------|------|

| City | State/Prov. | Zip/Postal Code |
|------|------|------|

Signature (if under 18, a parent or guardian must sign)

### Mail to the **Reader Service:**
#### IN U.S.A.: P.O. Box 1867, Buffalo, NY 14240-1867
#### IN CANADA: P.O. Box 609, Fort Erie, Ontario L2A 5X3

Not valid for current subscribers to the Romance Collection or the Romance/Suspense Collection.

**Want to try two free books from another line?**
**Call 1-800-873-8635 or visit www.ReaderService.com.**

\* Terms and prices subject to change without notice. Prices do not include applicable taxes. Sales tax applicable in N.Y. Canadian residents will be charged applicable taxes. Offer not valid in Quebec. This offer is limited to one order per household. All orders subject to credit approval. Credit or debit balances in a customer's account(s) may be offset by any other outstanding balance owed by or to the customer. Please allow 4 to 6 weeks for delivery. Offer available while quantities last.

**Your Privacy**—The Reader Service is committed to protecting your privacy. Our Privacy Policy is available online at www.ReaderService.com or upon request from the Reader Service.

We make a portion of our mailing list available to reputable third parties that offer products we believe may interest you. If you prefer that we not exchange your name with third parties, or if you wish to clarify or modify your communication preferences, please visit us at www.ReaderService.com/consumerschoice or write to us at Reader Service Preference Service, P.O. Box 9062, Buffalo, NY 14269. Include your complete name and address.